Maybe this time…

Zach reached for her arm. "Maggie…"

She looked up.

"Maybe I could take you to dinner while you're in town."

Maggie knew it wold be a mistake to see Sheriff Zachary Tate again. He was too darned sexy. Too handsome. Too everything. Her old flame aroused too many unwanted feelings in her.

Be careful, she told herself. *Be very, very careful. Twenty years may have passed, but there's still something between the two of you. Something that—if you ignore the danger signals and plunge ahead—could make past hurts seem like nothing compared to what might lie ahead.*

Say you don't think seeing him is a good idea. Say you'll be too busy. Say anything, as long as it's no.

She wet her lips. Looked up into those dark, warm, bottomless eyes. "I—" She stopped. "I'd like that.…"

Dear Reader,

'Tis the season to ask yourself "What makes Christmas special?" (other than a Silhouette Special Edition novel in your stocking, that is). For Susan Mallery, it's "sharing in established traditions and starting new ones." And what could be more of a tradition than reading Susan's adorable holiday MONTANA MAVERICKS story, *Christmas in Whitehorn?*

Peggy Webb's statement of the season, "The only enduring gift is love" resonates in us all as she produces an enduring gift with *The Smile of an Angel* from her series THE WESTMORELAND DIARIES. Along with love, author Patricia Kay feels that Christmas "is all about joy—the joy of being with family and loved ones." And we are overjoyed to bring you the latest in her CALLAHANS & KIN miniseries, *Just a Small-Town Girl.*

Sylvie Kurtz shows us the "magical quality" of the holidays in *A Little Christmas Magic*, a charming opposites-attract love story. And we are delighted by Patricia McLinn's *My Heart Remembers* from her WYOMING WILDFLOWERS miniseries. For Patricia, "Christmas is family. Revisiting memories, but also focusing on today." Crystal Green echoes this thought. "The word *family* is synonymous with Christmas." So curl up with her latest, *The Pregnant Bride*, from her new miniseries, KANE'S CROSSING!

As you can see, we have many talented writers to celebrate this holiday season in Special Edition.

Happy Holidays!

Karen Taylor Richman
Senior Editor

Please address questions and book requests to:
Silhouette Reader Service
U.S.: 3010 Walden Ave., P.O. Box 1325, Buffalo, NY 14269
Canadian: P.O. Box 609, Fort Erie, Ont. L2A 5X3

Just a Small-Town Girl

PATRICIA KAY

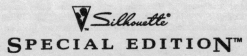

Silhouette

SPECIAL EDITION™

Published by Silhouette Books

America's Publisher of Contemporary Romance

This one's for the group—
Carla, Heather and Marilyn. You guys are the best!

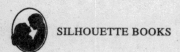 SILHOUETTE BOOKS

ISBN 0-373-24437-1

JUST A SMALL-TOWN GIRL

Copyright © 2001 by Patricia A. Kay

Visit Silhouette at www.eHarlequin.com

Printed in U.S.A.

Books by Patricia Kay

Silhouette Special Edition

*The Millionaire and
   the Mom* #1387
†*Just a Small-Town Girl* #1437

Books previously published as Trisha Alexander

Silhouette Special Edition

Cinderella Girl #640
When Somebody Loves You #748
When Somebody Needs You #784
Mother of the Groom #801
When Somebody Wants You #822
Here Comes the Groom #845
Say You Love Me #875
What Will the Children Think? #906
Let's Make It Legal #924
The Real Elizabeth Hollister... #940
The Girl Next Door #965
This Child Is Mine #989
*A Bride for Luke #1024
*A Bride for John #1047
*A Baby for Rebecca #1070
Stop the Wedding! #1097
Substitute Bride #1115
With This Wedding Ring #1169
A Mother for Jeffrey #1211
†*Wedding Bells and Mistletoe* #1289

*Three Brides and a Baby
†Callahans & Kin

PATRICIA KAY,

formerly writing as Trisha Alexander, is the *USA Today*-bestselling author of more that thirty contemporary romances. She has three grown children, three adored grandchildren and lives in Houston, Texas, with her husband and their three cats. To learn more about her, visit her Web site at www.patriciakay.com.

The Callahan Family Tree

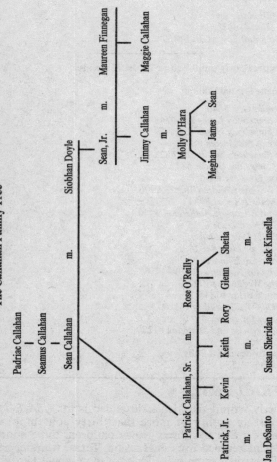

Chapter One

Hot and tired from her hour-long run in Central Park, Maggie Callahan slowly climbed the two flights of stairs leading to her third-floor apartment. Long ago she'd decided the absence of an elevator was an acceptable trade-off for the charm—not to mention cachet—of living in a brownstone on West 69th between Columbus and Central Park West.

Reaching her landing, she let herself into the apartment and headed for her miniscule kitchen. She stood at the refrigerator and gulped down orange juice straight from the carton while wiping sweat off her forehead with her free hand. Her pulse was still not back to normal, but she felt good. In fact, she felt terrific. This May morning was perfect—mild and balmy—with clear skies and low humidity.

Her thirst sated, she reached for a container of low-fat yogurt. Leaning against the kitchen counter, she ate slowly, enjoying the tangy lemon flavor. She was in no hurry. Her assistant, Rita DelVecchio, always opened the office at nine.

Rita didn't mind morning duty, as long as she could be on her way by four-thirty. A single mother, she had two kids and needed to be home to supervise their schoolwork and get their dinner ready early. Maggie, on the other hand, could still be found at her desk at seven or eight most nights. Their arrangement suited both women.

Maggie had just finished her yogurt and thrown the empty container in the trash when the phone rang. She eyed it, thinking the call was probably from Joel. Joel Nicholls, the hotshot producer she'd met last month and her current squeeze, had fallen into the habit of phoning her over his morning coffee. For the most part, Maggie was enjoying the attention—a new romance was always exciting—even though she knew the relationship would never go anywhere. She and Joel were just having a good time together. When one or both of them got bored, they would move on.

That was fine with Maggie. Except for a youthful romance that hadn't worked out, she had never met a man she cared enough about to give up her independence. And if occasionally she was lonely, well, that was another acceptable trade-off.

Walking over to the phone, she glanced at the caller I.D. display. But it wasn't Joel's number; it was her brother Jimmy's. Frowning, she snatched up the phone. "Hello?"

"Maggie? It's Molly." Molly was Jimmy's wife.

"Molly. Hi. What's up?"

"Maggie, I'm sorry, but I'm afraid I have some bad news."

The sweat that still hadn't dried turned cold and clammy against Maggie's skin. The last time she'd heard those words—just eight months earlier—it was because her father had died. She braced herself.

"It's your mother, Maggie," Molly said gently. "She's had a stroke."

Maggie sucked in a breath. "Oh, no!" She closed her eyes, afraid to ask the next question. "Is…is she okay?"

"She's alive."

Maggie let out the breath she'd been holding. "Thank God. When…" She licked her lips. "When did it happen?"

"This morning. Right after she got up, we think, because she was able to reach for the phone by the bed and dial 911." Molly paused. "It was a bad one, Maggie."

"Is she going to make it?" Maggie's lips formed a silent prayer.

''The doctors are hopeful. The problem right now is, they're not sure how much damage was done. From what they can tell, her entire right side was affected, but there may be other things that won't show up right away.'' Molly sighed, the sound carrying clearly over the wire. ''She may not be able to take care of herself at all. Sometimes stroke patients have to learn to walk all over again, and her speech is bound to be affected.''

A great sadness enveloped Maggie. Not walk or talk? Not take care of herself? Maggie couldn't imagine her indomitable mother in such circumstances. Even her father's death hadn't slowed her mother down.

Images of her mother—small and quick and never still and looking ten years younger than her actual age of sixty-eight—filled Maggie's head. Maureen Callahan had always seemed so healthy, so indestructible. There had been times when Maggie thought her mother would outlive her.

''You'll come home, won't you, Maggie?''

Maggie nodded, then realizing Molly couldn't see her, cleared her throat and said, ''Yes, of course. I'll check on flights as soon as we hang up. How's Jimmy taking it?''

''He's pretty shook up.''

Maggie nodded grimly. Her brother was a nice guy, but he wasn't much good in circumstances like these.

''He didn't want to call you.''

"I understand. Give him a hug for me. Tell him…" She stopped. Tell him what? That everything would be all right? It hadn't been all right for their dad. She took a deep breath. "Tell him I'll be there soon."

It didn't take Maggie long to make her arrangements. She was in her element when it came to coping with emergencies, and as long as she didn't allow herself to think about her mother, just put herself on automatic pilot, she was fine.

First she called her travel agent, who booked a seat on the one-fifty flight to Houston out of LaGuardia. From there Maggie would fly to Austin, where a rental car would be waiting for her. After that, it was only an hour-and-a-half drive to Rainbow's End—the small town founded by a Callahan ancestor—where Maggie had grown up.

After making her travel arrangements, she called her landlord to let him know she'd be gone for a while and how to reach her if he needed to. Only then did she call her office.

Rita answered the phone on the first ring. "Callahan Literary Agency," she said in her husky voice.

"It's me." Maggie quickly told her assistant what had happened.

"Oh, geez, Maggie, I'm sorry. What can I do?"

"Just keep things running smoothly, the way you always do. Think you can handle everything?"

"Don't worry about a thing."

"I'll take my laptop, so we can e-mail, and I'll also

have my cell phone with me, so if you need me quickly, you can call me.''

''I'll be fine. Don't worry.''

Maggie sighed. *Don't worry.* Easier said than done. ''Okay, let me think. You'll need to check with Kenyon's contract department and make sure they've made those changes to Allen Singer's new contract. Oh, and Judy Greenlee will probably call by the end of the week. You'll need to talk to her editor before then. Find out if they're going to send her on tour this time. If they don't, Judy's going to have a fit. She thinks it's time they recognized her as one of their stars.''

''Is she?''

Maggie grinned at Rita's skeptical tone. It hadn't taken her long to change from naive Brooklyn girl to hardened literary agent.

''She thinks she is. That's all that counts. Now you're sure you'll be okay?''

''Maggie, I'll be *fine.* Like you said, I can get in touch with you immediately if I have to. Now go home and don't worry about anything.''

''Thanks, Rita. After this I'm going to owe you big time.''

''And don't think I'll let you forget it!''

Maggie laughed, and they hung up.

Last of all, Maggie called Joel.

''How long will you be gone?'' He sounded annoyed.

Belatedly, she remembered she had promised to accompany him to Connecticut over the weekend. He was the keynote speaker for his college's annual alumni recognition weekend. "Look." She was feeling a bit annoyed herself. "I'm sorry about your alumni thing, but I certainly didn't plan for my mother to have a stroke." She waited for him to apologize for his insensitivity.

Finally he did. "I'm sorry, Maggie. I hope your mother is okay."

"Thanks." There was no doubt in her mind that he'd find some other arm candy for the weekend. She didn't consider *herself* arm candy, but she also didn't kid herself that Joel liked her for her intelligence. Not that he didn't appreciate an intelligent woman—she was sure he did—but he never would have given her a second glance if she hadn't been attractive, too.

After promising to call him to let him know how long she'd be gone, she spent the rest of the morning getting ready to go home.

Home, Maggie reflected as she stared out the window of the 737, was a place she'd spent most of her life trying to escape. And yet, Rainbow's End, Texas, was the kind of town she was sure many people would love to live in. Nestled in the hill country near Austin, it was home to fifteen thousand inhabitants and growing, although she was certain the city fathers hoped the town wouldn't grow too much.

She didn't blame them. Look what had happened to Austin when too many people decided they wanted to live there. Traffic was horrible, housing prices had skyrocketed, city services had deteriorated, and now, instead of being a place to escape to on the weekends, it was a place to escape from.

But desirable as Rainbow's End was to many, Maggie couldn't wait to leave. Despite her parents' dire predictions of doom, the ink was hardly dry on her high school diploma before she was off to New York to seek her fortune.

For the most part, she hadn't regretted her decision, even though she'd given up the man she loved in the process. Through her hometown paper and the occasional snippet of information from her mother or from Kris Diana, her best friend from high school, Maggie had kept up with Zachary Tate's life, and she knew his wife had died about a dozen years earlier, leaving him with three small children to raise.

God, she couldn't imagine how he had felt when it happened. His wife had committed suicide, and that alone must have been terrible. And then to be left with three young children. How had he done it?

He had a demanding job, too. At the time his wife had died, he'd been a deputy sheriff. A few years later, when the current sheriff had retired, he'd run for the position himself. Ever since he'd been the chief law enforcement officer of Peck County.

Over the years, she'd thought about Zach a lot.

She'd been so crazy about him. They'd begun dating when she was a sophomore and he was a senior, and by Maggie's senior year they were inseparable. Zach had assumed they'd get married as soon as she graduated.

And why shouldn't he? Maggie thought ruefully. That's what most Rainbow's Enders did. They got married young, had kids and stayed in Rainbow's End their entire lives. A weekend in Austin was a big deal for many of them.

But that life wasn't for Maggie. And when she'd told Zach she was too young to get married and had no intention of living out the rest of her life in a one-horse town, he'd been incredulous.

"I don't know why you're so surprised," she'd said. "I've been talking about going to New York forever."

"But I never thought you were *serious,*" he'd said.

She'd thrown her arms around him, pressed herself close. "Come with me," she'd urged. "Oh, Zach, it'll be so exciting. Just think of it. The two of us in the most exciting city in the country!"

"I *am* thinking of it. I don't like big cities. Besides, I have a job, remember?"

"It's just working for your father." Zach's father had a small landscaping business.

He'd stared at her. "Maybe I like working for my father."

She saw that she'd hurt his feelings, and she'd tried

to apologize, but she wasn't going to change her mind. Sure, she loved Zach, but she was too young to tie herself down. The thought of living in that pokey town forever, of having one kid after another, of never seeing anything, never *doing* anything, well, she knew she wouldn't be able to stand it. Heck, she wasn't even sure she *liked* kids.

Until the day she left, she'd really thought Zach would change his mind. But he hadn't. And two years later, he'd married Andrea Shoemaker, who had been one of Maggie's classmates.

Maggie would never forget the day she opened her mail to find the issue of the *Rainbow's End Register* that announced their wedding. Although at the time she was working full-time as a receptionist for a large literary agency and going to NYU at night and thought she was happy, it had hurt like crazy to read about Zach and Andrea, to see the photo of Andrea in her wedding dress. In that moment, Maggie realized she'd always secretly believed Zach would one day come to New York. That ultimately they'd be together.

Maggie sighed. Well, that was all water under the bridge now. An old story. She'd long been over Zach. She'd chosen her life and made a success of it. And by all accounts, so had he.

No regrets, she told herself, reaching for her briefcase. For the remainder of the flight she read a manuscript by an author she considered promising and tried to keep her mind off what she would face when she reached Rainbow's End.

"Sheriff!"

Sheriff Zachary Tate looked up. Standing in the open doorway of his office was his secretary, Jeannie. "I'm sorry, Jeannie. Did you say something?"

Jeannie, a plump fiftyish blonde, rolled her eyes. "Only three or four times."

Zach grimaced. "Guess I was daydreaming."

"Guess you were."

He fought a smile. It wouldn't do to encourage Jeannie. She was cheeky enough. "All right, what was it you wanted?"

"You need to sign these reports so I can get 'em in the mail this afternoon."

Zach stifled a sigh. He hated paperwork. Unfortunately, dealing with paperwork was more than two-thirds of what he did each day. Sometimes he thought longingly of the days when he was just a deputy sheriff, but he knew he couldn't go back.

And even if he could, financially it wasn't feasible. When you were raising three kids on one salary with no hope of supplemental income, you did not voluntarily give up a salary that was twice the amount you'd receive at a lesser position.

"So what were you daydreaming about?" Jeannie said as he signed the reports.

Zach would sooner cut out his tongue than tell

Jeannie the truth. "Just thinkin' about Friday's game." His older son Jason played basketball for the junior varsity team at Rainbow's End High School.

Jeannie grinned. "I know. That was some game, wasn't it?"

"Yes, it was." Zach had been so proud he'd nearly bust his buttons. The opposing team from Pollero, a neighboring town, had been ahead by two points with only twelve seconds left in the game. The Rainbow's End team had possession of the ball and managed to pass it to Jason— their best shooter—with two seconds on the clock. And Jason had scored a three-pointer to give Rainbow's End the win. Zach smiled again, remembering.

He had high hopes for Jason, who showed enough promise at fifteen that he might be able to get a basketball scholarship to a good school. Which would be a godsend since Zach's oldest, Hannah, was only a year ahead of her brother, and Zach had no idea how he would manage to pay for two of them in college at the same time.

On the one hand, he was proud of his kids for being smart enough and ambitious enough to want to go to college, but paying for it was a worry. Zach had been putting money aside, but he knew what he had saved wasn't nearly enough. Yes, a basketball scholarship for Jason would be the answer to a prayer.

Finishing up the paperwork, Zach handed it to Jeannie, who went back to her cubicle, leaving Zach free to return to the thoughts that had plagued him the entire day. Last night, on his way home, he'd stopped at the local supermarket to pick up milk and bread and a few other essentials. In the dairy department, he'd run into Molly Callahan, wife of Jimmy, Maggie Callahan's older brother.

Zach knew it was ridiculous to still think about a woman who'd dumped you more than twenty years ago, but he'd never been able to completely erase Maggie from his mind. He also never lost an opportunity to find out news about her family. So when he saw her, he gave Molly a warm smile and asked her how she was doing. And that was how he heard the news that Maggie's mother had had a stroke and Maggie was coming home.

He and the kids had been on vacation at Padre Island the previous summer when Maggie's father had died, so Zach hadn't known about it until they'd returned. By then the funeral had been over for five days and Maggie had already returned to New York.

And the other times she'd been home over the years, he hadn't known about it. Not that she'd returned often or for long. As far as he could tell, she had maybe come home five or six times, usually for family occasions like weddings or christenings. Occasions to which Zach was never invited. Not that he expected to be. He'd never run around with any of the Callahan brothers, and, after he and Maggie split up, he guessed her family felt it might be awkward for him if they were to meet again.

Molly didn't say when Maggie was coming, and Zach hadn't wanted to ask. So he'd just said he was sorry about her mother-in-law, and they said their goodbyes. Ever since, he'd been thinking about Maggie.

He wanted to see her again, if for no other reason than to put to rest the idyllic picture of her he'd carried all these years.

Damn, she'd been beautiful.

Tall and slender, with long legs and big blue eyes and curly auburn hair. She'd put a fire in his belly that had made him putty in her hands. He still remembered those feelings. How his heart would pound and his hands would tremble when he held her. How they'd neck in the front seat of his dad's pickup truck until they'd both be crazy with wanting each other. How she'd finally stopped saying no, they couldn't, and how, after that, they hadn't been able to keep their hands off each other.

He couldn't believe it when she'd said she was leaving him and going to New York. Up until the moment she was gone, he had thought she'd change her mind.

How could she leave? he'd asked himself over and over. They *loved* each other. He wanted to *marry* her. He'd thought she felt the same way.

But she obviously hadn't, because she'd left. For

months afterward, he kept thinking she'd realize what a crazy idea it was and come back to him. Pride kept him from calling her and begging, even though he was sick from missing her. He'd tried writing to her, but he'd never been any good at expressing himself on paper, so he gave it up, and she didn't write to him.

Her mother, who had always liked him, told him Maggie had a job and was taking classes at NYU at night. "I don't think she's coming back, Zach." Her eyes had been filled with sympathy.

He was sure Maggie would at least come home for Christmas, but she hadn't. When he'd called her house, her mother had said since Maggie was so new on the job, she would only have two days off, so they were going to New York to be with her.

When his birthday came and went in February without even a card from Maggie, he decided that was it. He wasn't going to waste another minute mooning over her. It was obvious she didn't give a damn about him, so he wouldn't give a damn about her. He started dating other girls then, and eighteen months later, he'd married Andrea.

Andrea.

As always, the thought of his late wife produced a mixture of guilt, sadness and regret. Theirs had been a troubled marriage from the beginning. For a long time Zach told himself the fault lay with Andrea, but in his more honest moments he knew he had to share some of the blame for their problems.

Sure, she was insecure and prone to depression, but maybe she would have been happier, maybe they'd have had a better chance at success, if he'd loved her the way he should have.

The way he'd loved Maggie.

Zach rubbed his forehead wearily. He didn't want to think about Andrea. What was done was done and could never be changed.

What was Maggie like now? he wondered. He'd give just about anything to see her. Maybe now that she was a big, successful literary agent she was hard and brittle and no longer as beautiful as his memories.

That would be good, he told himself. That would be real good.

Suddenly fidgety and knowing he was not going to accomplish anything more today, he got up, strapped on his gun, reached for his hat and strode out of his office.

"See you tomorrow," he said, waving to Jeannie, who stared at him with a question in her eyes. He never left the office early. Ignoring the question, he added, "Call if you need me."

Fifteen minutes later he was walking into the kitchen of the three-bedroom ranch house he and Andrea had bought three months after Jason was born. The scent of baking brownies filled the room. Hannah stood at the stove stirring something.

Zach smiled. God, she was a good kid. He'd bet there weren't many sixteen-year-olds who would so willingly take on the responsibility of supervising the household the way Hannah had done. "Smells good."

Hannah smiled back. "It's just spaghetti sauce."

Zach bent down and kissed her cheek. "I didn't expect you to be here early today."

"Choir practice was cancelled because Mrs. Kelly's little girl got sick at day care and she had to go."

Zach nodded absentmindedly, his attention caught by the stack of mail on the counter. He walked over and began leafing through it. Bills and junk mail. He tossed it back on the counter. "Where's Josh?"

"In his room. He said he was gonna do homework, but he's pro'bly—"

"—playing games," Zach finished.

Hannah nodded. "I told him not to, Dad."

"I'll go check. And what about you? Do you have homework?" Sometimes he worried that Hannah spent so much time being the mother of the house, she no longer had time to be a kid.

"Just English lit. I'll have plenty of time to do it after dinner."

Zach left her and headed for the bedroom his boys shared. Just as he'd thought, Josh was completely engrossed in a PlayStation game. "Hey," Zach said, walking over and tousling his twelve-year-old's black hair.

Dark eyes just like Zach's looked up. "Hi, Dad."

"I thought you were supposed to be doing your homework."

"I finished it."

"Really?"

Josh nodded. "Uh-huh. I didn't have that much. Only math."

"Where is it?"

"Right there. On my desk."

Each of the boys had their own desk. Jason's, reflecting his orderly personality, was neat. Josh's, mirroring his more casual approach to life, was covered in a jumble of papers, books and who-knows-what.

Zach walked over and saw a paper covered with math problems. He debated whether to shoo Josh outside or let him continue playing his game.

Zach didn't think it was healthy for kids to spend too much time indoors, and Josh, left to his own devices, would spend days buried here in his room.

But before he could say anything, Josh jumped up, saying, "Oh, man! I almost forgot. I'm s'posed to meet Travis at the school at five. We're gonna shoot baskets. Is that okay?" he asked belatedly.

"Sure, that's fine, as long as you're back by six-thirty for dinner. But you'd better hurry. It's almost five now."

Once Josh was gone, Zach headed for the other end

of the house and the master bedroom. He looked forward to the evenings when he could shed his official persona and just relax at home.

He removed the bullets from his gun and put them, the gun and his badge into the top drawer of his dresser, which he then carefully locked. Although from the time they were old enough to comprehend, his kids had been taught about the danger of guns, and they knew they were never supposed to touch his, Zach firmly believed it was better to be safe than sorry, so he never took any chances that one day one of them just might be curious enough to investigate.

Ten minutes later, dressed in old jeans and an older T-shirt, feet comfortably encased in old scuffed Docksiders, he walked back to the kitchen. Hannah was sitting at the table working on her homework. The brownies she'd baked were cooling on the counter.

"I forgot to tell you," Hannah said, looking up as he entered the room. "Nana called."

"Does she want me to call her?"

"Uh-uh. She said for you to drop by tomorrow." Hannah smiled. "She's making corn chowder. She said she'll make enough for us, too."

Zach's mouth watered just hearing the name of his mother's specialty dish. From the time he was a kid, her corn chowder, jammed full of sweet corn, butter, onions, chunks of ham and poblano peppers, had been his idea of heaven on earth. Washed down with some good Mexican beer, there was nothing better. "All right. I'll call her later. Right now, I'm going out back. I need to fix that fence."

"Oh, good. Mrs. Abbott was asking when you were gonna do it." Mrs. Abbott was their backyard neighbor.

Last week they'd had a bad storm and several boards in the back fence had come loose as a result. Since they had a pool, Zach felt—and obviously Mrs. Abbott did, too—that it was important to get the fence repaired quickly. After gathering the supplies he needed, he began working on the damaged section of fence.

While he worked, his mind wandered back to Maggie. He was determined to see her while she was home. He just wondered if he should call her. Or if he should try to make a meeting seem accidental.

Zach hated playing games, so maybe he should just give her a call. It would be only polite to inquire as to her mother's health, anyway. But if he called, there was no guarantee he'd get to see her.

By the time he'd finished the repairs, he'd made up his mind. Tomorrow night he would stop by the hospital. If, by some chance, Maggie wasn't there, nothing would be lost. He could still call the house.

But one way or the other, he was going to see her. It was time to lay this ghost to rest.

Chapter Two

It was seven-thirty before Maggie pulled the rented Taurus into the parking lot at Tri-City General, the hospital that served Rainbow's End, Pollero, and Whitley. The hospital had changed since she'd last been there, she saw. It looked as if a new wing had been added. That was a clear indication how much the area was growing. She wondered if Callahan Construction, the company founded by her father's younger brother Patrick, one of the most prominent employers in Rainbow's End, had built the wing. Probably, since his company had been the one to build the hospital initially.

She wondered how her uncle was doing. Last she'd

heard, he was still in good health. One of the good things about coming home would be getting to see him and her aunt Rose and all her Callahan cousins. Although Maggie wouldn't trade her life in New York for one here, she did miss her family, especially on birthdays and holidays.

After parking the car, she headed directly to the third-floor waiting area outside the CCU, where she'd arranged to meet Jimmy and Molly.

"Maggie," Jimmy said, giving her a big hug and a relieved smile. "I'm glad you're here." His bright blue eyes—a characteristic shared by every one of his kin, including Maggie—looked tired.

Maggie hugged him back. Although Jimmy was three years older, she had always felt protective of him. Maybe it was because as a kid he'd had severe allergies and was never able to do the things the other kids were doing.

When he released her, she saw that he was now teary-eyed. She felt a bit emotional herself.

Molly, hazel eyes filled with affection, stood off to the side, but once Jimmy moved away, she hugged Maggie, too. "Gosh, it's good to see you."

"You, too." The two women had been instant friends from the first day they'd met. Molly was good for Jimmy, Maggie knew. Sensible and calm, she was a perfect foil to his more impulsive nature.

After the initial greetings were over, Maggie was

ready to rush in to see her mother, but Molly stopped her.

"There are some things you need to know first," she said.

So they all sat down, and Molly and Jimmy brought Maggie up-to-date on her mother's condition.

"Right now she's almost completely paralyzed on her right side," Molly said. "And she can't talk."

"Can she understand you when you talk to her?"

"Yes," Jimmy said. "She understands, and she tries to talk, but..." He stopped, obviously choked up.

Molly took his hand; her eyes were soft with sympathy. "What comes out is gibberish," she continued for him. "But the doctors say that's normal. Gradually, as the undamaged tissues in her brain begin to take on some of the functions of the damaged tissue, her ability to speak should improve. Therapy will help enormously, too." Molly sighed. "She's going to need a lot of therapy, Maggie. Months and months worth."

Maggie nodded. "Where will she have it? Here?"

"Yes. In the beginning. Then when she's well enough to go home, she'll just come in for daily therapy on an outpatient basis."

"How long do the doctors think it'll be before she can go home?"

Molly shrugged. "They don't know. A week. Two.

A month. At this point, it's impossible to tell. It just depends on how much progress she makes.''

"She won't be able to be alone, though," Jimmy said with a worried frown. "Molly and me, we were talking about maybe bringing her to our house."

Maggie looked at their troubled faces. They had a small house and three children. Molly owned and operated a day-care center; she was rarely home before six-thirty. And Jimmy's job as an air-conditioning and heating repairman kept him busy six days a week, sometimes late into the evening. She knew what they were thinking. How could they possibly manage to take care of Mom, too?

"Look," she said, "let's not worry about that part right now. Let's just concentrate on getting Mom better and once she is, then we can discuss all our options."

Jimmy slowly nodded. "You want to go in to see her now, Mag?"

"Yes."

"Want me to go with you?"

Maggie gave him a grateful smile and nodded. So, together they entered the CCU and Jimmy led the way to their mother's curtained section. Maggie's heart ached as she stared at the pale woman lying in the bed. Her mother's eyes were closed, and even in repose, the right side of her face was contorted. Maggie swallowed against the lump in her throat. "Mom," she said quietly.

Her mother's eyes slowly opened. At first, they were clouded, but within moments they cleared and recognition dawned. She opened her mouth, but the only sound that came out was an agonized, "Mah Mah."

Maggie wasn't the emotional sort, but at the sight of her mother struggling to say her name, Maggie's eyes filled with tears.

"Mom, it's okay, it's okay. You don't have to talk." She bent over the bed and kissed her mother's cheek. Taking her mother's left hand, she gave it a gentle squeeze. She tried to smile, but it was hard.

Her mother whimpered, and her eyes stayed clamped to Maggie's. In them, Maggie saw fear and pain and mute entreaty.

"Don't worry, Mom. I know it's frustrating that you can't talk right now, but the doctors say you're going to be fine. It's just going to take some time." Maggie kept her voice as confident and reassuring as she could. "And I won't leave until you are. In fact, I plan to take as much time off work as necessary so I can stay here and be with you until you're completely back to normal."

Maggie could feel Jimmy looking at her, probably wondering where *that* had come from. Maggie couldn't have told him. She had suddenly just known it was the right thing to say, the right thing to do.

"We're all going to help you," she added and was rewarded with her mother's attempt to smile. Maggie kissed her mother again, whispered, ''I love you,'' then she and Jimmy said good-night and left to rejoin Molly in the waiting area.

''Her doctor said she'll probably be moved to her own room tomorrow,'' Jimmy said when they were once more seated in the waiting area.

Maggie looked at him. ''You don't sound happy about it. Isn't that good?''

''Well,'' Molly said, ''it's good in one way, but the trouble is, once she's in her own room, she won't have the constant monitoring she has now. One of us is going to have to be with her most of the time. At least until she can do a few things for herself.''

''That's not a problem. I can do it.''

''Oh, Maggie, you can't imagine how exhausting that can be. Believe me, I know. I went through this with my own mother in the month before she died. And I won't be able to help you much. I've already taken a lot of time off. And I'm terribly short-staffed right now. We're trying to hire someone, but—''

''Stop worrying,'' Maggie said, interrupting. ''After all, it's not like it'll be forever. I'll manage.''

Molly chewed on her lip. ''Well, I guess if you can be here during the day, one of us can come in the evening. And I know your aunt Rose will help out. She was here earlier today.''

Maggie nodded. ''See? It'll be okay. Now, what time are they moving Mom tomorrow?''

''The nurse said about ten.''

Maggie looked at her watch. It was eight-thirty. "I think I'll head on to the house now. Get unpacked and try to get a good night's sleep."

"That's a good idea," Molly said. "I'm tired, too."

The three of them left together, saying their good-byes in the parking lot.

"If you need anything, call," Molly said, giving Maggie another hug.

"Thanks, but I'll be fine."

As Maggie drove to her childhood home, she thought about what Molly and Jimmy had told her, then she thought about what she'd told her mother.

Could she honor her promise to stay in Rainbow's End until her mother was back to normal? What if that took six months? Or a year? Rita was a great assistant, but would she be willing to handle the lion's share of the work for that long?

Maggie had worked very hard to make a success of her agency. She couldn't afford to chance costly mistakes, and no matter how good Rita was, the bottom line was, the agency was Maggie's. Rita was just an employee.

But there was no sense stewing about it. None of those questions needed to be answered tonight. She had said what she needed to say to alleviate her mother's fear. Right now, that was the important thing.

Everything else could wait.

* * *

"Maggie, why don't you go get something to eat?" Molly suggested when she arrived at six-thirty the following evening. "The nurses tell me you haven't been out of this room since you got here this morning."

Maggie smiled wearily. Her gaze moved to the sleeping woman in the bed. "I hated to leave her alone."

"Well, I'm here now. You go on down to the cafeteria. And don't come back for at least an hour!"

"Okay, okay, I'm going." Maggie slung her leather bag over her shoulder. "But first I think I'll put on some makeup. I doubt I'm fit to be seen."

In the bathroom Maggie inspected her face in the mirror. She looked as tired as she felt. Molly had been right. It *was* exhausting to spend hour after hour at the hospital. Not to mention depressing.

But five minutes later, after brushing her hair and putting on fresh lipstick and a bit of eyeshadow and blush, she decided she would pass muster. Her spirits lifted the minute she left the room.

How did the nurses do it day in and day out? She couldn't imagine what kind of strength it took to remain upbeat and positive in the face of so much suffering and pain.

She was deeply grateful for everything the medical personnel at the hospital had done for her mother. They were so caring and optimistic and had reassured her over and over again that this helplessness her mother was experiencing would eventually lessen, that with work and determination her mother could once again be the vibrant, independent woman she had been only days before.

Oh, God, she hoped they were right. The idea that her mother might not be able to live on her own ever again was an ever-present worry, for Maggie knew Molly and Jimmy would then feel it was their responsibility to take care of her, and that just wouldn't be right.

Well, they would just have to cross that bridge when they came to it. If they were lucky, and the nurses and doctors were right about the possibility of her mother making a full recovery, they'd never have to deal with the problem.

Thoughts still on her mother, Maggie entered the cafeteria and headed for the main serving line. She was concentrating on the day's selections, trying to decide between a chicken and rice casserole or stuffed peppers when someone tapped her shoulder.

Startled, she whirled around and gazed in momentary confusion at the tall, commanding presence of a dark-haired, dark-eyed man dressed in a brown uniform. Then, recognition dawning, she nearly lost her cool. "Zach!" she cried.

"Hello, Maggie."

That smile. It had always had the power to turn her knees into water. Feeling just like a schoolgirl tongue-tied in the presence of the star quarterback for the football team, she told her heart to settle down and gave Zach what she hoped was a casual, isn't-it-nice-to-see-an-old-friend? smile in return.

"I heard about your mother," he said. "How's she doing?"

"She's holding her own."

"I'm glad. I always liked your mother."

Maggie nodded. Her heart was still going much too fast. And her stomach! Good Lord, she was a wreck. What was wrong with her that she couldn't handle seeing Zach again? "She always liked you, too," she managed to get out without sounding like a complete fool.

"Uh, Miss."

Maggie turned. A server was pointedly waiting for her to order, and Maggie belatedly realized she was holding up the line. "Oh, I'm sorry." She turned back to Zach. "Listen, Zach, I'd better—"

"Go ahead and get your food," he said. "I'll find a table. You don't mind if I join you, do you?"

"Uh, no, of course not." Maggie turned back to the patient server and said she'd have the chicken and rice. Her heart was thumping like a jackhammer. As hungry as she was, with this turn of events, she wasn't sure she'd be able to eat.

Calm down. What's the big deal, anyway? You've handled sticky negotiations between hard-nosed publishers and demanding clients without giving way to

*emotions or letting either of them know what you
were really thinking. Surely you can handle seeing an
old flame.*

She took some deep breaths and by the time she
got her food and a drink, paid for her selections and
picked up her tray, she had regained most of her com-
posure. Tray in hand, she looked around to see where
Zach was.

It wasn't hard to spot him. He definitely stood out
in a crowd. But then, he always had, hadn't he? If
anything, she thought as she headed his way, he was
even better looking than he had been as a young man.

Zach's mother was half Cherokee, and his Indian
heritage showed in his high cheekbones, his thick
black hair and dark brown eyes. And the snug brown
uniform, holstered gun, and Stetson he now wore only
added to his appeal.

Oh, yes, Zachary Tate was one magnificent speci-
men—the kind of man women couldn't help drooling
over.

Maggie wondered how many women had warmed
Zach's bed since his wife's death. She'd bet there had
been plenty who'd wanted to.

Suddenly, memories assailed her. Memories she'd
do well to try to banish if she hoped to pull off this
unexpected encounter without giving away how much
seeing Zach again had unnerved her.

He stood as she approached. He had taken off his
hat and she saw that his black hair was just as thick

and shiny as it had been when he was a kid. She'd always loved his hair, loved running her hands through it, loved feeling the springy texture, loved the way it smelled....

She swallowed. *Damn it, Maggie. Stop it.*

"Aren't you eating?" she said, after unloading her tray and sitting across from him. All he had in front of him was a can of soda.

"I had a big lunch." His eyes were warm as they studied her. "You're looking good, Maggie."

"Thank you." She was very glad she'd taken the time to fix herself up a bit. "So are you." More to have something to say than because it mattered, she added, "What are you doing here, Zach? Did you come to visit someone?"

He regarded her steadily for a moment. He'd always had that ability, she remembered, to observe without speaking. "The truth is," he said slowly, "I came to see you."

Maggie blinked. "Me?"

He nodded. "Yes. I was going to get something to drink, then head on up to your mother's room. It was just a lucky coincidence that you happened to come into the cafeteria while I was here."

Flustered, she wasn't sure how to answer.

"You're surprised."

"Yes, I guess I am." She spread her napkin across her lap.

"I don't know why. It's normal to be curious about

an old girlfriend, isn't it? I wanted to see what kind of woman you'd become.'' Amusement tinged his voice.

''And…?''

Again he gave her that slow smile. ''And I'm not disappointed.''

''My goodness, Zach,'' she said lightly, ''that's two compliments in less than five minutes. You never used to have such a silver tongue.''

''I was just a kid then. What did I know about sweet-talkin' a woman?''

''Sweet-talking? Is that what you're doing?''

He laughed. ''Eat your dinner. It's getting cold.''

Maggie picked up her fork. ''While I'm eating, tell me about your children. You have, what? Two girls and a boy?''

''Two boys and a girl.''

''And they're how old?''

''Hannah's sixteen. Then comes Jason, who's fifteen. Last of all is Josh, who's twelve.''

''Wow. Two teenagers.''

''Soon to be three. Josh turns thirteen in August.''

''I don't know how you do it.''

''It hasn't been easy, but we've managed because they're good kids. Hannah, especially, is wonderful. She does most of the cooking and a lot of the cleaning, although the boys are getting better about helping. And they all do their own laundry.''

''That's great.''

He nodded. "It was really hard the first couple of years after their mother died, but things are much easier now."

"Have you had any help at all?"

"My mother's helped. And Luke's wife has been good about pitching in."

Maggie smiled. Luke. He was Zach's kid brother and she'd always had a soft spot for him. "How *is* Luke?"

"He's doing great. He married a nice girl, and they've got two boys."

"What does he do?"

"He took over the business when Dad died."

"I wondered about that."

"What? My father's business?"

"Yes. When I left here, you were working for your father, and I thought…well, you led me to believe you were going to stay with him." This was an old source of hurt, for if he could leave his father's business to join the sheriff's department, why couldn't he have left it for her?

Zach shrugged. "Things change." For the briefest of moments, his eyes were shadowed.

There was an awkward silence, which Maggie broke by saying, "And now you're the Sheriff of Peck County."

"Yes. And you're a successful literary agent."

Their gazes held. She wondered if he had as many questions he wanted to ask but felt he shouldn't as she did. Like, did he have any regrets? Like, had he ever wished he'd come to New York with her? Like, was he happy with his life and his choices?

"How long are you planning to stay in town, Maggie?"

"I don't know. It all depends on how my mother does."

"What about your business? Can you afford to be away?"

"I have a great assistant. She can take care of most things, and if she runs into trouble, she can always call me or e-mail me. I do most of my business by phone, anyway." She grinned. "Have cell phone, will travel."

"They're great inventions, aren't they?" But the question was asked in an absentminded, rhetorical way, and she knew he was thinking about something else. He took a swig of his soda as, once again, silence fell between them.

Maggie ate some of her food as she cast about for something to say. In desperation, she finally blurted, "How's *your* mother doing?"

The question brought a smile. "Ma never changes. She spends most days in her garden or cooking or playing with her grandkids." The smile got bigger. "And she's still as stubborn and bossy as ever."

Maggie wondered if Zach's mother's attitude toward her had ever softened. Zach hadn't taken Maggie to his home more than a couple of times, because from the beginning it had been obvious that Awinita Tate didn't like Maggie and wouldn't pretend she did.

Maybe she always knew I'd hurt him, Maggie thought. *Or maybe she just didn't think I was good enough for him.*

"I was real sorry to hear about your father," Zach said, breaking into her thoughts. "The kids and I were on vacation when he died, or I would have come to the funeral."

For the second time in as many days, sudden tears stung Maggie's eyes, and after murmuring "thank you," she turned her attention to her plate so Zach wouldn't see them. When she had her emotions under control again, she wiped her mouth and put her napkin on her plate.

Shoving her chair back, she said, "I'm not very hungry. I think I'd better get back to the room."

Zach drained his soda can and picked up his hat. "I'll walk you back."

As they headed to the elevator and then rode up to the third floor, Maggie was amazed at how many people seemed to know Zach. And it was obvious they all liked and respected him, too.

She guessed she wasn't surprised. He'd always had a way about him that young and old alike responded to. She'd bet he was a very good sheriff.

When they reached her mother's room, Maggie started to say goodbye.

"If it's okay with you, I'd like to pay my respects to your mother."

Maggie hesitated. "I'm not sure she wants to see anyone but family."

He nodded. "In that case, I'll wait out here. If she doesn't want me to, I won't go in."

"It's just that she can't talk."

"Don't apologize, Maggie. I understand."

She pushed the door open and saw that Molly was helping her mother drink some water, some of which had dribbled down her chin.

Maggie smiled as her mother's eyes met hers. "I don't know if you're ready for company," she said softly, "but Sheriff Tate is outside and he'd like to say hello."

Her mother's eyes widened in alarm. Maggie immediately held up her hand. "No, no, it's okay. I'll tell him you're not up to it." Maggie knew Molly was giving her a questioning look, but she ignored it.

Outside, she found Zach leaning against the wall opposite her mother's doorway. A pretty blonde nurse in blue scrubs was standing talking to him, and from her body language it was obvious she found Zach attractive. She turned curiously as Maggie approached.

Maggie looked at Zach. "I'm sorry. She's just not up to visitors yet."

"That's okay."

The blond nurse said, "Well, I've gotta get going. Talk to you later, Zach."

"Sure thing, Jodie. Tell Mike I'll give him a call tomorrow."

After she had walked off, Maggie said, "Guess I'd better get back, too. It was real nice seeing you again, Zach. Say hello to Luke for me." She turned to go.

He reached for her arm. "Maggie…"

She looked up.

"Maybe, once your mother's doing better, I could take you to dinner."

Maggie knew it would be a bad mistake to see Sheriff Zachary Tate again. He was too darned sexy. Too handsome. Too everything. He aroused too many unwanted feelings in her. But even if he wasn't sexy and handsome, even if he didn't make her feel things she didn't want to feel, what was the point in seeing him again? They weren't friends. They had *never* been friends. They had been lovers.

Say you don't think seeing him is a good idea. Say you'll be too busy. Say anything, as long as it's no.

She wet her lips. Looked up into those dark, warm, bottomless eyes. "I—" She stopped. *Oh, God, I'm going to regret this.* "I'd like that."

Zach whistled as he walked across the parking lot to his car. He knew it was crazy to be so jazzed just because Maggie had said she'd like to go to dinner with him, but he couldn't help it.

He couldn't get over how beautiful she was—even more beautiful now than she'd been as a girl. But her appeal for him wasn't just that she was physically beautiful. Hell, he knew lots of beautiful women. The world was full of beautiful women.

No, there was something special about Maggie. There always had been. If asked, he wasn't sure he could put his finger on exactly what that quality was. He only knew that she'd always had the power to make him forget there was anyone else in the world.

Tonight, sitting across the table from her, it was all he could do to keep from reaching over to touch her. His hands had itched to feel her skin. To see if it was as smooth and silky as it used to be. To see if he could put that melting look into her eyes, the one that—years ago—had been reserved only for him. He hadn't been able to take his eyes off her mouth, either. He'd never forgotten that mouth, its softness, its sweetness, its heat....

The sudden glare of headlights coming straight at him snapped him out of his reverie with adrenaline-pumping abruptness. Jerking the wheel, Zach managed narrowly to avoid hitting the other vehicle. It took him a few minutes to regain control of his car, but once he did, he executed a quick U-turn, turned on his dome light and siren, and stomped down on the accelerator. The truck he'd almost hit was moving erratically in the opposite direction as he took off after it.

"Dammit, buddy," he swore. "You're drunker than a skunk. Get that truck off the road before you kill somebody!"

The words were no sooner out of Zach's mouth than he saw headlights coming toward the drunk driver, who was still weaving all over the road. Zach hadn't even realized he'd been holding his breath until the other car passed safely by the weaving truck. By now Zach was close enough to the truck that he could see there was a lone male inside. He also could read the license plate.

"Oh, hell!" he said. "Not again." He recognized the plate. The drunk was none other than Andrea's nephew Clint, who had finally acknowledged the siren and was braking to a stop. Zach pulled up behind him and wearily climbed out of his car.

"Hey, Zach, how ya doin', buddy?" Clint Shoe-maker said as Zach approached the driver's side. He gave Zach a lopsided grin, then hiccuped and started to giggle.

Zach sighed. "Hello, Clint." Although he'd rather do anything but, as a law enforcement officer, Zach was required to arrest the kid and haul his butt into the county jail for the night. He opened the door, grabbing hold of Clint so he wouldn't fall out.

"Hey," Clint said, "Whatcha doin? Wassa problem?"

"You know what the problem is. You're drunk."

"Me?" Clint squealed. "I'm not drunk. I kin hold my liquor better'n anybody."

"Sure, sure you can." While they were talking, Zach had marched Clint over to the patrol car. Opening the backdoor, he deposited him inside. "Just what I need," he muttered, "another go-round with your father."

Andrea's brother Billy—Clint's father—had always blamed Zach for Andrea's death. Relations between them had been strained ever since. Arresting Clint would just be pouring salt on the wound.

It couldn't be helped, though. The law was the law, and Zach had sworn to enforce it. This sure was a helluva way to end a good day, though, he thought as he climbed into the car and prepared to drive his passenger to jail.

And yet, maybe it was exactly the right way to end it. For, seeing Clint, being reminded of Andrea and her family and all his responsibilities, had successfully brought Zach back to the real world.

His world.

A world that hadn't interested Maggie Callahan twenty years ago and sure as hell wouldn't interest her now.

Chapter Three

Although it was the last thing Maggie felt like doing when she finally got home that night, she knew she had to call Joel. She should have called him last night, but she'd been too tired.

Sinking into the ancient leather recliner that had been her dad's favorite chair, she took out her cell phone and pressed the familiar numbers. Joel answered on the second ring.

"Hi," she said. "It's me."

"Hello, Maggie." He sounded cool.

Oh, hell. What was the matter with him? Was he irritated because she hadn't called him *last* night? She wasn't in the mood to assuage his touchy ego. "Just wanted to let you know I arrived safely."

"I see." Not only cool but angry.

"What's the problem, Joel?"

Silence. Then, "You could have called last night."

So she'd been right. Because she was tired, because she was worried, and because she'd known too many men who were self-centered and immature, she clamped her lips shut and refused to say anything else until he stopped his stupid pouting and began to act like a grown-up. The silence lasted a good ten seconds.

Finally he said, "How's your mother?"

"She's improving, but the doctors say it's going to be a long process."

"What does that mean?"

"It means I'll probably have to stay here awhile."

"Awhile? How long is awhile?"

Maggie sighed. "I don't know. No one knows. She has all kinds of therapy ahead of her. She has to learn to walk, talk, eat…all the things we take for granted, she'll have to relearn. It could take months."

"Months! You mean you're planning to stay there *months?*"

"I told you. At this point, I simply don't know."

"And while you're gone playing nursemaid, just what am I supposed to do?"

Maggie closed her eyes. "Look, Joel, I know you didn't sign on for this kind of thing, and that's fine. You're off the hook."

"Just what does that mean?"

''Well, since I have no idea when I'm returning to New York, and since that seems to be a problem for you, then I think it makes sense for us to call it a day.'' Softening her voice, she added, ''I've enjoyed being with you. We had some good times. So no hard feelings, okay?''

''You're *dumping* me?''

''Oh, come on, Joel. Don't act like the injured party here. When you think about it, you'll be relieved.''

His answer was to hang up on her. Maggie looked at the phone for a minute. She felt nothing. Not even regret. Wearily, she leaned her head back. Within minutes, she was asleep.

Just as Zach had feared, the first face he saw when he entered his office the next morning was Billy Shoemaker's. A former football player, Billy was starting to go to fat, the result of too much beer and too little exercise. Today his expression was murderous.

''You son of a bitch,'' he said. ''You just had to lock him up, didn't you?''

Zach stifled a sigh. ''Look, Billy, despite what you think, I didn't want to, but I didn't have a choice.''

''Don't give me that crap! You ruined Andrea's life, and now you're tryin' to ruin Clint's!''

''You know, Billy, if you really cared about Clint the way you say you do, you'd get him some help.

He's got a problem with alcohol, and you blaming everyone else isn't going to solve the problem.''

"He doesn't have a problem! Hell, Zach, he's just a kid sowin' a few wild oats. Just like you and me used to."

"Speak for yourself. I never drove if I'd been drinking."

"Oh, I forgot, you're *perfect*. You never did *anything* wrong. Aside from drivin' my sister to kill herself!''

Zach stared at his former brother-in-law. ''You can keep blaming me all you want, but I'm warning you. You'd do better to quit thinking about the past and start thinking about helping your son before there's another tragedy in the family. Last night I saw him weaving all over the road and stopped him before he had an accident. But the next time he drives drunk, he might not be so lucky. How are you going to feel if, one of these days, he ends up killing himself or worse, some innocent person?''

Without answering, Billy stormed out. Zach sank into his chair and rubbed his forehead. He hated these confrontations with Andrea's brother, but he didn't know what he could do to eliminate them. Billy seemed determined to despise him. Not even the fact that his bullheaded attitude toward Zach had impacted his relationship with his sister's children seemed to make any difference.

Thank God Andrea's parents didn't seem to feel

the same way. Retired and living in Sun City, a retirement community on the outskirts of Georgetown, an easy two-hour drive from Rainbow's End, they doted on their daughter's children. Zach was grateful they were able to get past the tragedy of Andrea's death because he felt it was important for his children to have a good relationship with their grandparents.

Breaking into his thoughts, Jeannie walked into his office carrying a steaming mug of coffee.

"Thanks."

"I figured you might need this." Her smile was understanding.

"Yeah, Billy can ruin a morning better'n just about anything."

"You know, you're right about Clint. One of these days he *might* kill somebody."

"I know."

"Why don't you talk to Judge Berlin? See if you can't get him to make Clint go into some kind of program?"

"I could try, I guess, but the judge is a real stickler for the law. He can recommend, but he can't force someone to enter a rehab program, not for a DWI. All he can legally do is fine him and throw him in jail. Since this is the third time Clint's been arrested, he can also suspend his license. But that's it."

"It's too bad. Clint's a nice kid. I'd like to see him straighten out."

After she'd gone back to her desk, Zach thought

about what she'd said. Clint *was* a nice kid. It was too bad his father was so stubborn and so determined to make Zach the bad guy when it came to episodes like this. Zach only hoped that one of these days Billy would wise up and make an effort to help his son, and that it happened before it was too late.

Maggie's first two weeks in Rainbow's End passed in a blur of long days spent in her mother's hospital room or waiting outside physical therapy. Maggie used the waiting time to call clients, send e-mail, and talk to Rita. Every few days Federal Express would deliver a package of manuscripts, contracts and other paperwork that needed Maggie's attention. It got so the driver began to ask about her mother's condition.

Evenings were spent filled with visits from family and friends. In free moments, Maggie wondered when she'd hear from Zach again, but after the first week passed without a call she decided he had probably changed his mind about taking her to dinner. He'd probably thought about it and come to the same conclusion she should have reached—that renewing any kind of relationship between them was pointless.

She was disappointed. It would have been fun to spend an evening with him. But since it wasn't to be, she had no intention of letting it bother her. Determinedly, she put him out of her mind and plunged herself into the daily routine of helping her mother climb back from the abyss of her stroke onto solid ground.

She and Jimmy and Molly were thrilled that Maureen—after her first depression lifted—began to exhibit signs of the determination and spunk that had carried her through a rough childhood, two miscarriages, the illnesses and deaths of her parents, and the untimely loss of her beloved husband.

By the middle of the third week, her mother had made so much progress her doctors were talking about releasing her into Maggie's care.

Maggie was elated, even though she now knew it would be impossible to cope on her own. She and Jimmy and Molly discussed the problem, and Molly had a suggestion.

"There's this woman, she's come in to help at the center when I've been shorthanded. Her name is Edie Spencer. She's really great, a hard worker. I think we ought to talk to her about helping out with Mom."

"Working with kids is very different from working with an older woman who's sick," Maggie pointed out.

"From what I remember, I think Edie has some experience along those lines." Molly shrugged. "It wouldn't hurt to call her."

As much as Maggie hated to bring up the subject of money, she felt as if she must. "Are you thinking about full-time help or part-time help?" Her mind raced. She could probably afford to pay someone to come in part-time, but she wasn't sure about full-time.

"If you're worried about money," Jimmy said, "we can pay our share."

"Your mom's insurance might pick up part of the cost," Molly said. "I can check on it."

"Okay," Maggie said. "Let's talk to this Edie."

So Molly called Edie Spencer and made arrangements for the woman to come and talk to them. Maggie liked Edie on sight. In her fifties, she was short and dark and had a pleasant, cheerful face and a strong-looking body. Best of all, when they took her in to meet Maureen, the two women seemed to hit it off. Maggie's mother actually smiled at Edie.

They decided Edie would start by coming to the house at noon and staying until eight. That way she would be there when Maggie brought her mother home from her morning therapy, and she could help with Maureen's meals and an evening shower or bath, which would give Maggie a break.

"My kids are grown and gone, so I could even stay overnight, if you needed me," Edie said.

When Maggie went home that night, she felt lighter at heart than she'd felt since that initial phone call from Molly. She decided to celebrate by calling Kris Diana to see if they could get together for some pizza and wine.

"I'd love to," Kris said. "How about if we meet at Rocco's in about thirty minutes?"

Maggie grinned. Rocco's was their old haunt, the place to go after football games and dances. Rocco Fennelli made pizza that rivaled anything Maggie had ever eaten in Little Italy, the kind with thin tender crust and gooey cheese. "Great. See you there."

Shedding her tailored slacks and blouse, Maggie donned her most comfortable jeans, paired them with her favorite T-shirt, slipped her feet into clogs, put on fresh lipstick and was out the door.

She pulled into Rocco's parking lot behind a red Honda Accord that turned out to be Kris's car. The two friends hugged. They'd talked on the phone a few times since Maggie had come home and Kris had stopped in to see Maggie's mother, but this would be the first time they'd have a chance to let their hair down and really get caught up.

"This is just like old times," Kris said when the two entered the noisy restaurant.

Maggie looked around. The place looked the same, and it was just as crowded as it used to be. "I see the kids still like it here."

"Oh, yes."

They headed for one of the empty tables near the back. Once they were settled in and had placed their drink orders, Kris glanced at a table a few feet away. "See that dark-haired boy in the red T-shirt?"

Maggie nodded. "Uh-huh."

"That's Jason Tate."

"Zach's son?"

"Yep."

Intrigued, Maggie studied the boy's face. Sure enough, there were the same high cheekbones, the same black hair, the same nose. In fact, Jason Tate looked uncannily like his father as a young man. "He's a nice-looking boy," she said as she turned back to Kris.

"Yes, he is."

"Do you know him?"

"Not well. But Kim does." Kim was Kris's fourteen-year-old. Kris smiled. "In fact, I think she has a crush on him."

"I can see why."

"I'm sure you can."

Something in Kris's voice caused Maggie to give her a sharp look. "What?"

"Oh, come on, Maggie. You know what."

"No, I don't."

"Gossip has it you were seen having dinner with our esteemed sheriff."

Maggie's mouth dropped open.

Kris shrugged. "Hey, what can I say? It's a small town."

"Kris, I wasn't 'having dinner' with Zach Tate. I ran into him in the cafeteria at the hospital, and he sat down with me while I ate." Maggie couldn't believe that anyone could construe their meeting as "having dinner." She pushed away the thought that she would happily have gone out to dinner with him if he'd called her as he'd said he would.

"You just ran into him, huh?" There was an element of disbelief in Kris's tone.

"Yes." Then feeling guilty about not telling the whole truth, she said, "Oh, all *right*. He admitted he purposely came to the hospital to see me."

Kris's elfin face broke into a huge grin. "I *knew* it! I swear, Maggie, I never see Zach that he doesn't ask about you. The man has been carrying a huge torch for a long time."

"Oh, Kris, that's ridiculous. Why, it's been twenty *years* since we broke up. We were just kids!"

"So? Romeo and Juliet were just kids, too."

"Trust me. Zachary Tate is *not* carrying a torch, huge or otherwise. He simply wanted to see how I'd turned out. Curiosity, pure and simple." She grinned. "He was probably hoping I was now fat and ugly."

"I doubt that."

"Ladies?"

The two women looked up. Their waitress put down their drinks—the house chianti for Maggie, a diet drink for Kris. Conversation was suspended while they placed their order, but when the waitress left, Kris said, "So come on, what did you two talk about?"

"You know, how's the job, how're the kids, how's life treating you. The usual."

"That's it?"

"That's it."

"Why is it I don't believe you?"

"*Kris!*"

Kris shrugged. "So I'm skeptical."

Maggie considered telling her that Zach had asked if he could see her again, but decided against it. Since he hadn't acted on the suggestion, there was no reason to mention it. Besides, Maggie wanted to drop the discussion of Zach and move on to safer territory.

Just then, Zach's son and the boys he was with got up in a noisy pushing back of chairs and teenaged horseplay. A few minutes later they were gone. Their departure seemed to deflect Kris's determination to make Zach their main topic of conversation. Soon their talk turned to Kris's husband John and his job troubles.

"He's afraid the company's going to be bought out," Kris said.

"Is that bad?"

"He thinks so. He says he's expendable in a con-solidation."

"I thought he was head of the human resources department for his company."

"He is, that's the trouble. The other company is bigger and has its own department heads."

Maggie nodded. "Surely he can find another job with his experience?"

"I'm sure he can. It's just that he gets so crazy when things are uncertain. John likes order."

By now their pizza—a large mushroom with green peppers and black olives—had arrived, and the two women enthusiastically dug in. For the rest of the evening, the talk remained easy and, to Maggie's relief, did not contain another reference to Zach. Instead they talked about Maggie's job and what it was like to be a single gal in the big city. Kris confessed her worries about Kim and how quickly she was growing up.

"Last week she asked me how old I was when I 'went all the way,' " Kris said.

"Ohmigod. What did you say?"

"Well, after I picked my chin up off the floor, I said I was a heck of a lot older than fourteen." Kris shook her head. "I don't know, Maggie. It's hard to know what's the right thing to say or do when you're dealing with your kids. She knew I was alarmed, and she said she was only curious, that I didn't have to get all worked up because she wasn't thinking about doing it or anything."

Maggie thought about Kim and what a sweet little girl she'd been. Girls grew up so fast today. "So what did you say then?"

"I told her I was very glad, but that if and when she was considering sex, I wanted her to come to me first, because there were things she needed to know."

"Lord, Kris, I don't know if I could've handled it like that. I'm afraid I'd have lost my cool. It's probably a good thing I'm not a mother. Actually, I think

I got passed over when they gave out motherhood genes.''

"Oh, Maggie, that's ridiculous. You'd make a wonderful mother. The thing is, we all start out clueless, but you learn as you go along.''

From Kim, the conversation moved to high-school classmates, then to Kris's two younger sisters. Before Maggie knew it, it was after ten and Kris said she had to go. "I get up at six, so I've got to be in bed by eleven or I'm wiped out at work.''

"I understand. I'm a working girl, too.''

"This was so much fun. Let's do it again soon,'' Kris said as they approached their cars.

"You can count on it.''

Kris put her arms out for a goodbye hug. "Gee, Maggie, I wish you lived here. I've missed you.''

"I've missed you, too. But—''

"I know. But you love being in New York and doing what you do.''

"Yes.''

As Maggie drove home she thought about what Kris had said. Yes, she did love being in New York and doing what she did. But tonight, listening to Kris, Maggie had to admit, if only to herself, that she had felt a twinge of envy. Because even though Kris was worried about her husband and concerned about her teenaged daughter's approaching womanhood and the problems that would entail, she had something Maggie didn't have. Kris was part of a unit. Sure, she had people who depended on her, but she also had people she could depend on herself. She had people who shared her victories and a shoulder to cry on when confronted with defeats. When it came right down to it, all Maggie had was a job.

Oh, come on, you're just a little depressed right now because of your mother and because you currently have no boyfriend. Kris probably has days when she envies you! Count your blessings. You have your independence, lots of friends and a really exciting life.

Maggie was so preoccupied with her thoughts that when, a few minutes after walking into her mother's quiet house, the phone started to ring, it startled her. Her heart immediately knocked in fear, because the phone never rang at night. Had something happened? Had her mother taken a turn for the worse? She grabbed for it, praying everything was all right.

"Maggie?"

Thank God. It wasn't the hospital. It was Zach. At the realization, her heart beat a little faster. "Zach. Hi."

"What's wrong? You sound funny."

"Nothing's wrong. The phone just scared me. I thought it was the hospital."

"I'm sorry. I didn't wake you, did I?"

"No, of course not. I've been out for dinner. Just walked in the door."

"Out?"

A slow smile spread across her face. Although he'd only uttered one small three-letter word, she knew he was imagining her out on a date. And that he didn't like the idea. "Kris Diana and I went to Rocco's for pizza."

"How *is* Kris? I haven't seen her in a while."

"She's doing great. Actually, she mentioned you."

"Did she?"

"Yes. Your son was there when we got there, and she pointed him out. He seems like a nice boy, Zach."

"Jason's a good kid."

"He looks a lot like you."

"Yeah, everybody says so."

For a few seconds, there was silence. Then they both spoke at once.

"So what did—" she said.

"So how's your—" he said.

They laughed.

"You go first," he said.

"No, no, you called me. You go first."

"I just wondered how your mother is doing."

"She's doing wonderfully. In fact, I think she'll be coming home this weekend."

"That's great, Maggie."

"Yes, we're all really pleased."

"Does this mean you'll be going back to New York soon?"

"No, I don't think so. Mom's a long way from

being able to manage on her own. We've hired someone to come in and help out part-time, but the rest of
the time either Jimmy or Molly or I are going to have
to be there. And since Jimmy and Molly are both
working, it's mainly going to be up to me.''

''You work, too.''

''Yes, but I have the luxury of being able to take
time off, and they really don't. Besides, they've had
the brunt of family responsibility for a long time. It's
my turn.''

''What if she can never be alone again?''

''Then we'll have some hard decisions to make.''

''It's tough seeing your parents grow older and get
sick, isn't it?''

''Yes, but it's also hard to lose a parent with no
warning, the way we did with Dad and you did with
your dad.''

''Well, I hope this all works out and your mother
has a full recovery.''

''Me, too.''

He was silent after that, and just as Maggie was
casting about for something else to fill the awkward
void, he said, ''One of the reasons I called is I thought
maybe we could have that dinner we talked about.''

''That...'' Maggie swallowed. ''That would be
nice.''

''How about Friday night?''

''Friday night sounds good.''

''Of course...'' He laughed. ''It may be tough finding a place you'll enjoy now that you're used to fine restaurants in the big city.''

''Shows how much you know about what happens to women when they hit forty. I eat Lean Cuisine most of the time.''

''You're not forty yet.''

''I might as well be,'' she said glumly. Turning forty later on this year was a sore spot with her.

He chuckled. ''Take it from one who's already there. Forty is a great age. Remember that old saying? Life begins at forty.''

''I never *did* believe that.'' Then she laughed, too. ''I'm only kidding. I'm perfectly happy to be the age I am. But I was serious about the Lean Cuisine. I really don't eat out much. So anywhere you take me will be a treat.''

''Tell you what. How about if we go to the Rainbow's End Inn?''

''That would be really nice. I haven't been to the Inn in years.''

They hung up after arranging for him to pick her up at seven. Afterwards, Maggie stood by the phone for a long time. She couldn't deny the kernel of excitement in her stomach at the thought of an evening with Zach. She also couldn't deny the knowledge that she was playing with fire. *People who play with fire get burned.*

Oh, that's ridiculous, she told herself. Going out with Zach once is no big deal. She wasn't going to fall in love with him again, and he wasn't going to fall in love with her. It was a perfectly safe, perfectly ordinary thing to do. They were just two old friends— she conveniently forgot she'd already decided they'd *never* been friends—going out to relax and talk about old times.

But the tiny kernel of excitement remained and that night Maggie's dreams were suffused with images of Zach. And when she awakened the next morning, she was filled with a sense of well-being. She told herself she felt good because she'd had a great night's sleep, but down deep, she knew she was lying to herself.

Chapter Four

"Gee, Dad, you sure seem happy this morning."

Zach looked at Hannah, who was liberally sprinkling her oatmeal with brown sugar. "Yeah, I guess I am feeling good."

"Any particular reason?"

Zach grinned. "It's a beautiful spring day and I'm having breakfast with my beautiful daughter. Isn't that reason enough?"

Hannah returned his grin.

"Beautiful daughter?" Jason said, entering the kitchen. "You mean this ugly thing?" He swatted at Hannah's ponytail.

"Hey, watch it!" she said.

He swatted her hair again, and the two of them entered into a good-natured tussle.

"Settle down," Zach said mildly.

Just then Josh came running in. One high-top sneaker was untied and his Houston Rockets T-shirt was half tucked in, half out. Zach mentally shook his head. Josh's dark hair was plastered to his head, but the cowlick at its crown refused to be tamed. "Better tie that shoe before you trip on it."

"Dad, I need five dollars," Josh said. He banged open a cupboard and reached for the box of cereal.

"What for?"

"That field trip to San Antonio. I *told* you."

"Oh, that's right. I forgot." Zach reached into his back pocket for his wallet.

"You need to sign my permission slip, too."

"Hey, Dad, I need some money, too," Jason said.

Zach sighed. "What's yours for?"

"Miss Chalmers is sending off for this writing book she wants us to have." Jason made a face. "It's fifteen bucks."

Zach stifled a second sigh. It seemed as if every time he turned around the kids needed money for something. Trouble was, none of these requests were for frivolous things. The field trip was to the Alamo, where Josh would learn about history firsthand—and in a way that would make an impression and stick with him, rather than reading about it in a book. And Jason belonged to an elite group of students that his composition teacher felt had real writing talent. But damn, sometimes Zach felt battered by the demands upon his wallet.

"What about you?" He looked at Hannah. "You need any money today?"

Hannah's smile was mischievous. "Well, I was thinking about buying that red Corvette I saw the other—" She broke off in giggles as Zach gave her a dark look.

Soon, all three kids took off in a flurry of last-minute searches for misplaced belongings, and Zach was left in a quiet, if disorderly, kitchen. He made quick work of the cleanup—he always cleaned up in the mornings since the boys had cleanup duty at night and Hannah already did so much—then headed for the bedroom where he collected his holster, gun, badge and hat.

It was time to start his day.

When Maggie arrived at the hospital Thursday morning, she was surprised to see her cousin Sheila waiting for her. "Sheila! Hi. What are you doing here?"

"I have a doctor's appointment across the street at eleven, so I thought I'd stop by here first and see how Aunt Maureen is doing."

Maggie eyed her cousin's rounded stomach. Sheila's little boy was only nine months old and here she was, six months pregnant with another child.

Maggie couldn't imagine having another baby so soon. Actually, Maggie couldn't imagine having a baby, period. And yet she had to admit motherhood and pregnancy suited Sheila. She looked adorable in a pair of overalls and a T-shirt. Her eyes, hair and skin glowed with good health.

"Where *is* my mother?" Maggie asked, eyeing the empty bed.

"The nurse said they'd taken her down to X ray."

"Did they say how long she'd be gone?"

Sheila shook her head.

"Well, since she's not here, why don't we go down to the lounge area where we can be comfortable? We'll be able to see her when they bring her back. Unless you need to leave right away?"

"No, I've got a good half hour before I have to go."

Once they were settled in the lounge, they chatted about Maggie's mother for a while, then Sheila said, "Jack and I were wondering if you'd like to come and have dinner with us tomorrow night."

"I would have loved to, but an old friend asked me out to dinner. Can I have a rain check?"

"Of course. Is this old friend male or female?"

"Actually," Maggie said casually, "he's male."

"Anyone I know?"

"Oh, I'm sure you do. Everyone knows him. It's Sheriff Tate."

"Really? I didn't know you two were friends."

"We've known each other since we were kids."

"He sure is one sexy hunk. Was he always so good-looking?"

Maggie smiled. "Yes, although truthfully, I think he looks even better now than he did as a kid. Maturity suits him."

"Jack is like that, too," Sheila said, her eyes turning dreamy as she said her husband's name.

Maggie thought it was sweet that Sheila was so in love with Jack. Of course, they were still newlyweds, having gotten married only a little over a year ago. She smiled, remembering how Sheila had called her when she'd thought Jack didn't love her. Maggie had been prepared to have Sheila come to New York to live with her and have her baby there.

But in the end it wasn't necessary for Sheila to leave Rainbow's End. Jack Kinsella had come to his senses and realized if he let Sheila go, he'd be committing the biggest mistake of his life. And by all accounts, he was now just as contented as Sheila seemed to be.

Maggie was glad for her cousin. Sheila was a pretty special person; she deserved to be happy.

"So where is our handsome sheriff taking you?"

"The Rainbow's End Inn."

Sheila gave her a funny look. "Is there something you're not telling me, Maggie?"

"I'm not sure what you mean," Maggie hedged.

"Well, the Inn isn't a place that people go for a

casual dinner. It's kind of a romantic spot. People usually save it for special occasions.''

Maggie made a noncommittal sound.

''He must think a lot of you to take you somewhere like that,'' Sheila pressed.

Maggie avoided her cousin's eyes, which were much too shrewd for Maggie's liking.

''Come on. You know all *my* secrets.''

Maggie rolled her eyes. ''Oh, all right. Many, many years ago, Zach and I were an item.''

Sheila smiled.

''Now don't jump to any conclusions. Tomorrow is just a dinner for old times' sake. Nothing more.''

Sheila's smile got bigger.

''I mean it, Sheila. There's nothing between me and Zach and there's not going to be. I have a life in New York, and he has a life here.''

''So?''

''So neither of us is interested in anything else.''

''Well, if you're not interested in Zach Tate, you're a rarity in this town, because most of the women in Rainbow's End would be more than happy to warm his bed, temporarily or otherwise.''

Maggie could have kicked herself. Here she was, a sophisticated woman of the world, yet Sheila's words caused her face to heat, and she knew it held a telltale blush. Sheila, however, was kind enough not to comment, and the conversation moved on to other things.

But after Sheila left, Maggie kept thinking about

what her cousin had said. And although she didn't want them to, those thoughts led to others.

Trouble was, Sheila had reminded Maggie of some things best forgotten. Like the fact that Zach Tate had been a wonderful lover. Inexperienced, yes, but instinctively generous and thoughtful, the kind of man who put his partner's pleasure first.

In fact, in all the years since, Maggie had never been with anyone who even compared to Zach.

But he could be the most fantastic lover on the face of the earth, and that still wouldn't change a thing. *Don't forget that, Maggie,* she reminded herself. *Zachary Tate is just an old friend, and that's all he ever can be.*

Hannah waved goodbye to Bonnie Fisher, who had given her a ride home, and slowly walked down the driveway to the backdoor. She blinked in surprise. Her dad's patrol car was in the garage. It was only four-thirty. He never came home this early. Was something wrong?

Heart beating faster, she hurried inside. "Dad?" He was nowhere in sight. "Dad!" she called in a louder voice. She dumped her backpack on the kitchen table and walked down the hall toward the master bedroom. The door was partially open, and she could hear the muffled sound of the shower from the bathroom beyond.

She felt silly to have been worried. Obviously her

dad had somewhere to go tonight. Probably a meeting. Or maybe even a speech. He was often called upon to give talks to civic groups. Retracing her steps, she went back to the kitchen and retrieved her backpack, then headed for her own bedroom.

Fifteen minutes later, she was in the kitchen rummaging through the refrigerator as she tried to decide what she might cook for tonight's supper. It looked as if it would only be her and Josh, because she knew Jason was working tonight and would eat at the restaurant. He'd recently gotten a weekend job at Burger Heaven, a local teen hangout.

Josh wasn't picky. Maybe she could just make some macaroni and cheese. She'd seen a box of the prepared kind in the pantry. And there was enough lettuce and some carrots for a salad. They were really low on milk, though. Maybe she ought to make a supermarket run. She'd just check and see what else they might need.

She shut the refrigerator and turned toward the pantry. Then she jumped, startled. Her dad was standing in the doorway watching her.

"Sorry," he said, smiling. "I didn't mean to scare you." He wore a pair of old shorts and a T-shirt, and his hair was still wet from the shower.

"Hi, Dad." She looked at his clothes. "I thought maybe you were going out."

"I am. But I don't have to get dressed for another hour."

Hannah waited for him to say where he was going. When he didn't, it made her curious. "You're not going to be here for supper, are you?"

He shook his head. "No."

"Then it's okay if I just make something easy for me and Josh?"

"I thought I'd give you some money and you could go out somewhere. Unless you have plans?"

Hannah sighed. "No." She'd hoped Kirk Brittain would ask her out, but he hadn't, and her two best friends both had dates, so that left her with nothing to do.

"Or you could order some pizza if you don't want to go out."

"Yeah, maybe we'll do that." Although Hannah would have preferred a burger or Chinese food, she wasn't keen on the idea of other people knowing the best she had to do on a Friday night was go out with her little brother.

"Okay, good."

"Where are *you* going, Dad?" If she hadn't been looking directly at him, she would have missed it. Her dad, normally so unflappable, got this funny look on his face and didn't meet her eyes.

"I'm, uh, going out to dinner with a friend."

Hannah, to her astonishment, realized her dad must have a *date*. Why else would he act like this?

He finally met her gaze. "What?"

She grinned. "You've got a date!"

"I…" He stopped. Smiled sheepishly. Shrugged. "Yes, I guess I do."

"*Dad!* Who is she? Anybody I know?" She tried to remember the last time her dad had taken someone out, and she couldn't. That's how long it had been.

"Just an old friend."

"An old friend? Who?" Hannah knew all her dad's old friends.

"You don't know her."

"Oh?" Now Hannah was *really* intrigued.

Pretending an interest in the day's mail, which he'd tossed on the kitchen counter earlier, he didn't respond.

"Dad?"

After a moment, he finally looked up. "You're not going to give up, are you?"

"Nope."

With an exaggerated sigh, he said, "Man, I sure do have a nosy daughter."

"*Da-ad.* You're *stalling*…."

"All right. Her name is Maggie Callahan, and she used to live here when we were both kids. Her mother's sick and she came home to be with her. I ran into her one day at the hospital and we're going out to dinner tonight. That's it. No big deal."

"You said she used to live here. Where does she live now?"

"New York."

"Really? Cool." Hannah had done a lot of reading

and research on New York, because in her secret heart of hearts, that's where she wanted to go to school, even though she knew the chances of that happening were probably zero. "What does she do?"

"She's a literary agent."

"Gosh." Jason would flip. He wanted to be a writer. And their dad knew a literary agent. Hannah could hardly wait to tell her brother.

"Now, is the third degree over?"

Even though there were a million questions she wanted to ask, Hannah nodded. Her dad was pretty patient, but he had his limits.

Later, after he'd gone out—looking pretty handsome, too—and she and Josh were waiting for their pizza to arrive, Hannah speculated on just how truthful her dad had been. He'd said he and this Maggie Callahan were just old friends. But he sure hadn't acted that way when Hannah had questioned him. He'd acted a whole lot more interested in her than he'd let on.

Hannah was dying to know what Maggie Callahan looked like. Suddenly, she had an idea. Her dad had a bunch of old yearbooks in the cupboard in the dining room. Maybe Maggie's picture would be in one of them.

Hannah looked in her dad's class yearbook first, but there was no Maggie Callahan among the graduating seniors. And the underclassmen didn't have individual pictures, just group ones. Still, why not look?

Turning to the appropriate section, she scanned the junior class pictures, but there wasn't any Maggie Callahan there, either. She debated whether she should even bother looking through the sophomore photos, but finally she did. And suddenly there she was. Maggie Callahan. Top row, third from the left.

Hannah squinted at the picture. Long curly hair, a pretty face. And she looked tall. And nice, Hannah thought. She had a nice smile.

An old friend, her dad had said. Did that mean they'd been friends the way Hannah and Mark Redding were friends? Mark had lived across the street from Hannah her whole life. They had played together when they were young and now they were real buddies and could talk to each other about anything, but that was it. Mark had a girlfriend and Hannah, well, Hannah wished she had a boyfriend, but not Mark.

Or had her dad and this Maggie person dated? And if they had, did that mean her dad might still be interested in her? Hannah thought about that for a while. How would she feel if her dad *was* interested in this woman? What if he married her?

Hannah and Jason had often talked about what it would be like if their dad got married again. They both had mixed emotions about it, although Jason said he didn't care one way or the other, unless, of course, the woman was mean or didn't seem to like them. Hannah wasn't quite so cool with the idea, even though she couldn't imagine her dad wanting to be with anyone who wasn't nice. Actually, it was hard to picture her dad with anyone, period.

Jason didn't remember their mother, but Hannah did. And even though it had been twelve years, it was still painful for Hannah to think of her mother's death in terms of suicide, so most of the time she didn't. She knew, from the counseling sessions she'd had, that the reason it had been so hard to face the truth— that her mother had taken her own life—had been because of the feelings of guilt that knowledge had caused in Hannah.

In her brain, Hannah understood she wasn't to blame for her mother's depression and unhappiness, but sometimes she still felt guilty. Her dad and Mrs. Ferrell, her counselor, and her Nana Tate had all explained that no one was to blame for her mother's death. That her mom had just had some severe problems, and she simply couldn't cope.

Mrs. Ferrell had also said her mother killing herself hadn't meant she didn't love Hannah and her brothers. "Don't ever think that," she'd emphasized.

Hannah wondered if her dad felt guilty sometimes, too. If he thought there were things he should have done and didn't. Maybe that was why he rarely dated anyone. Maybe he thought he didn't deserve to be happy.

But he *did* deserve to be happy. Everyone deserved to be happy. Wasn't that what Mrs. Ferrell had finally pounded into Hannah's head? That she couldn't blame herself for her mother's inability to face her problems and that she had to go on and live her life and be happy?

The arrival of the pizza interrupted Hannah's thoughts, but once she and Josh were busily eating, they once more turned to her dad and tonight's date.

She really hoped he had a great time tonight. And if something came of this date, if her dad decided he was ready for a relationship, then Hannah wasn't going to be selfish. She was going to be glad about it and what's more she'd make sure her brothers were glad about it, too.

Maggie felt like kicking herself for not bringing at least a couple of her dressier outfits home with her. All she had to wear to dinner with Zach that was the least bit appropriate was a short, cap-sleeved black crepe dress that she'd thrown into her suitcase as an afterthought. She guessed it would have to do.

She took particular care with her makeup and hair and, at the last minute, went rummaging through her mother's jewelry box to see if there was anything she could find that would jazz up the black dress.

Pearls? No. Too middle-aged. Cameo brooch? No. Too old-fashioned. Diamond drop earrings? No. Too delicate. Frustrated, Maggie closed the box. None of this conservative jewelry was her. She wore silver chokers and chunky earrings. Sophisticated, career-woman-from-the-big-city jewelry.

She sighed. Oh, well. She guessed she'd just make do with her diamond studs and the minimalist look.

She slipped on her black sling-back heels and had just finished tucking some tissues in her purse when the doorbell rang. She forced herself to walk leisurely toward the front door, even though excitement sizzled in her stomach. She couldn't help comparing tonight to all those nights in the past when Zach had come to pick her up. How she'd race to the door. How her heart would pound and she'd want nothing more than to fling herself into his arms.

Pushing the memories away, she opened the door.

Oh, my. He looked terrific. She loved the charcoal jacket, the black shirt and slacks.

"Hi." His gaze was warm and admiring as it met hers. "You look great."

"Thanks." She could feel herself flushing. Honestly, what was the matter with her? Wouldn't her friends in New York laugh if they could see her? Jaded Maggie, who never got excited over any man, acting as if she'd never been out with a good-looking man before.

"Ready?"

"Yes."

They walked out into the still-warm May evening. The scent of the gardenias in bloom on the shrubs flanking her mother's front door perfumed the air, and from somewhere close by, the strains of someone practicing a violin floated through an open window.

Maggie took a deep breath and thought how different her surroundings were from the ones she was accustomed to in the city.

"Sorry about the truck," Zach said. "It was either this or the patrol car."

"I don't mind." In fact, as he helped her up into the red pickup, Maggie was amused. She thought about Joel's Jaguar, the limousines he preferred when he wasn't driving himself, the BMW convertible she rented for weekend getaways. And yet she felt perfectly comfortable in Zach's truck.

What was it they said? You can take the girl out of the small town, but you can't take the small town out of the girl?

"What are you smiling about?"

"Just thinking how long it's been since I've ridden in a pickup."

For a few minutes after that, they didn't talk. Then, chuckling, Zach said, "When I walked up to the door tonight, I felt like a kid again."

Maggie grinned. "You, too?"

Reaching over, he squeezed her hand. "It's good to have you home again, Maggie."

His brief touch warmed her all the way to her toes. "Thanks. It's good to be here." The reply had been automatic, but once she'd said the words, Maggie realized she meant them.

She was sorry it had taken her mother's illness to get her there, but now that she was home, she was glad. Every once in a while, a person *should* go home, if only to remember who they were and where they'd come from.

Zach switched on the radio, and the inevitable country music that filled the cab only reinforced the feelings of nostalgia that Maggie felt so strongly. She didn't even like country music, yet she found herself humming along with the female vocalist.

In no time at all, it seemed, the hundreds of twinkling white lights in the trees surrounding the Inn appeared, announcing the entrance to the restaurant. "I'd forgotten about the lights," Maggie said.

Zach pulled into the circular driveway and the valet parking attendant jumped to attention. He opened Maggie's door and helped her out, then walked around to take Zach's place in the driver's seat.

Hand lying gently against the small of her back, Zach guided Maggie inside. She looked around with pleasure. Another thing she'd forgotten was how pretty the Inn was. A massive stone fireplace adorned one wall of the main room, and open French doors that overlooked a beautiful park-like setting of trees and flower-bordered walks lined the opposite wall.

The maître d' led them to a small round table where they would have a good view of the grounds. Flickering candlelight, a small crystal vase filled with pink roses, a snowy tablecloth and delicate crystal wineglasses all contributed to the romantic ambiance. "This is just lovely," Maggie said once they were seated.

Zach smiled, his dark eyes gleaming in the candlelight.

Heavens, he really was gorgeous. No wonder she'd been so crazy about him. What female wouldn't be? She was sure Sheila hadn't exaggerated when she'd said there wasn't a woman alive who wouldn't be happy to be with Zach.

Wouldn't he make a splash in New York? she thought in sudden amusement. Compared to the preponderance of self-centered young Turks, gays and looking-for-something-on-the-side bored married men that seemed to form the majority of available men in the city, Zach would be considered a lottery win.

Their waiter took their drink orders. Once he was gone, Zach said, "What's the latest on your mother? Is she still coming home this weekend?"

"Yes, probably on Sunday."

"That's great."

Maggie nodded. "She's done much better than they expected, better even than we'd hoped. She'll still need months of therapy, both physical and speech, but the prognosis is really promising."

"So does that mean you'll be staying awhile?"

"It looks that way."

He smiled. "I'm glad."

Against all common sense, against everything

Maggie knew was wise and smart, suddenly she was glad, too. But before she could say so, their waiter came back with their drinks, and in the minutes while he attended to them, Maggie knew it was a good thing she hadn't had a chance to say what she was feeling, because the last thing she wanted was to give Zach the wrong idea.

Once the waiter was gone, Maggie picked up the menu and, after a moment, so did Zach. Because she wasn't familiar with the relative merits of the Inn's offerings, Zach recommended his two favorites, the salmon and the scallops, both house specialties. "The New York strip steak is terrific here, too," he added. "And I'm told the sea bass is outstanding, even though I haven't tried it."

"Hmm," Maggie said. "I love sea bass. Maybe I'll have that."

Once their decisions were made, Zach leaned back in his chair and said, "Tell me about your job."

"You sure you want to hear? Your job is probably a lot more interesting."

He smiled. "That's a debatable point. Some weeks the most interesting thing that happens is a cat stuck in a tree."

Maggie laughed. "I thought the fire department got cats out of trees."

"Okay, so maybe I was exaggerating, but seriously, my job is three-quarters routine management and paperwork and one-quarter law enforcement. Now…tell me about being a literary agent.''

So Maggie did. Pretty soon she had him laughing as she described the way she'd outfoxed a particularly stubborn publisher who'd tried to get away with low-balling one of her most promising clients.

''You make what you do sound like a game.''

''That part of the job—negotiating a good contract—is like a game. A game of wits. A game of strategy.''

''More like a game of chicken, I'd say.''

She grinned. ''That, too.'' Then the grin faded. ''But there's a whole other aspect to what I do, and it's really the part I love the best.''

''And that is?''

''Discovering new talent. There's nothing better than reading something that excites you. Something you know is really good and helping find a home for it. And if the author of the work is someone you like and respect, that's icing on the cake.''

He nodded. ''So you're happy, Maggie? You're not sorry you left here? It was all worth it?''

Maggie's smile faded. ''I…'' She stopped, at a loss. What could she say? What did he want her to say?

''You don't have to answer that. I don't have any right to question you.''

Without thinking, she reached across and laid her hand over his. ''Yes, you do. No one has a better right." She sighed. "Maybe it's time to talk about this."

Their gaze held for long seconds. Turning his hand over, he clasped hers firmly.

Maggie swallowed. "I know I hurt you, Zach," she said softly. "But I was hurting, too. I didn't want to leave you, but I couldn't stay here."

"I know."

"For a long time, I couldn't understand why you didn't come with me. I..." She took a deep breath. "I thought you didn't love me enough."

He shook his head.

"I know. You *did* love me. Just as I loved you. But despite what we felt for each other, it just wouldn't have worked for us. It wasn't right. Not then. Maybe if we'd been older..." Her voice trailed off.

"It's okay, Maggie. I wasn't asking for an apology or even an explanation. I really just wanted to know if you were happy."

Maggie nodded. "For the most part, yes. Of course there are days when I wonder 'what if,' but who doesn't? We always wonder what our lives would have been like if we'd taken another road. Don't you?"

"All the time."

"But you have want you always wanted, don't you, Zach?"

His smile was crooked, self-deprecating. "For the most part."

Maggie smiled. "Are you making fun of me?"

He squeezed her hand, then let it go. "I'd never make fun of you." But his eyes twinkled.

Maggie was glad the atmosphere had lightened. Right now she wasn't sure she could have handled any more talk about the ways in which they'd hurt each other in the past. She felt too vulnerable and—*admit it, Maggie*—far too attracted to Zach. She was afraid if they'd kept on in that same serious vein for very long, she might have said something she'd deeply regret.

Be careful, she told herself. *Be very, very careful. Twenty years may have passed, but there's still something between the two of you. Something that—if you ignore the danger signals and plunge ahead—could make past hurts seem like nothing compared to what might lie ahead.*

Chapter Five

Zach had just poured his first cup of coffee and was sitting down to read the paper when the phone rang. He frowned at the clock. It was only eight-thirty. Who the hell was calling this early?

It had better not be the department. This was the first Saturday he'd taken off in a long time. And if it *was* the department, it had damned well better be a murder and nothing less to justify a phone call first thing in the morning.

He grabbed the phone, snapping out a curt, "Hello?"

"Well, you don't have to bite my head off!"

"Ma." He relaxed. "Sorry. I thought it was the department."

"Hmph," she sniffed, not mollified.

"Ma, I said I was sorry. Now what's wrong?"

"Wrong? What makes you think something is wrong?"

Even though she would try the patience of a saint, and Zach was no saint, he couldn't help grinning. His mother always managed to turn any question around so that the other person was the one having to answer instead of her.

"Well, I just assumed something must be wrong, since it's very early for a phone call." *Even for you,* he added silently.

"I knew you'd be up."

He almost hadn't been. It had been close to midnight when he'd said good-night to Maggie—a goodnight that included a kiss on the cheek, as opposed to the kind of kiss he'd have preferred to give her but knew would probably be a mistake. So it was nearly one before he'd gotten into bed and almost one-thirty before he'd fallen asleep.

Yet habit was hard to break. Six-thirty was his normal wake-up time, and this morning had been no exception.

"I called last night. Did Hannah tell you?"

"Hannah was asleep when I got home."

"She didn't leave you a note? I told her to leave you a note."

Zach rolled his eyes.

"She should have left you a note."

"She probably forgot. You know how kids are. Now c'mon, Ma, what's the matter? Do you need something?"

"I thought you'd raised your children to be more responsible, Zachary. Anyway, it's not what *I* need."

From long experience, Zach ignored the implied criticism of his parenting skills. His mother's remark came from force of habit, not because she thought there was anything wrong with his kids or the way he'd raised them. In fact, Awinita Tate was inordinately proud of her grandchildren. And Hannah was a particular favorite.

When he didn't answer, she said, "Did you have a good time last night?"

Ah. So that was it. Hannah must have told his mother where he'd gone. And probably with whom. Bracing himself, he waited for what he was sure was coming.

"I can't believe you didn't learn your lesson twenty years ago."

He'd been right. That was what this call was all about. The whom, not the what.

"Haven't you had enough trouble in your life?" she continued, her voice becoming more heated as she warmed to her subject.

Zach gritted his teeth. *Don't say it. Remember, she's your mother.*

"Some men have no sense when it comes to

women," she continued. "And I believe you're one of them, Zachary."

"You know, Ma, I—"

"What is she doing back in Rainbow's End, anyway? I thought she hated it here."

"Her mother had a stroke. Maggie came home to help out."

"Yes, I knew about her mother. But how did you know Maggie was home? Did she call you?"

Enough was enough. "Look, Ma," he said as evenly as he could manage, "I'm not going to talk about this. The only thing I'll say is, there's nothing for you to get all worked up about. But even if there was, it would be my business, not yours."

"Well! If *that's* the way you feel about it."

"That's the way I feel."

"You should be ashamed of yourself, Zachary. I'm your mother. You owe me respect."

"I respect you. But respect goes two ways."

"And what do you mean by that?"

"I mean you aren't showing me much respect. I'm a grown man, not a child. I don't need you to tell me how to live my life."

"When I see you doing something foolish, I have a duty to say something."

Zach counted to ten. Sometimes his mother drove him nuts. Sometimes he wanted to strangle her. When he was able to see the humor in her machinations, he told himself it would be justifiable homicide. Today wasn't one of those days. Today he was fresh out of humor.

"Zachary? Are you still there?"

"Yes," he said wearily, "I'm still here."

"I'm sorry, Zachary, if the truth hurts, but that woman is poison. If you can't think of yourself, at least think of your children."

Because every answer involved him saying something he knew he'd regret, he clamped his lips shut.

After several silent seconds had passed, his mother said huffily, "I'm very disappointed in you, Zachary."

And then she hung up.

Zach was shaking his head as he replaced the receiver. He loved his mother, and most of the time he liked her. But when she got into one of these moods...

Suddenly he chuckled. His mother reminded him of that old childhood rhyme about the girl with the curl in the middle of her forehead. That was Awinita Tate. When she was good, she was very, very good, but when she was bad, she was horrid.

Sobering, he reached for his coffee. Why did his mother dislike Maggie so much? No matter what she had implied over the years, he knew her feelings had nothing to do with the fact Maggie had dumped him all those years ago. Hell no, she'd been glad Maggie was out of the picture because she had disliked Maggie from the very beginning.

He'd never forget the first time he'd taken Maggie home to meet his parents. It hadn't been a formal thing, just an idea he'd had on the spur of the moment. He and Maggie had spent the day at the lake and they were on their way back to Rainbow's End when he'd said, "I need to stop at the house for a minute. Is that okay?"

She'd smiled at him. "Okay."

He still remembered how pretty she'd looked that day, smiling over at him like that. Her nose was sunburned and her hair was a tangled mess from swimming and the wind, but she was still the prettiest girl he'd ever seen.

He'd been so proud to introduce her to his parents, sure they'd think she was as wonderful as he did. His father hadn't disappointed Zach. Walter Tate had liked Maggie; that was obvious from the way he'd beamed at her and welcomed her. But it was almost immediately clear to Zach that his mother didn't. Her dark eyes turned flat and disapproving as she studied Maggie.

Belatedly, Zach realized maybe it hadn't been such a hot idea to come to the house after spending the day in the water. His mother was a stickler for what she termed proper respect for his elders, and maybe Maggie's disheveled appearance seemed like disrespect to her.

For the first time, he realized how the hole in the seat of Maggie's cutoffs and the skimpiness of her tube top and the way her nipples were outlined might offend his mother. Yet it also bothered him that his mother wasn't even giving Maggie a chance, that she was judging her on her appearance alone.

After all, she sure didn't like it when people judged him or his brother without knowing them. He hadn't experienced prejudice often, but there had been times when he was young when one of the kids in school had made remarks about his Indian heritage—probably parroting their parents.

His mother had been indignant when he'd told her, saying their heritage was a proud and noble one, and she didn't want him associating with anyone who didn't appreciate that.

Now here she was, making assumptions about Maggie without having any idea what Maggie was like.

"Your mother doesn't like me," Maggie said after they were once more back in Zach's father's truck and heading for Maggie's house.

"That's not true," Zach said, but even to his own ears his denial sounded weak. "It just takes a while for her to warm up to people. You'll get along fine once she gets to know you." He was determined that the next time he took Maggie to his home, they would both be dressed up, so that his mother could see Maggie in a different light. The way *he* saw her.

"I hope so," Maggie said.

"Don't worry, Maggie. It'll be okay."

But no matter how he tried, no matter how many times he'd taken Maggie home, it hadn't been okay. Awinita Tate had never warmed up to Maggie. And when Zach had tried to talk to his mother about it, she hadn't denied it. "But why?" he'd finally said in exasperation. "Why don't you like her?"

"She's not our kind, Zachary."

Her answer had infuriated him, and for the first time in his life, he'd lashed out at her, saying, "What are you saying? That I'm not good enough for her?"

She'd given him an incredulous look. "No, Zachary, I'm saying she's not good enough for you."

Thinking back on that conversation and how angry he'd been and how he'd gone for weeks barely speaking to his mother reminded Zach once again of how painful Maggie's defection had been.

Maybe his mother was right.

Maybe he really *was* crazy.

Because no matter what he'd said to his mother, and no matter what he'd told himself, he knew he hadn't taken Maggie to dinner last night simply for old times' sake. He'd taken her to dinner because she had always been irresistible to him.

"Was that Nana on the phone?"

Shaking off his thoughts, Zach turned to see a sleepy-eyed Hannah standing in the doorway. "Yes, it was."

She made a face. "I'm sorry, Dad. She called last night, and I forgot to leave you a note."

"It's okay, honey. Doesn't matter."

Hannah yawned and stretched. "Oh, good. I was afraid she'd be mad." Shuffling over to the pantry, she opened it and removed a box of cereal. "So did you have fun last night?"

"Who wants to know?"

Hannah grinned. "Your nosy daughter. Who else?"

"In that case, yes, I had a real nice time."

Hannah took a bowl out of the cupboard. "So are you gonna take your friend out again?"

Zach poured himself a second cup of coffee. "I think that falls under the classification of Dad's business."

Hannah smiled and poured cereal into her bowl. "That means yes."

"And why do you think that?"

"'Cause if the answer was no, you'd have said so."

Zach looked at his daughter, a girl almost too smart for her own good.

"Is Miss Callahan still as pretty as she used to be?" She opened the refrigerator and took out the gallon of milk.

"How do you know what Maggie used to look like?"

"I looked her up in your old yearbook."

Zach swatted at her, but she twisted out of his reach.

"Well, I was curious!" she said, laughing. "You always want to know about the people *I* date."

"I'm your father. I'm responsible for you."

"And I'm your daughter with your best interests at heart," Hannah said primly.

"Careful. You're starting to sound like Nana."

To the tune of Hannah's outraged protest, Zach escaped to the relative peace of the patio, where he spent the next hour reading the morning paper, listening to the mockingbirds and watching a couple of squirrels chase each other up and down the big live oak tree at the back of the yard.

Inevitably, his thoughts returned to last night. He wondered what his mother would say—for that matter, what his *daughter* would say—if they knew how he'd felt sitting there in the Rainbow's End Inn with Maggie. He'd told Hannah he'd had a real good time. Truth was, he couldn't remember ever enjoying himself more.

Maggie was good company. She was more than just a sexy, attractive woman. She was smart and funny and great fun to be with. She was also someone who cared about other people, and she knew how to listen.

In short, she was just about perfect.

Which meant if he had any sense of self-preservation at all, he'd relegate last night to the realm of pleasant memory and for the rest of her stay in Rainbow's End he'd stay as far away from Maggie Callahan as he could get.

Maggie's mother had only been home for two days, and already Maggie was worn out. Ferrying Maureen back and forth to rehab for her different therapies as well as helping Edie attend to Maureen's physical needs quickly took its toll.

Her mother's difficulty in communicating was probably the most formidable hurdle for all of them. It frustrated Maureen that she couldn't easily make her wishes known, and most of the time, the harder she tried, the worse it was. Maggie found herself trying to help her mother by guessing what she was trying to say, and that only infuriated her. Sometimes Maggie had to bite her lip to keep from saying anything and give her mother time to form the words herself. After just one day of this, Maggie went out and bought a slate and some chalk.

Eating was also a problem area. Because her mother's right side was still affected, she had difficulty chewing. Sometimes food dribbled out of her mouth, and tears of frustration would well in her eyes.

It hurt Maggie to see her mother like this, but she knew—from what the therapist had instructed—that it was best to let her mother do as much on her own as she could. So neither Maggie nor Edie did more than cut Maureen's food, and somehow her mother managed to get most of it eaten.

In between the tasks of caring for her mother, Maggie also tried to keep up-to-date on everything going on in her office. This proved to be nearly as hard.

"Maggie, you don't have to call here morning, noon and night!" Rita said after Maggie's fourth phone call of the day. "Everything is *fine*. I'd tell you if it wasn't."

"What about the Buckley contract?"

"I'm on top of it. Denise O'Toole said she'd courier it over in the morning."

"You're sure?"

Rita barely stifled her sigh. "I'm positive."

After Maggie disconnected the call, she grimaced. She hated feeling out of control and right now, every single phase of her life seemed to fall into this category.

The thought no sooner crossed her mind than the doorbell pealed, and when Maggie walked to the front of the house, she saw Zach standing on the other side of the screened door.

Yessirree, totally out of control, she thought wryly as her heart skipped at the sight of him. She'd finally admitted to herself how disappointed she'd been when several days had gone by since their dinner and she hadn't heard from him.

But despite the turmoil she felt, she managed to greet him casually, saying, "Hey, Zach."

"Hey, Maggie. How's it going?"

"Okay. What brings you here?"

"I was in the neighborhood and thought I'd stop by, say hello to your mother."

"That was nice of you." She unlatched the door and gestured him in.

Removing his Stetson, he walked into the entryway.

Maggie self-consciously pushed her hair away from her face. She was sure she looked a mess. "She's in the kitchen with Edie. C'mon back." Quietly, she added, "She has a hard time talking and gets frustrated over it, so don't—"

"I understand."

"Just bear in mind she may not be happy to see you, and if she isn't, please don't take it personally. It's just that she's embarrassed by her condition."

"Maggie, it'll be okay. Quit worrying."

Maggie was acutely conscious of him behind her as she walked down the hall and into the kitchen. Darn, she wished she'd known he was going to come. She'd have put on something a little nicer than the worn jeans and white T-shirt she now wore.

"Look who's here," she said brightly when they entered the kitchen. She hoped her mother wouldn't be rude. The last visitor they'd had—a woman who belonged to the Altar Society with her mother—hadn't gotten a very warm reception. Maggie knew it was because her mother couldn't bear having people see her like this, but Maggie had felt terrible about having to soothe the woman's hurt feelings. After all, she was only trying to be nice.

At the sound of Maggie's voice, both Edie and her mother looked up from the table where they sat over a game of checkers. The game had been Edie's idea. She'd said she thought it might help Maureen regain some coordination as well as entertain her. Maggie had been skeptical at first, but Edie had turned out to be right. Maureen liked playing checkers and instead of adding to her frustration over her limitations, as Maggie had feared, she seemed to enjoy the challenge the game presented.

"Why, hello Sheriff Tate," Edie said, giving him a big smile. "How nice to see you."

"Hello, Edie." He turned his gaze to Maggie's mother. "Hello, Mrs. Callahan. I hope it's okay that I came by. I've been wondering about you, but Maggie tells me you're doing great."

Maggie's mother smiled the odd, crooked smile that was one of the legacies of her stroke, and Maggie relaxed. It was going to be okay.

"Huh-huh-huh-huh," Maureen said with agonizing effort. Finally she managed to get the word out. "Huh-lo, Zach." She looked triumphant over pronouncing his name without stammering.

"I'll bet you're glad you're home," he said. "I know the one and only time I had to be in the hospital, I couldn't wait to get out."

Still smiling, Maureen nodded her agreement.

Maggie was astounded at how pleased her mother seemed to be over Zach's arrival.

"L-l-l-long t-time…" She stopped, exhausted.

"Since we've seen each other," he finished for her. "I know." Grinning, he glanced over at Maggie. "If you'd get this girl of yours home more often, I'd be a more frequent visitor."

Maggie wondered what her mother was thinking. She hadn't told her about going out with Zach. Avoiding looking at her mother directly, she said, "Why don't you sit down, Zach? Would you like a soda? Or a beer?"

"No beer. I'm officially still on duty." He looked at the clock on the opposite wall. "For another ten minutes, anyway." The clock read 4:50 p.m. "But a soda would be nice."

Maggie got him his soda and poured herself a glass of water. For the next thirty minutes the four of them visited, with Zach and Edie doing most of the talking. Maggie enjoyed listening, and from what she could see, so did her mother, whose gaze stayed riveted to Zach. Well, Maggie thought, her mother always *had* liked Zach.

At five-thirty, the timer on the oven dinged, and Edie got up. "Casserole's ready," she announced. Looking at Zach, she said, "We generally eat pretty early."

"Well," he said, pushing his chair back. "I guess that's my cue to shove off."

Maggie started to thank him for coming by, when her mother blurted out, "S-s-stay!" She was looking at Zach.

"Stay?" he said.

Maureen—blue eyes bright—nodded her head vigorously.

Zach looked at Maggie. Maggie smiled. "I think that means you're invited for dinner."

By now the casserole was out of the oven, and the aroma of cheese and tomatoes filled the room.

"Smells good," he said.

"It *is* good," Edie said. "My specialty. Enchilada casserole."

"You're tempting me," he said. Addressing his remarks to Maggie's mother, he added, "Since school's out, my kids are in Sun City with their grandparents for a couple of days."

"Sun City?" Maggie said. "In Arizona?"

"No. They've built a Sun City outside Georgetown," he explained.

Grabbing her slate, Maggie's mother printed out *Then you're staying*.

"Yes, Zach, do," Maggie said.

"With three such charming ladies inviting me, how can I refuse?"

After offering to help and being told there wasn't anything for him to do, he watched and made an occasional comment while Maggie fixed a salad to accompany their casserole and Edie sliced bread. He did help set the table, though, and by six they were all seated and ready to eat.

Several times during dinner Maggie felt her mother's eyes on her. She knew Maureen was studying her, probably trying to determine what Zach's presence meant to Maggie. Maggie knew her mother still harbored hope that someday Maggie would see the light and come home to Rainbow's End permanently. Maybe she had the idea Zach was just the person to help accomplish that.

It's not going to happen, Mom, Maggie tried to communicate silently. *No matter how much I'm enjoying seeing Zach again, nothing permanent can ever come of it. He has his life, and I have mine. And the two are worlds apart.*

After dinner, Zach insisted upon helping Maggie clean up the kitchen while Edie got Maggie's mother ready for bed. Now the cleanup was almost over, and he knew it was time to thank Maggie for dinner and then take off. Yet the empty house that waited for him was the last place he wanted to go tonight, even though normally he enjoyed a respite from being a parent and looked forward to the occasional weekend or week on his own.

He knew what was different about tonight.

It was Maggie.

He looked at her. She had pushed her hair back behind her ears, her lipstick had worn off, and little beads of perspiration stood out on her nose. No one seeing her tonight would guess she was a sophisticated career woman from the big city. Right now she looked like the girl next door and almost as young as she had looked all those years ago.

Maggie.

His gaze slowly swept the clean lines of her neck, the swell of her breasts, the flat stomach and rounded bottom, then slowly rose again.

He swallowed. He would have given anything to have the right to bend over and nuzzle that pretty neck. To put his hands under her hair and turn her face to his. To see if her mouth still tasted as unbelievably sweet as it used to.

Slowly, as if she knew he was looking at her, she turned, and their eyes met and locked.

Long, silent seconds passed as the air between them thickened. Then, almost imperceptibly, she swayed toward him. It was a good thing that at that precise moment, Edie called out from down the hall, because in another moment, he would have crushed Maggie to him, and that would have been a big mistake.

Maggie jumped and the glass she was holding dropped back into the soapy dish water. She wiped her hands on her jeans, dropped her gaze and said, "I-I'd better see what she wants."

Zach used the minutes she was gone to harness his wayward libido into some kind of control.

Damn!

He'd nearly done something really dumb-ass. The fact that Maggie had seemed to want him to kiss her just as much as he wanted to didn't make any difference.

Sure, the fire that had been between them as kids seemed to be alive and kicking, but what real difference did that make? he asked himself angrily.

The bottom line was, when Maggie's mother was well enough, Maggie was going straight back to her life in New York. And unless Zach was a masochist and enjoyed being dumped and left looking like a fool, he'd do well to remember that.

Chapter Six

That night and all the next morning, Maggie thought about Zach and how soon she'd see him again—or even *if* she'd see him again.

She couldn't get that almost-kiss out of her head, for that's exactly what it was. That moment in the kitchen when their eyes had met, she'd known he wanted to kiss her, *meant* to kiss her. She'd seen the intention in his eyes. And, oh God, she had wanted him to. The disappointment she'd felt when Edie called out, breaking the spell between them, had been so strong it was practically a physical pain.

And yet…hadn't there been relief, too? Because Maggie knew if she and Zach gave in to the strong physical attraction that was obviously still very much alive between them, it would not stop with one kiss.

And that would be a huge mistake. Huge. It had been hard enough walking away from him when she was a kid; Maggie wasn't sure she could do it again.

Yet what would be the alternative? Even more so than twenty years ago, Maggie's life was in another world. And Zach's life was here. And even if they could somehow get around the physical distance between them, there was the not-so-little matter of Zach's kids.

She couldn't even imagine herself a stepmother to three kids, two of whom were already teenagers and one who soon would be. She thought about Jo McIntyre, a non-fiction writer she represented. Jo had married a man who had two children in their early teens, and her life had become a nightmare. The kids hated her and constantly sabotaged her. Jo and her husband had ended up separating after only two years.

And then there was Alicia Blythe, an editor Maggie had worked with for a long time and who had become a friend. Alicia married a man with a teenaged son who had a drug problem. She'd gone through hell because of that kid and was still dealing with the aftermath.

As Alicia had said, it would be hard enough to deal with this kind of problem if the child were yours. But when he wasn't, it was nearly impossible. Anything you did was wrong. You didn't dare say anything.

After all, you weren't his mother. You had to bite your tongue and hope that the trouble would pass without leaving too bad a scar on your marriage.

No, that kind of turmoil wasn't for Maggie.

So stop thinking about Zach, she told herself. *Put him and his sexy body and his sexy eyes and his sexy smile out of your mind.*

She tried, she honestly tried, but telling herself to stop thinking about Zach proved to be extremely difficult. Unfortunately, her efforts weren't helped by what she began to think of as a conspiracy between her mother and Edie.

It started almost immediately after Zach left them on Wednesday. Edie fired the first shot.

"Maggie," she said while the two of them were helping Maggie's mother undress for bed. "I didn't know Sheriff Tate was a friend of yours."

"We've known each other since high school," Maggie said as casually as she could manage. She didn't look at her mother.

"S-s-s-s-sweet-h-h-h-hearts," her mother said.

"Really?" Edie said. "Well, that explains it then."

"Explains what?" Maggie said, in spite of telling herself it would be best to pretend disinterest in the subject.

"Why the sheriff couldn't seem to take his eyes off you," Edie said with a grin.

"Oh, Edie, that's ridiculous."

"Is it?" She winked at Maggie's mother.

Maggie's mother gave Edie one of her lopsided grins.

"So were you really sweethearts?" Edie asked.

Maggie shrugged. "It was high school. We went steady the way most kids do."

"What happened?"

"What usually happens to teenage romances. It ran its course."

"N-n-not ex-ex-ex-actly—" In frustration, Maggie's mother grabbed for her slate.

Maggie rolled her eyes. "What my mother is trying to tell you is Zach wanted me to marry him and stay here, but I wanted to go to New York."

"So you broke up?"

"Yes. Now…since you seem to have things under control here, if you don't mind, I'm going to go check my e-mail."

"Oh. Sure. Once I get your mom settled, I'll be taking off."

Maggie escaped with a sigh of relief. She hoped the subject of Zach was finished.

But Thursday morning, Maggie had no sooner gotten her mother settled at the breakfast table than she picked up her slate and laboriously printed, *What's going on with Zach?*

"Mom, will you quit thinking about him and eat your oatmeal? We're due at the hospital in an hour. We don't have time to fool around."

Her mother erased what she'd written and wrote, *Then answer me.*

Maggie met her mother's bright, eager eyes. "Look, nothing's going on. We're just old friends. I don't even know if I'll see him again. So don't make too much of yesterday, okay?"

In answer, her mother smiled. But she did pick up her spoon and began to feed herself. Maggie thought, as she had many times over the past weeks, how fortunate it was that the stroke had done most of its damage on her mother's right side instead of her left, for Maureen was left-handed and at least she could still write and manage soft foods like oatmeal, macaroni and pudding. It was only when her food required cutting that she needed help.

The rest of the morning passed without another mention of Zach, but just as Maggie began to think she might have heard the end of him, Edie again brought up the subject. "You know, Maggie," she said while they were eating lunch, "if you should happen to want to go out with Sheriff Tate of an evening, I'd be glad to stay overnight."

"G-g-good idea," Maggie's mother said.

The two women smiled at each other.

Maggie started to tell them both she was sick of the subject of Zachary Tate but knew it would be a waste of breath. They would take any protest as some kind of sign that she actually did care more than she wanted them to suspect. *I can't win,* she thought, so she just answered mildly, "Thanks, Edie. I'll keep that in mind."

"Oh, good," Edie said. "The sheriff seemed really pleased when I told him not to worry about your mother being alone if he wanted to ask you out."

It took a minute before Maggie realized what Edie had said. "You *what?*" In her agitation, she choked on a bite of her tuna sandwich and began to cough. When she finally stopped and could once again talk, she glared at Edie. "Edie, you had no right to talk to Sheriff Tate about me." She was mortified. What if he thought she had put Edie up to what she'd said? "Where'd you see the sheriff, anyway?" Then Maggie had a horrifying thought. "Oh, my God, you didn't call him, did you?"

"Maggie, I don't know why you're so upset," Edie said. "No, I didn't call him. I ran into him at the bank. We were both standing in line, and he thanked me again for supper last night and I told him anytime, 'cause I knew your mother would have said the same thing…right, Maureen?"

Maggie's mother shook her head vigorously. "R-r-r-right."

"So one thing led to another and I just happened to mention that I sometimes stayed the night if you had somewhere you needed to go in the evenings, that's all." Edie's expression was all innocence.

"You have never stayed the night," Maggie said.

She couldn't believe this conversation. Who could have imagined that Edie, who had never seemed the least bit nosy or interfering, would turn into such a busybody?

"Well, we'd talked about it before." She didn't seem in the least bothered by Maggie's indignation.

Maggie glared at her. "I wish," she said through clenched teeth, "that you and my mother and everyone else would just mind your own business!"

"Ma-Ma-Maggie!" her mother said. She grabbed her slate and wrote *Apologize!*

But Edie was unruffled. "It's okay, Maureen, she doesn't need to apologize. She's right. I *should* have minded my own business. I'm sorry, Maggie. I won't interfere in your love life again. It's just that Sheriff Tate is such a nice man, and he's obviously interested in you. I thought I was being helpful."

Maggie just shook her head. She could have responded with a dozen rejoinders. She could have said Zach had nothing to do with her love life or anything else that concerned her. She could have said even if he did, she could take care of her own love life. But again, what was the use? These two women were in cahoots to "help" her whether she wanted their help or not. She should have stuck to her first inclination and kept her mouth shut to begin with. "I accept your apology," she finally said. "Now can we please drop the subject?"

* * *

Zach was kicking himself. He couldn't seem to forget how close he'd come to making a fool of himself at Maggie's. All night Wednesday and all morning Thursday he kept remembering how he'd almost kissed her and how stupid that would have been.

Maybe his mother was right. Maybe he *didn't* have any sense when it came to women.

By mid-morning Thursday, he'd made a resolution. He was not going to see Maggie again. He had paid his duty call on her mother. There was no reason for him to go there again. End of story.

And then he ran into Edie Spencer at the bank and instead of discouraging her when she suggested she could sit with Maggie's mother if he wanted to take Maggie out, he *encouraged* her.

What the hell was his problem? Why, when it came to Maggie, couldn't he stick to his decisions?

He was cleaning off his desk, almost ready to leave for the day, when Daryl Barnett, one of his senior deputies and a good friend, poked his head around the open doorway. "Hey, Zach, you busy?"

"Nope. Just getting ready to go home. C'mon in. How's it going? Kathy doing okay?" Daryl's wife had just had foot surgery.

"Yep," Daryl said, walking into the office. "She's feelin' pretty good."

"Great. Glad to hear it. So what's up?"

"I was just wondering, you got any plans for tomorrow night?"

Zach shook his head. "Nope. Why? Something going on?"

"Yeah, we're havin' a little party at the house."

"*We?* You mean you and Kathy? But isn't she still recuperating?"

"Yeah, but her sister Kelly is here. In fact, that's why we decided to do this, so's Kelly can meet some people. It's not gonna be anything fancy, just a dozen friends or so."

"Couples, right?"

Daryl grinned. "Yeah. And we're inviting you for Kelly."

"Now, come on, Daryl, you know I hate—"

"I know. You hate blind dates. But you'll like Kelly. I guarantee it. Anyway, it's not a date. It's just a party. C'mon, Zach. It's no big deal. Kathy and I would really like you to come." He laughed. "In fact, the last thing Kathy said to me was *don't take no for an answer.*"

Zach sighed.

"I'm tellin' you, you won't be sorry. Kelly is really nice, lots of fun and a looker, too. Even prettier than Kathy."

"Better not let your wife hear you say that."

"Hey, she says it all the time. Kelly won all kinds of beauty contests when she was in her twenties. She was runner-up in the Miss Texas contest one year."

"She's younger than Kathy, I take it."

"Nope. Older. She's thirty-seven." Another grin. "Perfect age for you."

"What does she do?"

"She's a teacher. In Dallas. She's staying with us for at least a month—until Kathy gets on her feet again and can manage on her own."

Maybe this was just what Zach needed. Maybe this Kelly would turn out to be someone he really liked. Maybe then he could finally forget about Maggie. "Okay, you talked me into it. What time should I be there?"

Daryl grinned. "Seven o'clock. There'll be lots of food, so come hungry."

Zach almost changed his mind about the party, but he knew if he called Daryl and told him so, Daryl would argue with him and probably end up getting mad. After all, Zach had no real excuse for not going, especially with the kids still at their grandparents'.

So at seven o'clock, he pulled up in front of the Barnett house. There were already several other cars in the driveway and out front.

Daryl answered the door. Smiling widely, he said, "Hey, Zach, c'mon in. Everyone's back in the family room."

The big room that dominated the back of the roomy ranch house was noisy with conversation and laughter. Zach was relieved to realize he knew most of the people there. Two of the men were deputies, two others long-time friends of Daryl's that Zach had met before, and the other was Daryl's younger brother. The wives, too, were familiar.

To the tune of friendly hello's and hey's, Zach made his way through the room, returning greetings, until he reached Daryl's wife, Kathy, who was seated in a recliner with her bandaged foot propped up on a pillow. A pretty blonde with a sweet smile, she seemed delighted to see Zach. She lifted her face for a kiss.

Leaning down, he kissed her cheek. "Hey, pretty girl. You doing okay?"

"I'm doing just great, thanks to Daryl and my sister." She called over her shoulder. "Kelly! Come here. There's someone I want you to meet."

From the kitchen came a tall blonde, who was, as Daryl had promised, strikingly pretty, beautiful even, with classic features, wide green eyes and an even more lovely smile than her younger sister's.

"Kelly, this is Zachary Tate, you can call him Zach, though. He's Daryl's boss and our good friend. Zach, this is my sister Kelly Dixon."

Kelly gave him a warm smile, and they shook hands. "I've heard a lot of good things about you, Zach." There was an amused glint in her eyes.

Suddenly Zach relaxed. He could tell she understood exactly why he'd been invited, but rather than being embarrassed or feeling awkward, she was entertained by her family's attempt at matchmaking and did not take it seriously. "You came highly praised, too," he said lightly, returning her smile.

"I'll bet." Now she was openly laughing.

"They didn't exaggerate."

From then on, the rest of the evening passed pleasantly. Zach enjoyed Kelly's company and was glad he'd come. Yet he knew he probably would make no effort to see her again, and he was pretty sure she wouldn't lose even five minutes sleep over it, either. The truth was, as comfortable as they felt together, as easy as it was to talk to her and as good-looking as she undeniably was, there were no vibes between them.

When the evening was drawing to a close and people started to leave, Zach said, "I guess I should be going, too. Kathy's looking tired."

"Yes," Kelly said, glancing over at her sister. She turned back to him with a smile. "It was lovely to meet you, Zach. You're every bit as nice as they said you were."

"But—"

"But I think there's someone else in your life. Maybe someone my sister and her husband don't know about?"

Zach started to deny it. Then he shrugged and nodded. "You're right. There is. It's probably not going to work out, but tonight I realized I'm not willing to give up on it yet."

* * *

On Saturday afternoon, Edie hadn't been in the house fifteen minutes when she said, "I saw the sheriff again this morning. Funny thing. You can go weeks and not see a person, then bump into him two or three times in a row." She gave Maggie a sidelong look to see what she thought of this statement.

Maggie only made a noncommittal sound in response.

"He said to tell you hello," Edie continued. "Oh, and Maureen, he said to tell you he'd be by sometime this week. He asked if you needed anything. Wasn't that nice of him?"

Maggie's mother managed to say yes, then both women waited to see if Maggie would comment. But she was determined not to give them any encouragement and she kept her mouth firmly shut.

That night Maggie dreamed about Zach. In her dream they were young again. Young and in love. They were parked out by the lake and he was kissing her. Then the kissing led to something else and soon they were making love. The dream was so vivid that when she awakened the next morning, she felt bereft and her body ached.

For the first time since she'd come home, she wished she could pack up and leave. Go back to New York and her safe life. The thought stunned her, and she stopped brushing her teeth and stared at herself in the mirror.

Safe life? Where had *that* come from? She had

never thought of her life in New York as safe. In fact, she'd prided herself on the fact she'd *never* played it safe. That she was a woman who hadn't been afraid to take risks. She'd considered life in Rainbow's End to be safe—her life in the city to be edgy, challenging and exciting.

And yet, if she were being perfectly honest with herself, wasn't the fact she lived a life where she was only responsible for herself—a life without commitment to someone else—actually extremely safe...for her heart?

All day the question nagged her. She didn't like the picture of herself it presented. She wasn't a coward. She hadn't run away from commitment when she'd left Zach and gone to New York. She'd run *to* something, something bigger than what she'd left behind.

Hadn't she?

Zach waited as long as he could before dropping in on Maggie and her mother again. He hadn't wanted to wait, especially after seeing Edie again and knowing she was a willing ally if he wanted to spend time with Maggie, but he'd thought it was best to give Maggie some breathing room, maybe even time to miss him—although he knew that was probably wishful thinking.

Finally he could not stand waiting another day. Maggie was like a magnet, pulling at him even though he knew the wiser course would be to stay as far away from her as he could get.

This time he stopped by after dinner. His kids were home from their visit to their grandparents, but they all had something going on that night: Josh was sleeping over at a friend's house, Jason was working until eleven at Burger Heaven, and Hannah was baby-sitting and wouldn't be home until midnight. So his evening was free.

As he walked up the front walk of the Callahan home he thought what a beautiful evening it was. Warm, because it was already the middle of June, and the daily temperature was in the high eighties. The air was fragrant with the scent of summer flowers and newly mowed lawn. Down the street a bunch of kids were playing kickball and several of Maggie's mother's neighbors were standing outside, either watering lawns or talking.

Everyone waved to him as he went by. It was a mixed blessing to be the county sheriff and head-quartered in the small town where you'd lived all your life. On the one hand, he knew everyone, including all the troublemakers. On the other hand, they knew him, which included all his business.

Well, just about everything in life worth doing or having involved some kind of trade-off. He'd had that lesson rammed home when Maggie left him.

He rang the doorbell and wondered if Maggie would be happy to see him. He still didn't have an accurate reading of what she was thinking or feeling. He only knew what *he* was thinking and feeling.

And uppermost in those thoughts was the knowledge that no matter how dangerous and foolhardy it was to see too much of Maggie, he wasn't going to heed those warnings. Because Saturday night had shown him that no matter what might happen, he wanted to be with her for as long as he had the opportunity.

He needn't have worried. She smiled with genuine warmth when she came to the door and saw him, and it pleased him to see the quick flash of pleasure in her eyes. "Hi, Maggie."

"Hi, Zach." She gestured him in.

"How are things going?"

"Pretty good. Mom's made some great progress this week."

"I'm glad."

She led him into the living room where Edie and Maureen were watching TV. Zach greeted the two older women, told Maggie he'd be happy to have a beer when she offered, and settled himself in a chair.

After they'd visited for a while, Zach turned to Maggie, "That new Jim Carrey movie just opened out at Tri-City Mall. I thought maybe you might like to go."

Maggie looked startled. "Tonight? I don't th—"

"I know I haven't given you much notice." Zach had thought about calling her earlier, but figured it would be too easy for her to refuse over the phone.

"It's nice of you, but—"

"Why *don't* you go, Maggie?" Edie said, jumping in. "I'll be glad to stay until you get home." She smiled at Maureen. "We can play Scrabble." Addressing her next remark to Zach, she added, "Maureen plays a mean game of Scrabble."

Zach looked at Maggie.

"Well..."

He could tell she wanted to say yes. "Come on," he encouraged. "It'll do you good to get out for a while."

"You g-g-go, Ma-Ma-Maggie," her mother said.

Maggie grinned. "Oh, all right. You talked me into it. But I'll need to change. What time does the movie start?"

"It starts at eight," Zach said. "Why do you need to change? You look fine to me." She always looked fine to him. He couldn't remember a time when she hadn't looked fine.

Maggie looked down at her khaki shorts and black T-shirt. "It's just that I'd feel more comfortable in slacks. It won't take me long."

Ten minutes later, they were on their way.

That night, Zach had more fun than he'd had in years. Maggie was great company. She always had been. She took just as much pleasure in simple things as she did in more sophisticated outings like their dinner at the Rainbow's End Inn. As they laughed at Jim Carrey's antics and ate overpriced popcorn, Zach couldn't help but compare her to Andrea. Unfortunately, Andrea's depression had caused her to be negative a lot of the time. She was always finding fault, seeing what was wrong rather than what was right.

On the way home they had a spirited debate about the merits of the movie, which Zach enjoyed almost as much as the movie itself.

When they reached the house, Maggie turned to him and smiled. "Thanks for tonight, Zach. You were right. I did need to get out."

"It was fun, wasn't it?"

She nodded. "Yes, it was. I don't see many movies, so this was a real treat."

"Really? I would have thought you'd see a lot of movies."

"No. I work late most nights and on the weekends, there are always too many other things I'd rather do."

He wondered if those other things involved dating. He immediately realized what a dumb thought that was. Of course they involved dating. A beautiful, interesting woman like Maggie wouldn't spend her weekends alone. Envy stabbed him. "I don't see many movies, either."

Silence fell between them. After an awkward few moments, she reached for the door handle. "Well, I guess I'd better go in. Let Edie go home. Thanks again."

He touched her arm. "Maggie, wait."

Slowly, her eyes met his.

Before he could tell himself this wasn't a wise thing to do, he leaned over, placed his other hand under her chin, and raised her face to his. From the moment he touched his lips to hers, he was lost.

What he'd intended was to give her a casual kiss.

Certainly nothing to scare her off. But what actually transpired between them was as far from casual as a kiss could get. The little catch in her breath as his mouth settled over hers and the way she leaned closer fueled the desire that he'd managed to keep banked ever since he'd laid eyes on her in the hospital cafeteria.

His arms went around her as the kiss deepened. *Maggie, Maggie.* Her name became part of his heartbeat. She was familiar and yet she wasn't.

She moaned deep in her throat as one kiss became two and two became three. It was only when his hands found her breasts that she seemed to realize what they doing and where they were doing it.

"Zach, Zach," she said, tearing her mouth away. "We have to stop." Her breathing was ragged.

Shuddering, he forced himself to pull back.

Avoiding his eyes, she smoothed her hair and then her T-shirt.

"Maggie." His voice was gruff as he fought to get his body and his emotions under control.

"I've got to go in." She reached for the door handle again.

"Maggie, look at me."

"Zach, let's not talk about this, okay?" She finally looked at him. "I'd rather just pretend it didn't happen."

"Pretending won't change anything."

"Meaning?" There was a defiant edge to her voice.

''Meaning there's still something between us, and you know it. But if you want to pretend there isn't, fine.''

She licked her lips. ''I think that's best.''

Although he knew where she was coming from—hell, he knew better than anyone that they didn't have a future together now any more than they'd had twenty years ago—he still felt like shaking her. There was no way they were going to be able to pretend nothing had happened tonight. That kiss had ignited something too powerful.

Yet he knew if he didn't agree to go along with her, she might refuse to see him again. And that was something he couldn't chance.

''All right, Maggie.'' He reached over and squeezed her hand, and although she stiffened, she didn't pull away. ''We'll play it your way. I'll call you in a day or so.''

As he drove off, he knew that hopeless or not, he was going to continue to see as much of Maggie as she would allow. Because until she actually left again, there was always a glimmer of hope that maybe this time, things would be different.

Chapter Seven

Maggie couldn't fall asleep. She tossed and turned, reliving the last five minutes of the evening over and over again.

That kiss!

If only she'd pulled back. She'd known, in that moment after he'd laid his hand on her arm and said "wait" that he wanted to kiss her. So she couldn't plead ignorance about what had happened. Oh, no. She'd known. She'd looked into his eyes and seen the desire and the intent. Unfortunately, this time there was no call from Edie to save her, and she simply hadn't had the will or the strength to resist.

Face it, Maggie. You wanted him to kiss you, and

FREE FREE
BOOKS! GIFT!

PLAY BANGO!

AND CLAIM 2 FREE BOOKS AND A FREE GIFT!

BANGO
15	19	32	54	73
6	17	41	50	
13	22	FREE	52	
5	24	44	46	
8	21	35	47	75

BANGO
9	19	44	52	71
4	20	32	50	68
11	18	FREE	53	63
7	27	36	60	72
3	28	41	47	64

BANGO
38	9	44	10	38
92	7	5	27	14
2	51	FREE	91	67
75	3	12	20	13
6	15	26	50	31

★ **No Cost!**
★ **No Obligation to Buy!**
★ **No Purchase Necessary!**

TURN THE PAGE TO PLAY

PLAY BANGO!

AND GET THREE FREE GIFTS!

It looks like **BINGO**, it plays like **BINGO** but it's **FREE!**

HOW TO PLAY:

1. With a coin, scratch the Caller Card to reveal your 5 lucky numbers and see that they match your Bango Card. Then check the claim chart to discover what we have for you — 2 FREE BOOKS and a FREE GIFT — ALL YOURS, ALL FREE!

2. Send back the Bango card and you'll receive two brand-new Silhouette Special Edition® novels. These books have a cover price of $4.50 each in the U.S. and $5.25 each in Canada, but they are yours to keep absolutely free.

3. There's no catch. You're under no obligation to buy anything. We charge nothing — ZERO — for your first shipment. And you don't have to make any minimum number of purchases — not even one!

4. The fact is, thousands of readers enjoy receiving our books by mail from the Silhouette Reader Service™. They enjoy the convenience of home delivery…they like getting the best new novels at discount prices, BEFORE they're available in stores…and they love their *Heart to Heart* subscriber newsletter featuring author news, horoscopes, recipes, book reviews and much more!

5. We hope that after receiving your free books you'll want to remain a subscriber. But the choice is yours — to continue or cancel, any time at all! So why not take us up on our invitation, with no risk of any kind. You'll be glad you did!

YOURS FREE!
This exciting mystery gift is yours free when you play BANGO!

Visit us online at
www.eHarlequin.com

It's fun, and we're giving away
FREE GIFTS
to all players!

PLAY BANGO!

SCRATCH HERE! →

CALLER CARD

YES! Please send me the 2 free books and the gift for which I qualify! I understand that I am under no obligation to purchase any books as explained on the back of this card.

YOUR CARD ↘

BANGO				
38	9	44	10	38
92	7	5	27	14
2	51	FREE	91	67
75	3	12	20	13
6	15	26	50	31

CLAIM CHART!

Match 5 numbers	2 FREE BOOKS & A MYSTERY GIFT
Match 4 numbers	2 FREE BOOKS
Match 3 numbers	1 FREE BOOK

(S-SE-OS-12/01)

335 SDL DHZ5   **235 SDL DHZ4**

NAME   (PLEASE PRINT CLEARLY)

ADDRESS

APT.#   CITY

STATE/PROV.   ZIP/POSTAL CODE

Offer limited to one per household and not valid to current Silhouette Special Edition® subscribers. All orders subject to approval.

The Silhouette Reader Service™ — Here's how it works:

BUSINESS REPLY MAIL

FIRST-CLASS MAIL   PERMIT NO. 717-003   BUFFALO, NY

POSTAGE WILL BE PAID BY ADDRESSEE

SILHOUETTE READER SERVICE
3010 WALDEN AVE
PO BOX 1867
BUFFALO NY 14240-9952

NO POSTAGE
NECESSARY
IF MAILED
IN THE
UNITED STATES

if you had to do it all over again you'd do the same thing. In fact, if it happens again, if you find yourself in a position where you have the choice, you'll do exactly the same thing, and you know it.

That knowledge, more than anything, filled her with trepidation.

What was she going to do?

This course she seemed to be on was crazy. It would only lead to trouble and heartache. And not just for her. Zach would suffer, too.

You did it to him once. How can you do it again? How can you be so selfish?

And yet...

Wasn't Zach a grown man? Didn't he have the same power she had? That of making his own decisions? He certainly knew the risks of a renewed relationship with her. And it didn't look as if he were running from it. Didn't that mean that he might believe the rewards were worth the possible pain when it was over?

On and on her thoughts raged. The same questions, the same accusations, plagued her.

She finally fell asleep, but it wasn't a restful sleep, and the next morning she looked like hell. Even her mother commented, albeit by her slate board.

Didn't you have a good time last night? she wrote, the expression in her eyes one of concern.

Because Maggie had a headache, because she felt confused and vulnerable, and because she was no closer to a solution to her problem than she had been to begin with, she answered her mother more sharply than she'd intended.

"I had a great time, but if you don't mind, I don't want to discuss it, and I don't want to discuss Zach. Furthermore, I'd really, really appreciate it if you and Edie would stop talking about him and trying to push me into a relationship I have no desire to resurrect!"

Her mother's eyes widened, and Maggie was immediately sorry for her outburst. After all, her mother was just being a mother.

For the rest of the morning, her mother eyed Maggie warily, but as much as Maggie wanted to apologize, she decided it was much better to leave things as they stood. At least this way, her mother knew how strongly Maggie felt about her and Edie's machinations.

But, by the next day, the slight strain between them had eased, and, to Maggie's relief, the atmosphere seemed normal again. No mention was made of Zach by Maggie's mother or by Edie. Maggie wondered if the two women had discussed the subject when she wasn't in the room and decided it might be better to lay off for a while. It didn't matter. Maggie was just glad they had stopped bugging her.

It helped, too, that Zach didn't call and didn't stop by. When three days went by, though, without a call or visit from him, she began to wonder if he might have had second thoughts about continuing to see her.

She told herself if this was the case, she was relieved. But she knew she was lying to herself.

So on the fourth day, when she and her mother arrived home from the day's therapy sessions, and she found a message from Zach on the answering machine, she couldn't help the flood of happiness that engulfed her.

"I thought I might come by tonight," the message said, "unless you've got other plans?" Unspoken, Maggie knew, was another question: *unless you don't want me to?*

She forced herself to wait thirty minutes before calling him back. The whole time she could feel her mother's eyes watching her, waiting to see what she'd do. To her mother's credit, though, she did not say a word.

Finally Maggie called his office.

"So it's okay with you if I stop by tonight?" he reiterated.

"Sure," she answered, trying not to seem too eager, "we'll be here."

"Good." She could almost hear his smile. "I have to drop Josh off for a Scout meeting at the school at six-thirty. I'll swing by after that."

"All right."

That night, after an initial few minutes of awkwardness between them, the two hours Zach spent with them were relaxed and enjoyable. After a bit of coaxing from Zach, Edie stayed for the duration of his visit. Maggie made popcorn, and the four of them played a game of Monopoly amidst much laughing and teasing.

When the game was over—with Zach the winner and clearly never going to let them forget it—Maggie was persuaded to play the piano for a sing-along which even her mother made an attempt to join. Maggie hadn't played the piano in years, but like riding a bicycle, it was something you never entirely forgot, although she was rusty. Still, her audience didn't seem to mind.

They sang all the old songs from one of her mother's songbooks: "You Are My Sunshine," "Let Me Call You Sweetheart," "Heart and Soul," "She'll Be Comin' Round the Mountain," "Amazing Grace," and dozens of others.

It astonished Maggie to discover Zach had a good tenor voice and could sing beautiful harmony. Edie was an alto and couldn't hit high notes, so she sang everything an octave lower than Maggie. Maggie's mother, who couldn't manage most of the words, hummed along, sometimes humming harmony with Zach, sometimes melody with Maggie. Her eyes were bright with happiness, their expression bringing a lump to Maggie's throat more than once.

"I didn't know you could sing, Zach," Maggie said when they'd exhausted her repertoire.

He grinned. "I'm a man of many talents."

"He said modestly," she added, laughing.

"You two make a wonderful duo," Edie said. "Your voices blend just perfectly."

Edie, I'm going to smack you! Maggie gave the older woman a warning look, but Edie pretended not to see it.

Instead she turned to Maggie's mother. "Maureen, you look tired. I'll help get you ready for bed and let Maggie visit with Zach."

"I can only stay a few more minutes," Zach said, looking at his watch. "I'm supposed to pick Josh up at nine and it's almost that now."

"C-c-come b-back again, Zach," Maggie's mother said. "Tonight w-was wonderful."

He leaned over and kissed her cheek. "Don't worry, I'll be back. Good night, Mrs. Callahan."

Maggie's mother beamed with pleasure.

Once the two older women were gone, Zach said, "I think I'd better take off."

"All right. I'll walk you out."

Outside he said, "Thanks for letting me come tonight. I enjoyed it."

"I should thank you. I haven't seen my mother this perky in days. I forget how boring her life must feel to her now. You know how active she's always been."

He nodded. Lowering his voice, he said, "What about you, Maggie? Are you glad I came?"

Her heart skipped a beat as their eyes met. "You know I am."

''In that case, maybe you'd like to come with me to visit Luke and his wife Saturday night.''

''I'd love to see Luke again...and meet his wife. But I'll have to check with Edie.''

But, as it turned out, Maggie didn't need Edie to stay, because Molly said she and Jimmy would love to come and spend the evening with Maureen. ''We'll bring the kids and a bucket of fried chicken. Make a night of it.''

So, on Saturday night, Maggie found herself once more in Zach's company. The evening turned out to be another great one, and Maggie enjoyed herself tremendously. She'd always liked Luke, and his wife Norma was a darling. A petite brunette, she seemed filled with energy and vitality. She was a good match for Luke, who was much more laid-back.

''You know, I introduced these two,'' Luke told Norma about midway through the evening.

''Did you?'' Maggie said. ''I had forgotten that.'' But she hadn't. She just didn't want to admit that she remembered every single thing that had ever happened between her and Zach.

Over the next couple of weeks, Maggie saw a lot of Zach. He fell into the habit of dropping by the house for ten or fifteen minutes each day, ostensibly to say hello to her mother and Edie, but Maggie knew he wanted to see her just as much as she looked forward to seeing him.

A couple of times he spent the evening at the

house, evenings Maggie's mother and Edie both seemed to enjoy as much as Maggie did. Several times, he took Maggie out, either to a movie or to visit friends. One night they played poker with a couple they'd gone to high school with. One night they had dinner with Kris and John Diana. And one night they went to the movies with Maggie's cousin Sheila and her husband Jack.

Maggie smiled each time she remembered that evening. Sheila and Jack amused her, even as she envied them. Maggie couldn't remember ever seeing a married couple so in love. You could tell, even when they weren't looking at one another, that each was totally aware of the other. The sexual chemistry between them fairly sizzled. Maggie imagined if it were something you could see, it would be diamond-brilliant, arcing in the air between them.

Maggie constantly reminded herself that spending so much time with Zach wasn't wise, even though he had made no move to kiss her again and was treating her as no more than a good friend. But she did nothing to discourage him. Right now, she was living for the moment, and to heck with the consequences.

Even when she didn't see him, they talked on the phone. One night, they talked for more than two hours, and it was after midnight before they said good-night.

One night he finally opened up about his marriage. They were out back, sitting on the screened-in back porch. Edie had helped Maggie's mother get ready for bed and had gone home about thirty minutes earlier. Maureen was settled in her room with the TV and the remote control and had assured Maggie she was fine.

So Maggie had poured herself and Zach a glass of wine, and they'd gone out to enjoy the June evening. They talked lazily for a while about nothing of consequence, but gradually the conversation veered into personal territory and Andrea's name came up.

"It must have been terrible for you when she died," Maggie said.

Zach nodded. "Yes, it was. I had no idea she was in such bad shape. I knew she was depressed, but killing herself, that never entered my mind." He sighed heavily. "For a long time I thought it was my fault. Sometimes I still do."

"Oh, Zach."

"I didn't say that because I wanted you to feel sorry for me. The truth is, I probably do have to share some of the blame."

"What makes you think so?"

For a long time, he didn't answer. When he did, his voice was filled with an emotion Maggie didn't even try to identify, for to identify it might lead to questions better left unasked.

"Because I didn't love her the way I should have, and she knew it."

Maggie bit her lip and was glad of the darkness.

"I tried," he continued, "but some things can't be faked." He stared off into the distance.

No, Maggie thought, some things couldn't be faked. And some things couldn't be denied, either. She studied his profile—the strong nose, the chiseled forehead and chin, the solid body. Everything about him suggested strength and courage, honesty and dependability.

"Zach," she said softly.

In the darkness, his eyes gleamed as he turned to look at her.

"I'm no expert, but from what I know about suicide, there's not a lot anyone else can do to prevent it. Don't keep beating yourself up over it. Andrea had a choice, and she made it."

He nodded. "I know. And most of the time I feel sorry for her…and sad that she was so miserable and couldn't see any other way out. But other times…" His voice hardened. "Other times I get mad. What she did was selfish. All she thought about was herself. But her death affected everyone, especially the kids."

Maggie couldn't imagine thinking death was preferable to life, no matter what that life had dealt you, but she had never suffered from depression, either. "How old were the kids when this happened?" she asked softly.

"Hannah was five, Jason was four, Josh was one."

"So young…" And Zach was left to cope.

For a while, each was lost in their own thoughts.

"Hannah remembers her," he said finally. He drank some wine. "She had nightmares for a long time after it happened."

Maggie's heart hurt for his daughter. Such a little girl to suffer a loss like that. "Did...she understand how her mother had died, do you think?"

"Oh, she understood all right." He made no attempt to hide the bitterness in his voice. "Little kids understand a lot more than adults think they do."

"Poor kid."

"Yeah. I took her to a psychologist, and she had a couple of years worth of counseling before she was really okay." He grimaced. "My mother didn't approve of the counseling, but I ignored her objections and did it anyway. Best thing I ever did for Hannah."

"Good for you." Maggie frowned. "But why didn't your mother approve? I would have thought she'd want Hannah to get help."

"You know my mother, Maggie. She's very proud. She doesn't believe in showing weakness of any kind."

Also opinionated and narrow-minded. "Well, I'm glad you didn't listen to her. I personally think it's not weak to admit you need help. Just the opposite, in fact. It shows courage."

He smiled. "Thanks."

"What about the boys? How did they handle it?"

"Josh was way too young to know what was happening. He cried for a few days, probably without realizing why he was crying, but he quickly forgot her. Jason, I don't know about. He cried, of course, but I'm not sure he really understood what was going on. He seemed to forget pretty fast, too, and in all the years since, he's seemed completely well-adjusted. He's a good kid. They're all good kids.''

She heard the pride in his voice and felt a prick of envy. It must be wonderful to feel that way about your family.

''I'd really like you to meet them, Maggie.''

Her heart skipped. ''You would?''

''How about Sunday afternoon? Can you get someone to stay with your mother? I've got a pool. We can swim and cook out.''

''That sounds like a lot of fun. Okay, I'll see what I can arrange.''

There really wasn't anything to arrange once Maggie was sure there was someone to be with her mother, and that seemed to take care of itself. The next morning, before Maggie had even had a chance to mention Zach's invitation, her Aunt Rose called to ask if her mother felt up to coming over and spending Sunday with her.

''I'd come visit her, but I'm baby-sitting Sheila's Ryan and I doubt you want him tearing up *your* house,'' she said, laughing. ''You're welcome to come, too, Maggie, but I thought you might enjoy having a day to yourself.''

"As a matter-of-fact, I've had an invitation of my own."

"Well, good," her Aunt Rose said. "And don't you worry about coming home early, either. After Sheila picks up little Ryan, Patrick and I will bring your mother home and stay with her until you get there."

So now there was no reason she couldn't accept Zach's invitation, yet Maggie hesitated before calling to tell him. Did she really want to meet Zach's kids? Get even more involved than she was? But she *was* curious about them. In fact, she was dying to meet them, so she finally called him and said yes, she'd come.

On Sunday, Maggie arrived at Zach's house at two o'clock. She'd driven past the house before, so she knew what it looked like. It was a pleasant, one-story ranch style, the kind you saw everywhere in Rainbow's End, mostly brick with frame trim. The yard was neatly cut, the flower beds weeded and orderly, the front shaded by a giant live oak. A small magnolia tree, its glossy green leaves framing dozens of fragrant blossoms, stood between the house and the one next door. Altogether inviting, she thought.

Zach had told her to park in the driveway and come in through the back gate. As she approached the gate she could hear voices and laughter and the splash of water. She couldn't believe it, but she was actually nervous.

For the first time since Zach had asked her to come, she admitted that it mattered to her if Zach's kids liked her or not.

She took a deep breath before opening the gate.

"Maggie!" Zach, who had been sitting in a lawn chair, jumped up. "I didn't hear your car." His smile said how happy he was to see her. He walked over and clasped her hands, smiling down into her eyes.

The next few minutes were a jumble of impressions as he introduced her to his children. Hannah was a lovely girl with her father's dark hair and pretty hazel eyes that Maggie knew must have come from her mother's side of the family.

She smiled shyly as Zach introduced them. She wore a green two-piece bathing suit that wasn't quite a bikini and that showed off her youthful figure. "It's very nice to meet you," she said.

"It's nice to meet you, too, Hannah."

Jason came next. Up close, he looked even more like Zach than he'd looked the night Maggie had seen him at Rocco's. He, too, gave her a warm, welcoming smile and shook her hand firmly.

Josh was last. What a cutie, Maggie thought, looking at his fresh, freckled face. He looked the least like Zach, although he, too, had the thick, shining, black hair of his father.

"Hi," he said, putting out his hand the way his brother had done.

Maggie grinned.

After the introductions were over, Maggie took off her mesh cover-up and slathered suntan lotion over her skin while Zach went inside to get her a glass of lemonade. She felt a bit like someone else in the turquoise maillot—the only swimsuit she'd been able to find in her size at the local boutique—since she normally wore a plain black tank for swimming at her health club and hadn't brought it with her. But Zach seemed to like it, if the admiring look he gave her when he returned with her lemonade was any indication.

"Dad says you're a literary agent," Jason said once she was settled.

Maggie smiled. "Yes, I am."

He looked as if he wanted to ask her something else, and she was just about to encourage him when Hannah spoke up. "Jason wants to be a writer."

"Hannah," Jason protested, his face flushing.

"Well, it's true." Undaunted by her brother's embarrassment, she added, "He's really good."

Jason gave her a hard look, and Maggie had to smother a smile. She thought it was really sweet that Hannah was so obviously proud of her brother. "What kind of writing are you interested in?"

He gave a nonchalant shrug. "I don't know."

"Jason!" Hannah said. She looked exasperated.

"He mostly writes screenplays, and they really *are* good, Miss Callahan. And I'm not just saying that because Jason's my brother."

By now Jason's face was scarlet.

Maggie sneaked a look at Zach and could see he was trying not to laugh. "Well," she said, turning back to Hannah and Jason, "if you'd let me, I'd love to read something of yours."

"You would?" Jason croaked.

"Yes, very much so. I don't have a lot of experience with screenplays, but I do have one client who has sold a couple."

Hannah beamed and gave her brother a look that said *See?*

"Anything you could tell me would be great, even if it's bad," Jason said. He ignored his sister. "I can take it. I just want to learn and get better so that someday I can write for the movies for a living."

Maggie decided not to burst his bubble by explaining what the odds were of succeeding in the business he had chosen. Time enough for him to find out how difficult a task he'd set for himself. Besides, some people made it. All it took was talent, determination, a thick hide and a stroke of luck.

"Hannah's an artist," Josh piped up.

Now it was Hannah's turn to look embarrassed, although she recovered her aplomb quickly when Maggie questioned her.

"I'm not very good," she said, "but I'd like to be.

I'm hoping to go to an art school after I graduate.''
She darted a glance at her father. ''Dad wants me to
go to college, though.''

''Now, Hannah,'' Zach said mildly. ''What I said
was I thought you could study art in college and still
get a well-rounded education.''

''Did *you* go to college, Miss Callahan?'' Hannah
said.

Maggie smiled. ''Yes, I did. And why don't you
call me Maggie?'' She looked at the boys. ''All of
you.''

They continued to talk for a few more minutes,
then Zach shooed the kids into the pool, saying he
wanted some time alone with Maggie.

''You're right,'' she said once they'd gone,
''they're great kids.''

''Thanks.'' He watched, smiling, as they started a
game of Marco Polo.

''I was nervous about meeting them.''

Startled, he looked at her. ''Nervous? Why?''

Maggie shrugged. ''I don't know. I wanted them
to like me, and I was afraid they wouldn't.''

His expression was incredulous. ''Why would you
think they wouldn't like you?''

''Oh, come on, Zach. I'm spending a lot of time
with their father. It would be normal for them to feel
some resentment. Maybe even jealousy.''

He hesitated for a moment, his dark eyes pinning
hers. ''My kids aren't like that, Maggie. They're

smart enough to understand that I'm a man as well as their father. I think they want me to be happy.''

Maggie stared at him. She couldn't have looked away if she'd wanted to.

"Aren't you going to ask me if I'm happy, Maggie?''

"*Are* you happy, Zach?'' she whispered.

There was no hesitation in his reply. "I'm happier than I've been in a long time.'' For just a moment, his gaze left hers to rest on his kids, who were boisterously playing their game. "And my kids know the reason why.''

This time when their eyes met, Maggie's heart quickened. Suddenly she knew that she could no longer pretend they were just friends—not to him, and certainly not to herself.

Chapter Eight

Hannah eyed Jason, who was slumped in front of the TV set. It was Sunday night, the day after Maggie had come to swim, and this was Hannah's first chance to talk to Jason alone. "It was really nice of Maggie to say she'd read something of yours, wasn't it?" she said.

Jason looked up from the television program he was watching. "She didn't have much choice, did she? With *you* bugging her."

"I didn't bug her. I just told her your stuff was good. She's the one who said she'd like to read it."

"She'll probably think it sucks," he said glumly.

Hannah rolled her eyes. "Quit being so negative. Your stuff *is* great. I'm sure she'll like it."

But he continued to frown. "She'll probably just say she likes it because she won't want to hurt my feelings."

Hannah sighed. She didn't really want to spend hours building up Jason's ego. She wanted to talk about Maggie and her dad and their relationship. The subject of Jason's writing was only supposed to be the lead-in to her real goal. But she knew she had to be subtle, because boys could be weird when it came to discussing romance.

"I think Maggie's cool, don't you?" she said after a bit, keeping her tone as casual as she could.

Jason was once more concentrating on *The X-Files*. "Yeah, she's okay."

"I think she's more than okay. I think she's beautiful and smart. And Dad does, too. I can tell." When Jason didn't answer, Hannah said more forcefully, "Don't you think?"

Jason looked around. "Huh?"

Sometimes boys could be so *dense*. Hannah repeated her question.

Jason shrugged. "Yeah, I said she was okay. I hope Dad's not falling for her, though."

Hannah frowned. "Why not?"

"Because she's not gonna stay here, *stupid*, that's why not."

Hannah decided to ignore the "stupid" remark. "Dad's pretty good-looking and cool himself, you know. Maybe she *will* stay."

Jason raised his eyebrows. "I wouldn't get my hopes up if I were you. I mean, would *you* rather be here or in New York? Think about it."

That night, after Hannah was in bed, she did think about what Jason had said. He did have a good point, but she hoped he was wrong. She hoped Maggie and her dad would fall in love and get married, and Maggie would want to stay in Rainbow's End.

Why couldn't it happen that way? She could still keep her literary agency and just visit New York once a month or something. Like the movie stars did. They had private lives and lived with their husbands part of the time and then went off and worked somewhere else the rest of the time. If they could do it, why couldn't Maggie?

Hannah smiled, thinking how perfect that would be. Then maybe Hannah herself could go to school in New York the way she wanted to. Maybe she could even live in Maggie's apartment! Wouldn't *that* be cool?

Hannah had done some research and chosen the School of Visual Arts as the one she wanted to attend. She could just see herself in New York. She'd wear cargo pants and black boots and black turtleneck sweaters and big silver hoop earrings and a black leather jacket and she'd carry a huge black backpack with all her art supplies in it and she'd ride the subway and she'd go to all the museums and art galleries on the weekends and she'd hang out in Central Park on warm days in the spring and she'd eat hot dogs from street vendors and those big pretzels and she'd have lots of friends that were interested in the same things she was interested in.

Oh, it would be so *excellent*.

Still, Jason's prediction worried her. She began to wonder if there was anything she could do to help make things turn out the way she wanted them to. After stewing over the problem for a long time, she finally decided the first step in her campaign would be to get to know Maggie better.

Starting tomorrow.

On Monday afternoon, the doorbell rang at just a few minutes past two. Maggie opened the front door to find a smiling Hannah Tate on the doorstep. Trying not to show her surprise, Maggie said, "Well, hello, Hannah."

"Hi."

The teenager's smile was so fresh and lovely, her eyes so bright and eager, Maggie couldn't help but respond. "Come on in," she invited.

How cute she looked, Maggie thought as Hannah entered the hall. Only the young could get away with no makeup, short shorts, skimpy T-shirts and hair pulled back and fastened with a rubber band.

"I was just passing by," Hannah said, "and thought I'd stop for a minute." Then she ducked her head. "No, that's not true. I—I wanted to see you. To talk to you about something."

Touched, Maggie laid her hand on Hannah's shoulder. "I'm glad you came. Let's go back to the kitchen. I'd like you to meet my mother and her companion."

"Oh, that's right," Hannah said. "Your mom's been sick. I forgot. Maybe I *shouldn't* have come."

"Don't be silly. In fact, my mother is feeling much better. The only thing is, she still has difficulty talking at times, but she's fine. And she likes visitors." Maggie mentally crossed her fingers. Her mother liked *some* visitors. Maggie hoped Hannah would be one of them.

Five minutes later, Maggie knew she'd been foolish to worry for even a second. No one could help liking Hannah. The girl exuded friendliness and a natural charm that was impossible to resist. Maggie's mother fell under the teenager's spell instantly. Of course, it helped that Hannah was a well-brought-up girl who greeted both Maureen and Edie courteously and showed genuine interest in the ensuing conversation.

Maggie waited ten minutes or so, then she offered Hannah a soda, and the two of them walked out to the screened-in porch where they could talk privately.

"I wanted to ask you about a school I'm interested in," Hannah said. "See what you think of it."

"Okay, although I should warn you, I don't know much about art schools."

"But you live in New York."

"Well, yes, but—"

"This school is *in* New York."

"Oh." No wonder Zach wasn't keen about Hannah going to an art school, if the school that interested her was in New York.

"It's the School of Visual Arts," Hannah said. She drank some of her soda and watched Maggie's face.

Maggie bit the inside of her lip and tried to think how to answer. She knew Zach would not appreciate her encouraging his daughter to do something he was not in favor of, but she wanted to be honest with Hannah. Even so, she would have to tread carefully. "Of course, I've heard of it. In fact, I have a friend whose son is going to school there."

Hannah's eyes lit up. "You *do?*"

Maggie nodded. She wasn't a close friend of Phoebe Miller, but she had worked with the publicist on two separate occasions, one just this past spring, which was how she knew about Phoebe's son.

"Does he like the school?"

"Yes, he likes it a lot."

Hannah sighed. "I've been reading all about it on the Internet, and they have exactly what I want."

"Which is?"

"I want to study illustration and graphic design."

"You can do that at any number of schools and colleges," Maggie pointed out.

"I know that, but I don't want to go to college.

Why should I waste my time studying all kinds of things that don't interest me when I can go somewhere and get exactly what I want from *professionals* in the field?''

The girl had a good point, Maggie thought. Still, she hesitated to say so, because she knew Hannah would latch on to anything she said and use it to try to persuade Zach to come to her way of thinking.

''There's a lot to be said for getting a well-rounded education,'' Maggie finally said.

Hannah frowned. ''That's what Dad is always saying.''

''You know, Hannah, your Dad has your best interest at heart.''

''I know, but—''

''New York is very different from Rainbow's End. It's an exciting city with a lot to offer, yes, but it's also a scary place, especially for a young girl.''

''*You* went there when you graduated.''

Maggie sighed. ''I know. And my parents didn't want me to go, either.''

''Are you sorry?''

How to answer? Maggie wondered. After all, this was Zach's daughter. Should Maggie tell the girl that there had been lots of lonely times, times when she wondered if she'd made the right choice? Should she tell her that Saturday, looking at Zach's home and meeting his children, she had felt twinges of envy and loss?

Yet their two circumstances were not the same. Maggie had had to give up a terrific man, a man she deeply loved, to achieve her goal. Hannah was not in the same position. Hannah just wanted to go to the school of her choice. She wasn't proposing to make a new life thousands of miles away from her family and loved ones. After she got her education, she would come back home.

"Naturally I've sometimes wondered what my life would have been like if I'd stayed here," Maggie said carefully. She wasn't sure how much Hannah knew about the past, so she decided not to bring up Zach's name. "I think people always wonder about the road they didn't take."

Hannah eyed her thoughtfully. "I know you and my Dad dated each other when you were young."

Maggie kept her face impassive. "Oh? Did he tell you that?"

"Uh-huh."

Maggie was dying to know what else Zach had said, but there was no way she was going to ask.

"I don't have a boyfriend." This last was said sadly.

Maggie smiled in commiseration. "Maybe that's best, especially if you end up going somewhere far away to school."

Hannah nodded. For a few moments, they sipped at their drinks, each lost in her own thoughts. Then, almost shyly, Hannah said, "There *is* a boy I like a lot."

"Is there?"

"Uh-huh. His name is Kirk." She sighed heavily. "He doesn't know I'm alive, though."

Maggie looked at Hannah's shining black hair, her long tanned legs, her fresh-faced beauty. "I find that hard to believe."

"It's true," Hannah said dejectedly. She sighed again. "He's dating this girl. She…she's blond and she has big boobs."

Maggie put her hand up to hide her smile, although Hannah wasn't looking at her.

"And everyone knows she puts out," Hannah added. By now a flush had crept into her cheeks.

Maggie wanted to put her arms around Hannah and tell her that although right now this Kirk's preference for the unknown blonde with the big boobs might seem important, in the end it was probably the best possible thing that could ever have happened to Hannah.

In fact, Maggie hoped this crush she had would last through her senior year and that old Kirk would continue to prefer busty blondes who "put out" over sweet Hannah. That way Hannah would emerge from high school unscathed, untouched and with no regrets.

"I could tell you you're better off," Maggie said, "but you probably wouldn't believe me."

"All my friends have boyfriends," Hannah said.

This time she looked at Maggie. "'Course, I wouldn't be caught dead with most of them.''

Maggie laughed, and after a few seconds, Hannah laughed, too.

"You're particular, then," Maggie said.

Hannah nodded.

"What's so special about this Kirk?"

"Oh, he's just so...cute."

Maggie smiled. Silence fell between them again, and Maggie watched as a noisy blue jay chased a squirrel across the yard.

"Maggie?"

Maggie turned to Hannah.

"I really like talking to you. Is it okay if I come and visit again?" Hannah asked shyly.

Something warm tugged at Maggie's heart. She smiled. "Nothing would please me more."

"What a nice girl," Edie said after Hannah left.

"V-very nice," Maggie's mother said.

Maggie smiled. "Yes, she is."

"Did you know her mother, Maggie?" Edie asked.

"She was in my graduating class, but we weren't friends. She ran around with a different crowd." The truth was, back then Maggie had spent most of her time with Zach, and what was left was spent with Kris. "Why?"

"I was just wondering what she was like."

"I really don't know."

"Must have been real hard for the sheriff to raise those kids on his own."

"Yes, I'm sure it was."

"They seem to have turned out okay, though. He's done a good job."

"Yes, he's done a great job."

"That girl of his sure seems to have taken a shine to you, Maggie." Edie chuckled. "You could just see the hero worship in her eyes when she was talkin' to you."

Maggie nodded. She hoped she was up to the responsibility of being someone's idol, for it was clear to her, too, that whatever she said to Hannah was going to carry a lot of weight with the teenager.

Yet along with the concern this realization brought, it also made her feel good that Zach's daughter admired her and respected her opinions enough to ask for advice.

She wondered if Hannah would tell Zach about coming here today. And if she did, what would his reaction be? Would he be pleased? Or would he worry that Maggie might corrupt Hannah by influencing her in ways he disapproved of?

She hoped not. Suddenly it was very important to her that Zach trust her, that he understand that Maggie would never do or say anything to undermine his relationship with Hannah.

So if she doesn't tell him about today, you'd better.

Otherwise, when he does find out, he'll think you were hiding it from him.

In fact, the next time she talked to Zach, if he didn't bring up the subject, Maggie would.

But Maggie hoped it wouldn't come to that. Even though Hannah had not acted as if she wanted her visit kept a secret from her father, Maggie would feel better if the disclosure came from the teenager and not Maggie herself.

Zach pulled into the driveway a little before six. He was tired. It had been a rough day, starting at noon when one of his newest deputies had walked into a convenience store in the middle of an attempted robbery. The robber, gun in hand, had swung around and fired at the deputy. The first shot missed, and, before he could fire again, the deputy shot and killed him.

Everyone concerned, including the deputy, was badly shaken. It had taken Zach the better part of the afternoon to conduct an investigation and get a coherent statement out of the traumatized clerk and the equally traumatized deputy.

Killings were rare in the department, and Zach wondered if this one had been necessary. The deputy involved was young and had only been on the job four months. Maybe a veteran of the department would have been able to stop the robber by wounding him rather than killing him.

Yet it was far better for the robber to have died

than the clerk, the deputy or some innocent bystander. Even so, Zach took the responsibility of the investigation and subsequent debriefing of the deputy seriously and would make sure the deputy received adequate counseling and follow-up.

And then, to top off an already stressful day, just before quitting time, Jeannie had given her notice.

"I'm so sorry, Sheriff," she said, "but Buddy's retiring, and you know how we've always planned to move to Tucson to be near Michelle."

Zach had rubbed his forehead wearily. Jeannie was like his right hand. Indispensable.

"I don't want you to worry, though," she'd said. "I'll stay on until we find someone, and I'll train her. It'll be okay. You'll see."

Remembering, Zach grimaced. All he needed now was for Maggie to say it was time for her to go back to New York or for there to be some crisis with one of the kids. His mother always used to say trouble, like death, came in threes. If that was true, he still had one trouble to go.

Because he tried never to bring concerns over work home, he told himself to forget about today. Then he cut the ignition and climbed out of his patrol car.

When he walked in the backdoor, he was greeted by Hannah humming and peeling potatoes at the kitchen sink. The sight of his cheerful daughter immediately lifted his spirits.

"Hi, Dad," she said with a bright smile.

"Hi." He walked over and kissed her cheek. "You look happy. Have a good day?"

"Uh-huh. How about you?"

"Mine wasn't that great, but I don't want to think about it." He picked up the stack of mail and started leafing through it. "Where's Josh?"

"He went to Brian's house. Is that okay?"

"Sure," Zach said absentmindedly. "Jason's working, right?"

"Right. He gets off at eight."

"So what did you do today?" Mondays were Hannah's day off from her summer job as a pool attendant at the country club pool. He ripped open the water bill, hoping it wasn't going to shoot his budget. They hadn't had rain in weeks, and he'd been watering the lawn a lot.

"I did some laundry, and this afternoon I went over and visited Maggie."

Zach had only been half listening. But at the mention of Maggie's name, his head shot up. "What'd you say?"

Elaborately casual, Hannah said, "I stopped by Maggie's house this afternoon."

Zach stared at his daughter.

"Don't look at me like that, Dad. I just wanted to talk to her, that's all."

"About what?"

Hannah laid down the paring knife she'd been using and wiped her hands on a dish towel. "About school and stuff. *Girl* stuff.'' Bending down, she opened a cupboard and took out a pot.

"Girl stuff," Zach repeated.

"Yeah." Hannah smiled. "Maggie's really cool. I like talking to her." She began cutting the potatoes into chunks which she dropped into the pot.

Zach felt a mixture of pleasure that Hannah approved of Maggie and sadness that his daughter so clearly missed a mother to confide in. And maybe there was some envy, too.

"She said I could come anytime," Hannah added.

"You know, Hannah," he forced himself to say, even though this was something he had been trying to forget, "Maggie probably won't be staying around here much longer."

Hannah's eyes, so like Andrea's, regarded him seriously. "Did she say so?"

"She didn't have to say so. Her life's in New York. She's only here until her mother's well enough for her to go back."

"Maybe she'll decide to stay permanently."

Zach fought to keep his expression from betraying his feelings. He shook his head. "I don't think so, Hannah."

"Don't be negative, Dad. Remember what you've always told me. Think positive."

Zach couldn't help but smile. "Being realistic isn't the same as being negative."

"Well, she's not gone yet."

He tossed down the mail. "On that note, I'm going to go change into my swim trunks and get in some laps. Unless you need help here?"

"Nope. I've got everything under control."

I wish I did, Zach thought as he headed for his bedroom. *I sure as hell wish I did.* And sitting at the top of the list of things that felt out of control were his hopeless feelings for Maggie and the certainty that no amount of positive thinking on his part or the part of his daughter would make one iota of difference to the eventual outcome of the situation.

When the phone rang at nine-thirty that night, Maggie knew the caller was Zach.

"I hear my daughter paid a call on you today," he said right off.

She smiled in relief. "I wondered if she'd mention it."

"Why wouldn't she? It wasn't supposed to be a secret, was it?"

"No, of course not."

"So what did you two talk about?"

Maggie hesitated, wondering just how much she should divulge. "She wanted to talk about a school she thought I might know about. Stuff like that."

"What school?"

Maggie could almost hear his frown. "An art school."

"Why would you know about art schools?"

"This one's in New York."

"New York!"

"Now, Zach..."

"She's not going to any school in New York. I hope you didn't encourage her."

At his tone, Maggie couldn't help it. She bristled, and her tone reflected her feelings. "No, Zach, I didn't encourage her. I wouldn't do that, because I knew exactly how you would feel about it. However," she added when he started to say something, "I think the idea does have some merit and maybe you should keep an open mind."

"You know what, Maggie?" he said in a tight voice. "You forfeited the right to give me advice about my kids or anything else when you walked out on me twenty years ago. So don't start now."

For a long moment, his words hung in the air between them. Then very quietly, Maggie said, "You're right. I apologize. And now, Zach, if you don't mind, I'm really tired and I think I'll call it a night."

Without waiting for his answer, she broke the connection.

Zach stared at the phone.

Why had he said that? Why had he deliberately said something he knew would hurt her and drive her away?

Two hours later, sitting in the dark out on the patio,

he was still mulling over the question, although by then he pretty much knew the answer.

He was scared. Scared of the way he felt about Maggie. Scared of what was ahead.

What the hell, he thought wearily. He drained his drink, the third he'd had since the aborted phone call. Maybe this was for the best. As he'd told Hannah, Maggie would be leaving soon, anyway, and the more time he spent with her, the harder it would be to let her go. At least this way, he still had some pride left.

Maggie didn't sleep well and awakened with a headache. Zach's words had stung, even as deep down she knew they were true. She *didn't* have any right to give him advice about his kids. Or anything else.

But it still hurt to know he didn't trust her, that he thought so little of her that he would dismiss her opinions out of hand.

I would never do or say anything to jeopardize Hannah's welfare or his relationship with her, and I would certainly never undermine his authority. Doesn't he know that?

Lost in her thoughts, she jumped when the phone rang just a little after seven.

"Maggie? I didn't wake you, did I?"

Her heart constricted at the sound of Zach's voice. "No. I've been up for a while."

"Maggie, I'm sorry about last night."

"No need to be sorry. What you said was true."

"No. No, it wasn't. I just…oh, hell. I don't know why I said that. I guess it bothered me that Hannah told you something she hadn't told me."

Suddenly Maggie felt better. Zach hadn't lashed out at her because he didn't trust her. He'd said what he did last night because, since Andrea's death, Hannah and the boys had been *his* territory. He'd just been protecting his turf. That, Maggie understood. That, she could forgive. "It's okay, Zach. I'm not mad."

"You're not?"

She smiled. "No."

"Thank you. I felt like a real jerk last night. I was afraid I'd hurt your feelings."

"Oh, come on. I'm a big girl. Anyway, as I said last night, you were right."

"No, I wasn't. What I said was unfair."

It made Maggie feel good to know he felt this way, moreover to know he had the guts to admit it when he thought he was wrong. She couldn't remember the last time a man had apologized to her, for anything. "Zach, I told Hannah she could come by anytime. Is that okay with you?"

"Of course it's okay."

"You're sure?"

For a moment, he didn't answer, and some of the warmth Maggie felt began to evaporate.

And then he said, "I can't think of anyone I'd

rather have Hannah spend time with than you, Maggie.''

That night, Maggie fell asleep with a smile on her face.

From then on Hannah was a steady visitor. And she wasn't the only one of Zach's children to find her way to the house. When Maggie read the screenplay she'd been given by Jason and discovered that not only was it good, it was *very* good, she told him so, and soon he was showing up on the doorstep at regular intervals. Maggie soon became his confidante, not only hearing about his hopes and dreams for his writing, but about the girl he liked and a classmate who was giving him trouble.

Like Hannah, Jason was a sensitive kid, although in typical male fashion, he tried to hide his softer side. He reminded Maggie so much of the way Zach had been as a kid, she couldn't help but love him.

Before long, even Josh had found his way to the Callahan house. It got so he biked over almost every day, lured by the peanut butter and chocolate chip cookies Maureen had resumed baking with Edie's help, and by the presence of his older siblings.

''You've certainly made three conquests,'' Zach said one evening after the entire family had been invited for dinner with Maggie and her mother. He and Maggie were sitting out back on the screened porch while his kids and Maggie's mother played Monopoly inside. Every once in a while, they could hear shouts of laughter and good-natured teasing.

Maggie smiled. It gave her great pleasure to know his children liked her and wanted to be around her, even as it frightened her, too. For she was beginning to care about them too much. It had been bad enough when it was just Zach she hated to leave when it was time to go back to New York, but now…now it was going to be horrible when she finally left. She would miss them all terribly.

"Penny for your thoughts," Zach said softly.

"I was just thinking how much I'll miss them when I leave to go home."

He didn't answer for a long time. When he did, his voice was devoid of emotion. "Yes, well, I'm sure they'll miss you, too."

Maggie didn't know what she'd expected him to say. All she knew was that his answer made her heart ache. *Won't you miss me?* she wanted to cry. *Why don't you say it? Why don't you ask me to stay?*

But if he did, what could she answer? Did she really want to give up everything she had worked so hard to accomplish?

So she swallowed her hurt and made a noncommittal reply, and, soon after, he left.

That night, Maggie fell asleep with a heavy heart.

Chapter Nine

The following morning, as Maggie was driving her mother home from therapy, her mother said, "M-Maggie, there's s-something I—I've been wanting to talk to you a-about."

Maggie smiled at her mother. "Your speech is improving every day, Mom."

Her mother nodded. "I-I'm trying h-hard."

"I know. I'm proud of you." Her mother had gained flexibility in her right hand, too, and she was walking without the aid of the cane she'd used up until about two weeks ago. "So what was it you wanted to talk about?"

"It's about Z-Zach."

Maggie flipped on her right-turn signal. "What about him?" she answered warily.

"D-do you know wh-what you're doing, Maggie?"

"What do you mean?"

"You kn-know what I mean."

Maggie hesitated. Should she pretend righteous indignation? Ignorance? What?

"M-Maggie."

Maggie sighed.

"I-I'm not t-trying to make you feel bad, I-I just, I like Zach v-very much."

So do I.

"Even s-so, wh-when it was just him, I th-thought, well, he's a grown m-man, he can t-take care of himself. B-but now his kids are c-coming over all the t-time and they're g-getting attached to y-you and I just think s-someone's going to g-get hurt and it might b-be those k-kids—"

She broke off with a gasp as Maggie swerved to avoid a parked car she hadn't seen because she'd been too concerned with what her mother was saying and too upset by the guilt that flooded her when her mother brought up the subject of Zach's children.

Heart thudding, Maggie pulled over to the curb. She turned off the ignition and closed her eyes. She felt ridiculously close to tears.

"M-Maggie," her mother said gently, placing her hand on Maggie's arm. "I-I didn't mean to upset you."

Maggie took a deep breath. "I know you didn't."

"I just...y-you need to think about what the outcome of all th-this is going to b-be, Maggie. B-because if Z-Zach is thinking you're g-going to stay this time, and y-you're not, then it w-won't just be him you hurt when you go. Th-those kids will be hurt, too."

Those kids will be hurt, too.

Her mother's warning was all Maggie could think about. For days, those six words played in her head, over and over again. Maggie wanted to believe her mother was exaggerating, but down deep, she was terribly afraid her mother was right. The kids did seem to be thinking of her in terms of a stepmother.

In terms of a stepmother someone who was going to stick around. Maybe they didn't realize that's what they were hoping would happen, but subconsciously, she was afraid that's exactly what was in their minds.

Maggie thought about how Hannah now told her everything that happened in her life. How she asked for Maggie's opinions and her advice. How she had started hugging Maggie hello and goodbye. How she wanted to know all about Maggie's life and her friends. And in particular, how she talked about her father all the time, constantly praising him and pointing out his good qualities.

Jason was the same way. Maybe he didn't show his admiration as much as Hannah did, but it was there in his eyes and in the way he hung on to every word Maggie uttered.

And Josh.

Maggie swallowed against the lump in her throat. Josh was adorable. A goofy kid one minute, a serious almost-adolescent the next, Josh had stolen her heart. Just that morning he'd stopped by on his way to a friend's house and given her a bouquet of black-eyed Susans. Those half-wilted flowers had been one of the nicest gifts Maggie had ever received and they now occupied a place of honor in the middle of the kitchen table, where every time Maggie looked at them, she couldn't help smiling.

She stared out the kitchen window. A sparrow was sitting on the lip of the bird feeder mounted outside. *Why can't life be simple?* she wondered. Why do we have these agonizing choices to make?

She knew it wasn't fair to keep encouraging Zach's kids to think of her as a possible permanent fixture in their lives. And that's what she'd been doing. Maybe, on some level, she'd even *known* she was doing it.

Oh, God, I never meant to hurt them.

No, maybe not, but by playing at being their mother, by encouraging their confidences and enjoying their adulation, she had done nothing to prevent that eventual outcome.

So now what?

"Zachary?"

"Ma! You're back." Zach's mother had gone for

her annual summer visit to her sister in New Mexico. "I didn't think you were coming back for another couple of weeks." Zach pushed some paperwork aside and propped his feet on his desk.

"I changed my mind. Six weeks of Nuna was long enough."

Zach grinned. His aunt Nuna and his mother had a love/hate relationship that defied description. Both were stubborn women with strong opinions, and neither was afraid to express them. It had always amazed him that they could spend six hours together—not to mention six weeks—without killing each other. Yet, ever since his father had died, his mother had spent a good part of the summer in New Mexico. When his kids were little, she used to take them with her. For the past couple of years, though, what with summer jobs and friends, they hadn't wanted to go.

"I'm anxious to see the children," his mother said. "Can you come for dinner tonight?"

"Thanks, Ma, but tonight's not a good night. Jason's working till eleven and Hannah's sleeping over at a friend's house."

"Well, you and Josh come, then."

"Why don't we just wait until tomorrow? I'm pretty sure all the kids can come then." He didn't want to tell her he and Josh were taking Maggie and her mother out for pizza tonight, because he wasn't in the mood for another lecture.

"But—"

"Tomorrow would be better," he said firmly.

"Oh, all right." Her voice rang with disappointment. "Then maybe I'll stop by for a while later. At least I can see Josh."

Damn. "Josh and I won't be there. We'll just see you tomorrow, okay? What time do you want us?"

If he'd hoped to divert her, it didn't work, because she ignored the question and pounced on the "Josh and I won't be there" part of what he'd said. "Where are you and Josh going?"

"Out for pizza."

"Oh. Just the two of you?"

It was no good. He could lie and say yes, but why should he? "No. We're taking Maggie and her mother out."

"Maggie? You mean she's still here?"

"Yes."

After a long, pregnant silence, she said coldly, "I see."

No, Ma, you don't see. You never did see. "Listen, Ma, I have to go." He rustled some papers. "What time should we come tomorrow?"

At first he thought she hadn't heard him. Finally she answered. "I'll expect you at six."

"All right. See you then."

For the remainder of the day, the conversation niggled at the back of his mind. One of these days he was not going to be able to keep his temper in check.

Mother or not, he was going to say something he shouldn't, and then all hell would break loose. He just hoped it wouldn't happen tomorrow night.

Zach, Hannah and Josh arrived at Zach's mother's house promptly at six. Hannah hadn't been thrilled about coming. She'd had other plans. But Zach had asked her to change them, and after thinking about how disappointed her grandmother would be if she didn't come, Hannah said she would.

His mother opened the door with a welcoming smile.

She looked great, Zach thought. She was a tall, sturdy woman strongly reminiscent in appearance of her Cherokee ancestors, and her hair was still as thick and almost as dark as it had been when she was young. She wore it the way she always had, in a thick braid down her back.

"Where's Jason?" she said after giving them all hugs.

"He's working until six-thirty tonight. It'll probably be seven before he can get here."

She frowned. "I don't know why you let Jason take that job, Zachary. You know I don't believe in children working during their school years."

The subject of jobs had been an ongoing bone of contention for a while now. "I worked for dad from the time I was old enough to push a lawnmower," Zach pointed out mildly. He was determined not to let her goad him into any kind of disagreement in front of the kids.

Ignoring this as she ignored anything she didn't like, she fussed over Hannah and Josh, saying, "I brought you both something from New Mexico," then smiled benevolently as they opened their gifts.

"Oh, Nana, I love them!" Hannah said. "Thank you!" She held up a pair of silver earrings in the shape of stars. "Look, Dad, aren't they beautiful?" Throwing her arms around her grandmother, she kissed her.

"You're very welcome, Hannah."

Josh, too, was thrilled with his gift—a hand-sewn leather wallet. He grinned at his father. "Pretty soon I'll have a driver's license to put in here."

Hannah rolled her eyes. "In three more years."

"I can get a hardship license in two years," Josh said.

"A hardship license!" she scoffed. "Why would you need a hardship license?"

Josh made a face at her. "If Dad says there's no way for me to work without driving, then I'll get one."

Both children looked at Zach.

"Since you won't even turn thirteen until next month, and since you have no job to speak of, this is a premature discussion, so let's drop it." Zach's tone invited no further argument.

They continued to talk about the New Mexico trip

and what Zach's mother had done there and what was going on with their cousins until Jason arrived. As Zach had predicted, it was close to seven. He, too, opened his gift from his grandmother—a fine-looking silver belt buckle—and then the family went into the kitchen where Zach's mother proceeded to put out an enormous quantity of food, including Zach's favorite corn chowder.

Dinner went smoothly, with no mention of Maggie, and Zach began to think he might weather this visit with no dissension. Then, just as his mother was serving dessert—blueberry cobbler and ice cream—she looked at Josh and said, "Did you have fun last night?"

"Huh?" He had been staring at his bowl, but at her question, he looked up.

She put a dollop of ice cream on his cobbler. "I just asked if you'd had fun last night. You went out for pizza, didn't you? With your father and his friends?" There was a slight emphasis to the word *friends.*

"Oh, yeah," Josh said.

If Zach hadn't been so annoyed over his mother's tactics, he would have laughed. A typical kid, Josh was totally oblivious to her motive for questioning him.

"So did you have fun?" she repeated.

"Yeah, we had a good time." He began to eat his cobbler. "We went to Rocco's."

"I thought you might be bored," she persisted in her single-minded way. "After all, it's not like Mrs. Callahan and her daughter are *your* friends."

Josh stopped eating and looked at his grandmother, who had finished serving the ice cream and was now returning it to the freezer. He frowned. "Maggie's my friend. So is her mother." He looked at his sister and brother. "We *all* like them, Nana. They're really neat."

"That sounds like you've been spending a lot of time with them."

Zach stared at his mother, who looked back impassively.

"Do you know, Maggie, Nana?" Hannah asked.

"Yes, I know her."

"We like her a lot," Hannah continued.

Zach knew that Hannah, like Josh, was unsuspecting and probably thought her grandmother wanted to hear good things about Maggie.

"Like Josh said, she's really neat," Hannah went on happily. "She's so easy to talk to. I've been going over to visit her a lot this summer."

Zach's mother's lips tightened.

"She's been reading my work," Jason chimed in. "She thinks it's good. Did you know she's a literary agent in New York?"

"Yes, I'd heard that."

Zach couldn't believe his children didn't hear the edge in his mother's voice, but he was grateful they didn't. No matter how much his mother might deserve it, he didn't want them to think less of her. "Guess who we saw at Rocco's." He addressed the comment to his mother.

"I have no idea."

"Oh, yeah!" Josh said. "We saw Jenny!"

Jenny worked for the landscaping business started by Zach's father.

Zach's ploy worked. His mother really liked Jenny and wanted to hear all about her. But even though he'd successfully turned the conversation away from the subject of Maggie, he knew he hadn't heard the end of it.

Sure enough, when dinner was over, his mother shooed the kids into the living room to watch TV, "so your father and I can talk a bit in peace."

Once they were gone from the kitchen, she offered him a cup of coffee, then poured one for herself. Her dark eyes pinned his. "This situation with Maggie concerns me, Zachary."

"There's nothing to be concerned about."

"When you persist in a relationship that is doomed to failure, as your mother, I think I have a right to be concerned, especially when you expose your children to someone who is—"

"Ma, you can stop right there, because I don't intend to discuss Maggie with you. I've told you before—if I choose to see Maggie or any other woman, it's *my* business. And another thing," he added before she could answer, ''I also don't want you pumping the kids for information the way you did earlier.''

''Well! If *that's* the way you feel!''

''That's the way I feel.''

She pressed her lips together and glared at him.

''Look, Ma,'' he said in a softer voice, ''I don't like talking to you like this, but you've got to let me live my own life.''

''Fine. Live your own life. What do I know? I'm only your mother.''

It was no use. She wasn't going to budge from her stubborn stance. He drained his coffee and got up. ''It's getting late, and I've got a full day tomorrow, so I think we'll be going. Thanks for dinner. I'll call you in a day or so.''

''Your mother's right, Maggie. Zach's definitely thinking marriage.''

Maggie traced the condensation on her glass of iced tea. She and Kris were having a late lunch together. ''Do you really think so?'' Until the moment Kris had echoed Maureen's concerns, Maggie had been hoping Kris would say Maggie's mother was making a problem where none existed.

''Yes, I do. I saw the way he looked at you that night when the two of you came over. He's in love with you. He's hoping that this time, you'll choose him.''

"But he *knows* I live in New York. That I have a *business* there. I mean, he must realize…"

"You haven't exactly been *discouraging* him."

"I know."

"I mean, what's the guy *supposed* to think? Especially since the signals you're sending are what he wants to see."

Maggie sighed. She had no answer for Kris's logic.

"You know, Maggie, one of the things I've always admired about you is your honesty. The fact that you're such a straight shooter. That you tell it like it is and you don't play games."

Maggie nodded.

"Zach doesn't play games, either," Kris said softly.

"I know."

Kris's eyes were filled with sympathy. "Then you also know what you have to do. Unless…"

"Unless what?"

"Unless you're having doubts yourself?"

Maggie started to say she didn't know what Kris meant, but stopped.

"*Are* you having doubts?"

Maggie swallowed. Was she?

"I'll be darned. You *are* having doubts."

"Maybe I am."

Kris leaned back in her chair and studied Maggie for a long moment. "I'm glad I'm not in your shoes," she finally said.

"Gee, thanks."

Kris smiled. Then the smile faded. Reaching across the table, she squeezed Maggie's hand. "I can't tell you what to do. You've got to make that decision yourself. But I'm always available to listen and give moral support."

That night, Maggie knew it was time to have a serious talk with Zach. She'd been wrong when she'd asked him to pretend that nothing had happened between them after that night when he'd kissed her. Something *had* happened, and something was still happening. It was time to get it out in the open and find out where they were going from here.

Maggie's decision to initiate a talk with Zach was easier to think about than actually to do. For one thing, several days went by before she heard from him again. Hannah volunteered the information that he was tied up with a training class and would be back on Friday.

But on Friday, Edie had a family birthday dinner to attend, and Maggie's brother and his family were spending the week at the beach, and her aunt Rose and uncle Patrick also had plans, so she and Zach spent the evening with Maggie's mother.

Then, as he was leaving, he said, "The kids left today. They're spending this week with Andrea's sister Arlene and her family in Houston."

"You know, I'd forgotten about Arlene. How is

she?'' Arlene was a couple of years older than Maggie, but from what Maggie remembered of her, she'd been really nice.

"She's great. She and her husband have two kids. Their son is the same age as Jason, and their daughter is a year younger than Hannah. My kids get along really well with them and look forward to spending part of their summer vacation there.''

"So she doesn't feel the same way her brother feels.''

"No,'' Zach said. "She's like her parents. She wants to keep a good relationship going. Anyway, I thought maybe I could cook dinner for you tomorrow night. That's if you can get Edie or someone to stay with your mother.''

"I'll see,'' Maggie promised, thinking this would be the perfect time for her to talk to Zach. They'd have privacy, and they could really hash things out.

That night she had a hard time sleeping. She kept dreaming of Zach and his children. In one of the dreams they were standing on top of a hill, and she was trying to climb up to where they were, but no matter how many times she gained a foothold, she kept falling back. In another, she was the one at the top of the hill, and they kept trying to reach her, with no more success than she'd had.

Maggie was practical. She wasn't into dream interpretation or symbolism or anything similar. Yet even she could understand the significance of these dreams.

She was nervous all day Saturday. If only she knew what she wanted, things would be so much easier. *My trouble is, I want everything. I want to keep my career and my independence, but I want Zach and everything he represents, too.*

Edie had consented to come and spend the evening and arrived at six. "I'm going to stay all night," she announced as she walked in the door. "So don't worry about coming home early."

"Thanks, Edie."

"You look nice," Edie added approvingly as Maggie gathered up her purse and her keys and prepared to leave.

Maggie had debated over what to wear, finally settling on a green sundress that she'd bought at the local boutique the previous weekend. Funny how in New York she mostly wore black and beige, but in Rainbow's End she gravitated toward color. She was sure there was some significance in that, too.

As she drove to Zach's she told herself to be calm, but the butterflies in her stomach refused to be banished. The thing was, after tonight there would be no more ambivalence or indecision. After tonight she would either have a future with Zach...or she wouldn't.

Zach had obviously been watching for her, because

she'd no sooner stepped out of her car than the front door opened and he walked out to meet her.

He looked wonderful, she thought. He was wearing loose-fitting khaki pants and a black T-shirt which showed off his impressive chest to advantage. His dark eyes shone with admiration as he gave her the once-over. "Nice dress," he said.

"Thanks." She handed him the bottle of shiraz she'd brought. "A gift for the host," she said lightly.

He looked at the label. "My favorite."

Putting his hand on the small of her back, he guided her up the steps and inside.

And in that moment, she knew exactly why she'd been so nervous all day. It wasn't because she planned to talk to Zach about their situation. Or even that the whole course of her future would be decided tonight. It was because she had known, on some level, that they would do more than talk.

They were going to make love.

Chapter Ten

Zach led the way into the dining room. "I thought we'd eat in here tonight."

Maggie looked at the table, which was beautifully set with pretty china, silver and cloth napkins. Zach had even put candles and a crystal vase filled with flowers on the table. She smiled, pleased that he'd gone to so much trouble. "The table looks nice."

"Thanks."

"This is the first time I've seen it when it wasn't stacked with the kids' things."

Zach grimaced. "I know. Unfortunately, they've gotten into the habit of dumping their stuff here, and I've let them get away with it."

"Jimmy and I used to do the same thing when we were kids. Drove my mother nuts."

He grinned. "That wasn't all you did that drove her nuts."

Maggie chuckled, remembering how her mother would leave the front and back porch lights blazing when Maggie was out with Zach. As if that would stop them from doing anything they weren't supposed to be doing, she thought wryly. They'd just found other places to do it, like the old lake road and certain corners of the park. Remembering, her pulse quickened and her gaze slid away from Zach's.

"Enough reminiscing," he said. "Would you like a glass of wine?"

"Sounds good."

"How about some merlot? I've got a bottle open."

"Great." She followed him into the kitchen and watched as he poured her wine. Leaning against the counter, she sipped the wine and watched as he finished chopping carrots for their salad, then deftly cut a tomato and added it to the bowl.

She enjoyed watching him. Zach was a sexy, thoroughly masculine man, but he looked at home in his kitchen. She guessed he'd had plenty of practice preparing meals, for Hannah hadn't always been old enough to do the cooking. Once again, she marveled that anyone—let alone a man—could manage a demanding job plus raise three young children with no regular help. His accomplishments made hers feel miniscule by contrast. After all, until this summer she'd never had to worry about anyone but herself.

When he finished the salad, he asked her to put it on the dining-room table. Setting down her glass of wine, she took the salad bowl and walked back into the dining room. By the time she returned to the kitchen, he was removing a casserole from the oven.

"Mmm," she said. "Smells good. What is it?"

"Some recipe Luke's wife gave me. It's called Chicken Delight." He laughed. "I know, it's a ridiculous name. It does taste good, though."

He was right, Maggie thought later. The casserole—filled with tender chicken, mushrooms, broccoli, rice and cheese—had been delicious. With it they'd had the salad and crusty French bread, more of the wine—lots more of the wine—and later, a mouthwatering key lime pie. "Don't tell me you made this pie," she said with a satisfied sigh.

He shook his head. "No, I bought it at that little bakery in the shopping center on Fifth Street."

"If I'd known their stuff was this good, I'd have been there weeks ago." She grinned. "It's probably a good thing I didn't know about them. I think I've already gained ten pounds since I've been home."

"You don't look as if you've gained an ounce." His gaze swept her approvingly.

"You were right," she said lightly, trying to ignore the inner flutter his admiration had created.

He gave her a crooked smile. "Right?"

"Yes. That first night I saw you...in the cafeteria at the hospital?"

"Yes." He was frowning, obviously still confused by the connection.

"You said you'd learned to sweet-talk. You were right. You have."

He made a comic face. "Sweetheart, you ain't seen *nuthin'* yet."

Maggie laughed. "You'd better stick to law enforcement. You'll never make it as a comedian."

Soon after that, they cleared the table, and even though Zach insisted they should just stack the dishes in the sink and he'd take care of the cleanup later, Maggie wouldn't hear of it. "I *hate* facing dirty dishes late at night or in the morning. Let's do them now. With two of us, it won't take any time at all."

A half hour later, everything that could go into the dishwasher was there, and the rest had been washed, dried and put away. When they were finished, he poured two more glasses of wine and suggested they go into the living room. "I've got a new CD. We can listen to music and relax."

Maggie was afraid the CD would be by one of the country singers he seemed to favor, but he surprised her. It was a collection of James Taylor's greatest hits.

"How'd you know I'm a James Taylor fan?" Maggie said.

"Oh, come on, Maggie. Don't you remember? Your mother was always playing his stuff when we were kids. You knew all the words and would sing along.''

Maggie smiled. She had forgotten. Suddenly she was filled with nostalgia for those days.

''Put your wine down,'' Zach said. ''Let's dance.''

As ''You've Got a Friend'' rolled silkily off Taylor's tongue, Zach drew her into his arms, and they danced in slow circles around the living room. Maggie closed her eyes as Zach pressed her closer. Whoever invented dancing had been a sadist, she thought, for if this wasn't torture, she didn't know what was. The feel of Zach's body moving against her caused her own body to ache with need, and she knew he was feeling the same torment.

When the song ended, he whispered, ''Maggie.''

She pulled back a little so she could see his face. In his eyes there was a question.

She only hesitated a moment. Then she reached up and pulled his head down to meet hers. The moment their lips touched, Maggie knew she was lost. She melted against him, and he crushed her to him.

How long they stood there kissing, Maggie didn't know. She only knew that here in Zach's arms was where she belonged. Where she'd always belonged.

Soon kissing wasn't enough. Without quite knowing who did what or how they managed to get there, Maggie found herself in Zach's bedroom, their clothes thrown wherever they tossed them.

And then they were on the bed, naked bodies entwined, hearts beating wildly as they rediscovered each other. Each touch, each stroke, each searching kiss, fueled the desire that had been building over the past weeks until Maggie was trembling with need.

"Maggie, Maggie," Zach said again and again.

She gasped when he entered her, moaning as he plunged deeply. She twined her legs around him and met him thrust for thrust. *Zach, Zach.* His name was a song in her heart, his mouth a remembered feast, his strong arms and slow hands a gift she'd been denied for too long. Combined they took her on a journey that climaxed in a shattering explosion of feeling that shook Maggie to her core. Zach gripped her tightly as her body shuddered and trembled under his. Only then did he allow himself his own release. When he cried out, Maggie's eyes filled with tears.

She had forgotten what it was like to make love when the lovemaking was as much about emotion as it was about sensation. *I love him,* she thought. *I love him.* Yet in some ways, this realization made her feel worse. Wonderful sex was one thing. Love was quite another. She could walk away from wonderful sex. But could she walk away from love a second time?

This time around, what she felt for Zach wasn't a kid's love based mostly on hormones. It was a deeper and more complicated emotion. This time she loved the person he had become, and she was almost certain he felt the same way.

Dear heaven.

What were they going to do?

Maggie could see no way around their problem. The only way they could be together was for her to give up everything she'd worked so hard for. Because Zach belonged here, even more so than she belonged somewhere else.

Yet, even as she told herself this, she waited for him to declare himself. She knew it was crazy, but somehow she felt that once he said he loved her, once he asked her to marry him, they might be able to see their way clear to some kind of future together.

Zach knew what he felt for Maggie wasn't just physical. He loved her. How he loved her! And he wanted to be with her. Not just tonight or for the remainder of her stay in Rainbow's End, but forever.

Holding her close like this, sharing what they'd shared tonight—he wanted that for always.

Yet how would that be possible? If it wasn't possible to be together twenty years ago, it was even less possible now.

Did he have the right to ask her to give up her career and take on not only him, but his kids, too? He knew she really liked his kids, but liking and living with them and being partly responsible for them were distinctly different things.

Although the decision was painful, he knew that no matter how much he might want to ask her to stay, he couldn't do it. It simply wasn't fair.

And yet, he had to say *something*. Cradling her close, he kissed her temple. ''Tonight was wonderful, Maggie,'' he said softly. He stopped, wishing he could at least tell her he loved her. But saying he loved her without making a commitment to her seemed like a clichè.

The silence stretched awkwardly. Then, sighing, she pulled away and sat up. ''It *was* wonderful, but we both know it was a mistake.'' So saying, she rose from the bed and reached for her clothes.

He wanted to cry out that making love with her wasn't a mistake, that he would never be sorry, but he knew if he did, he would give away his feelings. And if she really felt what had happened between them tonight was a mistake, he sure as hell didn't want her to know how differently *he* felt. So he said nothing, because it was bad enough he'd fallen in love with her all over again; he didn't want to make a public fool of himself, too.

It hurt like the devil to admit it, but it was now clear to him that Maggie didn't love him. She was attracted to him, sure. They'd always had that going for them. But she hadn't really loved him when they were young, and she didn't love him now—at least not the way he loved her.

Face it, Zach, he told himself. She chose her life in New York a long time ago.

Resigned now, he kept silent while she dressed. She didn't look at him, just put on her underwear and slipped into her sundress. Zach's heart ached as he watched her, but he didn't get out of the bed until she disappeared into the bathroom. Then he hurriedly pulled on his own clothes and waited.

He tried not to think. Time enough for thinking after she was gone. Now he'd just concentrate on getting through what was left of their time together tonight without giving himself away.

It seemed a long time before she emerged from the bathroom. He heard water running and the flush of the toilet. Finally she opened the door. Their eyes met briefly, then she dropped her gaze. He studied her face to see if she was feeling even a fraction of what he felt, but her expression gave away nothing.

Maggie. Look at me. Tell me I'm wrong.

But she didn't look at him. And when she spoke, all she said was, "Thank you for everything, Zach. I had a lovely evening."

Five minutes later, she was gone.

Maggie lay in bed and relived every moment of the evening. What had happened? Had she been completely wrong about Zach? Was it sex he'd wanted all the time? Is that what all this attention was about this summer? Getting her into bed? Was this payback time?

Maggie prided herself on the fact she rarely cried. But tonight she couldn't help herself. The tears came, and once they did, she couldn't seem to stop them. Eventually, she cried herself to sleep.

The next morning, Maggie was downstairs before six. She turned on the coffeemaker and while the coffee brewed, filling the kitchen with its rich fragrance, she brought the morning paper inside. She felt like hell, and she knew she looked bad. She was afraid her mother would know something was wrong unless she was able to put on a damn good act.

"Get a grip," she told herself. "You've weathered a helluva lot worse than this. So you had sex with a guy you thought cared about you more than he does. Big deal. You're a grown-up. You'll get over it."

Anyway, this was for the best. Her life was thousands of miles away from here; she'd always known that. So even if Zach *had* said he loved her and asked her to stay there, it would have been impossible. Now she could leave Rainbow's End with no regrets.

She was still talking to herself when she heard her mother stirring. Fifteen minutes later, her mother slowly walked into the kitchen. She wore a cotton robe and she'd combed her hair. "I th-thought I smelled coffee," she said, giving Maggie a smile.

Maggie forced herself to return the smile. "Sit down and I'll get you some."

Her mother complied. She didn't say anything until

Maggie put the cup in front of her. "You're c-certainly up early t-today."

Maggie picked up the Lifestyle section of the paper. "I couldn't sleep." She didn't meet her mother's eyes.

Maureen reached for the front page, and for about ten minutes they drank their coffee and read the paper in silence. Just as Maggie began to relax her mother said, "Did you have a nice time last night?"

Maggie kept her voice offhand and light. "Uh-huh, I sure did."

"You came home early, that's why I w-wondered."

"Yes, well…" She started to say something about Zach's children, but she realized her mother knew they were gone for the week. "I was tired." The moment the words were out, she wanted to take them back.

"Oh? You d-didn't seem tired when you left."

Damn. Why was it her mother seemed to have a sixth sense about her and always knew when Maggie wasn't telling the truth? She laughed, but even to her own ears, her laugh sounded fake. "I probably had too much wine."

Her mother didn't comment, and Maggie wondered what she was thinking. "Are you hungry, Mom? I was going to make some pancakes."

"Th-that sounds good."

Maggie bustled about—mixing the batter, heating

the griddle, setting the table. All the while she could feel her mother's shrewd gaze on her.

But to Maggie's great relief, her mother didn't mention the previous evening again. And by the time breakfast was over, it was time to get ready for church, after which they had been invited to her cousin Keith's house for dinner.

Normally Maggie enjoyed seeing her relatives. Today, though, she wasn't looking forward to it, because for the most part, they were a happy bunch. And she didn't feel very happy. Normally, too, Maggie found Sunday mass relaxing. She wasn't deeply religious, but the ancient rituals, the sun pouring through the stained-glass windows, the wonderful music and the beauty of the liturgy never failed to soothe her and remind her that her problems were insignificant in the scheme of things. But today she couldn't lose herself in the service. Today her thoughts stubbornly remained rooted in her own unhappiness.

After mass, they went back to their house for a quick change of clothes. Maggie's mother donned lightweight cotton slacks and a knit top. Maggie put on cropped linen pants with a matching top.

By the time they arrived at Keith and Susan's, it was one o'clock, and the street and driveway were already filled with cars.

"L-looks like everyone is h-here," Maggie's mother said as they walked up the front walk.

"Yes." Maggie recognized Jack and Sheila's SUV,

her cousin Kevin's pickup truck, her cousin Glenn's sports car, her cousin Patrick's Bronco, her cousin Rory's old Mustang and her uncle Patrick's Buick. Yes, the clan was all there. Maggie braced herself and rang the doorbell.

To an outsider, the Callahan clan could be, and often was, overwhelming. Not only were they a large family, they were also boisterous and demonstrative. They did nothing quietly. The first person Maggie saw when she walked inside was Kevin.

"Maggie!" He came over and threw his arm around her shoulders.

She couldn't help smiling. Of all her male cousins, Kevin was her favorite. He'd been in her high-school graduating class, and they'd always been buddies, probably because he had a streak of wildness in him that matched hers.

"I haven't seen much of you lately," he said. There was a devilish twinkle in his eye. He lowered his voice. "I hear that's because you've been spending a lot of time with a certain law-enforcement officer."

Maggie put on her best smile and answered in the same vein. "Don't believe everything you hear."

He raised an eyebrow. "I got this from a trusted source."

She rolled her eyes. "I can't believe the way people gossip in small towns."

While this exchange was taking place, Maggie's

mother had been the object of much attention and fussing. Maggie and Kevin joined the group surrounding her.

"Hi, Maggie," said Susan, Keith's wife. "Glad you could make it."

Maggie liked Susan—a pretty, no-nonsense girl whom Keith had married a few years earlier. This was a second marriage for Susan. Her first husband had been Keith's best friend. He'd also been one of Zach's deputies and had been killed in the line of duty. Zach still felt terrible about Paul's death—one of the few they'd ever had in the sheriff's department.

Susan had a thirteen-year-old son, Scott, from that marriage, and she and Keith had a daughter, Megan, who was eighteen months old. Maggie wondered if it had been easy for Keith to take on a child fathered by another man. He certainly made it look easy, she thought as she watched him ruffle the boy's hair. In the times she'd been around them, she'd seen nothing but love in Keith's dealings with the boy, and it was obviously reciprocated.

Maybe it would have been that way with me and Zach's kids, too.

Pushing the hurtful thought away, Maggie greeted the rest of the family. As always, she was struck by how good-looking they were. The men were all tall, with almost-black hair and the intense blue Callahan eyes that Maggie had also inherited.

"Callahan genes are strong," Maggie's mother had

said more than once. Maggie had to agree. Unfortunately, their less desirable qualities—like stubbornness and quick tempers—had also shown up in most of them, including Maggie.

Sheila, the only Callahan girl aside from Maggie, showed evidence of the dominant Callahan genes, too, although her eyes were a soft gray, inherited from her maternal great-great grandmother.

"Our colleen has eyes the color of the Irish sky," her father was fond of saying.

The younger generation were, if anything, going to be even better looking, Maggie thought. Patrick Jr.'s four girls were beautiful, and Sheila and Jack's little Ryan was adorable. And Keith and Susan's Megan—with her chubby cheeks and dimpled smile—stole Maggie's heart.

Keith gave Maggie a hug and asked her and her mother what they'd like to drink. While he went off to fill their orders, Susan announced that dinner would be on the table in twenty minutes, so she hoped they were all hungry. "I'll call you all when it's ready."

"Can I help you?" Maggie asked.

"Sure. C'mon back to the kitchen."

Susan put Maggie to work mixing the dressing for the coleslaw while Jan, Patrick Jr.'s wife, sliced the ham. Jan was a breast cancer survivor, but no one would ever know she'd had her share of dark days, because you never saw her when she didn't have a smile on her face or something good to say. She and

Patrick had gotten married young—as young as Maggie and Zach would have been if they'd gotten married when Maggie graduated from high school the way Zach had wanted.

Stop thinking about Zach, she told herself sternly, turning her attention back to her assigned task.

When the food was ready, Maggie, Jan and Susan carried it into the dining room, then Susan called the rest of the family. They trooped into the dining room with the same noisy exuberance they brought to every gathering. As always, Maggie's Uncle Patrick was given the place of honor at the head of the table, even though this was Keith's home.

Maggie thought it was great, the way they all deferred to the patriarch of the family. She loved her uncle. He was a lot like her father, and she'd adored her father.

Her aunt Rose was shepherded to the other end of the table, and everyone else took whatever seat they fancied. Maggie found herself sitting between Kevin and Glenn. Rory was across the table from her. "How'd I get so lucky?" she said.

"I don't know whether to take that remark as a compliment or a complaint," Kevin said.

"I'll never tell," Maggie said, grinning.

"Gotta be a compliment," Rory said. "After all, how many times does a New York woman get to be surrounded by three handsome, eligible men?"

"Two of whom are about to become rich," inserted Glenn with a grin.

"Really?" Maggie said. "Do you have the inside track on the lottery or something?"

Now it was Kevin's turn to grin. "Nope. Jack gave us a tip about a new dot-com company about to go public, and Glenn and I jumped at the chance to make some money."

Maggie winced. She'd lost a substantial amount of her savings when she'd invested in the technology sector a few years back and the market took a dive.

"Don't worry, Maggie," Jack said. "This isn't a risky investment."

"Yeah," Shelia interjected, "there's no way I'd consent to anything risky. Not with kids to think about." She glanced over at her father, who was noticeably silent. "Dad doesn't approve."

Maggie's Uncle Patrick just shrugged his shoulders. "I'm old-fashioned. The most risk I'm willing to take with my hard-earned money is blue-chip stocks."

"Can we please talk about something else?" her aunt Rose said. "Everyone knows how you feel, Patrick. But the boys have already invested their money, so let's all hope things go the way they want them to."

"Ma's right," Kevin said, turning back to Maggie. "So, cuz, you never did tell us how it feels to be surrounded by three handsome, eligible, about-to-be-rich men.''

''Oh, brother,'' Sheila said. ''It's getting thick in here.''

From then on, the banter flew back and forth, punctuated with guffaws and an occasional serious remark. Even so, Maggie was glad when the meal was over and dessert had been served, because she could see that her mother was tiring and they could legitimately say their goodbyes without anyone protesting.

Maggie herself was exhausted. All the pretending had taken its toll, and all she wanted now was to go home and, while her mother was napping, escape to the privacy of her bedroom where she could lick her wounds and try to figure out where she was going from here.

Chapter Eleven

The last thing Zach wanted to do Monday morning was interview potential secretaries, but Jeannie had been adamant. On Thursday she'd told him that when she'd said she'd stay until he found someone, she'd expected him to begin looking immediately.

"I can't stay forever, Zach. Buddy's anxious to get moved before hunting season starts."

So now, when all he wanted was to be alone, he was faced with interviewing three young women, the first of whom had arrived a few minutes earlier and was now filling out an application.

While he waited to talk to her, he tried to keep his thoughts from straying back to Saturday and Maggie, but he couldn't seem to stop himself from thinking about the way they'd parted.

Why are you feeling sorry for yourself? You knew she was going to leave eventually. It's not like she ever led you to believe anything different.

He guessed it was one thing to know something, another to actually have it happen. But he would survive this. He'd survived her leaving him once; he could do it again.

A noise outside his door snapped him back to his surroundings. He saw that the girl had finished with her application and was now standing uncertainly in front of Jeannie's desk. Before he could wonder where his secretary had disappeared to, he saw Jeannie coming. A few seconds later, she ushered the girl into his office.

"Sheriff Tate, this is Emily MacMillan." Jeanne smiled brightly and handed him the girl's application.

"Have a seat, Miss MacMillan," Zach said, indicating the chair Jeannie had moved in front of his desk earlier. Fleetingly, he wondered how old this girl was. She hardly looked older than Hannah, even though she'd tried hard to look professional in her navy-blue dress and sensible pumps.

The girl smiled nervously and sat.

Zach scanned her application and the attached resumé, noting that she'd graduated from high school three years earlier, so she was probably close to twenty-one. Two years of junior college with an Associate Degree in Business. One year of working in the office of a local supermarket. Her typing and computer skills seemed up-to-date, but he expected no less. Jeannie would have weeded out those candidates whose skills weren't.

He turned his attention back to the girl. Twenty-one, he thought. So young. Only five years older than Hannah. He wasn't sure he'd feel comfortable with her. What could they possibly have in common? Still, he knew he needed to give her a fair shot at the job, so he took his time questioning her.

Thirty minutes later, he told her they would let her know, and Jeannie showed her out.

"Well?" Jeannie said expectantly once the girl was gone.

"I don't know. She's awfully young."

Jeannie grimaced. "I know. I was worried about that. Good skills though, and she's bright."

"Who's next?"

"Carol Karpinsky. She'll be here at eleven. She's older—thirty-two, if I recall—and she has great experience."

"Karpinsky? She related to Joe Karpinsky?" Joe was a friend of Zach's brother.

Jeannie shrugged. "I don't know. Is it important?"

Zach shook his head. "Who else is coming today?"

"This afternoon you'll be talking with a woman named Betty Harvey. She's in her forties."

Zach sighed.

"You hate this, don't you?" Jeannie said.

"How can you tell?"

She laughed. "I'm not sure if it was the scowl or the sigh that gave it away."

"Trouble is, I don't like change."

"Most men don't."

"Oh, come on. Most *people* don't."

"No, I stick by my original statement. Men do not like their lives disrupted. They do not like to be inconvenienced. Women are much more adaptable. We just figure we can't change things, so we roll with the punches."

Zach rolled his eyes. "I'm not even going to *try* to dispute that, 'cause I have a feeling I can't win."

"What a shame," Jeannie said with a grin. "I've finally got you trained, and now I'm leaving!"

The interview and her teasing had helped Zach stop brooding, and he plunged himself into work until his eleven o'clock appointment arrived.

Carol Karpinsky turned out to be Joe Karpinsky's wife. A pleasant-looking blonde, she and Zach immediately hit it off. When the interview was over, he gave Jeannie thumbs up, saying, "I'll still talk to the woman coming this afternoon, but as of right now, I'm sold on Mrs. Karpinsky. Did her references check out?"

"Everyone I talked to raved about her."

"She said she was laid off. That check out, too?"

"Yes. The company had a big downsizing last month."

"Okay, it's settled then."

"If you're that happy with her, maybe I should cancel the afternoon appointment. Why waste her time?"

"You're right. Call Carol Karpinsky and offer her the job. If she says yes, cancel the other woman."

Zach was busy the rest of the day and didn't have much time to think. But eventually the day was over, and he had to go home to his empty house.

After looking over the mail and listening to two messages on his answering machine—neither of which was from Maggie, dashing a fleeting hope—he walked back to his bedroom to change clothes. Entering the room, he took one look at the bed and knew he couldn't stand to be there tonight.

He had no idea where he was going to go. He only knew he had to find a place that held no memory of Maggie.

"M-Maggie, are you sure this is what you want?" It was Tuesday evening. Edie had just gone home after assuring Maggie that she could handle things from now on, and Maggie was free to go back east if she wanted to.

Maggie looked at her mother. "I'm sure."

"You don't s-seem happy about leaving."

"I'm fine." Maggie knew her mother wanted to

ask her what had brought on this sudden decision to leave, and she was grateful she hadn't. Maggie knew if she was forced to talk about Zach, she might break down, and that was the last thing she wanted to do in front of her mother.

Not that her mother wouldn't be sympathetic. She would. It was just that Maggie felt bad enough. At least now, she still had some pride left.

"I'll miss you," her mother said.

"I'll miss you, too."

"When will you leave?"

"I was able to get a seat on tomorrow's flight."

"So soon!"

"There's no reason to wait." Although Maggie did wish she'd have a chance to say goodbye to Zach's kids, but they wouldn't be home before the weekend. Still, maybe it was for the best that she wouldn't get to see them. She might do or say something to give away the fact that she wasn't entirely happy about the way things had developed between her and Zach. And that would never do.

No, better that she make a quick getaway. She could write the kids later and apologize.

But the next day, as she finished her packing and prepared to leave, she felt half sick thinking how Hannah would feel when they got back home and discovered Maggie had gone. She didn't doubt that Zach would figure out something to tell his daughter, something that would not paint Maggie in a flattering light.

She zipped her suitcase shut.

Fine, she thought. *Let him blame me. I'm used to being the bad guy.*

But it wasn't fine, and she knew it. It might never be fine again.

On Thursday, Zach decided he had to talk to Maggie. He knew it might not be wise, but he couldn't let things go on like this without at least trying to explain to her how he felt.

He debated whether to wait until he got home to call or whether to call before he left the office, then maybe go over and talk to her in person. Because down deep, he really wanted to see her, he opted for the second choice. So at four-thirty, he closed his office door and pressed the familiar numbers.

The phone rang twice.

"Hello?"

Zach recognized Edie's voice. "Hi, Edie. It's Sheriff Tate."

"Oh, hello, Sheriff."

"Um, Edie, is Maggie around?"

"Maggie?"

He frowned. Why did she sound so surprised? "Yes, Maggie. I'd like to talk to her if it's convenient."

"Uh, Sheriff, uh…Maggie's gone."

"Oh. Well, what time do you expect her back?"

She didn't immediately answer, and he began to

think she hadn't heard him. Just as he started to ask the question again, she said, "Sheriff, Maggie's gone for good. She went back to New York yesterday."

At her words Zach felt as if someone had landed a sucker punch to his gut. Gone. Maggie was gone. Without even a goodbye.

"Sheriff?"

He cleared his throat. Tried not to sound as stunned as he felt. "I see." For the life of him, he couldn't think of anything else to say.

"I'm sorry," Edie said, her voice ringing with sympathy. "I thought you knew."

"No," he said after a numb moment. "No, I, uh, I had no idea."

Neither of them said anything for a long moment. Then Edie said, "Look, Sheriff, I'm really sor—"

"It's okay," he said, interrupting. "It's not your fault. Listen, Edie, I've got to go. My secretary's calling me." Without waiting for her to answer, he hung up.

For a long while, he simply sat there, staring at the silent phone. He couldn't believe Maggie was gone. You're such a fool, he thought furiously. Such a damn stupid fool!

Suddenly he couldn't sit there another minute. Getting up, he grabbed his hat and stalked out.

"Sheriff?"

Without turning around, he said, "I'm gone for the day, Jeannie. See you in the morning."

He drove home blindly. Thank God the kids were still at Arlene's, because he wasn't sure he could have handled seeing them. Not now. Not yet.

When he got to the house, he changed into his swim trunks. Then he went out back and dove into the pool.

He churned through the water like a man possessed. Back and forth. Back and forth. Trying not to think.

How could you do this again, Maggie? Wasn't it enough that you ran out on me once? Would it have killed you to at least call this time and say goodbye?

Finally, exhausted, he pulled himself out of the pool and collapsed onto the chaise.

Hannah couldn't wait to get home. She'd had a great time at her aunt Arlene's house—that wasn't the problem. It was just that she couldn't wait to talk to Maggie and tell her what had happened.

For the entire flight home, she daydreamed, remembering how she and her cousin Lisa had gone to the pool party that a friend of Lisa's had had on the Sunday after Hannah and her brothers had arrived in Houston and how all the kids there had been really nice and really friendly and how one of them had brought *his* cousin who was visiting him from Austin.

Hannah was still pinching herself as she thought about how cute Tom was and how she could immediately tell he liked her. He was eighteen, two years older than her, and already graduated from high school.

He wasn't like most of the boys she knew. He was so much more mature and interesting. Now that she'd met him, she couldn't imagine what she'd ever seen in Kirk Brittain. Kirk seemed a baby compared to Tom. Hannah couldn't imagine Tom being interested in a girl just because she had big boobs. If that was true, he would have picked another girl to spend the day with at the pool party, because there were a couple of them there that had really big boobs. But he hadn't. He'd picked Hannah.

Hannah smiled dreamily. Oh, she couldn't wait to tell Maggie all about him. She knew just what Maggie would do. She'd smile and say, *See? I told you you'd meet someone special one of these days. Someone just right for you.*

And Maggie had been right. Tom *was* special. She'd only had to spend one day with him to know that. And he thought she was special, too. It made her feel all warm inside to remember how he'd looked when he'd told her so. He hadn't been embarrassed or anything.

And he wanted to see her again. That was the best part. Since he'd be going to school at UT this fall, and he had a car of his own, there was no reason Hannah couldn't see him, either.

Oh, it would be so great. She'd be dating a college man! Brittany would be so jealous.

Sunday hadn't been the only time she'd spent with Tom. He had taken her to the movies on Tuesday night. Of course, his cousin Craig and her cousin Lisa had been there, too, so it wasn't a real date or anything, but he'd managed things so that he sat next to her, and he'd held her hand through the entire movie.

Hannah shivered as she relived how she'd felt sitting there in the dark with her hand in his. She'd wished so much that they were alone, especially when they got back to her aunt Arlene's. She was sure Tom would have kissed her good-night if they had been. He'd whispered in her ear, though, before he and Craig left to go home, saying he would call her when she got back to Rainbow's End.

And now she was almost there! In fact, their plane had already banked in preparation for landing.

They touched down five minutes early, and when she and Josh and Jason exited the jetway, the first person she saw was her father. He was grinning, obviously happy to see them. She waved, and he waved back.

When they got closer, she saw that he looked tired. He must have worked hard while they were gone. She gave him a hug and then they all trooped down to baggage pickup to get their luggage.

On the way home, her dad asked them about the week. The boys, as usual, hardly told him anything, so Hannah found herself answering most of the questions. She didn't mention Tom, though. First she wanted to discuss him with Maggie, see what Maggie thought about the best way to break the news to her dad that a college man was interested in her, because her dad could be overprotective at times, and Hannah didn't want to do or say anything to screw this up. Tom was too important to her.

"So you had a good time?" her dad said once they were on the highway leading to Rainbow's End.

"Yeah, it was great."

"I'm glad."

"We went to Astroworld, Dad," Josh chimed in. "It was cool. I rode this one coaster—it's called the Texas Cyclone—six times! I got to ride in the last car, too, because I was tall enough this year. You have to be five feet two to ride the last car. It was cool, wasn't it, Jason?"

"Yeah," Jason said.

Hannah rolled her eyes. Sometimes her brothers were so childish. She couldn't imagine getting all excited over a *roller coaster!* "What did you do while we were gone, Dad?"

"Mostly work. I did get a new secretary hired, though."

"That's good. What's she like?"

"She's nice. You'll like her."

Hannah wanted to ask him if he'd spent much time with Maggie, but she felt kind of funny about it. Sometimes her dad didn't like being questioned about personal stuff. She'd wait until they got home, then tell him she wanted to call Maggie. Then he might mention what they'd done together this week.

After they put their suitcases in their rooms, she walked into the kitchen. Just as she'd thought, her dad was there. Good. Here was her opportunity to bring up Maggie's name. "Dad," she said casually, "I think I'm going to call Maggie before I unpack. There's something I want to tell her."

He frowned. "Um, Hannah…"

"What?" She already had the phone in her hand and had started to press the numbers.

"Hannah, put the phone down."

She stopped with the number only half completed.

"Please hang it up, Hannah."

Totally confused, she put the phone back into the base unit. "Why can't I call her? It's only eight o'clock. She won't be in bed yet."

"Maggie's not there, that's why."

"Oh." Disappointment coursed through her. "Oh, well. I'll just have to talk to her tomorrow." Darn. She'd really wanted to talk to her tonight.

He shook his head.

"What are you shaking your head for?"

"You can't talk to her tomorrow, either. When I said she's gone, I meant she'd gone back to New York."

Hannah gaped at him. "Gone back to New York? When? Why?"

"She left on Wednesday."

"But, *Dad!*"

"I don't know why you're surprised. You always knew she lived in New York and was going home someday."

Hannah couldn't believe her ears. Maggie. Gone? Gone without even saying goodbye? Sudden tears sprang to her eyes. "I-I just can't believe it. Why…why would she leave like that? Did something happen? Did you two have a fight?" She knew her voice was rising, but she couldn't seem to stop it.

Her father seemed to sag. For the first time, Hannah wondered if the reason her father looked so tired had anything to do with Maggie.

"No," he said wearily. "We didn't have a fight."

"Then why did she go?" Hannah could no longer hold back the tears. She hated that she was acting like such a baby, but she couldn't seem to help it.

"Ah, Hannah, sweetheart, don't cry." Her dad walked over to her, putting his arms out to hug her.

But Hannah shook her head. Suddenly all she wanted was to be alone. "I-I'm sorry, Dad. I don't want to talk about it any more. Okay?"

She whirled and ran from the room.

Zach hadn't thought he could feel worse than he'd felt the past week, but seeing the tears on his daughter's face and the hurt and disappointment in her eyes had nearly undone him.

We all loved you, Maggie. Why couldn't you have loved us, too?

Chapter Twelve

August 13th

Dear Hannah,

I have been thinking about you and your brothers ever since I left Rainbow's End. I wish I could have said goodbye in person, but I had some urgent business in New York that couldn't wait, so I decided I would just have to write to you and tell you how sorry I am I didn't get to see you before I left.

I won't be coming back to Texas anytime soon. My mother is doing so much better now, and she really doesn't need me anymore. Edie will stay on with her until she can manage on her own again, so I know she'll be fine. I hope you'll keep dropping in to see them. I know they both enjoyed your visits every bit as much as I did. Getting to know you was one of the best things about my time at home this summer.

I hope you had fun in Houston. Your dad told me that you really like being with your cousins, so I'm sure you did. Houston is such a great place to visit. I used to love to go there.

I guess school will be starting soon. Your junior year! I have a feeling it will be a great one for you.

I'd really like to hear from you if you feel like writing to me. I'll be curious about what school you and your dad finally decide upon, and if it should happen to be the School of Visual Arts here in New York, I would be happy to take you under my wing and introduce you to my city.

How are your brothers? And your dad? I hope everyone is well. Tell them I miss them.

Maggie looked at the line she'd just typed.
Tell them I miss them.
Did she really want to say that? She certainly didn't want Zach to think she was mooning over him, even though she was. Angry with herself now, she deleted it.

Then she hit Print. Once the letter came off the printer, she signed it, *With Love, Maggie.*

August 17th
Dear Maggie,

I was *so* glad to get your letter. When I came home and my dad said you'd gone back to New York, I was so disappointed. I mean, I guess I always knew you'd be leaving here, but I felt terrible that I hadn't had a chance to say good-bye to you.

Oh, Maggie, the most wonderful thing has happened to me! I've met a boy. Well, really, he's a man, not a boy. His name is Tom Crandall and he's going to be a freshman at UT this year. He wants to be an architect (he's artistic, like me) and he's so cute. I met him in Houston. He was visiting his cousin just like I was visiting mine and we were both invited to this pool party and we just liked each other right off. We talked and talked and talked and he told me I was one of the most intelligent girls he'd ever met. (Me! Intelligent!!!) He also said I was pretty! (I'm blushing just thinking about it.) I saw him again a couple of nights later and since I've gotten home, he's called me twice and the best part— on Saturday he's driving over to see me and meet my dad. Oh, Maggie, I think he's the one.

Maybe it wouldn't be so bad to go to UT after I graduate, after all.

You asked about my brothers. They're both fine. Dad said to tell you he's fine, too.

I miss you, Maggie. I wish you were still here. But I'm glad you want to write to me. Write soon! Oh, and if you want to e-mail me, my e-mail address is listed at the bottom of this letter. I have my own computer (I don't have to share the one my brothers use) so it'll be private. Hope to hear from you soon!

Love, Hannah

PS: The 2445 part of my e-mail address is our street address, but you knew that. *g*

Maggie smiled at the letter—it sounded so much like Hannah—although the part about "Dad said to tell you he's fine, too" hurt. It hurt a lot. She guessed Zach just wanted to be sure she knew that he wasn't missing her at all. Well, fine. If he was fine, so was she. In fact, she was great! And in her next letter, she'd tell Hannah so. Maybe she'd even e-mail her today. In fact, there was no time like the present. She booted her laptop and opened her mail program.

Date: August 20th
From: Maggie Callahan
To: Hannah Tate
Subject: E-mail is a great idea!

Dear Hannah,

I got your very welcome letter today. I smiled as I read it. It sounded just like you! Tom sounds wonderful. An architect, huh? That's a great profession. My cousin Kevin is studying architecture at UT, too. Kevin is older, actually, the same age as me, and we used to be great friends in high school. Anyway, he says UT is a wonderful school, so if you do decide to go there next year, I know you'll be happy. I have to admit, though, I was sort of hoping your dad would let you come to New York. It would have been so much fun to have you here. Maybe, when you're a bit older, you can come and visit me in the summer.

I've been really busy since I got back. Just catching up with all my reading is a full-time job! This weekend I'm going to a writer's conference in Maine. I'm looking forward to it. You never know when you might discover the next John Grisham—or even a good-looking guy! I haven't gotten back into the social swing yet, but that's because New Yorkers usually go away for the month of August. Next month things will heat up again.

Glad your dad is doing so well. Tell him and your brothers I said hello. And write soon. Tell me how your date with Tom went and how your dad liked him.

Love, Maggie

Maggie looked at what she'd written. The stuff about work and her social life was so much bull, but she'd be darned if she'd tell Hannah, who might pass it on to Zach, that she was having a horrible time settling back into her life in New York.

How was it she'd never noticed how dirty the city was? Or how people rushed about so fast they barely had time to think, let alone say hello or smile at you?

Maggie buried her head in her hands. Oh, who was she kidding? There was nothing wrong with New York. It was her! She was the one who'd changed. And it was all Zach's fault.

She sighed and scanned the e-mail again to make sure she didn't want to make any other changes. She stared at the line she'd written about good-looking guys. She almost took it out, then thought *what the hell*. She'd leave it in. Finally, she pressed Send.

Date: August 21st
From: Hannah Tate
To: Maggie Callahan
Subject: Tom

Dear Maggie,

I was *thrilled* to see your e-mail in my e-mail box tonight. This is why I love e-mail so much. If we kept on writing letters it might be *weeks* before I heard from you!

Well, Tom came on Saturday just the way he

said he would. You should have seen how *excellent* he looked (excellent is what we say at school if a guy is really, really cute and cool). He had on really cool cargo pants and a black T-shirt (did I tell you he has blond hair?) and my heart nearly stopped beating when I saw him. My dad really, really liked him. Tom knows how to talk to adults, and he and my dad hit it off right away. I could tell my dad was impressed with how polite Tom is and how serious he is about school (they talked about Tom's courses and what he hopes to do after he graduates) and how respectful he is when he talks about his family.

Did I tell you his parents are both teachers? Well, they are. His dad teaches English at Austin Community College and his mom teaches biology at the high school where Tom graduated. And he has a younger sister—she's fourteen and her name is Heather—he said she's a pain! *g* And he has a baby brother. His baby brother is only three years old. His name is Brian. Isn't that neat? I love little kids. Tom said he wants me to meet them all and asked my dad if I could come to Austin next weekend to visit. Dad said he'd have to talk to Tom's parents first, make sure it was okay.

Oh, Maggie, I'm so *happy*!!!!!!!!!!!!! I'm

grinning like an idiot. Oh, I almost forgot. I would *love* to come to New York to visit you. Maybe next summer?
Love, Hannah

Maggie knew it was ridiculous to be envious of a sixteen-year-old girl, but everything Hannah had written about her feelings for Tom brought back aching memories of what it felt like to be in love for the first time.

Tears filled her eyes, which infuriated her. What was *wrong* with her? Why couldn't she get past this? Why did she continue to dwell on what had happened between her and Zach? Get over it, she told herself. It's done, over, *history*.

Angrily, she closed her laptop. What she needed was to get away from every reminder of him. And that included Hannah. Maybe it wasn't such a good idea to stay in touch with the girl. Maybe she should just phase out their correspondence. If she waited longer and longer before replying, eventually Hannah would get the hint, and the relationship would die a natural death.

Date: August 24th
From: Maggie Callahan
To: Hannah Tate
Subject: The Weekend

Dear Hannah,

Sorry I didn't answer your e-mail sooner. This week has been hectic. Well, I guess we'll both be away this weekend—me at my writer's conference, you at Tom's house. I'll be looking forward to hearing from you when you get back. Have a wonderful time!

Love, Maggie

Date: August 27th
From: Hannah Tate
To: Maggie Callahan
Subject: The Weekend!!!!!!

Dear Maggie,

I had a *wonderful* time at Tom's house! Oh, his parents are *so* nice, and I adored his sister and his baby brother. They were all so wonderful to me. On Saturday we went out on Lake Travis—his family has a boat—and spent the day. Saturday night we had Mexican food at their favorite restaurant. I shared a room with Tom's sister Heather. She's really cute and we had fun together. Sunday morning we all went to church together, then we went to his grandparents' house for lunch. And then he brought me home.

Oh, Maggie, I'm in love!!!!!!!!!! I'm soooooo

happy. I just wish everyone could be as happy as me.

Love, Hannah

PS: I went to visit your mom on Friday. She's doing great, but she misses you. So do I. <g>

When Zach was tempted to go into Hannah's room and search through her trash to see if he could find Maggie's e-mail, he knew he was in bad shape.

He knew he had to forget about her. But it was a helluva lot easier to tell himself this than to actually do it. Sometimes he wondered if he would *ever* forget about her.

Well, he had no one but himself to blame for his state of mind. He'd always known it was madness to get involved with her again, but he'd gone ahead and done it anyway.

So now he'd have to suffer the consequences.

Maggie was too depressed to answer Hannah's e-mail right away. The writer's conference had been horrible. Her talk had not gone well. There had been no one who interested her as a potential client. And as for good-looking guys, who even cared? With her track record, she'd be better off swearing off men forever.

"Dad?"

Zach looked up from his desk to see Hannah standing in the doorway. "Hannah! This is a surprise. What are you doing here?"

"I wanted to talk to you about something."

"Sure, honey. Come on in. What's on your mind?"

Hannah closed the door, then sat down in front of his desk. She looked so serious, Zach felt a pang of worry.

"Dad, if I ask you something, will you be honest with me?"

"I'm always honest with you, Hannah."

She nodded and bit her bottom lip.

"You're scaring me, Hannah. What is it?"

Taking a deep breath, she said, "Jason and Josh and me, we...well, we thought you really liked Maggie."

Zach went still. "I do really like her."

"No, I mean *really*. We..." She swallowed. "We thought maybe you were going to ask her to marry you."

Zach had always been truthful with his daughter. With all his children. He saw no reason not to tell the truth this time, too. He nodded. "I wanted to marry her, Hannah. The problem is, she doesn't love me."

Hannah stared at him. "Are you *sure,* Dad?"

"I'm sure."

"How do you know she doesn't? Did she say so?"

"She didn't have to say so."

"But *Dad*..."

"Hannah, please. I know you mean well, but there

are things you don't understand." He made himself smile, even though inside he was a miserable wreck.

"Just tell me one thing, okay?"

He sighed. "Okay."

"Did you *ask* her to marry you?"

"No. There was no point. Her life is in New York, and she made it very clear that she was going back. Now please quit worrying about this. I'm sorry it worked out like this, but that's life. Things don't always turn out the way we hope they will."

Hannah sighed. "Well..."

"It's okay, Hannah, really."

"Well," she said again. She stood. She still looked unhappy.

"I'll see you later," he said, giving her a gentle smile. What a good kid she was.

For a second, he thought she was going to say something else. Finally she smiled back.

After she was gone he thought that he might be unlucky in love, but he was awfully lucky in his children.

When Hannah got home, she was really glad to see that Jason was there and Josh wasn't.

"Jace, we have to talk," she said.

He looked up from the computer keyboard. "What about?"

So Hannah told him about her conversation with their Dad. "Can't we do something?"

"I don't know," Jason said. "This is heavy stuff. I don't think it's a good idea to butt in."

"But *Jason!* Dad loves Maggie. He admitted he wanted to marry her. Maybe if he'd asked her, he'd have found out she wanted the same thing, too."

"Has she told you that?" Hannah had told her family she was corresponding with Maggie.

"No, but I think she *does* love Dad. Isn't there *anything* we can do?"

Jason thought for a while. "I do have an idea," he said slowly.

Hannah grinned. "What? Tell me what it is."

When he'd finished, she said, "Oh, it's *perfect*. Just perfect! Do it!"

"I hope you're right," Jason said. "'Cause if it doesn't work out, and Dad finds out we did it, he's gonna be really ticked."

"It'll work out. I just know it."

"Fed Ex delivery just came for you, Maggie."

Maggie looked up to see Rita coming through the doorway. She dropped a Federal Express overnight envelope on the desk. Maggie frowned as she read the return address. Jason Tate? Picking up the envelope, she said, "Thanks, Rita."

She opened it slowly, then extracted the half-dozen pages it contained. Then she smiled. He'd written a short story. Settling back in her chair, she read:

Will You Be Our Mom?
A short story by Jason Tate

Matt Thompson missed his mother. He missed her a lot. She'd been dead for nine years now, which was almost as long as Matt's brother Billy had been alive. Matt himself had only been five when she'd died, and his sister Linda had been seven.

After their mom died, their dad told them their mom had been too sad to live, and that it hadn't been their fault she died. He said it wasn't anyone's fault, but for a long time Matt was sure his dad was wrong, that he'd just said that because he didn't want Matt and Linda to feel bad. Billy was too little to feel bad.

Matt was convinced that his mother hadn't wanted to live because Matt had been bad. He thought about how she would cry and say things like "you kids are driving me crazy!" and "leave me alone, just leave me alone."

It was only after he got older that he realized his dad was probably right. It really wasn't his fault his mom had been so unhappy that she'd killed herself.

He wished she hadn't, though. He wished he and his brother and sister had a mom to come home to the way his friends did. He'd always wished that.

Sometimes he and his sister talked about their

dad getting married again. Linda said she hoped it might happen, but Matt wasn't sure. What if their dad married someone they didn't like?

Linda said they didn't have to worry about that. Their dad was too smart to marry someone who wasn't nice. Anyone he would pick would be great and someone they'd like a lot. But Matt wasn't convinced about that, either. It was his feeling that they'd gotten along without a mother just fine for a long time and maybe it was too late to change things.

And then one day their dad started dating a woman named Carrie. She was someone he'd known when he was young. After awhile, he brought Carrie home to meet Matt and Linda and Billy, and they all liked her. They liked her a lot.

But Carrie was only visiting in their town. She actually lived far away, and even though they hoped she might decide to stay in their town and marry their father, she didn't. She went back home.

When Linda asked their dad why Carrie had left and said they'd thought he was going to ask her to marry him, he said he had wanted to marry her, but the truth was, she didn't love him.

"Are you sure?" Linda asked. She couldn't imagine anyone not loving their dad. He was a really great guy.

Their dad said he was sure.

"But did she tell you that?"

"She didn't have to say it," their dad answered. "She has a life somewhere else, and that's what she wants."

Linda told Matt what their dad had said. She wondered what they could do to help because she was sure her dad was wrong, that if he'd just asked Carrie to stay, she would have. "I know she loves him," Linda said.

Matt said maybe she didn't, and maybe they should mind their own business, but Linda persuaded him that it wouldn't hurt anything to try to help their dad. "He's so sad all the time," she said. "He wasn't sad when Carrie was here. He was happy."

So Matt wrote Carrie a letter. In it, he told her how much they all loved her and how they wished she hadn't left them. "Dad loves you, too," he wrote. "But he thought you didn't love him." He ended the letter with, "We want you to come back. We want you to be our mom."

Maggie could hardly read the last line of the story, she was crying so hard. *Those kids. Those wonderful kids.* When she was all cried out, she wiped her eyes, blew her nose and repaired her makeup. She reread the story, then she swiveled her chair around and gazed out the window at what she could see of the

New York skyline while she thought about her life and what it was she really wanted.

It didn't take long. Less than an hour later, she walked across the hall and tapped on Rita's door.

Chapter Thirteen

Rita stared at Maggie. Her brown eyes behind her glasses were wide with shock. "Are you *serious,* Maggie? You're really thinking about leaving New York?"

"Yes, I am."

"But you've worked so hard to build the agency."

"I know, but none of that work will be wasted, not if you become my partner." Maggie cradled her coffee mug in her hands. "You've pretty much taken over the management of the place now, anyway."

"I know, but you do the lion's share of the work with the clients."

"Don't you *want* to assume more responsibility in that area?"

Rita twirled her pencil thoughtfully. "Sure, I'd like to, but I'm not sure I can manage everything."

"You did it while I was gone this summer."

"Yes, but I knew it was only temporary then. I don't know if I want that kind of pressure on a permanent basis." She made an apologetic face. "I have the kids to think about, Maggie. I can't spend ten- and twelve-hour days working the way you can."

"Tell you what," Maggie said. She'd thought about this part, too. "How about if we hire an office manager? Someone to man the phones, take over the bookkeeping and paperwork, maybe even do some of the preliminary reading and screening? If we did that, you'd be free to do more work with the clients and I'd be free to spend the majority of my time in Rainbow's End. You'd probably even be able to work the same hours as you do now."

"Can we afford that?"

"I think so. Anyway, before long I'm sure you'll be signing up new clients of your own and there'll be more money coming in."

Rita smiled. "You certainly have a lot of confidence in me."

"It's not misplaced."

"But you *do* plan to spend *some* time in New York, right? You're not going to do all the work from Rainbow's End?"

"No. Right now I'm thinking I'll come into town about every six weeks or so—you know, just to wine and dine editors and some of the marketing people and to touch base with you and whoever else we have working here.''

''Are you going to keep your apartment?''

''As much as I'd like to, I don't think that would be a wise thing to do. Much too expensive.''

''Then where will you stay when you come to town?''

Maggie shrugged. ''At one of the small hotels.''

''But that'll be just as expensive, won't it?''

''Not even close. I'll probably only be here two or three nights at a time.'' She set her mug down and leaned forward. ''What do you say, Rita?''

''I have to admit…it's tempting.''

''Then why are you hesitating?''

Rita's smile turned self-deprecating. ''Guess I'm scared.''

''Why not at least try it? How about a six-month trial period? If it works out, when it's over, I'll sell you a half interest in the agency. We'll be equal partners.''

''Maggie! Do you mean it? I'll be a *partner?*''

Maggie grinned. She had just come up with the idea of selling Rita part of the agency, and she was pleased with herself. She should have thought of it before now. If Rita had a stake in the success of their venture, she'd work even harder to make sure their arrangement worked out. ''An *equal* partner,'' she emphasized. ''We'll share whatever profits there are.''

''Oh, Maggie!''

''So you'll do it?''

''Yes! Yes, I'll do it!''

''That's wonderful, Rita. I know this is going to work out beautifully.''

For the second time in four months, Maggie was headed home. It had only taken her a week to get things squared away in New York.

She'd subletted her apartment for the duration of the lease, talked to all her clients, then assigned half of them to Rita. She'd also interviewed several recent college graduates and hired one of them to work as the office manager/receptionist with an eye to training her to learn the business the way Rita had been trained.

Once those things were taken care of, she'd packed up everything in her apartment that she wasn't leaving for the new tenant and arranged to have it put into storage until she had a permanent address.

Last of all, she'd said goodbye to all her friends. They were sad to see her go, but a couple of them admitted they were envious, too.

''I hope this all works out well for you, Maggie,'' Alicia Blythe said.

Maggie hoped so, too.

She'd also called her mother and told her what she

was planning, but she'd sworn her to secrecy. After all, there was always a chance his kids were wrong and that Zach wouldn't want her now. Maggie wasn't sure what she'd do if that happened. Probably she'd have to slink back to New York with egg on her face.

Well, it wouldn't be long before she'd know. Her flight landed in Austin in less than an hour. By two o'clock, she should be in Rainbow's End. By three, she would be at Zach's.

Just the thought of seeing him again caused butterflies to race around in her stomach.

Zach had taken a day's vacation to try to get some things done around the house. He'd spent the past hour working on the back fence again. Another section had come loose, and this time the problem wasn't a storm, it was wear and tear and wood that had started to rot.

He grimaced. The entire fence really needed to be replaced. He'd known that for a while, but he hadn't wanted to spend the money. The trouble was, money seemed to go out a lot faster than he could bring it in.

He wiped the sweat off his forehead with the bottom of his T-shirt. It sure was hot. Nearly as hot as August. Of course, it was only the first week of September. And in this part of Texas, it didn't normally start to cool off until October.

He would have to go inside and get cleaned up

soon, because he was supposed to talk to a group of seniors over at the community center tonight. He wondered if Maggie's mother and Edie would be there. He hadn't seen either of them since Maggie left.

Maggie.

Why couldn't he stop thinking about her? He wondered if Hannah had heard from her lately. His daughter hadn't mentioned any recent e-mails, and Zach sure didn't want to ask. It was bad enough that Hannah knew he'd wanted to marry Maggie and that she hadn't been interested.

Behind him, he heard the gate creak open. He frowned. It was too early for Josh, wasn't it?

He turned around, and for a moment, he couldn't believe his eyes. Standing there with an uncertain smile on her face was the woman who haunted all his thoughts and dreams, the woman he'd never expected to see again, the woman he'd loved for more years than he could count.

"Maggie," he whispered, stunned.

"Hello, Zach." She walked toward him. She was wearing that green sundress, the one she'd worn the night they'd made love, and her unruly hair was tied back with a green ribbon. It blazed with golden highlights under the afternoon sun. Her legs were bare, and she wore sandals. She looked incredibly beautiful.

He just stood there. His heart was thundering. What

did this mean? he wondered. What was she doing here?

He was afraid to hope.

Why didn't he smile?

Suddenly Maggie was scared to death. He hadn't moved, either. Their eyes met. She searched his for a clue as to what he was thinking and feeling, but she couldn't read his expression.

Finally he spoke. "You've come back."

"Yes." She swallowed. Was he glad? *Oh, Zach, please don't say it's too late.*

"Why?"

She took a deep breath. This was the hardest thing she'd ever had to do. What if he no longer wanted her? "I came back because I love you."

For just a second, something flickered in his eyes. It was gone in an instant, but in that instant, it had given her reason to believe everything might be okay. "Because this is where I belong," she added softly.

"What about New York?" he said. "What about your life there?"

"Everything I want is here."

Another long moment passed. Maggie held her breath. Then, just as she began to think maybe she'd been wrong, maybe he *didn't* love her anymore, he said, "Are you sure, Maggie? Because if you're not, don't say you are. Don't get my hopes up again. It's too hard when you leave."

Maggie's eyes blurred with tears. "Oh, Zach," she said in a trembling voice. "I'm not going anywhere unless you throw me out."

His smile blazed across his face. She didn't care that he was all sweaty or that his hands were grimy or that his clothes were covered with dirt from the fence. She wouldn't have cared if he'd just climbed out of a barrel of tar. She flew into his arms, and he crushed her to him.

He kissed her hungrily, as if he could never get enough of her, and she returned his kisses with all the passion and love and joy that filled her being.

How long they would have stood there kissing, Maggie didn't know, because they only stopped when they heard the gate bang open. They jumped apart to see Josh staring at them.

"Maggie!" he shouted. "You're back!" He came barreling toward her and flung his arms around her.

Maggie hugged him. Her heart was so full. "Yes, I'm back."

"To stay?" he squealed.

"That's up to your father," she said softly. Her eyes met Zach's over Josh's head.

"Okay, Josh, that's enough," Zach said. "Let Maggie go. She and I have things to talk about."

Josh grinned. "I get it. You want me to scram."

"Just for a little while."

Once Josh had disappeared into the house, Zach put

his arms around her again. "I hope you meant it when you said this was where you belonged."

"I've never meant anything more in my life."

"In that case, Maggie Callahan, I love you and want you to be my wife. Will you marry me?"

"Oh, Zach, yes. Yes, I'll marry you."

Zach laid his forehead against hers. "How about tomorrow?"

She laughed. "Is that possible? Don't you have to wait for a license in Texas?"

"I think it's just three days. We can be married by the weekend."

"The weekend!"

"Why not? If I could, I'd marry you today." He tipped her head up and kissed her again.

Standing there in his arms, Maggie decided if she were to die at that exact moment, she'd die the happiest woman on earth.

Six weeks later

"Maggie, please quit fidgeting!" Kris admonished as she fussed with Maggie's veil.

Maggie rolled her eyes. She thought it was ridiculous for a nearly forty-year-old woman to wear a long white dress and veil like some kind of virgin bride, but neither her mother nor Kris nor Edie nor Molly nor Sheila nor anyone else in her family or circle of friends would even hear of Maggie being married in anything else.

"You've never been married before, and you're the only daughter I have," her mother had said. "P-please indulge me, Maggie."

How could Maggie say no when her mother looked at her that way? She couldn't.

So here she was, standing in the middle of the bride's dressing room at Holy Family Church, where she would soon be walking down a flower-decked aisle to the strains of the "Trumpet Voluntary."

"There," Kris said with a sigh of satisfaction. She stood back. "Just look at yourself. Oh, Maggie, you look gorgeous. That dress is perfect for you!"

Maggie turned to study herself in the mirror. She had to admit, the wedding gown suited her. Heavy satin and simply cut, it fell in a long, elegant column that complemented her tall, slim frame. The creamy shade was perfect with her auburn hair, too.

It still amazed her they'd been able to find a dress like this one on such short notice, for it was only six weeks since she had returned to Rainbow's End. But Kris had known exactly where to go and had taken Maggie to the small bridal shop in Austin where the owner was a whiz at alterations, and sure enough, they'd found this dress, and Maggie had fallen in love with it.

Originally Kris had tried to talk her into waiting until Christmas to get married, saying Christmas weddings were so beautiful, but neither Maggie nor Zach had wanted to wait.

"We've wasted enough time apart," Zach said. In fact, after the first euphoria of knowing they would finally be together, he'd wanted to elope. But Maggie knew it would break her mother's heart if she eloped, so they'd compromised.

Now it was the last weekend in October and a beautiful autumn day—bright, sunny, and in the sixties with just a hint of crispness in the air. "A perfect day," Kris had pronounced.

And inside the church at this very moment were all of Maggie's family and friends, and even some of her clients, many of them having trekked here from New York and California.

She was touched that so many people wanted to share this day with her and Zach, and now that it was here, she was glad she'd gone along with her mother and agreed to this traditional wedding. It would be something for her to remember when she was old and gray. Something she could tell her grandchildren— well, technically *Zach's* grandchildren, but as much as she loved his kids, she knew by the time they had kids of their own, she would think of them as hers, too.

She smiled as she remembered how thrilled Hannah had been when she'd come home that Monday and found Maggie there.

"I *knew* you'd come," she'd cried. "I *knew* when you read Jason's story you'd come."

"What story?" Zach had said.

So then Hannah and Maggie told Zach all about how his two oldest children had schemed to bring them together.

"I can't believe you kids did that, Hannah," Zach said, but both Maggie and Hannah knew he wasn't mad.

"Well, it worked, didn't it?" Hannah said with a cheeky grin.

Jason, too, was pleased to find Maggie there and took his father's mock reproof over his matchmaking with good humor. "Hey, Dad," he said, "anytime you need help, you can count on me."

Later that night, Zach had read the story himself, and Maggie got all choked up watching him, because she could see he was just as moved by it as she had been.

Afterward, they'd both agreed that his kids were remarkable.

"Ready?" Kris said now, breaking into Maggie's thoughts and bringing her back to the present.

Maggie took a deep breath and nodded. Suddenly, she had butterflies in her stomach.

They left the bride's changing room, and as they entered the narthex, Maggie saw that her uncle Patrick, who was giving her away, and Sheila and Hannah, her bridesmaids, were already there waiting, along with Louise Kelsey, the wedding coordinator.

Sheila and Hannah looked lovely, she thought. They were dressed identically in flame silk—a shade that looked terrific on both of them. Each carried a bouquet of gold baby mums and trailing ivy.

Maggie looked at Sheila, amazed that her cousin was back to her naturally slender self, even though it had only been seven weeks since her baby daughter had been born.

Maggie's uncle looked great, too, in a black tux paired with a flame-colored cummerbund.

Kris, who was serving as Maggie's matron of honor, wore forest green—which complemented her blond hair—and carried a bouquet identical to the bridesmaids'.

"Oh, there you are!" exclaimed Louise, a small birdlike woman. She hurried over to meet Maggie and Kris. She fussed around Maggie, adjusting her dress and her veil, then she handed Maggie her bouquet, a delicate arrangement of baby roses and ivy. "It's almost time," she said.

Maggie nodded. Her uncle had walked over and now stood beside her. "You look beautiful, Maggie." His bright blue Callahan eyes were misty. "Your father would have been so proud."

Maggie's own eyes filled. "Thank you," she whispered.

"Now remember how we did it last night," Louise said. "You'll go first, Hannah. Then Sheila. Then Kris. And last of all, Maggie and her uncle Patrick."

She had no sooner gotten them lined up than the first majestic notes of the processional sounded.

Maggie slipped her right hand through her uncle's left arm, and he smiled down at her.

"Now," said Louise in a stage whisper to Hannah.

Hannah, head held high, began the hesitation step. Sheila turned around and gave Maggie a brilliant smile. Then she, too, started down the aisle. Kris was next. And then it was Maggie's turn.

Clasping her hand firmly against his arm, her uncle whispered, "Ready?"

"Yes."

Maggie felt as if she were in a dream as they slowly made their way in unison toward the altar. Everything looked so beautiful. The sun shone through the stained-glass windows and gilded the church with jewel-toned color. The air was sweetly perfumed with the scent of roses and the myriad fragrances worn by the women. White ribbons and ivy adorned the ends of the pews.

Everyone she passed was smiling: there was Rita, there were her two favorite clients, there was Edie, there was her mother's next-door neighbor, there was Maggie's old piano teacher. As she drew closer to the front pews, she saw her aunt Rose and all her cousins—Kevin and Rory and Glenn and Keith—and all their spouses and children.

In the first pew on the left sat Jimmy and Molly and their three, along with Maggie's mother, who looked beautiful in blue lace. And on Zach's side, the first pew held Jason and Josh and Zach's mother, who had finally unbent toward Maggie. Awinita Tate, elegant in gray chiffon, even managed a smile.

Zach hadn't told Maggie what his mother said when he'd let her know he and Maggie were getting married, but Maggie could imagine. Still, his mother had unbent enough to be, if not warm, at least civil to Maggie when they were in each other's company.

Zach, with uncharacteristic cynicism, had told Maggie his mother's improved attitude had a lot more to do with her fear that her beloved grandchildren might drift away from her than it did with anything else, but Maggie didn't care. She was just glad her soon-to-be mother-in-law wasn't going to make life more difficult than it needed to be.

Behind Awinita, in the second row, were Luke's family and some of Andrea's family. The rest of Zach's side of the church was filled with hundreds of his friends and deputies. In fact, the entire church was full.

Finally Maggie and her uncle reached the front, and Maggie saw Zach for the first time that day. Her heart lifted in happiness as their eyes met. He looked so handsome and resplendent in his black tux, his eyes filled with love as he watched her approach. Next to him stood his brother Luke, who was serving as best man.

Her uncle handed her over to Zach and the two of them turned to face Father Pasquale for the beginning of the ceremony.

Throughout, as Maggie listened to the beautiful words and repeated her vows, then listened as Zach repeated his, she thought about how this ceremony was only the beginning. She and Zach had a lifetime to spend together, a lifetime in which they would love one another and cherish each day. The road wouldn't always be smooth; she knew that. But it didn't matter, because whatever life dealt them in the future, they'd be together, and together they could handle anything.

* * * * *

The Street of the City

Frannie was a working girl who lived on the poor side of town. Across the river glamorous people glittered in high society.

Wealthy Val Willoughby, impatient with his shallow world, was captivated by Frannie's sweet sincerity, and gladly crossed the river to court her.

But sophisticated Marietta Hollister considered Val her personal property and jealously resented his association with such a common girl.

Her spiteful vindictiveness threatened to poison both Val's reputation and Frannie's.

Bantam Books by Grace Livingston Hill
Ask your bookseller for the books you have missed

#7	THE BEST MAN
#13	IN TUNE WITH WEDDING BELLS
#28	WHITE ORCHIDS
#35	PARTNERS
#38	SPICE BOX
#43	DAWN OF THE MORNING
#44	THE BELOVED STRANGER
#47	THE STREET OF THE CITY
#54	THE OBESSION OF VICTORIA GRACEN
#60	MIRANDA
#61	MYSTERY FLOWERS
#62	THE CHRISTMAS BRIDE
#63	THE MAN OF THE DESERT
#64	MISS LAVINIA'S CALL

The Street of the City
Grace Livingston Hill

BANTAM BOOKS
Toronto • New York • London • Sydney

THE STREET OF THE CITY

*A Bantam Book / published by arrangement with
Harper & Row, Publishers, Inc.*

PRINTING HISTORY

Lippincott edition published in 1942

Bantam edition / February 1977
2nd printing . . . April 1977
3rd printing . . . November 1977
4th printing . . . September 1983

ISBN 0-553-23429-3

Published simultaneously in the United States and Canada

PRINTED IN THE UNITED STATES OF AMERICA

H   13 12 11 10 9 8 7 6 5 4

Chapter 1

THE RIVER WOUND like a crystal ribbon at the foot of the hill below the house, a clear shining pathway of solid ice, blue as the sky above it, until it curved about the hemlock bluff where the tall feathery trees cut it sharply with dark delicate points against its shining surface. Then beyond, the gleaming pathway swept toward the town, and on to the dingy group of munitions plants, and farther to the open spaces banked by the buildings where airplanes were made.

The old lady was sitting in her sunny window with a bit of sewing, now and again glancing out the window, and following the bright course of the river. She had been watching the river for years, in all seasons, but she loved it best in this shining garb of winter, with its solid pavement of bright ice in its soft white setting of snow.

Lady Winthrop, as her friends called her, had come to the house as a bride. It was a pleasant house on the hillside with the river at its feet, and she had had long years to get acquainted with her river. She knew and loved every phase of it. How it had been with her in every change of her life. How she had communed with it during the early days of her young wifehood, shyly watching, learning slowly its quiet moods: singing with it when there were twinkling sparkles on its bosom; or gathering comfort from its steady peace when there was sorrow in the house, sadly, patiently waiting when gray skies spread gloom over its stolid surface; or, in times of storm and stress, watching its steady strength, hurrying on angrily, as if so much depended upon its haste.

And sometimes when her life had given quiet, and a space for thoughtfulness, she had seen in that river as it were a way into the Heavenly City. Especially was

1

this so in the winter evenings at sunset, when the sun, a great ball of fire, was going down in the break of the distant mountains and casting ruby light over the ice like flaming gold. Often taking a moment out of her busy life she would stand at her window watching it, and would repeat softly to herself: "And the street of the city was pure gold, as it were transparent glass."

Or later, when the sun was slipping over the rim of the world and its last brilliancy flared over the ice like a great conflagration, she would murmur: "And I saw as it were a sea of glass mingled with fire."

But today Lady Winthrop was not seeing fire in her river. It was early morning and she was watching for her day's parade of people, passing by on that pathway of ice. Groups of workmen walking by the river because it shortened their way, rather than going around by the bridge and the road. Bevies of laborers hurrying to their tasks, rough clad, striding along at the edge of the stream with grim, set faces, or bandying rough jokes with raucous laughter. Some wore the hard determined look of men who were in this warfight to make the most out of it; and others bore themselves as men who had sacrificially laid aside their work in their chosen field of labor to do what was to be done for right's sake and for loyalty to their country.

But there was one young man who had been going by for several days now, in fact ever since the fierce cold came that locked the river into a deep floor of crystal. He had appeared that first morning after word had gone out that the skating was fine, and he had come sailing smoothly into view with gleaming skates that almost seemed to be tipped with silvered magic, and had glided by with quick firm strokes, and such assurance and grace as only a natural gift can acquire.

He was young, yet not a boy, for his movements had that control that belongs to maturity.

Lady Winthrop had watched him every day, wondering who he was, where he came from, and what was his place in this new world that the war had brought suddenly into being?

Lady Winthrop liked to watch his tall straight form

moving with such easy precision down the bright ice. She had been watching him morning after morning now, since the ice had been so fine. She felt glad and comfortable in looking for him because the cold had been so steady. The ice would not be gone, nor spoiled by rain, or a heavy snowfall, not today, anyway. The sky was clear. There would perhaps be several days yet when he could go down this same way to wherever it was he went in the morning, and he would probably return the same way in the evening. Each day she studied him from her post in the window, caught a glimpse now and then of his vivid young face with the determination of manhood in its lines, and liked it, wished she might see it nearer by. She had even climbed to the attic and searched in an old trunk till she found an old pair of field glasses that she had not used since Judge Winthrop died, a relic of their happy days together and the summer and winter trips they used to take.

She studied him one night as he came back from his day's work, and after that keen look put down her glasses, quite satisfied that he was worth her interest.

And so this morning she had settled down by her window, field glasses on the table beside her, watching for him. It was almost the time he usually came by, and she wanted another good look at him to be sure he wasn't someone she used to know a few years ago. She was lonely and sad. Her own two boys were long since grown up, and away at the war, one a naval commander in the Far East, the other an officer in the army. She had given them freely, and would not spend her days in sighing for them, but she was trying to get all the cheerful interest she could find in the things about her.

And now suddenly there came into view another skater, a young girl, so tiny she almost seemed a child. She had seen her two or three times before, skating almost uncertainly the first time, as if somehow her skates were untried, or perhaps rusty and had been idle a long time. But here she was again like a little bird, flying along as if she had wings. The skates looked brighter now, or did she imagine that? She had probably been polishing them up. At any rate she seemed to make

swifter progress than the first times. And she was a fine skater, very graceful, like a bird of swift wing. Lady Winthrop might be old, and she no longer took frequent trips by herself down the slope of the hill, but she could remember the feel of her own skates long ago when she too used to glide down that long smooth stretch of ice, and she felt the swing of her body as if she were out there skimming along. She felt the exhilaration of the keen bright air, the cut of steel on ice, and drew a deep breath of wistfulness. Oh for the days when she could skate! How great it would be if even just for one day she could have her young skill and strength back, and go down that bright path toward the city herself!

And then suddenly she laughed aloud at herself, a sweet old trill of a laugh. She was actually envying that young girl!

Who was she? A student? Or perhaps a teacher in one of the city schools. But she looked so young, and why had she never seen her before? She might be a worker in some defense plant, a stenographer or typist. They gave good salaries in some of those places she had heard. She hoped her salary was adequate for her needs. It was not many times she had seen this girl go down her Crystal Street as she called it, and yet here she was thinking of the child as if she were a friend!

The girl wore such a look of steady purpose, the look of a worker, not just a girl out for fun or exercise. Ah! Here was another skater of whom she would like to know more. She must find out who she was if possible. Perhaps she came from one of those new houses across the river, the small ones built alike up around the bend of the hill. She could see them from her kitchen windows; they were small frame houses, high on the bluff. She must find out about her. Perhaps the servants could discover who she was.

And that young man must be a stranger in the neighborhood, too. Did his people live up in that new suburb farther up the river, the place they called Cliveden?

How well those two skaters would look together!

Did they know one another? Queer thoughts for the dear old lady to have about two young people who were utter strangers to her, two people she had only seen from a distance a few times!

She watched the girl go gliding down the river, till she disappeared at Hemlock Rocks, and a moment later reappeared beyond them again and skimmed away into the silvery distance. A mere little speck of a girl in simple garb, with a graceful motion. That was all she could see even with the glasses.

But she could not help thinking again how well those two skaters would look together. If they only knew each other. Both of them living up in the same direction, perhaps they did, and perhaps some day she would see them come down by her house together.

But where was the young man? It was almost five minutes past his usual time for going by. She hoped nothing would hinder him. It would seem as if the day held a big disappointment for her if he didn't come. It would be something left out from what she had come to expect of a day, not to see him. And that was silly of course, because it had been only four or five days that she had been seeing him at all. She couldn't expect it to go on forever. There would presently come a thaw and spoil the ice, or a snow storm and spoil the skating— unless a crowd came out and swept it clean, and that would hardly be likely, sweeping the whole way to town!

Then suddenly she heard footsteps crunching hastily through the crusty snow up the hillside. Young, hurried, frightened footsteps, a quick insistent pounding on the door beside her window, and a little girl's voice full of fright calling wildly:

"Oh, please, *please* won't you help me? Please won't you come quick and open your door? Something has happened to *my mamma!*"

Lady Winthrop hurried to open the door.

"Why, *my dear!*" she exclaimed. For there stood a little girl about five or six years old, a very tiny little girl, with no hat or coat on, and shivering, with her small, red, cold hands clasped tightly, and tears flowing

down her cold round cheeks. Her large beautiful eyes were full of terror.

"What is the matter?" asked the old lady tenderly. "Come into the house and let me close the door. It is very cold!"

"Oh no, I can't come in," said the child excitedly. "I must go to my mamma! Won't you come with me *quick?*"

"Why, you poor child! You are trembling with cold. You poor little thing! Who are you, and what is the matter with your mother?"

"I'm Bonnie Fernley," wailed the child frantically, "and I don't know what is the matter. My mamma just dropped down on the floor with her eyes shut, and she didn't answer me when I called her. She was clearing off the table and all the dishes she was carrying are broken on the floor! Oh, *won't* you come *quick* and make my mamma wake up?"

"Oh, my dear! I'm lame and I can't come myself, but I'll send somebody! Where do you live?"

"Right across the river in that red brick house. Come out here and I'll show you."

"Wait, child! Who is your doctor? I'll telephone him." The child began to cry again.

"We haven't got any doctor. We just moved here! Oh, I must go quick! My mamma is all alone!"

"Wait!" said Lady Winthrop sharply. "You can't go that way! You have no coat on, and it is very cold!"

"No! *No!*" said the child jerking away. "I can't wait!"

The old lady reached to the couch and caught up a soft bright knitted afghan, wrapping it quickly around the little shaking shoulders. Then she swung the door wide and looked out on the white morning scene, and her shining glass pathway. And then straight into the scene at the upper bend of the road wheeled the tall skater coming at full speed.

The old lady did not pause to consider. She lifted her soft frail hands, hollowed them about her lips, and made a deep sound like a big boy calling to his mates, a sound that boomed out and became a far-reaching "Hal-

loo! Hal*loo!*" and then turned sharply into another syllable, *"Help! help!"*

The skater looked up sharply as the word rang out with a carrying quality that an old lady would not have been supposed to be capable of sending out.

"H-ee-lp!" cried Lady Winthrop with all the power of her frail little body thrown into the cry.

And now she was standing out in the center of her porch, her little lavender shawl fluttering wildly, with bright strands of her lovely silver hair caught by the sharp morning breeze. She was waving her hands frantically as she cried.

The skater threw up his head attentively and faced her, whirling almost in a circle and coming about in front of the old house on the hill and the pretty old lady.

"Are you calling *me?*" he shouted, coming to a halt on his shining runners and looking up.

"Yes!" answered the old lady, nodding her white head excitedly.

"What's the matter?" called the young man.

"A woman in trouble!"

"Where? Up there?"

"No, over across the river. This child will show you."

She put the little girl before her, pointing to her, and the child started to plunge into the snow, and come to him.

"Wait!" shouted the young man, "I'll come up and carry you. There's a big drift there!" and he swung to the edge of the river deftly, and began breaking a way for himself up the crust of the snowy hillside.

Lady Winthrop took her handkerchief out of her pocket, softly, swiftly, wiped the little tear-wet face of the child, and tucked the afghan closer about her shoulders. Then she lifted her head and watched the strong firm steps that broke into the white crust of the hill. The young man was looking up now, taking the hill in great strides, studying the two on the porch.

"I'll carry that child," he announced as he arrived. "Sure, I can manage that all right. Are you coming, Madam?"

"No," said the old lady sadly, "I have a sprained knee, and I'm very unsteady on my feet. I'm afraid I couldn't make the grade. Both my servants are out on errands. I'm here alone."

"Well, can you tell me where I am going, and what I am to do when I get there?"

"This child's mother has been taken sick. She will tell you. They are strangers to me, have just moved into that red brick house across the river. She says her mother is lying on the floor. That she fell."

"She wouldn't answer me," said the baby catching her voice in a sob. "Her eyes were shut tight!"

A tender pitying look came over the young man's face.

"And what is their name?" he asked. "I imagine there ought to be a doctor at once."

"Yes," said Lady Winthrop, "I was just going in to telephone my doctor. His office hours will be over but I think I can catch him. The name is Fernley, isn't that right, dear?"

The child nodded.

"It's number ten Rosemary Lane," she added. "It's the old brick house. We just moved there last week. Our things haven't all come yet."

"I see," said the young man. "Well, let's get going. Lady Winthrop, you had better go inside. The wind is pretty sharp this morning. Better get warm at once, or there will be two sick ladies instead of one."

The old lady looked up surprised.

"You know me?" she asked.

"Sure," said the young man with a pleasant grin, "go in and get warm!" He plunged sharply down the crusty hill with the child held firmly in his arms. He landed in a smooth glide on the ice and flew away upstream.

The old lady watched for an instant to make sure the child would be all right with this engaging young stranger, and then turned swiftly in to her telephone, not even stopping to shiver, though it was a good many years since she had permitted herself to be as cold as she was now. There had always been that afghan to

throw about her if anyone came to the door and she had to stand a moment talking to them. But she wasn't thinking about being cold now. She was thinking of that little child, and a poor mother lying unconscious on the floor. She must get the doctor before he started on his rounds!

She waited frantically for the number, wondering what to do if the doctor was gone. Was there some other doctor she would feel like sending in his place if her doctor was not available? Then she was relieved to hear the doctor's voice answering.

"Yes, Mrs. Winthrop? You're not ill, I trust? Yes, of course I recognized your voice. There isn't another voice like yours. You see I sent Miss March out on an errand, and I was just leaving myself, that's how I happened to be taking the call. Is anything the matter?"

"Not with me, doctor, but I am afraid there is terrible trouble across the river from me, and I don't know what to do about it. I sent the servants to the city shopping for me, and I'm here alone for the moment. They have a lot of errands and will be some time, I'm afraid, and *this* may be a matter of life and death. Doctor, *could* you possibly go right away and see? A little child came rushing across the ice to my door screaming for help. She said her mother had fallen down on the floor and wouldn't answer her when she called. She was half frightened to death, nearly frozen, and crying bitterly. She had come across the river without hat or coat and was blue with cold and shivering. Perhaps the woman has only fainted, but you know I can't walk over, and I thought someone ought to investigate at once, for maybe she is dying. The child said they had just moved here and didn't have a doctor. Can you take the time to go?"

"Of course. I'll go at once. Where is it?"

"Number ten Rosemary Lane, a little old red brick house across the river from our house. The name is Fernley."

"All right, I'll go at once. And I'll be reporting back to you afterwards. Don't you worry, and don't think of

going out yourself. It would be suicidal for you. There is a glare of ice everywhere, and the wind is bitter. Good-by! I'm leaving immediately."

She turned from the telephone and hurried over to the window again, but the skater and the child had disappeared. She stood there a moment watching to see if the young man would be coming back, but the river was empty, no skater in sight either way.

With a sigh she turned away from the window, suddenly aware that she was very cold. She went to the hall closet and took out a warm soft old-fashioned shawl wrapping it close about her, remembering the little shivering child who had come crying for help.

Back at the window there was still no sight of anyone. If only Joseph and Hannah would come she would have them drive her over at once to find out what this was all about anyway. It was hard to have to be helpless and wait. And that poor woman over there dying perhaps. Was the young man staying in the house all this time, or could he possibly have gone by while she was getting her shawl? She could see the river perfectly from the telephone and she had been watching the window every minute. She hadn't been a second getting that shawl. Probably he was doing something for the sick woman. Of course. Reviving her perhaps, if it was a faint. But would he know how? Not every young man was versed in First Aid in such an emergency. This young man was at the age when he would have recently been away to college. They didn't have much time to study up First Aid in college, did they? Although if they were in athletics they might have some experience. Of course her own boys if they had been here would know what to do; at least enough to keep the woman alive if she was still living. And this young man looked like a wise fellow. He had intelligent eyes. Who was he, anyway, and how had he happened to know her name? Had she ever seen him before? The boys nowadays grew up so fast. And then of course she hadn't been around among the young people of the neighborhood so much as she used to be when her own boys were at home and had the house full of friends all the time.

How the years raced by her in panorama as she anxiously watched the icy pathway of the river! Oh, if she only hadn't sent Hannah and Joseph off this particular morning! They could have gone later just as well. What could that skater-boy do anyway for a desperately sick woman, even if he did know enough to bring her back to consciousness?

She wished she could see the little brick house more clearly. The big elm tree in her back yard almost hid its front door. Was that somebody coming out now? Probably if she went out on the kitchen porch the vision would be clearer. But no, she musn't, the wind was very sharp. She shivered now at the thought of facing it again as when she had called the young man. She mustn't risk getting bronchitis again. No, she couldn't go outside without fixing up very warmly, and that would take a lot of time. Likely she would fail to see the young man if he came back. But that surely was a car parked by the side of the little brick cottage. Probably the doctor had arrived. And, ah—there was the young man, coming cautiously down the snow toward the river, just as he had walked up her lawn. And now he was dashing out on the ice and skimming along. Probably she had made him late to something, asking him to help. He might be a worker in one of those munition places, and would be late arriving, maybe be docked in his pay, or even lose his job. But what else could she have done? She had to call someone, and he was the only one in sight. And he was a gentleman, she was sure of that. He had it written all over him, even in a leather windbreaker. He would never let her know she had inconvenienced him.

If he was late he wouldn't likely stop to speak to her now, though he had said he would be back. But, perhaps the doctor had understood, and promised to stop and let her know.

Then she saw him coming, and suddenly he whirled to face her house, and came dashing up, stepping in his same footprints as if they were stairs.

She opened the door and stepped out anxiously, but he called:

"Don't come out, Lady Winthrop. The cold is something fierce. I'll come in. The doctor sent you a message."

She stepped back into the house, and he was beside her almost at once, taking care, she noted, to keep his skate-shod feet on a rough mat at the door.

"She's a pretty sick woman," he said as he closed the door behind him. "It took me some time to bring her to, but the little kid brought some water, and told me where to find aromatic ammonia, and when I got a few drops of that down her throat she began to rouse. I got her on the bed and covered her warmly, rubbed her hands and feet. They were like ice. We put a hot blanket around them. They had a good warm radiator in the room. That helped to heat the blanket. But we couldn't find a hot water bag. The doctor said did you have one or two you could lend him, and a couple more blankets. Their goods haven't all come yet. And the doctor asked if you would please telephone his office boy and ask him to bring over his other medicine bag, and get hold of Nurse Branner and bring her right over to the house?"

"Why surely. There's the telephone, suppose you call the office and talk with the boy while I get the blankets and things. The number is 75–J."

As she hurried away she heard the young man's efficient voice giving directions to the doctor's office boy, and rejoiced that she had so able a helper. This young man was going to stand right by as long as he was needed. Then she heard him coming down the hall after her, walking very carefully, not to hurt her floor.

"Can't I help you?" he asked, and he stepped gingerly up and took the blankets from her, then reached for the two hot water bags that were set so neatly together on a high shelf in the bathroom.

"Thank you," said the old lady. "And now suppose we fill these bags from the teakettle in the kitchen. I happen to know it is full of hot water and standing over the simmerer. You can wrap the blankets around the bags and that will keep them hot and save a lot of time."

"That's a good idea!" said the young man. "You've been through a lot of sickness in your lifetime and you know what to do."

"Well, I couldn't have done much if you hadn't responded to my call. And it couldn't have been easy walking up that hill with skates on, either."

The young man grinned, and, turning, was soon plunging down the hillside, the big blanket-wrapped bundle held firmly as he sprang out on the ice and went skimming away again. What a fellow he was! How wise and brisk and efficient!

Lady Winthrop found she was quite weak with excitement when he was gone, and she sat down suddenly to rest and get her breath.

"Well," she said aloud to herself, "to think all this would happen the first time I sent Hannah and Joe away at the same time, when I was alone. If Joe were only here with the car I'd have been over there myself long ago seeing what I could do to help that poor woman. And now here I am, just a go-between. But perhaps that's needed just now more than anything else, to do the telephoning."

Then she got to thinking about that little brick house up the river and the people who had just moved in. Would they have plenty to eat? Food fit for a sick woman? The sick mother and the baby girl who had come across the icy way alone. She must see what food was quickly available in the refrigerator, in case somebody came back again. At least she could send it over by Joseph when he got back. Neither the woman nor the little girl would be able to do any cooking, of course.

There was a good bowl of chicken soup Hannah made last night. She always made enough for two or three days. And there would be some breast of chicken of course, there always was. She decided to fill one thermos bottle with the hot soup, and the other with hot coffee. So she went to work, making delicate little chicken sandwiches, heating the soup and the coffee, and working happily in her own kitchen, where her faithful servants had not allowed her to lift a finger to work for years. It was fun, she told herself.

Yet all the time she was watching out the kitchen window, looking for somebody to come down the river. She worked swiftly to be ready if anyone came. And then she saw her young knight come out of the brick cottage and down the icy pathway, and she hurried into the living room to be ready to open the front door for him in case he came up again.

He came. With that grave competent smile on his face.

"She's recovered consciousness fully now," he announced as he stepped inside the room and shut the door after him. "The doctor isn't sure yet how serious it is, but at least she is able to speak. He says it looks to him as if it might be merely a case of exhaustion from having worked too hard on too little food. Of course the heart might be more affected than he can tell at present, but he hopes it isn't serious. And the first thing that woman said when she came to herself was, 'Don't let my daughter know I fainted. Please don't! She'll be so worried, and she mustn't lose her job! I'll be all right now.' The nurse got her right into bed of course, and she's warm now. The nurse is going to try to make something for her to eat, but there doesn't seem to be much that's suitable in the house. The doctor told me to ask if you can spare a little milk for immediate use. The child says her mother ate no breakfast this morning."

"Milk? Why certainly! Here's a whole bottle. Wait, I'll get a basket. I have some other things ready. Coffee and chicken soup in thermos bottles, and some chicken sandwiches. I thought that mother had been too used up to do much cooking. And here, put in a loaf of bread and a carton of butter. Some oranges too might come in handy."

"That's great, Lady Winthrop, I'm sure they'll all come in for use and everybody grateful, including the nurse and doctor. I don't think the people are exactly poor, just pretty hard up for the present, moving expenses and the like. The daughter has a job down at the first munitions plant. She hasn't had it but a week or so, and I judge from the few words the mother said that

she's afraid she might lose it if she came home to look after her mother."

"Poor child!" said the old lady. "I wish I might go over and help. I will when my car gets back. You see I had a bad fall, and sprained my knee and strained my ankle and I can't walk very far, especially on snow and ice. I have to go everywhere in my car. It is providential that you came along. You've been wonderful!"

"Oh, I haven't done much. I'm glad you called me."

"Yes? Well you see I was watching for you. I've seen you go skating by on the river for several days. I knew you hadn't gone by yet but it was your usual time, so I just watched for you. I hoped maybe you'd come. Who are you, anyway? Ought I to know your name? You seem to know mine."

The young man smiled.

"No, you wouldn't remember me. I'm Mrs. Haversett's nephew, Val Willoughby. I stayed here with my aunt Mrs. Haversett for a year when I was a kid, while my mother was taking treatment with a specialist in Vienna. I've been here several times since for a few days at a time. But I'm not surprised you don't recognize me. It was a good many years ago. When mother came back we went to the west coast to live, and my trips east since have been brief and hurried."

Lady Winthrop was studying the young man's face, and gradually comprehension came to her eyes.

"Willoughby! Oh, you were little Valiant Willoughby, weren't you? Yes, I remember the sturdy little boy with the round eyes and wide grin. It was your eyes and your grin that made you seem familiar when you came up the hill. And what are you doing here now? Visiting your aunt again?"

"Well, not exactly visiting. I'm staying at my aunt's of course, but I'm here for work now, not fun. I have a job down at the airplane factory."

"Oh, you have! Well, aren't you going to be very late to it? And it's all my fault of course."

"Well, yes, I'll be later than usual. But I'm in a way my own boss. Nobody will say anything. I'll explain of course that it was an emergency, though I'm not really

answerable to anyone but myself. But I guess I had better get going. They'll be needing these things across the river, and then the doctor thought I had better stop and tell the daughter. She might blame us for not letting her know. The doctor feels it might be serious later perhaps, although he thinks when the woman gets something to eat she may rally and be really on the mend. He says she's probably been going on her nerve for several days. Perhaps longer. Well, so long! I'll be seeing you again. I'll let you know tonight how things go."

She watched the young man striding down the snowy way on those treacherous-looking skates. How nimbly he trotted down that crusted slope! How skillfully he skimmed out upon the glassy surface of the river and went on his way with the basket balanced so easily on one arm.

She watched him out of sight, till presently she saw him returning, and when he neared the foot of the hill he lifted his cap in a courteous bow, and pointed on down the stream. He was hurrying now to the city.

She opened her door and waved a frail hand in acknowledgement, and got another wave from the cap in his hand as he turned and sailed off toward Hemlock Rocks.

Chapter 2

WHEN FRANCES FERNLEY was ready to go to her job that morning she turned back and looked at her mother.

"Oh, mother, I wish you'd promise me something. Promise me you won't do a stroke of work until I get back. There are hardly any dishes, and Bonnie can do those. I promised her she might, and you know she's very careful handling them. Besides, the ones we are using are just the old cracked ones anyway, and even if

one broke it wouldn't be much loss. Now mother, you will go right upstairs and lie down and get a real sleep, won't you? I'm so worried about you. And you know I can't keep my mind on my work when I'm worried. If you would just promise me I know you wouldn't break your word. Please, mummie!"

"All right," said the mother with a weak shimmer of a smile on her tired, worried face.

"You know the rest of the goods will probably come late this afternoon," went on the girl, "and we all want to be fresh and rested to get things in apple pie order before we sleep. You know you can do a lot more if you are really rested, mother. And there isn't so much that needs doing now before the other furniture gets here. You take a good long nap on your bed, and then about eleven o'clock you and Bonnie run over to the store and get what we'll need for dinner. That's enough for you to do today. Will you *really* do that, mother?"

"Why, yes, surely, I'll rest. Now run along quick, Frannie, or you'll be late for your work."

So the girl had stooped and kissed her mother, and then gone carefully down the wooden steps to the ice, stopping to make sure the lacing of her skating shoes was fastened firmly, then went skimming off down the ice, looking back to wave good-by and blow a kiss to Bonnie at the window.

As she went skimming along in the bright morning air her thoughts were with her white-faced mother whom she realized was working too hard. It was all too evident. She tried to think how she might make these few hard days at the beginning easier for her. Of course, she could have stayed at home today and helped more, but she had a good job with an amazing salary for such a young beginner as she was, and both she and her mother felt they must not trifle with it, especially not now right at the beginning of things. A little later when she was sure of herself, and could take some time to help get settled, perhaps she could find a young girl who would come in to do some of the heavier work, or a stronger, older woman to take the

burden from her mother. For the mother had warned her that they must not spend any more of their tiny capital in hiring help until it was absolutely necessary, and until Frannie was sure she was going to be satisfactory to her boss and that her job was dependable. She must not take success as an assured thing until she had been tried out by her superior.

So, against her strong intuitions she had gone away that morning, hoping that all would be well until she got back, and resolving to enquire around and find out whether there was a woman she could get who would be right for them. Maybe some of the women who lived in those smaller houses over in that far row. And yet those houses must of course be filled with people who had money, for they had to be *bought*. They were not for rent. And that took money, more downpayment than they owned. The little tumbledown brick where they lived was quite old, and just ready to fall apart, or they would not have been able to rent it.

Another thing that worried her was that they had no very near neighbors. Those houses in that far row were at such a distance that she was not sure if they were even finished. Maybe nobody lived in them yet. That made her a little uneasy to leave her mother and sister alone all day. Suppose something happened! There would be nobody nearby to go to for help. But of course nothing would happen. Not in the daytime. And pretty soon they would get in a telephone so mother wouldn't have to go to the store for groceries. The store was five blocks away. But they had been so delighted at the idea of living near to the river. It would be so lovely in the summer. And now too, all frozen this way, it was wonderful, and it was saving her carfare too. She was going to get Bonnie a pair of skates and teach her to skate. She was not too young to learn. When she got home this evening she would look in some of the big boxes that had come yesterday and see if possibly her own first skates weren't there somewhere. The ones her dear father had taught her to skate on so very long ago.

So she hurried along, over the smooth ice, so glad the

way was clear, so glad it had not snowed in the night. It was wonderful weather; five whole days, ever since they had moved, there had been clear cold weather. Of course it couldn't last much longer, and then she would have to start earlier to walk to the bus that would take her to the plant.

She sighed at the thought. It was so much pleasanter going this way, no crowded buses, no stuffy air. Just this grand cold snap in the tingling crisp air and sunshine. It made the blood simply dance in her cheeks, and gave her such a free feeling, almost as if she were really happy again, the way she used to be before her father died, and there were not so many burdens to bear. Mother looking so worn and sad, so worried at her having to go off into the world and work. Oh, of course mother didn't mind her working. But she did hate to have her go off into conditions that were all strange and new to her. Mother had old-fashioned sweet ideas that a girl ought to be guarded, and not have to go and work in offices among men. Mother wanted to know the people herself among whom her daughter worked all day. Well, poor little mother. Some day perhaps she would understand that it wasn't bad. It was really very nice and orderly, and the men among whom she worked were kindly, pleasant, most of them real gentlemen, in spite of the fact that many of them wore rough working garments. And then there were a number of boys, just like the high school boys with whom she had so recently been associated. Some young college men too, who had been debarred from military service because of some physical defect, or weakness. They were fine and kind and she had a feeling that everybody in the plant was wonderful.

She had come out into the world of business with the idea that she must be on her guard wherever she went. But she was gradually coming to feel that attitude had been a mistake. All the men she met were so helpful, so ready to tell her what to do when she asked a question, that she gave her sweet shy smile in return without any withdrawal, and gave to all who came about

a sense of her wholesomeness and friendliness and willingness to serve. It gave her a happy satisfied feeling. She must make her mother understand how kindly and in earnest everyone was, and that perhaps would keep her from her constant worrying.

So it was with an almost light heart that Frannie sat down on the snowy bank to remove her skating shoes, and slip on her other shoes for the day, and then tucking her skating shoes into the ample pockets of her old coat, she ran lightly up the steps that led to the door of the building where she worked.

As she went toward her desk two young men stood at the end of the room and talked, watching covertly the different people in the room.

"There she comes," said one with a weak face, and pale eyes. "Isn't she a honey? Gosh, she's a sight for sore eyes. And look how she walks. She arrives on skates by the river! And can she move? Just like some little bird! Boy! I'm telling you!"

"Yes, she sure is a smooth little number," said the other, who went by the name of Spike Emberly, "I think I'll make a date with her for tonight and try her out as a dancer."

"Not on yer life you don't," growled the other. "She's my find. You keep hands off or you'll be sorry!"

"Oh, *will* I?" leered the boy with the mop of dark curly hair and bold eyes. "How do you know but *you'll* be the sorry one? Well, here goes! Watch me!"

He strode ahead and fell into step with Frannie as she walked toward her desk. She looked up startled into the bold black eyes.

"Hello, beautiful!" he greeted her with the kind of grin that did not belong in her social stratum. "I've been waiting for you. Want to make a date? How about going places tonight? Take you to a swell joint fer dinner. Good eats, good drinks, and then we'll go a-dancing. That okay with you?"

Frannie gave him a frightened look and lifted her chin with gravity.

"Thank you, no!" she said with finality. "I am busy this evening."

"Then how about tomorrow evening? That'll give me more time to make arrangements."

"Thank you, no. My evenings are all occupied!"

"Say, now, that's too bad. You really ought to take a day off now and then. Your health won't stand that kind of life. A little fun now and then is what you need. Tell me where you live and I'll call for you. You wouldn't know what you're missing till you try it. Come on, you try me out once and see if you don't have the time of your life. Where do you live? I'll call for you about seven-thirty, or eight. How's that?"

"Definitely, *no!*" said Frannie, turning sharply toward her desk.

And then the pale-eyed boy stepped up on the other side.

"What did I tell you, Spike, a dame like this one wouldn't be seen with a guy like yerself. She's *my* girl, I told you. You lay off her, Spike Emberly. She's going places with me. We have a previous engagement, haven't we, lovely?"

Frannie gave a frightened glance around and saw that the head of the department was just entering the room at the far end, so she settled down quietly into her chair and ignored the two, her cheeks growing white with annoyance. So, this very morning when she was so sure that all the young men in the plant were perfect gentlemen, here had come these two to disprove it. Well, she certainly would have to make them understand that she wanted nothing to do with them. Utter strangers! How upset her mother would have been if she had overheard what they said. Not, of course, that there was anything actually wrong about it, except that free-and-easy intimate way that seemed to be the vogue these days among young people. Perhaps she was growing prudish, but she certainly didn't like the way they had talked. Like picking her up on the street.

But the young men had cast an eye toward the doorway too, and noted the manager coming in their direction.

"Well, good-by, dolling," said the one called Spike. "Here comes the big boss. I better get on with my job,"

and he vanished out the opposite door. But the other lingered, his eyes on her face impressively, his voice lowered to confidential tones:

"Just in case you're interested," he said, "my name is Kit Creeber, and I'm meeting you down on the ice at closing time. So-long baby, till t'night!" Then he made the tour of the room, stopping to speak to three other girls on the way, as if he had messages from someone in the office for them.

Frannie was engrossed in polishing her typewriter, and seemed not to be aware of his presence, but she was exceedingly annoyed and no movement of his escaped her notice. Now, what was she going to do tonight? How could she get away without meeting him? But meet him she certainly would not do, no matter if she had to go out the front way and take a taxi home to avoid it. Of course that would cost a lot, and she didn't know the vicinity well enough to find a bus going home. Perhaps some of the other girls could tell her at noon. She looked despairingly around on them. There wasn't one that she felt friendly with yet. Perhaps that was her fault. Her mother had always told her that she was far too shy and retiring. She must overcome this and make friends of course, but how she hated the idea of those two fellows who had approached her this morning. Was she just silly? Perhaps she ought to have laughed them off, but somehow she just couldn't. The boys at her old home had never treated her that way. They were polite. But there! She must forget this and plunge her mind into her work. Perhaps at noontime she could ask a few questions about how to get home by bus, just casually of course. She wouldn't let anybody know that those boys had been fresh with her. Perhaps they wouldn't think there was anything wrong with what they did anyway.

Then the buzzer on her desk sounded and she picked up her pencil and pad and made her way to the inner office for dictation, and the two impudent young men passed out of her thoughts for the time.

The man for whom she was taking dictation was a kindly, reserved, elderly man with iron gray hair and a

stern face. He wasted no time in his work, and Frannie's fingers flew to keep pace with his gruff voice. When at last she went back to her machine she was fairly breathless with the speed she had been going. She sat down at her typewriter and began to work, determined to finish all these letters before the noon hour.

She had been working nearly two hours at top speed when she became aware of two people coming straight toward her desk. One was Mr. Chalmers, her chief, and by his side a strange young man. At least she had never seen him in the plant before.

"Miss Fernley," Mr. Chalmers said, "this young man has a message for you, from your mother, isn't that it, Mr. Willoughby?"

The young man bowed, but Frannie turned white.

"Oh, my mother?" she exclaimed, springing to her feet, one small hand fluttering to her throat. "Has something happened?"

"Please don't be frightened," said the young man. "Your mother isn't very well. But she's resting now, and I'm sure she's going to be all right. She didn't want you to be told, but the doctor thought you might be upset if you were not told at once. He told me to assure you that at present there is nothing for you to worry about, and he will see that you are notified if there is any need for you to come home."

"But—I don't understand—!" said the girl frantically. "How did she get a doctor? She was all alone with just my little sister, and she's only a baby yet."

"Well, she's *some baby!*" said the young man emphatically. "When your mother fainted she ran across the river on the ice and told Lady Winthrop, and she sent her doctor over, so everything is all right now. We put your mother on the bed and the doctor brought his pet nurse along, so your mother isn't alone now, and you don't need to worry. She was most anxious that you *do not* come home until the day's work is over."

"Oh, that will be all right," said the chief kindly. "I can excuse you right away if you are anxious to go to your mother."

"Oh, but I *must* go!" said the girl frantically. "We

have just moved in there, and there isn't anything in
the house to eat yet. I must go and see that she has
food. I'll just finish that important letter you wanted
to have go at once, and then I'll go. It's almost done!"
She turned toward her typewriter with a quick nervous
little movement, but young Willoughby put out a detaining hand.

"Listen!" he said. "You needn't worry about food.
Mrs. Winthrop sent over a thermos bottle of chicken
soup, and another of coffee. She sent bread and butter
and chicken and a quart of milk too. You needn't
worry at all about something for them to eat. They
have plenty. I took it over myself. Mrs. Winthrop knew
you had just moved in and thought you might not be
prepared for illness, so she sent over some things that
were suitable for an invalid and a child. You don't
need to worry at all. And your mother was most anxious
you should not be told. It was the doctor who felt you
ought to know, as you might wish another physician
called or something. So I agreed to tell you. But I'm sure
your mother is in good hands. When I left she was eating spoonfuls of chicken broth and they were telling
her she was to stay right there in bed and get a good
rest. The nurse is staying of course. It just happened
that she left a case this morning, and was glad to get a
place where she could be useful until her next case
comes on."

"Oh!" said Frannie, struggling to keep the tears back,
"that is all very kind and wonderful. But I'm sure I
ought to be at home. Mother will be so unhappy having
strangers have to come in and look after her."

"No," said young Willoughby, "she will be much
more troubled if you do anything to upset your job just
now. I know for I saw her face when she begged them
not to tell you. In fact the doctor told me he was giving
her something to make her sleep for a little while, and
by the time you get home she'll be just waking up and
won't think there was anything much the matter perhaps."

"Oh, you are very kind and thoughtful. But we have
never had to be such a lot of trouble to strangers."

"Well, don't think of us as strangers, call us neighbors," said the young man with a confidence-inspiring
smile that somehow loosened the tightness around the
girl's heart, and made it possible for her to breathe
again. She wavered a pale little white smile in answer.

"You see, I'm sure you can trust the doctor. He's
very skillful. He is Dr. Ransom, Lady Winthrop's own
physician. And besides, he promised me he would go
back again just before noon, and then will go straight
to his office and from there telephone me how things
are going. I am sure he will do that. And I promise to
telephone you here immediately. May I do that, Mr.
Chalmers?" He looked toward Frannie's chief, who
bowed assent graciously, and Frannie began to feel as
if the reeling ground beneath her feet was gradually
steadying.

"Oh! That will help a lot," she murmured. "But—
the movers will be coming this afternoon with the rest
of our furniture, and there will be nobody to tell them
where to put things!"

Her practical young eyes had taken on their frightened look again.

"Mother would never lie still and let that go on.
She will get right up and go to work unless I'm there!"

"Not with Nurse Branner there!" laughed Valiant
Willoughby. "You don't know her if you think that
could happen. But I do. She nursed me through a brok-
en leg once and believe me there isn't a thing that woman doesn't understand and can't take charge of. You'll
find she'll ferret out the most suitable spot for every
article and have it placed there right on the dot, and no
patient of hers will get out of bed and go to work.
She'll see to that! Now, will you be good, Miss Fernley?
And I give you my word of honor to phone the latest
news from your home at noon or know the reason why.
Does that satisfy you?"

"Thank you so much. That will be wonderful. Now
I can go back to my work."

Then Mr. Chalmers interrupted.

"Miss Fernley, I'm afraid it is going to be a strain on
you to finish those letters I gave you this morning. If

you like I'll call Miss Dart and let you read them to her and she can take them down and type them, and then you can go home."

But Frannie's business pride rose to the front. She clutched her precious notebook firmly and shook her head.

"No indeed, Mr. Chalmers, I'd rather do them myself. You explained so fully what you wanted in some of the letters that I would hate to have you have to do that all over again. No, I'm sure since Mr. Willoughby has been so kind, that everything will be all right. I know that my mother would much rather have me stay here and make good than to rush home, since she has a good doctor and an efficient nurse. I would be silly to worry about her. I'll bring the letters to you when I have them finished, and if there are any changes to be made I'll have plenty of time to recopy."

"Well, if you are sure you won't worry—"

"No, I won't worry," promised Frannie with a grave, capable smile.

The two men glanced at the girl with approval.

"Well, good-by Miss Fernley," said Willoughby. "I'll be calling you around noon. And thank you, Mr. Chalmers, for your courtesy to us both."

The young man walked away, and the chief gave one keen look at his secretary, and then slowly made his way back to his own office, while Frannie settled down to do some of the most tensely careful work she had ever done in the line of typing. She somehow felt that her skill was in question, she was being put to the test, and she must not let even her anxiety for her beloved mother steal her thoughts away from the duty of the moment. This must come first, even before her mother. She *must* make good here if she was to be able to carry on and keep the little family together.

So with resolute will she turned her thoughts from the picture of the precious mother lying on the floor unconscious, and the little carefully-guarded baby sister flying alone across that great expanse of ice to call a stranger to help, and put her mind entirely on her work.

Valiant Willoughby, walking swiftly down the flag-

stones of the street that ran between the plant where Frannie worked, and his own headquarters which were about a quarter of a mile farther on down the river, was thinking of that girl, that sweet fine young girl! With what charming self-control she had taken the startling news he had brought her, though it was most evident that it had shocked her tremendously. How sweet her eyes had been as she lifted them with that frightened, almost pleading look. Grave, lovely eyes, they were, though she seemed not much more than a little girl.

And how quickly she had rallied to see where her first duty lay! Though it was plain it had been a struggle, because her heart was bidding her fly without delay to her sick mother. She seemed to be a rare girl, and really beautiful, though she was plainly dressed, with no pretense at the make-up and painted finger nails of most girls. Strange he should notice that in such a time, when he was not considering the girl as a girl at all, only as a human being, a young working woman with a family to support!

Well, he hoped the doctor would be on time with his news from the sick room, and that there would be something in his message that would give a possibility of cheer to that brave little girl when he relayed the message at noon.

So he went on to his own place of work, and was presently immersed in duties that were fully as engrossing as Frannie's. And the hours pranced on swiftly as hours have a way of doing when one is working hard, and noon not far away.

And then, before she realized how late it was, for she had not been keeping her mind on the time, but looking ahead to see how much work was still to be done, there came a summons from the office boy, "Miss Fernley, telephone! Mr. Chalmer's office!" and Frannie with her heart beating wildly hurried to the office. Oh, would there be bad news? Should she have gone home anyway? And then as with trembling hands she took up the instrument, there was that pleasant reassuring voice of the young man.

"Good news, Miss Fernley! Your mother is sleeping

quietly, a natural sleep. The doctor did not give her the sleeping tablets after all. She took the nourishment well, and fell right to sleep. Perhaps she was just very tired. The doctor says her pulse is decidedly stronger, and you have nothing to worry about. The nurse says she is glad to have a place to stay till her next case, so you can just trust her to look after things till your regular time for returning."

"Oh, that's wonderful!" breathed the girl softly. "I can't thank you enough for taking all this trouble."

"It wasn't trouble. It was a pleasure," said Willoughby. "And now, what about the return trip for you? Can I help in any way? I can easily get the car and take you back, much faster than if you went on the bus."

"Oh, no, thank you. You've taken too much trouble already. I shall get home all right."

"Why, it wouldn't be any trouble. I'd be glad to help you in any way I can. What time do you get done there? I didn't think to ask Mr. Chalmers."

"Why, we usually go out at five, but Mr. Chalmers said I might go as soon as I finished the letters for the day. However there were a great many letters. It was a heavy mail this morning. I can't tell how long it will take me. But *please* don't trouble any more about me. You have been very kind already. And I have my skates. It doesn't take long to get home on the ice. Thank you so much for all your kindness."

Skates? So she was a skater! He couldn't help but admire her independence.

"Well," he said in a genial tone, "run along then and get done as quickly as possible. I'll be seeing you later."

Frannie hurried back to her desk with a warm glow on her cheeks. How nice it was of that young man to offer to take her home. How wonderful it was that people had been raised up to look after her mother in her stress! But she simply must not think about it or she would get to crying. Poor dear little mother all alone with strangers!

And now what would mother think they ought to do? Perhaps she would have to give up her job for a while—until mother was better. Mother wouldn't like

the idea of strangers in the house, even kind strangers. And as for that nurse, well, even if she was *very* nice, they couldn't afford a nurse. Nurses were very expensive. But she must not go into that now or she would get it all mixed up with the letters she was writing and would lose her job by careless work, and that would be worse than giving it up.

So she resolutely put it all out of her mind and went to work again. With no thought whatever of lunch, she plunged into her job and did her level best, though she had a neat little bundle of crackers and cheese and an apple tucked away in her locker, that might have helped out a little. But her only ambition was to get done and get home, home to her mother and her little sister and find out what she had to do next.

Of the two boys,—the *very* young men,—who had endeavored to gain an acquaintance with her that morning, she hadn't even thought all day, not since the tall young stranger had come down the aisle with Mr. Chalmers and brought her word about her mother. And if she had thought of them they would have been like the passing of a bad dream. They were nothing to her. She felt years beyond them. Even her dread that they might try to annoy her had passed beyond her memory.

So she worked on, now and again an eye toward the clock that loomed like a sentinel at the far end of the room. She was running a race and the clock was her judge, her arbiter. Breathlessly she worked, with strangely perfect precision, all keyed up as she was, not daring to turn a particle of thought away from the matter in hand. It was as if her whole life depended upon the outcome of her work that day.

Occasionally she drew a weary breath, and pressed cold fingers to tired eyes.

Then she slid another sheet of paper into her machine and typed on, her fingers in perfect rhythm with the timing of her goal.

And at last the final letter was typed, letter perfect, and ready for inspection.

Her eyes went to the clock again that ticked solemnly on with no evident intention of finishing the afternoon

just yet. It was twenty whole minutes to five! She had
finished! There was time to take the letters to Mr.
Chalmers, and find out if he had other orders for her
before she left.

Quietly she put her materials away in the machine
drawer, covered the typewriter, and rose with her sheaf
of letters in her hand, walking over to Mr. Chalmer's
office. And just a moment later the two young men, Kit
and Spike, strayed casually across the hall and paused in
the open doorway, lingering long enough to look down
toward Frannie's desk, and note that it was empty.

"She's gone," said Kit. "I bet you scared her off."

"Scared? That baby?" said Spike, "Not her! She's
only independent. Or perhaps she's got away early to
steal a march on us and laugh at us tomorrow. Come
on. It's near five. I'm going down and get my skates on,
and be ready for what happens. There's no need hanging around here."

"It isn't five yet," reminded Kit. "I already got so
many marks against me for getting out early I can't risk
getting in bad with old Jimsey. Let's go back to the
room and make like we're awful busy."

"Okay! Go if you like. I'm getting my skates on. I'm
not taking any chances on losing that little number.
She's a honey and no mistake."

"Oh, well, if you think we can get away with it, I'm
agreeable," said Kit, and discreetly they stole by devious
ways to their lockers, stealthily procured their skates,
stuffed their caps in their sweater pockets and vanished
out the basement door. They chose a sheltered spot to
attire their feet with gleaming runners, and then struck
out on the ice, far enough away from the plant not to
be noticed by any chance watcher.

"I'll tell you one thing," said Spike wisely, "that gal
won't appear till the stroke of five. She's not one to
slide out of things. She'll stay till the last minute or I
miss my guess. She's conscientious. When you fall for a
conscientious dame you've got to get wise to her ways,
and go slow and easy. She won't break the tidy little
rule she's got in her life, not even if she falls for you,

so you better go slow and easy. She's got to think you're
a nice guy like her own folks, or she won't look at you!"

"Oh, you don't say so!" said Kit. "Who taught you
all that, I'd like to know?"

And just then Frannie walked out of the basement
door, her skating shoes on a strap over her shoulder,
and sat down on the wooden step to put them on!

With wary furtive glances about to make sure the
coast was clear of anyone who could make trouble for
them, the boys struck across the ice and circled up to
her, Spike dropping neatly down on his knees before her
and boldly putting out intimate hands to the small shoe
she was attempting to lace up.

"How about me doing that for you, beautiful?" he
said, smiling boldly into her frightened face just above
him as he grasped her foot.

"No! No thank you!" said Frannie, pulling her foot
away and trying to rise. She clutched her other shoe in
her hands and held it almost as a weapon. "Please
don't!" she protested. "I *prefer* to do it myself!"

She tried to put dignity in her frightened voice, but
the bold young bully held her foot like a vise, and she
had to drop back again on the step.

"Let go of my foot!" she said sharply, and lifting the
other shoe with its skate she brought it down smartly
on the bold fingers, making Spike howl in protest.

"You little hell-cat!" he shouted. "What do you think
you're doing?" and with his smarting hand he came at
her angrily, and tried to seize the shoe from her, but
she realized her danger just in time, and hit him a
sharp rap again across the knuckles, which caused him
to howl still louder and dance angrily about on the ice
holding his bruised hand in the other one and shouting
to his companion to help him.

"Hi, there, Kit, get that shoe away from the little
fiend. Come on, we'll make her skate home on one foot.
We can do it. You grab her on one side and I on the
other. I guess she won't be so high hat any more with
us. Grab her now before she has a chance to strike
you! Pin her hands behind her! *Quick!* Don't let her

get another clip at you. Hold her elbows! That's it!
Now, I'll wrench this skate out of her hands and then
she won't have a chance, and will have to do just what
we tell her. Take it easy there, girlie. If you don't fight
you won't get hurt. We're not going to hurt you,
girlie. We're just going to show you a good time. There,
there, now take it easy! Don't try to yammer. We'll take
care of you, beautiful!"

With a final yank he tore Frannie's skate from her
tense fingers, and she let out a piercing scream. Then
suddenly a voice spoke thunderously: "What do you
fellows think you are doing?" and Spike was lifted from
behind by his collar and wafted through the air in a
circle that sent him hurtling on his back across the ice
to a safe distance, where he lay, stunned, utterly astounded that this should have happened to him. Why,
he was the big bully of his neighborhood! Nobody ever
got *him*. What happened anyway? He tried to lift a
maimed hand to pass it over his bleared eyes. Who was
that guy, anyway? What wouldn't he do to him when he
got up out of this!

But he wasn't out of it yet, and where was that
Kit? Was he punishing the guy that butted into their
frolic? And what had become of the girl? She couldn't
go very far with only one shoe and one skate on. Where
was the other?

He wanted to look around, but somehow he was too
sore in his muscles to turn around and look. He had to
lie still a minute longer.

"Kit! Oh *Kit!*" he murmured, and wondered why his
voice didn't seem to carry farther. He tried again. "Kit!
Oh, I say, *Kit!*" Nothing happened. Then he tried his
piercing whistle that always waked the echoes, but the
whistle didn't seem to pan out right. His lips were stiff
and wouldn't work. Did that girl get away after all?

At last he managed to roll over, raising himself on
one elbow to look around him. Blinking into the
late afternoon sunlight he made out two figures skimming together far upstream, but look as he might he
could not see Kit anywhere. He must have made good
his escape.

Chapter 3

MARIETTA HOLLISTER was considered a beautiful girl. She wore severely tailored tweeds in the daytime, and affected the latest hair-do and make up, though she tried never to go to extremes. She considered herself very conservative. She kept the length of her finger nails within quiet bounds, and of late their color had resembled more the seashell pink of a young rosebud, rather than drops of blood. Perhaps it was because a young man she much admired had expressed dislike for the bloody looking hands of many girls of the day. Some of her friends considered her eccentric, but she went on her way serenely.

She took a deep interest in war work of various kinds. She attended class in First Aid religiously, offered her services as an ambulance driver, got up entertainments for the soldiers' camps, and was put on numerous committees for the various defense activities, patriotic and otherwise, to say nothing of keeping up her social obligations. She was a very busy and eager young woman, ready to set everybody right on everything, and in such a lovely way that they were not antagonized. She lived in the big colonial house on the hill, on the estate to the left of the Haversett House, where Val Willoughby was staying with his aunt and uncle. She was considered one of the most desirable and charming girls in the neighborhood.

Marietta had known Valiant Willoughby when they were children. Whenever he was in the neighborhood they had played together and taken each other for granted. She had just discovered his return, having not seen him during the four years he was in college.

It was that same morning that Marietta got up with a new plan in her mind. As it involved Valiant she

proceeded to call up his aunt's house as soon as she had had breakfast.

"Oh, good morning Nannie!" she called as she recognized the old servant's voice answering her. "Nannie, is Val there? Oh, has he gone *already?* Why, I supposed he went down on the eight thirty train. You mean he goes this early every morning? What? You say he *skated* down? Why, how ridiculous! I should think it would tire him all out for the day. Well, he's gone then, and I can't speak to him. Does he come home to lunch? No, of course not. That would be too long a journey, wouldn't it? But Nannie, let me speak to Mrs. Haversett, please. That is, if she isn't busy. Oh, good morning, Auntie Haversett! This is Marietta. I called to speak to Val but Nannie tells me he is already gone. Can you tell when he will be home? Not till five? How provoking! I wanted to talk something over with him. I wonder if he would come over and take dinner with us tonight, then I can have time to talk things over with him. Do you think he will come?"

"Well, my dear, I'm afraid I can't say positively. Sometimes he has to stay all the evening at the plant. It depends on whether they are finishing some army order or not. I didn't have any talk with him last night. He was late coming home, and I was just going out. And this morning he was off before I got up. I am afraid he is very uncertain just now, my dear. But I'll tell him of course when he gets back, only it won't do to count on him too much. He is most uncertain. You know war work comes first."

"Why, how perfectly horrid!" said the girl indignantly. "I thought Val was in charge of a department or something. Can't he arrange his own hours?"

"I'm afraid not, my dear. He is in charge of something, I forget just what they call it. But nobody can arrange his own hours just now. The government arranges those matters, and we'll just have to be patient until the great work of defense gets going thoroughly, and it becomes apparent just what is the best method of working."

"Well, it's all wrong, I say, to waste time and good

men that way," said the girl. "A man can't keep on working indefinitely without his proper rest, and he needs a little play time too, time to do just exactly what he pleases. Don't you think so, Auntie Haversett?"

"Well, in ordinary times, yes, I should think so," said the older woman thoughtfully. "But in these times of stress, my dear, people who have charge of important matters have to put aside their own wishes you know——"

"Oh, certainly, I know that as well as you do, but it isn't the way to run things, and I should think if Val is in charge of things he could regulate his hours according to common sense."

"Well, I don't know how much power he has yet. Perhaps those things will work out. But in the meantime I'll tell him what you want, and I'm sure if he can make it he will come."

"Thanks awfully, Auntie Haversett. I'm really planning something quite important. It's a scheme to raise money to get shelter places ready for the children down near the munitions plants—in case of raids, you know. There are a lot of little children living down there on the flats near the plants where their fathers work, and there should be refuges with fully trained nurses in charge, ready for sudden needs. You know those places down there would be the very first spot an enemy would bomb in case of a raid. And I thought if we were to get up a series of dances for the younger set, the ones who aren't really doing anything much yet, and charge plenty for tickets, we could get quite a lot of money in no time. There's nothing like a dance to get the youngsters interested. And of course we *regular* young set would be there to run things for the kids. I'm quite sure it would be popular. That's what I want to talk over with Val. If he will help me start it I'm sure it will take like wild fire. Don't you think he would be interested? And don't you think the project seems fairly inspired, Auntie Haversett?"

"Well, I don't know, my dear. It sounds as if you were planning a lot of hard work and a lot of fun for somebody. But as for Val, I'm not altogether sure how the idea would strike him. I really haven't seen enough

of him since he has been here on that job to know how he reacts to such things any more."

"But he always was so ready to help in any good thing," said the girl positively.

"Yes, I know he was. But these war times are unpredictable times, and there is no telling how anybody would react to any proposition. And of course there are so many things that defense workers are not free to discuss that might make a difference, too, in any plans."

"Well, I can't see how such a thing as that could possibly carry any objections, can you?"

"Well, no, it doesn't seem so on first sight, does it, dear?" said the older woman thoughtfully. "But, as I say, I don't seem to be able to judge just what reaction *any*one will have to anything any more. And of course Val is changed in some ways. He's a lot quieter than he was. By the way, Marietta, did your mother go to the club meeting yesterday? I was wondering what they did about the special war fund? Did you happen to hear her say whether they were going on with their plans for that play, or were they just going to ask for voluntary contributions? Of course everyone is begging for something now, and it does seem as if it was hopeless to try to sell tickets to any more things."

"Why, no, I didn't hear mother say anything about the club meeting," said Marietta, "I haven't been at home much in the last day or two, but it does seem as if something that has been planned and looked forward to for so long ought to be carried out, don't you think so? Of course I know some of the actors have gone to camp, and Jason Allenby can't be here. He went to England by clipper plane yesterday, you know. But surely there will be somebody who could take his place. I think Val would be a wonderful substitute to take that part. I'll remember to suggest it to him tonight. I'll suggest it to the committee, too. Well, Auntie Haversett, you'll be sure to tell Val to call me up as soon as he gets home, won't you?"

"Yes, I'll tell him when he comes, dear, but you mustn't be surprised if you don't get a response right away. He may not come home till very late."

"All right. But, Auntie Haversett, isn't there some way to call him up at the plant?"

The lady looked troubled.

"I'm afraid not, Marietta. That is, one could of course, but it isn't expected, except in emergencies."

"Oh, I see. And you wouldn't think this was an emergency?"

"Well, I'm afraid not, dear."

"Of course I could drive down there and ask to see him," said the girl speculatively.

"Oh, my dear! Is it that important? If I were you I would just forget it. Because really, I think Val is so extremely busy and so absorbed in his work just now, that it isn't in the least likely he'll have time for social affairs until things get going. You know the government is urging intensive work."

"Oh dear! Well, I suppose we'll have to put up with it for a while, but I don't see why other work isn't just as important. Well, good-by for the present, Auntie. I must be getting back to my work. I'm on a new committee this morning and I must hurry."

So Marietta went to her new committee which was at nine o'clock, followed by another at ten, and a third appointment at eleven, but her eager and prolific brain had already solved her problem. That afternoon at a quarter to five with determined mien and assured voice she called up Val Willoughby's plant.

But Val Willoughby was not in his office.

"Has he gone home yet?" demanded the efficient voice.

"I couldn't say, Miss," answered the man who was detailed to look out for phone calls.

"Well, you know whether he is coming back to the plant, don't you?" asked Marietta impatiently.

"I couldn't say, Miss. Mr. Willoughby is a very busy man. He doesn't tell us where he is going. He may be back tonight and he may not. He doesn't have to tell us what he does. He might be outside in the yard. He might be over to the other building. Or he might be gone into the city to see somebody. I don't know. He comes and he goes."

"Well, really!" said Marietta. "I shouldn't think that was very efficient work. Well, if he comes in will you ask him to call me? This is Miss Hollister. The number is Cliveden 725. Will you write that down?"

"Oh sure! But I ain't sure I shall see him. I'm going off duty now, and the other man hasn't come in yet. I'll write the number here. Mebbe he'll see it, I don't know."

And, desperately, at last Marietta hung up.

But Val didn't call her. He was out on the ice dealing with the two young bullies who had set out to play a joke on a girl they thought was too stupid and too young to get it back on them.

Spike came to somewhat while Willoughby was helping Frannie on with her other skate which he had retrieved from a distance whither it had slid at Kit's last frantic yank before he had sighted the enemy coming toward them. He had given the girl's shoe a quick fling across the ice, and then suddenly vanished in a way he knew and had often practised in his early youth. So when Willoughby returned with the shoe in his hand enemy number two had disappeared from off the face of the earth.

Val dropped down before the girl and helped her put her skate on. Then taking her hand he set her upon her feet, and looked her over.

Her hair was awry, the little green cap sat crazily on her brown curls, there were tears on her white cheeks, but not in her eyes, and with brave determination she was holding her trembling lips fairly still.

"Are you sure you are able to go on home this way?" he asked her, looking into her wide eyes that had been so frightened when he first came up.

"Oh, yes," she said, with a catch in her voice. "Yes, I can go on! I'm so sorry I made you trouble again! How wonderful that you should have come along just now! I don't know what I should have done!"

He smiled.

"I'm glad I was here. Who were they? Do you know them? Have they troubled you before?"

"No, I never saw them before till this morning. They

stood in the hall when I went in and were awfully fresh. They asked me to go dancing, and when I told them no they insisted they would meet me out here at closing time. I didn't answer them, and I forgot all about them, or I would have gone out the front door and taken to the river down beyond the next street. I never knew any boys like that."

"There are a lot of tough fellows down in this neighborhood of course," said Willoughby, "but I don't fancy they will trouble you again. Perhaps we had better curve over in the direction of that one and see if he is coming to, or whether I ought to send someone to look after him."

Then still holding Frannie's hand protectively he set out slowly at first, watching the prostrate form of Spike sprawled across the ice.

"He's coming to," said Willoughby. "I saw him move his arm just now. Didn't you? There! He's turning his head. He'll be himself presently. I'll just stop at the next corner and tell the plant night watchman to take a look at him, and send for an ambulance if necessary, or a taxi, if he can't navigate himself. I wonder where his companion is."

"He won't come back while you are here," said Frannie in a low trembly voice. "He's a coward. I watched his face when you took the other one off and flung him out on the ice. He was scared to death. And I don't think he has any very great love for his pal either. He won't want it known that he was mixed up in this affair."

He looked at her and smiled.

"You certainly are a brave girl," he said fervently. "I watched you defend yourself while I was sprinting to the spot and you never flinched once. I was afraid you might faint."

"I don't faint," said Frannie seriously, as if it were a thing to be deplored. "I just don't know how."

"Fine! That's wonderful. There are not many girls who could claim that. But, aren't you feeling pretty well broken up after all this? I think we had better steer in to shore at the next street and take a taxi."

"Oh, no, please! I'm all right. Just a little shaky, but I'll be steady in a minute or two. Skating isn't any effort."

"Oh, isn't it? Well, that may be so at times, but after a brisk fist fight such as you've been through I can't think it is the best thing. We'll just steer for that corner, and take the next bus."

"Please, no," said Frannie frantically. "It rests me to skate. It really does. And I should be frantic hanging around waiting for buses and changing from one to another. You don't understand. It does steady my nerves to skate."

He studied her face an instant.

"Oh, very well," he said, "but you're going to let me help steady you. Here, cross your hands. I think we can travel faster and easier this way." He took her mittened hands in a firm clasp, and they sailed off together. It was easier that way, of course, and she gave him a thankful little smile.

"You're being very kind to me, a stranger," she said. "I can't ever thank you enough."

"Don't try," he said with a smile. "And besides, you're not a stranger, merely a neighbor. Now, let's forget it, and have a good journey. That will rest you more than trying to be grateful. See that color in the sky, and how it reflects from the ice. It's like sailing into a pavement of rubies."

"Yes, isn't it lovely? That's one great reason why I like to come this way. It's so beautiful, any time of day, especially morning and evening. I dread so to have the weather change and spoil the ice."

"Yes, that's right. Weather has a good deal to do with it. I feel that way myself, watching the sky every morning when I wake up. Rejoicing when the sky is still clear and bright. But say, where did you people come from when you moved here? Was it from far away?"

"No," said Frannie. "It was only about seventy miles north, but it was in the country. We went to stay with my grandmother after my father died. Grandmother was quite ill and needed us. But she died three weeks

ago, and mother and I felt we should come down here where I could get a job. I think I was most fortunate in finding such a good job, just by answering an advertisement in the paper. We came from a little place called Bluebell, and that is the reason our goods are coming in sections. There wasn't a regular mover to be had, and so an old farmer, a friend of my grandmother's, is moving us, a little at a time. That's why you found our little house so bare. But I think the rest of the things are coming today. The farmer borrowed a larger truck and is bringing his son with him to help, so we can soon get in order, I hope. He thought they might get here before dark tonight."

"Well, perhaps they'll be there when we arrive. I'd like to stick around awhile and help a little if I may."

"Oh, but you've already done too much!" said Frannie.

"It seems to me that I've somewhere heard that there's a kind of law, perhaps it's in the Bible, that the reward for doing something is that you get the privilege of doing something more a lot greater. Anyway that seems a pretty good rule to me. I've enjoyed what I've done so far immensely."

"That's a beautiful way to look at it," said Frannie wistfully.

"There are other compensations, too," said the young man with a smile. "I feel that I have made some very lovely friends, besides renewing the acquaintance of one whom I knew several years ago when I was a youngster. I mean Lady Winthrop. It was she who called me from the river and sent me to your mother. I want you to know her also. I know you will love her."

"Oh, yes, and I shall want to thank her, too," said Frannie eagerly. "Tell me about it again please. That is something I shall not want to forget."

So he told her about it, more in detail, as they skimmed along on the sunset-colored ice, her mittened hands held firmly in his gloved ones, his strength steadying her balance. And the way did not seem long in such company.

And then they were in sight of the little brick house,

and saw that two trucks were drawn up by the sidewalk.

"Oh, the furniture has come!" cried Frannie. "I'm so glad. Now mother can have her blankets and pillows. I'm afraid she wasn't warm enough last night."

"Oh, but Lady Winthrop thought of that too, and sent over some blankets with the first load I took across."

"How dear of her!" said the girl, her face brimming over with gratitude. "I'm eager to know her. She must be wonderful!"

"She's all that!" declared the young man, guiding the girl to the steps. "Well, here we are! Now, let me unfasten those shoes and put on your other ones. And may I suggest that after the shock, and the unusual experience you had this afternoon, you save yourself as much as possible? I'm going in and help, and I want you to give me orders instead of doing things yourself. Will you? Please promise me, for I shall be worried that I let you skate home if you don't."

"But I feel quite all right, *really*. You made the journey so much easier than it would have been if I had skated alone."

"Well, I'm glad of that, but I want your promise all the same, because if you don't keep it I shall have to tell your family what you have been through, and I know you don't want that just now. Anyhow not till your mother is well and up and around."

"Oh, no, I wouldn't have her know it for anything. She has been awfully worried lest I would get in with a tough set, and I'm afraid she wouldn't want me to go to work any more, and would worry all the time I was away. Please, you won't tell her, will you?"

"Not if you keep your part of the contract. You've just got to sit down as much as possible, and get to bed as early as possible, or you certainly won't be able to go to work in the morning."

"All right, I'll be very careful. And thank you so much for all you've done."

"Oh, but you've already thanked me. Now, let's go in and see what we can do to get this household settled for the night. And by the way, if the morning is clear

and the ice still good, are you going to skate down to work again?"

"Oh, yes, of course."

"Well, then, may I have the pleasure of accompanying you?"

"Why, that would be lovely, but—you mustn't feel that you've got to take me over as a continual burden."

"Oh, it wouldn't be a burden. It's nice to have a skating companion, and it certainly helps to eat up the miles. Now, here we are, and the door is wide open for us. The furniture seems to be mainly inside the house, doesn't it? Just a few more pieces. Here, I'll help with this couch. It's a little awkward for two to handle. And then in a minute I'll hunt up the nurse and introduce you."

And so at the doorway of the little brick house they parted and Frannie rushed up the stairs to find her mother.

At the closed door she paused, startled. Her mother's door! Had something dreadful happened this afternoon? Was her mother worse? Oh, she ought to have come home before! She knew she should not listen to the persuasions of strangers, not even to the voice of caution for her job. She should have come at once.

Softly, cautiously, with trembling fingers she grasped the doorknob, firmly, and turned it ever so softly. Why, it didn't open! It seemed to be locked! What had happened? She glanced wildly around, and then called softly.

"Bonnie! Oh, Bonnie!" And then in a desperate wail: *"Mother!"*

Suddenly she heard small footsteps downstairs, Bonnie hurrying to answer. Bonnie at the foot of the stairs, her important young face bright with grown up responsibility.

"Here I am, Frannie," she whispered, "Mother's asleep. You mustn't wake her up."

"Oh, Bonnie *dear!*" grasped Frannie, the tears rushing to her eyes. "How is she? Is she worse?"

"No indeed!" said the little girl with childish gravity. "She's a great deal better. But Nurse Branner is trying

to keep her quiet till the men are gone so she won't try to get up."

And then suddenly the key turned in the lock and the door was opened by a pleasant-faced nurse in full uniform.

"Oh, this is Frannie, isn't it?" she said in a low clear voice. "Come right in. Your mother is awake now and has been asking for you. Don't let her talk too much. She wants you to give directions to the movers where to put things. Just be as quiet about it as you can, and smile a good deal!" She gave Frannie a knowing look that changed Frannie's tears into sunbeams.

"Of course," smiled Frannie, giving a quick wipe to her wet lashes. Then she stepped to the side of the bed and knelt beside her mother:

"Oh, mother dear! To think you've been sick and I wasn't here!" she whispered, but there was a bright smile of relief on her face as she said it. "But you're better now, mother dear, aren't you? And what wonderful neighbors we have! Bringing a nice nurse and a doctor. I was so happy when I got the message that you were being taken care of. I wanted to fly right home of course when I heard you had fainted, but they said you sent word I mustn't, so I stayed. But mother, I did a lot of praying all day."

Her mother smiled peacefully.

"Yes, dear, there wasn't any need for you to come home. I was perfectly all right. Just a little faint. I was only tired, and perhaps some worried about your going off alone on that dreadful ice."

"Oh, mother dear! But the ice was lovely, as smooth as glass."

"Well, I'm glad you're safely home again," sighed the mother with a smile of relief, "and I suppose I'll get used to it. Only really, my dear, I didn't need to be put to bed. I could perfectly well have kept up and gotten dinner for us, I'm sure."

"Why, yes, of course you could," smiled the nurse cheerfully. "I told you that when I was putting your nightgown on, don't you remember? You *could* have got up and gone to work, of course, but since I was here

and there really wasn't anything important to do all day but what Bonnie and I could do, it didn't seem worth while, did it? You know, Miss Frannie, I wouldn't have felt comfortable to stay here without doing something to help pay my board," and she gave a merry little twinkle of a wink toward Frannie. "So you see, Bonnie and I got everything fixed up as well as we could without bothering your mother, and just let her have a rest. And then that nice Lady Winthrop sent that lovely lunch over to us, and we certainly were in fine shape to enjoy it. Your mother ate a whole cup of the chicken broth, and we put some in a cup in the tin pail with snow around it, and had enough for her this afternoon when she woke up. She really enjoyed it a lot, didn't you, Mrs. Fernley?"

The mother's eyes assented with a sweet smile.

"How lovely that was, mother," said Frannie, catching the idea of cheerfulness from the nurse. "Wasn't it grand of Mrs. Winthrop to be so thoughtful? You thought we would be so lonely among strangers for a long time, and you were going to miss the dear Bluebell people. But even Bluebell couldn't have been any kinder."

"Yes," said Bonnie who had come upstairs importantly to join in the conversation, "there was hot water bags, and a n'ice bag, and blankets and soup. It was grand!"

The mother lay there looking at her children and smiling almost hopefully now, relaxing on her pillows, realizing after many hard days that someone was caring and helping, and she could lie still and get rested before she had to get up and go on with her troublous life.

"And now, Mrs. Fernley," said Nurse Branner, "what were those things you wanted your daughter to look after when the movers came? They have brought in some of the larger pieces and I did my best to have them placed where you said, but maybe she had better run down and see if everything is just as you planned. I think you've talked long enough for a little while, so you take a nap while she goes, and Bonnie and I will get the kitchen to rights. I saw them bring in the barrel

of dishes and we can rinse them off and get them in the cupboards so we'll be all ready for supper. You shut your eyes and be real rested when the doctor comes back before supper, won't you? I want him to think we've done a good job of nursing you, you know, so you can get up sooner."

"Oh!" said the sick woman with a troubled look. "I really ought to get up now. I'm feeling quite well enough," and she lifted a frail hand and tried to raise herself to her elbow.

But the nurse gave her a soft little push back to her pillow.

"No, you don't pull any tricks like that on me, my lady!" laughed the nurse. "I promised the doctor I'd keep you perfectly quiet in bed until he came back tonight, and I mean to keep my promise or he wouldn't let me nurse for him any longer."

So the nurse puffed the pillows up, drew the blanket a little closer, opened the window just a crack, watched the tired eyelids droop down, and the sick woman's breath come softly, steadily, until she knew she was on the way to sleep again. Then she slipped away to see what Bonnie was doing in the kitchen, and whether the movers were anywhere near through their work.

Chapter 4

DURING THE DAY Marietta had more or less perfected her plans for the defense of her country. After all she would be the one to plan, and she expected it to be an easy matter to bring Val Willoughby to her way of thinking. Of course he hadn't always been easy to move. He never by any chance saw things, even the things of mere play, exactly as she did. But he was polite. She could always count on that. And in things that did not seem to him to matter he always gave in to the lady. He

had been trained that way. Though she could recall times, a few of them, when he had stood out against her in the matter of what he called fair treatment to someone else, even someone whom she disliked very much. He never would consent to let anyone be put out of the game for some trifling matter. He always insisted that one child was as good as another, even if the one was the small meek daughter of the cleaning woman, who had to come along with her mother because there was no place for her to stay alone while her mother was working. Marietta saw no reason for that child to be called into their game, but Val insisted that she should be asked. Val used to be queer that way. He said little Annie was lonely, and he took special pains to teach her how to hide so that she would not be too easily found, how to run to the base when opportunity came. Marietta never had liked that in him. She felt that it somehow took from her some of the prestige that should have been hers. She wanted all the attention herself. She felt it was her due.

Marietta was not unduly proud, though she was well aware that she was beautiful and better dressed than most of the other girls. On the strength of all that she assumed a precedence for herself that gave her the right to rule, to order the lives and goings of her companions, and such menials as should be related to their individual groups. And when an occasion arose in which some unfortunate friend balked her plans, either intentionally or otherwise, Marietta usually dealt out a punishment in the form of cold words and sharp looks; sometimes followed by honeyed forgiveness and restoration to high favor if they were duly repentant.

Val Willoughby formerly was one of her most devoted subjects at the age of ten to twelve years. But advanced prep school and then college had removed him from her immediate neighborhood, and she had had little contact with him of late, except for a few isolated hours now and then when he stopped off on his journeys for a brief visit with his aunt. But now that he had come back to be with his aunt indefinitely, or at least "for the duration," Marietta fully expected to take

over again, and this "defense plan" as she called her scheme of a series of dances, was the first move in that direction. She was therefore greatly annoyed not to be able to get in touch with him at once to make him aware of his part in the activities.

So it was with a deeper frown than mere annoyance would have caused that Marietta turned from the telephone at last and wondered what to do next. She wasn't often balked so fully and so continuously as this. Surely, *surely* Val would come home to dinner presently. She would wait a little longer and call again. Then she interviewed the cook and had their own dinner hour delayed a half hour, just to allow time to get hold of Val.

Meantime Val was helping the Fernley family move in, and watching Frannie as she went capably about, directing the arrangement of furniture, putting dishes and pots and pans away in the cupboards, showing that she had calculated to a nicety just where everything would fit and be convenient.

He watched her gracious young face as she thanked her former neighbors for bringing their goods so safely. She urged them to stay a little while and let her get them some supper before they would begin the long drive back to Bluebell.

"No, Frannie," said the older man speaking for them both, "we gotta get back. I promised mother I'd get back along the edge of dark, and she'll be worrying till we get there. And don't you worry about us. Mother, she put up a lunch for us, and she sent you some of her raisin cookies you like so much. Here they are. I calculate you'll have enough to do to get supper for your own family without any of us added to it, so if you're sure that is all you need we'll just be hurrying right along. We'll be back some day next week with the pianna. Then that's all your things, but don't forget, if you should need anything else of us, don't hesitate to write us, or telephone my son's house and he'll let us know."

So they were gone, and Frannie turned to thank the

young man who had helped her so materially all day.

"You've been just wonderful!" she said again.

"Nothing like that," said he smiling. "I've been having the time of my life. It's fun to help other people get settled. Say, this is going to be a real handy little house, isn't it? I never dreamed there would be so much room here. And now, what do we do next? Don't we have to get supper? And by the way, how did you find your mother?"

"Why, she seemed really bright, although I could see she is still very tired. She has been through an awful beating, it's true, and I suppose we didn't realize what it was doing to her, although I'd been terribly worried about her. But she really is getting a good rest. She went to sleep when the nurse told her, like a tired little child. I'm so thankful for that lovely nurse. I can see she knows how to manage mother. If I'd been here alone with her I'm positive she'd have gotten right up and tried to get supper. But isn't that a car stopping at the door? You don't suppose those men have come back, do you? Perhaps they forgot something."

Willoughby looked out of the side window.

"That's the doctor," he announced. "I'm glad he's come. Now we'll know just how your mother is. I was hoping he would come before I left. Shall I open the door? You know he won't be surprised to see me here. He and I really opened this hospital together this morning, you remember. Come in, Doctor Ransom. This is Miss Fernley."

Frannie looked up to meet the kindly eyes of the old doctor and her heart gave thanks at the instant confidence he gave her.

"Oh, is my mother very sick?" she asked him, her keen young eyes on his face, a sweet wistfulness in her voice.

"Why, I trust not, my dear," assured the hearty voice of the old doctor. "I thought she was doing very well when I was here at noon. How does she seem now? Where is the nurse?"

"She's upstairs with mother. Will you go up? The

movers have just gone. I hope the noise wasn't too much for her!"

The doctor smiled at the anxious young face.

"Why, I don't see why that should harm her," he said. "Suppose we go up and see. I think your mother is simply tired out and needed a little rest. I'm sure she's going to be all right very soon. Val, suppose you wait here till I come down. I want to see you a minute."

"Yes, sir, I'll do that," said Willoughby.

Very quietly the doctor entered the sick room, and Mrs. Fernley's eyes opened instantly, as if his coming were what she had been waiting for even in her sleep. The doctor's presence was like a ray of sunshine in the little room. He came over and sat down on the chair by the bed with a cheery smile.

"Well, little lady," he said, "how are you feeling by now?"

He peered keenly into her eyes, and put a fine soft hand over her wrist with a friendly motion, searching for the pulse which had been so weak that morning. Then he looked up at the nurse and gave an almost imperceptible nod of his head.

"Yes, Nurse, this is a good strong pulse," he said decidedly. "You've done a good job of nursing here to-day. I think this lady will be coming around in a very few days. What do you think?"

The nurse smiled at Frannie.

"Yes, I thought she was getting along nicely," she said happily.

Frannie's heart rose, and her joy was reflected in her happy eyes.

"Oh, I'm so glad!" she breathed. "I was so afraid I should have come home, even though you did send me word it wasn't necessary. I knew those movers were coming, and I knew mother would worry about that."

"Yes, but my dear child, you didn't realize that your mother was too ill at first to worry about anything, except that you should not be disturbed. And then as she got a little rested, there was the nurse, and she didn't take long to get acquainted."

"No, I didn't know all that," murmured Frannie

gravely with a bit of a sigh. "But you see I knew mother, and how used she was to worrying."

The doctor gave her a quick glance of comprehension.

"I see!" he said understandingly. "Well, we must fix it so that she won't do any worrying, at least not for a while."

"Yes," said Frannie with a suddenly troubled look in her eyes. "But that won't be so easy to arrange."

"Oh, I think there'll be a way to arrange that," said the doctor comfortably. "You leave it to me. I'll find a way. Now, nurse, how much of that medicine have you got left? I see. Well, I'll give you something else to go with it."

It was quiet in the room while the doctor was preparing his medicine, and giving now and then a crisp direction to the nurse. Frannie listened with a growing confidence. Then he rose and looked down at the patient.

"Good night, Mrs. Fernley. I hope you will eat a nice little supper, and then go to sleep and sleep until morning. I shall expect to find you greatly improved by morning when I run in again, but remember, if you want to get well quickly you must do just as the nurse says."

"But doctor," said the invalid, "I should have told you. We are really poor people. We can't afford to run up doctor's and nurse's bills. I'm sure I shall not need you again in the morning."

"There, there, my dear, we're not running up bills. This is just a neighborly visit on my way home, so you needn't worry. In fact I like to be good friends with my patients, and I like to run in and get acquainted with them now and then. Now, Nurse Branner, is that all, or do you want to ask any questions?"

He stood a moment at the door talking with the nurse, and Frannie stole near to her mother and softly kissed the frail hand that lay on the pillow.

The mother smiled, and murmured, "I'll be all right, dear child. Don't you worry!"

"No, I won't, mother, if you do just as you are

told. Now I'm going down and hunt some supper for you."

"Just some milk will do," said the mother softly. "Don't go to any trouble for me. I'll be all right."

Frannie kissed her again and stole downstairs after the doctor.

"Don't worry about her supper," said the nurse softly as she passed her at the door. "I saved a cup of that chicken broth for her."

Frannie flashed her a grateful glance and sped on after the doctor, who was standing in the room below with his hand on young Willoughby's shoulder, and a comradely look on his kind, benevolent face. They might have been talking about personal affairs, or business matters, or even political and defense programs, but in reality the doctor was saying:

"My boy, I wonder if I can rely on you to keep me in touch with how things are going in this family. That little mother has gone just about as far as she could go, and not slip over the border entirely. And yet I believe that with reasonable care she can snap out of this trouble entirely and recover her normal health. But there has got to be somebody watching for at least a few days, or maybe even weeks, and so I am hoping they will let the nurse stay here awhile—just as an accommodation to her you know, that is, ostensibly—and keep a watch out. You see it happens most fortunately that Nurse Branner has just come off a year's case. And the people with whom she formerly boarded have suddenly gone to California. Of course we would take her into our home if necessary, but my wife's sister and her daughter are with us this winter, and it makes it a little crowded to take in another at present, so she has really been expecting to look for a new abiding place. But she is enough of a Christian, and enthusiastic enough as a nurse, to get interested here and stay awhile, as long as she is needed. So the matter of money does not need to come into the picture at all. So then, could I depend on you, Val, to see what you can do with the family to see this thing straight, at least until the mother is out of

danger? I know you haven't much time, but are you so situated that you could run over here early in the morning and then phone me how things are, so that I won't have to leave home until after my office hours are over? They ought to have a telephone here, but of course that can't be done tonight, and I ought to be in a position to get word from the nurse early. Can you do that?"

"I can," said Willoughby with a pleasant ring to his voice. "I'll be glad to help in any way I can. I think they are unusual people."

"Yes, you're right, my boy. Well, thank you. I'll be depending on you," and with a smile of reassurance at Frannie the doctor strode out to his car and was soon driving away.

But as Frannie and Val lingered for a moment watching him, another car drew up before the house and stopped. It was a big, old-fashioned car with plenty of room, a shining exterior, and an old lady sitting on the back seat alone.

The chauffeur helped the old lady out, and she started up the walk.

"Why, Val Willoughby!" she said. "I wondered if you would happen to turn up around here again. That's nice. You can introduce me to my new neighbors, can't you?"

The young man came quickly to her side and offered his arm.

"I surely can, Lady Winthrop. I'll be delighted. This is Frances Fernley. I think they call her Frannie. She is the young lady, I believe, whom you have admired so much, skating down the river."

Frannie looked up surprised, and flashed a shy smile at the old lady.

"And you are the wonderful neighbor that came to our assistance when my mother was taken sick, aren't you?" said Frannie. "I've heard all about you and I'm so glad to be able to thank you. I know my mother will want to thank you herself as soon as she is able to see anybody. Won't you come in? We're not really in order

yet. Our things have just come. I don't know what we would have done without those blankets you sent, so few of our own came in the first load. And the hot water bags! And the food! I was so relieved when I heard you had sent my mother that wonderful chicken soup."

The old lady held the girl's soft hand in a warm clasp.

"You dear child!" she said. "I was so glad to know of something I could do. And your dear little sister! Is she all right? I was so afraid she would take cold going out across that awful ice without a coat."

Then Bonnie appeared smiling.

"I'm all right," she said shyly. "That soup and chicken you sent over were just *grand!*"

"Were they, my dear?" said the old lady with a pleased smile. "Well, I've brought you some things for supper. One couldn't be expected to get meals when there is sickness going on, and moving too. Here, Joseph, are you bringing the basket?"

"Yes, Madam, I'm right here!" said the old serving man walking up behind her. "Shall I just take it inside to the kitchen?"

"Oh, yes. Bonnie, you show him the way to the kitchen. And now I'll sit down for a minute so I will feel I know you, and then I must go." Lady Winthrop dropped into a big chair by the door, and looked around her smiling, taking in every little detail without in the least seeming to do so.

"This is a very attractive house," she said. "I can't see it well from my windows, but I think it might be very lovely in the summer. You'll need some vines. I have plenty of ivy slips. If you want them in the spring I'll send them over. I think a brick house always looks lovely with English ivy growing over it."

"Oh, we would love to have that," said Frannie eagerly, "and I know mother would be delighted. The only objection she made to the house was that it looked so bare and stark. Mother loves trees and vines and flowers."

"Well, that's interesting. I'm sure she and I will

have a lot in common. Only I'm not able to go out and work among my flowers any more. I had a fall and it left some of my joints and muscles rather stiff and balky, though Joseph knows how I like the garden, and he fixes it the way I used to have it. But soon the spring will be coming again and you can see it for yourself. Do you like flowers?"

"Oh, I love them," said Frannie with eagerness in her eyes. "Mother used to have an old-fashioned garden up in the country where we've been since father died, and it was lovely. Mother seems to know just how to make flowers grow. She charms them into bloom."

"Well, I want to get acquainted with her just as soon as she is better. And now, my dear, I think I had better go, because I want you to eat that supper while it is nice. I want your mother to have that milk toast right away while it is still hot. It's well covered in a hot dish, and the nurse will understand how to fix it. I put in a couple of little bags of tea lest you hadn't had time to go to the store yet. Well, good-by dear, and don't you worry. *You* can't afford to get sick, you know, not till your mother is well anyway. Now, Val, are you coming with me? I want to talk to you a few minutes. How would you like to eat dinner with me? It was all ready to put on the table when I came away, and I told the cook I might bring you back with me if you were here. It won't take you any longer to eat with me than if you went home, and I won't hinder you if you want to leave immediately after we finish."

"Why, delightful! Of course I'll come," said the young man.

Then he cast a quick look and smile toward Frannie.

"Are you sure you don't need me for anything before I go?"

"Oh, no," said Frannie shyly. "You've been wonderful. I couldn't think of troubling you any longer. And really there's nothing more to be done."

"All right, good night then, and I'll be seeing you in the morning. You heard me promise the doctor. And besides, if you are planning to skate down we might as

well keep each other company, if you don't mind. It looks as if the weather was going to be all right for the ice at least for another day or two. Good night."

Frannie stood at the door a moment and watched the big car swing away up the road to the bridge. There was a warm feeling around her heart. How nice and pleasant they all were! How glad she was for their friendship. How nice it had been for the young man to protect her down at the plant, and come home with her. And how he had helped the movers.

She went into the house with a smile on her lips and hurried out to the kitchen to investigate the big basket that had been left there. She found Bonnie and the nurse already there looking at it.

What nice things they found in that basket! Milk toast made out of homemade bread, light as a feather, browned just right, and with that delicious cream dressing over it, piping hot.

The nurse had the cup of tea already made, and they lost no time in conveying it to the invalid, who ate hungrily, appreciatively, and dropped sweetly to sleep soon after.

Down at the dining room table, which Bonnie had been setting to the best of her ability, the three sat and ate the meal that had been prepared for them. Broiled chops, enough to have some left over for the next day, chopped creamed potatoes cooked to perfection, spinach and peas, a dish of applesauce and a small delicious custard pie. How good everything tasted, and how grateful they all were!

"And now," said the nurse, assuming charge of the little household, "you two girls run upstairs and make up your bed. I didn't know where to find the sheets or I would have done it. Don't worry about me. I've taken that cot the movers brought and put it in your mother's room. If you've got an extra blanket and quilt or something just lay them out and I'll be fixed fine. I want to watch your mother and give her the medicine through the night, you know. And you girls ought to get to bed right away. You said you had to start early in the morning, Frannie, and there'll be breakfast to get.

I saw some cereals among your stores on the pantry shelf. Would you like me to start some oatmeal? You ought to have a good hot breakfast, Frannie, before you go to work. I can start it while I wash up these few dishes. And I'll squeeze a little orange juice, too. I see there are some oranges here."

"That will be lovely, Miss Branner. But I could do all that," said Frannie.

"No, we'll work together," smiled the nurse. "Run along and get that bed ready."

So in a very short time Nurse Branner had martialed the little household into bed, and except for a dim night light in the sickroom the little house beside the silver way was in darkness, until late that night when the old moon dropped over the brow of the hill, and reaching down for a brief space gilded the edges of the mossy roof, and glinted for a few flashing seconds from the window panes behind the gaunt hemlock tree.

The weary little family who slept behind those modest old brick walls felt great content at the refuge they had found, deep gratitude to the God who had provided it for them, and dreamed pleasant dreams of a comfortable future.

But out on the dark frozen river there stalked two figures. One, a tall man in a warm sumptuous overcoat, furred to his chin, hands in his pockets, rubber shod, had his hat drawn over his eyes. The other was short and thick set in a heavy sheepskin-lined windbreaker, rough shoes spotted with plaster, and a soft hat that had seen many years of service.

"There it is," said the tall man, "right behind that line of houses. As neat a piece of land as you could get for the job. And I should think it ought to be had for a song. The house is just ready to drop down anyway. But suppose they won't sell."

"Oh, they'll sell all right," said the other, commonly known as Mike.

"But there's somebody living there, isn't there? I'm sure I see a light. A blue light."

"Only renters," said Mike. "I seen 'em move in last week. Only had one truck load of stuff as far as I could

see. They might even be only squatters. I don't think they're anything to worry about, Mr. Granniss. It would be dead easy to drive 'em out."

"Not if they have a contract. You couldn't do a thing if they have."

"Oh, they wouldn't have a contract. Not plain folks like that. And besides, if they have, it would be dead easy to get the house condemned, and then the owner would have to tear it down, and he'd be glad enough to take what's offered him, in a case like that."

"H'm! I see!" said Granniss. "Well you go ahead, Mike, and see what you can do about it. It certainly would be a convenient place for our powder plant, right on the river and all. I suppose perhaps there might be a kick from some of those grand residents across the river, who think they own the earth with a gold fence around it, having a powder plant so near, but they wouldn't be able to do a thing about it of course after we had bought it. Don't let a word get out about this, Mike, till we get it all settled."

"That goes without sayin', Boss. And you wouldn't have trouble with those swells over there anyhow. They're too far off. And besides, they don't even look over across the river. They wouldn't touch one of those people on the other side with a ten foot pole. They're too snooty. But say, Boss, did you take notice to them new houses going up on our side? They'd be just the place for our workers to live. And only two of 'em is rented, so far. That'd mean you could house your workers right off the bat after you got your plant built, and that don't take any time at all these days."

"That's so, Mike! Well, suppose we walk over past the brick house, and get a little closer so we can see it better. And we'd better not talk while we go by. Some one might hear us and report on us. You can't even trust a sleeping woodchuck these days. Then we'll get back to my car and go get some sleep. Meantime you get in touch with your owner. Better do it by long distance phone. This thing has got to be settled at once if it is going to be any good to me. And tomorrow

night, same time, same place, you'll find me. Let me know how you come out."

"Okay!"

Then the two figures shuffled silently across the river, and up nearer to the river bank, even pausing a moment at the very steps where Frannie had sat to take off her skates, and looked up at the house a moment. The house with the blue light in the upper front window, and the silver edges to the old mossy roof. Then they turned and shuffled away to the car that was parked on a side street back of the half-finished houses, higher up the hill.

Chapter 5

VAN WILLOUGHBY WENT to supper with Madam Winthrop. He had always admired her, even from a child, and he felt that what she had done for these stranger-neighbors was a beautiful act. She was going to be a good friend to the newcomers, and somehow he was very glad of that. For some unanalyzed reason he had taken a deep interest in these Fernleys himself. He hadn't thought it through for himself yet, but he was glad they would have such a friend as this gentlewoman. Moreover she had two sons whom he used to admire, both older than himself. He must find out about them, where they were and what they were doing. So he accepted her invitation with alacrity. He was too late for the formal dinner at his aunt's house anyway, and might as well enjoy himself. And it wouldn't be necessary for him to let his aunt know. She understood that he often had to stay late at the plant, and would not have waited dinner for him.

The dinner was delicious of course. All Hannah's dinners were. And they lingered talking for a long time.

Lady Winthrop was telling of incidents of her sons' experiences in camp, telling where she *thought* they were located now, and how she wasn't sure just when or where they would be moved. They spoke briefly of the terrible things that were beginning to happen over the world, of the possibilities if the war should come nearer, the safety regulations.

"We have a wonderful storm cellar, of course," said the old lady. "Not that we've ever used it for storms in our time. The grandfather who built the house came from the west where they had so many tornadoes, and he insisted on a storm cellar. So, in a way, I suppose we are prepared for raids. I had them come and inspect the foundations and they are solidly reinforced. So I've had supplies taken down there, in case there should be a need. Of course I don't suppose a quiet country house like this would be the object of a raid, but I thought we might be able to help others who have no refuge. And I've provided rolled up black shades which can be quickly adjusted for a sudden blackout. I think we must comply with the requests of those in charge of course, but it is hard to realize that such terrible things could actually come to our peaceful land."

"Yes, that's right. It surely is," said the young man seriously. "It doesn't seem possible that such a state of the universe can possibly fit in with the Creator's scheme of things for the world, either, does it? But perhaps He's just disgusted with us all and has given us over to do our own ways. Weren't there some old fellows in the Bible times who had to have a lesson to teach them how they had abused their privileges? I don't really know much about such things, but lately when I've been spending my days planning instruments of punishment for our enemies, I've been wondering what God thinks of it all. I guess my mother's way of teaching me when I was a kid has made me think such thoughts. What do you think about it all, Lady Winthrop? You used to know my mother, and I have a kind of memory that she thought you were the best Christian she knew. Have you reasoned it all out?"

"Why, no, not *reasoned* it out exactly. I never was

enough of a Bible student to do that. I think it is better just to *trust* it out. I believe God has it all planned though and there's a reason for everything that happens. Some of it undoubtedly must be warning to sinners if not actual punishment for unbelief."

"But there are a lot of good people suffering through this war, aren't there? How do you account for it that God lets so many of what you would call real believers suffer? Do you mean you think some of those who *seem* to be such good people are really sinners in secret?"

"Oh, no, I didn't mean that. Though there might be some of course. But don't you remember the story of the blind man when you went to Sunday School? Don't you remember how the disciples asked the Lord, 'Did this man sin, or his parents, that he was born blind?' And you remember the Lord's answer, 'Neither hath this man sinned, nor his parents; but that the works of God should be made manifest in him.' "

"You mean," said Willoughby, his eyes bright with thoughtfulness, "that perhaps this war is in some way going to show that God is working through it all? Going to show that God isn't dead, and hasn't forgotten?"

"Yes, I think it may be something like that. God is using these evil nations and their ungodliness, and hatred, and especially their hatred of His chosen people, the Jews, to show the world that He means all He has said in the Bible. And I think we are going to discover pretty soon that everything that is happening in the world, all that is in the newspapers, and on the radio every day, has been written long ago in detail, in the Bible."

"You don't mean it!" exclaimed Willoughby. "Do you mean to say that the Bible has anything to say about this present war? About the things that are going on all over the world today?"

"Why of course. Didn't you know that? We have a wonderful class that meets here once a week and we've been studying about that."

"I'd like to come and hear about it," said the young man. "Would that be permissible?"

"Wonderful!" said the old lady with sweet satisfac-

tion on her face. "I've been wishing we could get some of the young people to come, for I know they would be interested if they could just hear even a few minutes of it. It is fascinating."

"That's great. Surely I'll come. If there is anything in the Bible that shows God is aware of this awful war I would like to know about it. You know, Mrs. Winthrop, I think this war business has made us all think more seriously about what we're here for."

"Well, maybe that is one of the good things about the war then," smiled the old lady. "They say so many of the young people are just going on gaily as if life was all a game, and had no end. I'm glad if a few of them are beginning to think. I knew my boys were, but they are older than you are."

"Yes, they are older and they are doing great things in the service. I only wish I could be over there where they are."

"Don't say that, Val. You are probably just where the Lord meant you to be. You're doing most valuable work where you are. I just heard about your plant today. Mr. Strong, the head of the committee for war plants, told me that your plant is one of the most valuable in the country, and they were especially favored in having a young man in as responsible a position as you are, who had your training and ability. He felt you were doing far more there than you could have done in any other capacity, and I was proud to say that I knew you."

"Oh, thank you, dear lady. That means a lot to me. It's almost like having my mother send me commendation, because I know you were her friend, and she honored and loved you."

Presently she took her caller into the library and showed him some letters and pictures her sons had sent her, and then some of the books on prophecy that her class had been studying.

"That one is written by a friend of our teacher," she said. "He has made quite a study of prophecy, and I think he is one of the most fascinating writers we have. Take it along with you and read it if you like. I've

finished reading it. Do you have any time to read?"

"Well, a little, now and then, when I'm not too late coming home at night," he said taking the book and opening it interestedly. "Thank you. I'd like to read it. It looks interesting."

"Oh, it is!" said the old lady enthusiastically.

And so, while Marietta over in her own home, ate a belated dinner, and hovered uneasily near the telephone until it was time to go to an engagement, waiting and expecting Val to call her, Willoughby was discussing prophecy and war probabilities with a lovely lady four times Marietta's age, and enjoying every minute of it. Before Val went home they talked a little about the new people who had come to reside in the plain little brick house across the ice, and what could be done for them.

"You and the daughter came home together, didn't you? You both skated home, didn't you? Do you know, I was watching for you although I didn't know that that girl was the Fernley one. I never saw where she came from before, only noticed her as she went skimming by, and admired her. She seems quite an attractive little thing, doesn't she? Was she much worried by the news you brought her?"

"Yes, she was," said the young man. "She wanted to drop everything and hurry right home, until I finally made her understand that the doctor did not think it necessary, and had promised to telephone at noon just how things were, and that her mother was very insistent that she should not be told lest she would think she had to come home and perhaps lose her job. Her boss was very kind and offered to let her go at once, but that seemed to bring her to her senses, and she braced up and stayed. She seems to be a girl with a good deal of character."

"Yes," said the old lady. "Of course I only saw her a short time, but she impressed me as being very sweet besides being pretty. I do hope her mother will soon get well. That little Bonnie is a darling child, but she's too young to be left alone with an invalid. I'm glad the nurse is there."

"Yes," said Willoughby, "they certainly need her.

But I'm not so sure they will keep her long. I think even now they see through the excuse that she needs a place to stay, and they are very proud. But I guess they cannot afford to pay nurses' prices."

"Well, there'll probably be a way to work it out till she is better, and in the meantime they'll get very much attached to that nurse. She's rather wonderful, you know."

"Don't I know! She nursed me once, and she's swell! But say, is that clock right? Don't tell me I've stayed here all the evening, wasting all your time! I ought to be hanged at dawn. But I've enjoyed every minute of it, and I hope you'll let me come again sometime."

"I certainly will, and I hope you'll come often. Though when you get really settled down to this part of the country again I expect there'll be so many girl-rivals that I shan't see much of you," smiled Lady Winthrop. "But I shall cherish the memory of this evening, anyway."

"Girls?" said the young man with an indifferent shrug, "don't worry! I don't waste much time with them. That little skating girl today is about the most sensible one I've seen since I was a kid. But I don't believe she has time to use socially, and she might not care for my society if she did. She's a most independent little lady. Besides, she lives on the other side of the river, and when the ice is gone that makes a wide barrier for people who haven't much time to themselves these strenuous days."

"Well, that river was anything but a barrier today. I don't know what would have happened if that child hadn't crossed the ice. Not many of those houses near them are inhabited yet."

"That's true," said Val, "I was thinking myself how none of that today could have happened if the river hadn't been frozen."

"Yes," said the old lady with a soft little contemplative sigh, "it's a great river! I call it my street. It has always reminded me of the words 'And the street of the city'—the Heavenly city, you know, 'was pure gold,

as it were transparent glass.' And evenings when the sun is setting I always think of the 'sea of glass mingled with fire.' "

"Say, that's beautiful, Lady Winthrop! I feel I am greatly privileged to know you."

"There, young man, don't go to imagining I am anything unusual. It's just some fanciful ideas that came to me from time to time when I was reading my Bible, or looking at my river. They are not my ideas at all, just a sort of vision the Father gave me. Perhaps I should have kept them to myself. But I'm alone so much I get to thinking out loud."

"Heavenly thoughts!" said Val in a grave sweet voice. "I shall like to catch the vision with you. I'll be thinking of that when I go skating down your 'street of the city.' Well, now I must go home! Do you see what time it is? You are more fascinating than any people I know —Around here, anyway."

And after he was gone the old lady stood thoughtfully a moment looking at the chair where he had sat.

"Nice boy!" she said softly. "Almost like one of my own. I wonder if he will really ever come to a Bible class. Maybe just once. He's very polite. He might think that necessary. Well, he's a nice boy, anyway. And how he has fitted into the need of the day! I hope he comes to see me often."

Meantime Marietta was making another angry attempt to reach Valiant Willoughby. He heard the violent ringing of the telephone as he unlocked the front door of his aunt's house, and no one seemed to be answering it. The servants must have retired, and his aunt was out on one of her endless committees which had succeeded her former endless bridge parties.

He stepped over to the telephone and his clear impersonal voice came like a draught of ice water to Marietta's angry spirit.

"Yes?" he said.

"Well, for pity's sake! Are you actually there at last, Val Willoughby! Where on earth have you been keeping yourself all day and all the evening? I've fairly been driven to call out the police to search for you."

"Oh, it's Marietta, isn't it?" he said amusedly.

"It certainly is. Did no one tell you? I left messages that you were to call me the minute you came in."

"Well, I just this minute entered the door, and came immediately to the telephone. Is there something I can do for you?"

"Yes, there certainly is. In the first place I invited you to take dinner with me. I had something to talk over with you. Something quite important. Do you always stay as late as this at the plant?"

"No, not always," said Willoughby. He was not one who told all that he had been doing to everyone who asked.

"But do you mean that they actually keep you at the plant till all hours of the day or night? I think that's outrageous. Something ought to be done about it!"

"No, not usually. Not unless there is something important to keep me there," he said. "I'm sorry about the dinner invitation, but as it happened I had another invitation to dinner, and I didn't come home at all until just now. But what else was it you wanted of me, Marietta? You know I'm not my own master all the time now, and can't be depended upon to be always at home at my usual hours."

"Well, that's absurd! You can't be a slave to your work. You've got to have a little time for yourself. I think you ought to make a stand for that. If you don't *I'll* have to get to work. I happen to know some of the head men interested in that plant of yours and I shall certainly tell them what I think of the way they are treating you."

"Listen, Marietta, you'll do no such thing, do you hear? I'm in no need of your fine official hand in my affairs. I know what I am doing, and these are strenuous days you know. This is no time for a man to baby himself and cry out for playtime when the world is at war. My work has to do with government defense."

"Well, so has *mine*," said Marietta loftily. "And that's why I want your help. I know you are utterly loyal to our America, and would be a grand one to take hold of this plan of mine, and help me make it a great

success. It's quite an important matter, and I want to talk it all over with you and get ready tonight to start right in and do something really worthwhile."

"Well, Marietta, that sounds very interesting of course, and it would probably be interesting to work with you, but I really couldn't promise to get into anything that involves much time or thought. I'm *busy*, Marietta and can't count on my hours at all. What is this scheme of yours, and just how do you want my help?"

"Oh, I can't tell you over the phone, Val," said the girl impatiently. "Can't you come over *now* and I can outline it for you? I don't want to waste any more time."

"Now! Why girl alive! Do you know what time it is?"

"Oh, what difference does that make? We've stayed up much later than this at parties, many a time!"

"Not me, lady! I never was one of those late birds. My work means a lot to me and I have to be early at the plant tomorrow morning!"

"Now Val, don't be stuffy! Come on over now, this minute. It won't take so long for me to explain, and I'll have a nice little snack for you to eat while we're talking. Good eats and good drinks. Come on! An hour or two longer won't make any difference in the long run."

"I couldn't do it, Marietta. I'm a working man and have to save my best faculties for my job."

"Now Val! I didn't think you'd stand me up that way! I tell you this is important work. It's for the good of your country!"

The young man was silent for an instant, considering.

"What's the nature of your scheme," he said. "What is it you are so anxious for me to do?"

"Why it's a perfectly wonderful scheme for raising money and furnishing entertainment for the soldiers in camp. It's something I know you can do. I've practically got the thing all thought out, and if you'll just run over a few minutes I won't keep you long."

"Nothing doing, lady," said Val. "I've got to be in

my little bed within the next ten minutes. And I wouldn't have time for raising money and getting up entertainment. Sounds childish to me. What do you mean, get up games for the soldiers? Seems to me they ought to have brains enough to get up their own games."

"No it's not that, Val! Don't be stupid! It's to do some really serious planning to have a steady income for such things. You see I'm planning to get up a series of dances for the younger set, with a few of us older young folks to sort of sponsor and chaperone them. I just know it could be made popular among the young crowd, and we'd get a lot of money. Of course we'd make them pay a good price for their tickets. And it would be awfully popular among their parents if you and I and a few others of the really solid set of young people were sponsoring it. You were always popular everywhere, and just your being in the scheme would give it a boom right off at the start. The kids would be crazy to join it and there would be enough of our own set to have really a good time for *us*. Don't you see? While we are carrying on something worth-while for the younger ones, helping *them* to do defense work, too, you know. And *you*, Val, you need something really restful and relaxing once a week at least."

"Hold up a minute, Marietta. Do I understand that you are proposing a series of dances once a week for which I should be partly responsible? Well, right at the beginning, lady, *nothing doing!* I never was interested in dances in my life, and I don't propose to stop my man-sized job now and start in playing with kids. Seriously, Marietta, you don't seem to know what this war is about."

"Oh, now Val, you don't really understand. Do come over a few minutes and I'll make you see what a perfectly swell plan it is."

"Not possibly, Marietta. You'll have to excuse me now. My time is up and I'll have to hang up. Sorry to disappoint you, but you picked the wrong man for a thing like that. I've grown up since you and I used to play prisoner's base, and fight who should be allowed in. Good night, Marietta. See you sometime soon for a

few minutes when I get a chance, but I can't say just when it will be."

Valiant Willoughby hung up the receiver and went upstairs with a bound. Was Marietta really as silly as she sounded? What had life done to her? Was she as much of a snob as she used to be, or had she acquired a semblance of courtesy? Her voice didn't sound like it, but maybe he was mistaken. He really would have to run over some time and renew his acquaintance. But, how would she compare with that little girl he had brought home tonight? Getting herself a difficult responsible job; going there on skates; fighting her way against those two bullies; coming home to take the responsibilities of a family upon her frail young shoulders. Marietta: well educated, rich, not a responsibility in the world, and all she could think of to help her country's necessity was to get up a series of dances, where she could have a good time among her kind. Bah! Well, maybe he was misjudging her. He would go and see her sometime and give her a chance to prove herself, whether she was worth-while.

And then the very next afternoon about closing time she appeared on the scene at the street door of his plant, in her gorgeous sport car, wearing becoming furs of sable, her gold hair in a long sleek bob with the ends duly curved in the latest twirl. She sent a boy to Willoughby's office to say that she had come to take him home, and would he please come out to the car *at once!* She wanted to see him about something important.

Chapter 6

BUT VALIANT WILLOUGHBY had just gone out the back way and was hurrying up the frozen river to the plant where Frannie worked. He didn't intend she should run any further risks tonight.

And so while Marietta waited impatiently for the office boy from the front office to go all over the plant hunting for Willoughby, he was kneeling on the ice fastening Frannie's skates, and hadn't even seen the beautiful vision in her sport car who had set all the office boys around the place agog with envy of "the young boss." At last the boy came back apologetically and said they couldn't find Mr. Willoughby. They thought he must have stepped out somewhere.

"But that's the same tale you had for me yesterday when I called him on the telephone," said Marietta impatiently. "Isn't he *ever* here?"

"Why, yes ma'am. He works here. That is, he's all over the place usually. We never know just where to put a finger on him. He's been here all day, more or less. He just keeps track of every worker under him and never gives you a break if you get tired or lazy. He's right on the job. But you know a fella can't just do that and be in one spot all the time. For after all he's the young boss. He *works,* you know."

Marietta stared at the youth who had a comical grin in one corner of his mouth. She couldn't believe that just a common workman was capable of sarcasm, but somehow it sounded that way, almost the way Val had sounded last night. Well, there was such a thing as being almost too patriotic, perhaps. Certainly Valiant Willoughby was taking his obligations seriously. She must do something about this.

"I'll wait," she said resignedly, and sat back luxuriously. "As soon as he comes in you tell him I'm here," she added crisply.

"Okay!" said the youth with a polite grin, and bounded up the steps to the office.

So Marietta sat in her car, the admired of all the workers from all the shifts as they came forth from building after building. She even carried on a mild flirtation with a couple of the young fellows she knew who lived in her neighborhood and were filling in the time until they were called to the army or navy by taking a temporary job.

"Doesn't this place ever shut down for the night?" she asked them petulantly.

"Shut?" they exclaimed in a breath. "I should say not! Nothing shuts down any more. Didn't you know that, Marietta? This country has gone mad on work. We work when we ought to be sleeping, and we sleep when we ought to be working, and when we get almost used to that they lay us off. I suppose that's good for our moral characters, but somehow I can't see it. What are you waiting for? The young boss? Well, he's hard to find. You know there are times when he works all night as well as all day. He's a kind of superman, you know. But I think he went home early tonight. I heard him asking one of his subs to take over for him while he went somewhere. I don't believe he's coming back tonight. You might as well call it a day and quit. But I'll tell him in the morning that you were here for him. That is if I can get speech with him. He's a hound for work. He doesn't hang around much talking."

So at last Marietta decided to take the two young men to their homes and then stop at the Haversett house, hoping to find the lost Willoughby there.

But Valiant Willoughby was putting up curtains for Frannie Fernley, and hadn't turned up at his home yet. And though she waited until after time for her Red Cross class, he did not come. She began to wonder on her frantic way to her class, if by chance this could be intention and her old playmate could be evading her? But she didn't really think that seriously, for she had a fairly good opinion of herself and her charms, and would find it hard to believe that any young man would not be glad to go with her anywhere.

Frannie hadn't seen anything of her two tormentors at the plant that day, and as she was intimate with none of her fellow-workers she heard nothing of them. Besides, they were employed on another floor from the one where she worked, so she did not know that they were both at home nursing black eyes and bruises. And she was so well cared for that she had no fears of a repetition of their annoyances.

"You really mustn't go out of your way to look after me," she protested when she saw Willoughby come sailing up as she came out of the lower door with her skates in her hand. "I truly am not afraid of those boys. I haven't seen anything of them all day. I think they had enough yesterday."

"Yes? Well, I hope they retain that impression," said the young man. "It's just as well they should see you have friends who will protect you."

"Thank you! That's awfully kind of you," said Frannie, "but you know you can't go around being a daily nursemaid to me. An utter stranger! And of course I must learn to fight my own battles!"

"Well, it was very evident yesterday that you are quite able to do that, but I don't want those hoodlums to think you're entirely on your own. So now for a few days while this ice lasts we might as well take the trip together."

On the way they talked about the war, and about Frannie's life.

"You've been to college," said the young man, giving her a quick look when she spoke of classes in some advanced studies.

"Yes, I had a year and a half till father died, and then we came to this part of the world and I had to hunt a job."

There was just the breath of a sigh on the girl's lips, but there was no cloud in her eyes.

"You didn't mind?" he asked.

"Why, yes, I minded. But it couldn't be helped of course, and I was only too glad to be in shape to work. I had to take care of my family, you know. Mother wanted to work and make me stay at college of course, but she wasn't well enough. As it was she wore herself all out taking care of grandmother. That's why I wanted to get them down here where I would be near them and could see that mother took it easy."

"That was pretty plucky of you," said Valiant pleasantly. "But you must look out now that you don't work too hard," he warned. "You can't afford to get sick, at least not till your mother gets well."

"Oh, no, I won't work too hard. Why, you ought to see the way Nurse Branner watches over me. She made us all go to bed last night the minute supper was over and the few dishes washed. And she made oatmeal for us. She's great! I wish we could afford to keep her on for awhile. But of course I know we couldn't, even if we had a lot of money. She's an important nurse. Other people need her."

"Yes, I suppose she is," said Willoughby. "But she'll be there for a little while, anyway, the doctor said, and that will help. You haven't much more to do to get settled, have you?"

"Why, no, not so much. We're going to put the curtains up tonight and a few pictures, and then we'll feel like living. The rest can be done a little at a time, or not at all if we don't want to."

"Ah! I see! That's where I come in. I was wondering where I could work into the picture."

And so, in spite of her protests, Val walked into the little brick house, saluted the nurse who appeared in the kitchen door smiling, and said, "Now, bring on your curtains! I'm the man they sent up from the interior decorators to put up draperies and hang pictures."

"Well, Mr. Willoughby, that's nice," said the nurse. "Frannie says the windows are all washed. It certainly will be fine to have your help. You've got such nice long arms. But how about sitting down with us and having a little bite of supper first? I made some soup this afternoon, and it's grand and tasty if I do say so as shouldn't. Doesn't it smell good? Carrots and onions and barley and potatoes, and tender meat from the soup bone. It's cooked all the afternoon."

"Well that's great!" said the young man. "I'm hungry as a bear. The menu sounds very alluring."

"Better sit down now," said Miss Branner. "Everything is ready to put on the table. You sit here, Mr. Willoughby, and Frannie, you take the head of the table and pour the coffee."

It was good soup, and Val Willoughby was hungry. So was Frannie. Such a pleasant, friendly, merry time they had eating it, just as if they had known one another

for years. And then there was a luscious apple pie, and delicious cheese they had brought from the country.

When the nurse went upstairs to take the sick woman her tray and settle her for the night, the two young people jumped up and began to clear the table.

"Oh, but you mustn't do this," said Frannie in horror, as she saw the young man gathering up the dishes in an orderly manner as if he had been doing it all his life.

"And why not, I'd like to know," said Val, fitting the four plates neatly together, gathering the silver by itself. "Haven't I eaten here, and should I not help to put things back into place? You see I want to get at those curtains right away, and we can't do that until our consciences are free from these dishes. Is this the dish pan? I'll wash and you dry and put them away, for I don't know where they belong."

"But truly, you don't need to do this. There aren't many, and I can do them in no time after the curtains are up."

"Yes, but that's exactly what I don't want you to have to do. You see I'm concerned about you, all you went through yesterday, and then going to work so early again today. How did you get through the day? Weren't you all shaken up? You're such a little thing, and you took quite a beating from those two boys you know. And I wasn't at all sure you wouldn't have more trouble with them today. They are not the kind who give up a fight. Don't relax your vigilance. They'll try to catch you unawares. They may lie low for a while though, for it's my opinion that one of them had a pretty good case of black eye and wouldn't want to appear in public, not for a while, if you ask me."

"I hate to be the cause of any workman losing time," said Frannie with a troubled look.

"They deserved it," said Val, setting his lips in a stern line.

And so they worked together and soon had all the dishes washed and put away. Then Frannie produced the curtains.

They went to work chattering pleasantly, getting well acquainted and feeling like old friends.

And there went another day when Marietta couldn't find her old playmate to take dinner with her. Even though she had gone to the plant to find him, and then called up the Haversett house. Strange, she thought. He hadn't been at home to dinner for two nights. She would certainly have to go and have it out with Auntie Haversett, for she was determined to get Val to help her with her plans.

But Val was showing his skill at putting up curtain rods, and advising about which curtains would fit best in certain places. He was really having a good time at it. This little girl he was helping was so much in need of help, and so utterly free from superficial airs and graces that he felt the atmosphere was just easy, pleasant, unrestricted. He hadn't thought of Marietta since he talked with her on the telephone the night before. He assumed that she had gone elsewhere for help. Marietta was seldom at a loss to find somebody to kowtow to her beauty and her father's wealth.

About that time out on the ice two figures walked again with their eyes toward the little brick house.

"Well, how did you make out, Mike?" asked the tall man whose name was Granniss. "Get in touch with the owner?"

"No, not yet. He's gone west on business. May be back tomorrow or next day, they weren't sure."

"M-m-m! Well, we haven't any time to spare, Mike."

"I know sir. I tried to find out the man's address. I meant to wire him, or find out what train he might be on, but nothing doing. Nobody knew where he'd gone or what for. But they said his brother-in-law was coming home tomorrow and he might know, so I'll try again tomorrow."

"Better make it snappy, Mike, for I got wind of another place I might get if this one fails."

"I'll do me best, Granniss, devils can't do no more you know," and Mike snickered apologetically.

"Yes, I know, but you've got to do better than any

devil if you want to work for me, Mike. Understand?"

"Okay," said Mike sullenly, and tried to think what he should offer next as an alibi.

"Say!" said Granniss. "Isn't that the house over there where that light just went on in the front room? Why, there's a man standing up at the window doing something to a curtain. I thought you said there weren't any men in the family, just two women. I thought you said that was the reason we wouldn't have any trouble working this racket."

"I didn't hear of no man there," said Mike. "Mebbe it's just some workman they hired."

"If they are poor people as you thought, they wouldn't hire a man to put up their curtains, would they? They'd put them up themselves."

"That's right," said Mike, perplexed. "Well, mebbe it's some neighbor, or the grocery boy or something. Mebbe it's some man works at the plant where the girl works."

"That's bad," said Granniss, "her making friends so soon. We don't want any man in on this, not if we're going to carry it through quickly. A man might block things and hold us up."

"Well, I couldn't say who he is. I never heard about any man. Mebbe some more of them movers come back to bring something."

"Well, there's no time to waste," said Granniss determinedly. "It seems to me you could have found that owner somehow, or his agent. I don't believe you half tried."

"Say, looka here! I guess it's as much to me as it is to you to get this thing started quick."

"Okay. See you get a hustle on and get some action. I ought to have things under way by the end of this week."

The two men drifted by on the far side of the river, and when they finally turned to go back again, the front room of the little brick house was dark, and a skater shot by them and disappeared into the shadows up-river, but the memory of a man putting up window

curtains in the distance stayed in the minds of those
two men as they went on to find their parked car, and
caused the man Granniss to call to the other as he left
him that night:

"You make sure you find out something about that
lease, even if you have to go to the owner's office and
pump his office boy, or his secretary, for information.
There's always a way to find out things if you just
know enough to pave your way with a little dough. I've
surely given you enough to use that way, and I want it
used! Understand, Mike?"

"Okay!" said Mike heartily.

Val Willoughby got back to his aunt's home a little
after ten o'clock, and was presently called to the telephone by the butler who was still on duty. Again it was
Marietta's indignant voice that challenged him.

"What's the idea?" she demanded haughtily. "Are
you trying to avoid me? Here I've spent another whole
evening racing after you. I even went so far as to drive
down after you at the plant at what I judged to be closing hours, and waited endlessly without success. Nobody knew where you were nor when you would return, if you did. Now I should like to know where one
finds you? Are you always completely evanescent?"

"Why, I'm sorry, Marietta. Nobody told me you
were looking for me. Where were you? What time?"

"I was parked right outside your office door for at
least an hour, from quarter of five on, and then I chased
you everywhere I could think of. What on earth do you
do with yourself, and when do you usually leave the
office?"

"Why, I don't have any special time. But usually
around five unless there is a stress of work. Sometimes,
I told you, I'm needed there nearly all night. But I'm not
always in the office. I'm here and there and everywhere."

"So I understood," said the girl coldly. "Just where
were you tonight?"

"Tonight I was out on an errand," said Val firmly. "It
took more time than I had expected. But now, Marietta,
what was it you wanted? I'm sorry I should have been so

unavailable when you wanted to get me. Is there anything important, that you were so anxious to find me?"

"There certainly is," said the girl haughtily. "I was delegated by our district committee to contact you and find out if you would undertake to organize and be warden of the air raid group in this neighborhood. You were unanimously chosen to do that, and when they found I knew you, they asked me to give you the papers and tell you what was wanted of you. It certainly hasn't been an easy job locating you. As this is a request from the citizens in our neighborhood, and not a private plan of my own, I suppose you'll be a little more affable about it than you were about my request last night."

"Well, Marietta, I'm sorry I wasn't affable last night, but what you asked was utterly out of the question. And as for this, it is equally impossible. I am a worker you know, under government orders, and my time is not my own. I would seldom be available at the times when a warden was wanted. Remember my work is defense work!"

"Well, I certainly think that is perfectly ridiculous. You can't be busy *all* the time!"

"Not all the time of course, but enough of the time so that I could not be depended upon for any other job that was important. But really, Marietta, don't you do anything but go around contacting people for jobs? Isn't there some small favor I could do for you for old time's sake that would make you understand I am not merely trying to be rude?"

"Why, yes, there is. I'd like you to take me to the orchestra concert tomorrow night. Then perhaps we'd have a little time between numbers to talk seriously."

Val made a wry face at the telephone, but answered in a pleasant voice:

"Well, now that's a simple request. Yes, I could try to do that. Of course you have to understand that if a stress should come I might have to get a substitute at the last minute. But I'll really try, Marietta, and you know I enjoy symphony concerts extremely. It ought to be a very pleasant occasion, and I'll do my very best to

appear at the right time. I'll ask my aunt if I can borrow her car."

"Don't bother," said Marietta. "I have a new one of my own that I want to show you. I go everywhere in it, semi-officially you know. And as I want to talk over some of my defense plans I shall count that a trip for the country's good. All right, Val, and get here at quarter to eight. That'll be plenty of time. Now I'll say good night and let you get some much needed rest, or you'll fall asleep at the Academy of Music. Good night!"

He turned from the telephone with a sigh. So, that was that! He'd be as nice to Marietta as possible, but he would make her understand that he had no time this winter to attend her on her various activities. He could still hear her insistent voice ringing in his ears as he went about preparing for rest. And it flashed across his mind that there was a vast difference between her and that little Frannie who was so gay and sweet, and so free from demands of any sort. Was that the reason why he enjoyed helping her so much, and why the picture of the simple little home lingered so pleasantly in his memory?

Chapter 7

BUT MARIETTA DID not dismiss the subject of the conversation she had just held with the young man as easily and quickly as he had done. She flung herself down on her luxurious chaise longue with a petulant look on her face. She had won, it is true, a whole evening to herself with Val Willoughby—with reservations —for she didn't at all feel sure of him even now, since he said he might have to call up and cancel any engagement he made. But what was one evening? For he seemed perfectly capable of talking around a thing without once coming to the point to say anything but a

decided no. And what was it all about anyway? The excuse he gave of work seemed to her altogether too trivial for a young man from his class in society. He might have an important job, yes, but he wasn't a day laborer, was he? He surely could get someone else to take his place when there was need. And wasn't courtesy and precedent in the class of real need? It was just unthinkable that a nephew of Mrs. Robert Haversett should be so tied down to any kind of a job, even for defense, that he couldn't take time off for social duties, and she didn't mean to accept that excuse any longer. She would go to some man of importance in the defense world and find out just how much Val's talk really meant. But of course there was some other reason. Could it possibly be a girl? Another girl than herself? She couldn't believe that. If she chose to run after a man and honor him with her smiles, of course he would prefer herself to any other girl. That went without saying. She had grown up in that belief, and had never seen reason to doubt it. Well, if it was another girl, she must find out the girl and deal with her. There was usually a way. But of course the main thing was to make herself important to the man. She would have to work fast and well if she had only this one evening to start with, and that cluttered up with music, besides. He would likely be stuffy about talking while the music was going on, too. Well, she would have to do her best. She must just keep him on her mind until she found the way to conquer him.

It was the next day when she was talking with one of her friends at a committee meeting that she began her work. Deborah Hand was one of those girls who always asked questions and managed to find out a great deal about this and that, so Marietta began to talk about the old crowd, but didn't mention Val Willoughby herself. She knew better than to begin that way if she wanted to find out anything really worth while about a person, and also retain her own prestige and importance. But it wasn't long before Deborah got around to think of him herself.

"Do you see much of Val Willoughby since he came

back to our neighborhood?" she asked and fixed her keen gray eyes on Marietta knowingly. She and several others of their group had spoken of it a number of times lately, wondering if Marietta had renewed her attentions to Val, and if he was succumbing nicely.

"Oh, yes," said Marietta casually, as if it were to be expected. "I see him or talk to him almost every day. He's looking awfully well, don't you think? But he's so horribly busy he can hardly ever get off. Isn't this war simply horrid, driving some of our men to the ends of the earth, and keeping the rest of them so busy you can hardly get speech of them."

"Yes, I suppose the war is responsible for the lack of young men these days," sighed Deborah. "Well, let us hope it will soon be over."

"Yes, it will be a relief when it's over," said Marietta, "but you know I've been really interested in what we are all doing. It makes quite a change from the regular monotony of life. And then the uniforms are so becoming to some. I just love mine. And it's awfully interesting to be doing something really important. Something men respect you for doing, don't you think?"

"Oh yes," said Deborah listlessly, "but somehow I'm not so awfully interested. I just loathe making bandages, and studying all those First Aid things. I never can remember whether you stand up a person who has fainted or lay them down, and it's gruesome to have to lie down and let them bandage you up as if you had been hurt. I had to do that the last time, and I thought I should expire before they finally undid me and let me act like myself. Personally I think it's silly, don't you? I never would even *try* to revive somebody who had fainted. I'd just ring the bell for my maid and make her do it, or send for a doctor and a nurse."

"Well, you know if there was a raid you couldn't always get your maid. She might even be hurt herself. Really I think it's a good thing to know what to do. You could at least tell somebody else what to do."

"I suppose you could," said Deborah. "Well, personally I hope it's soon over, though if the people in charge want to keep on playing the game I suppose it

will last as long as they want it to. But to go back to
the crowd. I'm glad Val Willoughby is looking well. I
haven't really seen him close enough to tell. Only twice
skating on the river with a girl. I thought perhaps it was
you till they got nearer to the house and I saw she was
smaller than you. She's a tiny little thing, graceful as a
wand, and skates like a bird. Do you know who she
is? They go down in the morning together and skate
back around five or five-thirty. At least I've seen them
twice now, and they do skate divinely together. Last
evening I happened to be up in our attic looking down
the river at the sunset, and I saw them coming back.
They went to a red brick house on the opposite bank. I
thought I'd remember to ask you the next time I saw
you who the girl was."

Marietta had fine control over her facial muscles. She
never by so much as a flutter of an eyelash gave evidence that she was astonished at the news she was receiving. The smile on her face was one she often locked
there on occasion, not to be lifted till called for, and
she turned an imperturbable serenity upon her friend
Debbie.

"Why, could it have been one of the Haversett
nieces? You know they are growing up fast, and they
perfectly adore their uncle Val. Even when they were
almost babies they fairly dogged his steps, everywhere
he went. I used to think they were a perfect nuisance,
myself. You never could go anywhere with Val but
they were underfoot."

Deborah looked thoughtful.

"Oh, perhaps it *was* one of them," she mused, "but
—he stooped over and unfastened her skates, and she
went up the steps and into that little brick house that
has been empty so long. He went up the steps too and
went in. You know someone is occupying that house
now. Some working people, I suppose."

"Oh, very likely they were going after a cleaning
woman then, for her mother."

"But I thought those nieces were off at boarding
school somewhere."

"Why, yes, they were," said Marietta calmly, "but

they often come home for the week-end, or for a party here among their set, or something like that, you know."

"Oh! Well, that might have been the explanation. But if you ask me, that girl didn't look like either of those nieces. She seemed older, more sophisticated. Well, perhaps not sophisticated, I wouldn't use that word for a girl that lived on that side of the river—not in a little tumble-down house like that brick one. However, I saw him go skating with her twice, and that wouldn't be likely to happen with his nieces *twice,* would it, and have them stop at the same place? Well, I don't know. I always thought Val Willoughby was a pretty decent sort of a fellow, with such an aunt and all, but of course boys do go wrong and get silly over a pretty face. Of course I didn't *see* this girl close by, and she might not be pretty at all, but I did think his attitude looked very attentive."

"Nonsense!" said Marietta sharply. "Val Willoughby isn't at all that sort of fellow. I know him too well. He hates anything sordid like that. I've heard him say so. And besides, remember how well I've known him since childhood. That would be practically impossible, for Val to have an affair with a common sort of girl."

"Yes—well, I *thought* you knew him pretty well, and that's why I mentioned it. I knew you would know whether it could be so or not. And then of course if he was tempted by some pretty face that works in his office or something, I thought perhaps we ought to rally around him and keep him out of temptation. We might get up a skating party and go down to meet him nights or something. I fancy that would drive away any little cheap girl that was attempting to interest him."

"I don't fancy that will be necessary in the least, Deb. I tell you *I know Val!* And anyway if one attempted to break up anything that way and take him by storm it would simply work the other way with him. We'd have to be very subtle about anything we did. He's keen, Val is, and he'd see right through anything like that and resent it. No, Debbie, I'm certain there's some very simple explanation to all this. I'll try and find out about it myself. I'm going out with him tomorrow night,

and I'll ask a few simple questions that will bring the situation out in the open. If there's anything going on I'll nip it in the bud, and don't you worry about it. I know Val too well, and he knows better than to try to deceive me. We've known each other too long and too well."

"Well, I shall be just dying to find out who it was he has been skating with," said Deborah Hand. "But I'm not so sure as you are that Val isn't capable of a little sly flirtation now and then. That holy look he wears so much would crack sometime if he didn't have any chance to relax now and then."

"You're talking as if Val were a hypocrite," said Marietta, "and he's anything but that. It shows you don't know him very well." Marietta's tone was cold and indifferent in the extreme.

"Oh, well, you needn't take that tone, my dear," said Deborah indignantly. "One would think it was a personal matter with you and I never thought you cared enough for him for that."

"Of course not," said Marietta with contempt in her voice, "but you know really, he is a very old friend, and I don't like to hear him maligned."

"Well, I didn't malign him, my dear. I just said I saw him with a strange girl and I wondered who she was. But of course you know Val Willoughby always was kind to every stray kitten he found in the alley. Always insisted they had a right to play with us all as much as if they were one of us. Don't you remember that child of the scrub woman who always had to play hide and seek with us on Wednesdays because Val thought she was lonely? But you know, Marietta, that's a dangerous position for a young man to take. If he carries that out in his life his wife will certainly have plenty of heartaches. And somebody ought to warn him. He'll get into something very unpleasant if he doesn't look out. A breach of promise case, or something like that. You know those cabaret beauties are utterly unscrupulous."

"Oh, for heaven's sake, shut up won't you, Debbie! I simply won't hear you talk that way about a friend

you've known for as many years as I have. I'm ashamed of you. Val has sense enough to look out for himself, I'm quite sure, and what's more he's principled against such sordid things."

"Well, principles don't always save people from bad breaks. I think if you're a good friend of Val's you ought to warn him!"

"How about doing it yourself, if you think you know so much about him? As for me I don't believe any such tales as you're trying to spread, and I'd rather not talk about it any longer. Suppose you tell me what they did at the class last night. I simply couldn't get away from home. I was waiting for a long-distance call from New York, and it didn't come till very late. Who did they use for the victim last night? Clara? My word! She must have been a handful to roll over after they got her bandaged. Aren't these First Aid classes simply a scream? I always enjoy them, and I'm learning a lot, too."

And so no more was said about Val Willoughby, but neither girl forgot the matter. Deborah had watched her victim sharply as she insinuated some things that she did not really know, or see; and Marietta with all her nonchalance resolved to search this matter through and find out just who that girl was—if there *was* really a girl. She didn't half believe it. For Val had been known for years as the boy who never had had a crush on a girl.

Skating! Could that be where he went, that he disappeared so utterly just before closing time from his office?

And if so, could it be some secretary, or some worker in his plant with whom he went up the frozen way? But she had always understood that there were no women in that plant, even as secretaries. She had made particular inquiries about that, thinking she might even apply for something herself. Not that she was fitted for anything really practical, in lines needed in an office. That was the trouble with Marietta. She thought she could succeed anywhere, just by being her lovely self,

wealthy, popular and beautiful. She felt that of course she would be an asset to any business to which she condescended to lend her exquisite presence.

But this skating girl, she really had to be tracked down and investigated. She couldn't have any common girl poaching on her preserves, and Val certainly was that. She could remember Auntie Haversett telling her to give the dear little boy a sweetheart kiss, just one little sweetheart kiss, baby dear. And she could remember the stolid look on the face of the little boy during the transaction, for even at that age Marietta registered definitely those things which had to do with her popularity. She could still remember the challenge in his angry red face after her kiss had been administered, for he had not received it graciously. Indeed he had jerked away and said, "No! No! I don't wanta!" and he had rubbed his fat red cheek indignantly with a crumby black hand, that erased even the memory of her delicate touch. So, ever since, she had been in the position of setting the seal of her rights upon the reluctant young man.

Certainly this skating girl must be investigated!

So Marietta set herself to investigate.

The little old run-down brick house! She cast an eye across the frozen river. The little brick house was over there down river from where she lived. It had been there always, but she had never given particular attention to it. It was dark now, save for a tiny blue light in the second story front window. Why should they have a light like that? A night light? Was the girl sitting up reading? But one could not read by a blue light of that sort. She must find out about this. Perhaps it was a spy who lived there, and that light was a signal. Marietta had fantastic ideas sometimes, especially if someone she disliked were connected with it. If she could only prove that that girl was a spy, and was trying to find out some secrets from Val about his plant, her way would be clear before her. For Val was loyal to his country. She was sure he was. He wouldn't have anything to do with a girl who was a spy, if he knew it. So she stood for a long time looking out her window and trying to think out a

plot by which she could rid Val of the girl, when she
didn't even know the girl by sight yet. But underneath
it all was a boiling rage that Val should dare refuse to
go places with *her,* and yet take up with a girl of "this
sort." Of course she did not know just what she meant
by "this sort," as the whole thing was made of her
imagination. But she decided not to let another day go
by without finding out about that girl, and she spent a
good deal of her brain energy studying out just how
she was to go about it.

In the end she decided to go to the house on some
one of the canvases connected with defense drives.
Selling bonds! Could she get these people to feel that
they must buy some bonds of her?

The Red Cross. That would be a good number to
urge, and when she once got into the house she would
be able to find out a lot of things. Marietta was not
shy about prying into others' affairs, especially if they
belonged to what she termed "the lower classes." And
of course these people, or this girl, whoever she was,
belonged to the lower classes or she wouldn't be living
in a little old ramshackle house like that. And on the
"other side" of the river too. The only thing she
couldn't seem to fathom was Val's taking up at all
with a girl from the other side of the river. He was
aristocracy, and had no right to as much as look at a
girl from the other side of the river. Not when he had
plenty of nice girls to choose from on the right side.

So Marietta got up early the next morning and wrote
out all the plans she had made the night before. She
intended to go at once to that little brick house across
the river, and at least see that little sneak of a girl who
seemed to think she could take over the really most
eligible young man in the neighborhood. Scores had
gone to camp and there weren't so many to depend on
as there used to be.

After she had her list written out carefully so that
she would be provided with an idea in a hurry that
would fit any contingency, she arrayed herself in her
most stunning uniform and started out in her shining
new car.

Chapter 8

MARIETTA DROVE UP the road to the bridge and over the bridge to the despised "other side," turned down the old river road, past the tiny new houses that represented "the laboring class" to her aristocratic mind, and at last reached the little brick house.

She sat a moment in her car surveying the place. This was the place where that obnoxious girl lived! It needed painting terribly. Strange that even a laboring man should be willing to live in such a run-down looking house. If he was worth anything surely he could find a few minutes a day to paint at least around the windows and the door. The door was simply impossible. Dirty fingermarks and scratches as if heavy boots had kicked it for years. Well, of course no decent girl could come out of a house like this. Poor Val! What had possessed him to take up with a girl from a house of this sort? It probably was just another case of the scrub woman's child. Well, she would have to do her best. She turned to get out of her car and then looked back at the windows. Why, there were *curtains* at the windows! That was astonishing! Perhaps somebody in the house had ideas.

Slowly she went up the path and tapped at the door. She could hear hurrying little feet coming from the region of the back of the house. A child! Well, perhaps it would be as well to meet a child first, then she would not have to stand at the door in this cold wind and talk. Getting in would give her an advantage.

Bonnie opened the door and smiled up at the beautiful girl in the lovely fur coat, and a real uniform showing beneath. She was charmed with the haughty visitor, and opened the door a little wider. Marietta stepped in and looked about her curiously. Why, the

curtains which had looked rather nondescript from outside, were clean and quite attractive, as if someone with taste had selected them. Probably some rich person for whom the mother worked, washing or scrubbing perhaps, had donated them. Or they might even have been stolen from some clothes line in the wealthy part of the city. Such things had been done.

"Won't you sit down?" said Bonnie politely. "We aren't in very good order yet. We just moved in last week." The child did the honors in a quaint old-fashioned way, and Marietta looked at her astonished.

"Is your—mother, or your—sister at home?" she asked sharply.

"My mamma is sick," said Bonnie. "She's been very sick upstairs in her room. The doctor said she mustn't see anybody yet."

Marietta instantly decided that the mother was drunk and this was probably an excuse.

"Well, haven't you a sister?" she asked.

"Yes, I have a sister, Frannie, but she has gone to her work in the city. She is a secretary down at a munition plant. She won't be home till supper time. She goes to her work on her skates. She's a very nice skater," and Bonnie smiled engagingly.

Ah! That was the girl. Then she did skate. Probably Val had been lured by her skating.

"Well, isn't there anybody here at all that I can talk to? Someone who is older than you are?"

"Oh yes, there's the nurse. She's very nice. She could talk to you, only I think she's giving my mamma a bath now. You could wait for her, or I will talk to you. I know more about the family than she does, because she's only been here since yesterday."

"A nurse!" said Marietta. "Do you have a nurse?"

"Yes, we had to, 'cause my mamma got so sick, and Frannie had to go to her job."

"Oh!" said Marietta, wondering what she had got into. Was the woman sick with some contagious disease, perhaps? Marietta had a good imagination, and could always go a step ahead of the facts. "What is the matter with your mother? Has she got anything that's

catching? Any contagious disease?" Marietta involuntarily stepped toward the door—her hand on the knob—preparatory to escaping if necessary.

"Oh, you mean anything like measles and whooping cough? Oh no, it's nothing like that. She just fell down when she was clearing off the breakfast dishes, and her eyes shut and she couldn't answer me. They said she fainted. The doctor said she was all tired out and needed a rest."

"Oh," said Marietta relaxing from her alarm and dropping down in the hair cloth chair by the door. It was then that she noticed that several of the chairs in the room looked like simple old antiques. Could they have been given to these people? Where did they get fine old chairs? There was nothing to show that they had money. If they had they would never have come to live in this dreadful little house, whose wall-paper was soiled and faded, and looked as if it had served large families for a century or two.

"And you have a *nurse?*" asked the bewildered caller. "Is she some relative who is living with you?"

"Oh no," said Bonnie with her sunny smile. "She's just a nurse. The nice doctor sent for her and she came, and she's wonderful. She knows how to do almost everything."

"Yes, nurses usually do," said Marietta dryly. "But this nurse, is she an old woman? Somebody without any home?"

"Oh no," said Bonnie affably, "she's a nice lady and she has a home somewhere I guess, only she's staying here now because my mamma is sick and she wants to help her get well. She loves to help people. She has a pretty white uniform. It's not like yours, it's white all over, and a pretty white cap, and she always smiles. But say, are you a soldier?"

"Well, no, not exactly. I'm just a person who has signed up to help in the war."

"But you have a uniform like a soldier. What do you do? Go out and pick up dead soldiers and take them to the hospital to be mended?"

"*Mercy* no!" said Marietta, shivering. "What put that idea into your head, you crazy infant?"

"Why, because our nurse said people in uniforms were all doing something to help the poor soldiers, and I wondered what you do to help them."

Then suddenly there was a step on the stairs and the nurse came down bringing a tray.

"Oh, Bonnie, have you a caller?" the nurse said cheerily. "Why didn't you call me? Was something wanted?"

"Why, I don't know," said Bonnie. "I forgot to ask that. But I did tell her to sit down. Was that right?"

"Yes, that was right, dear. Why, Miss Hollister, is it you? Aren't you lost over on this side of the river?"

"Well, almost," laughed Marietta unpleasantly. "But I might ask the same thing of you, Miss Branner. You don't usually nurse over on this side, do you?"

"Why, I nurse wherever I'm needed," said the nurse calmly.

"But isn't it unusual for people in these walks of life to be able to pay a nurse of your class?"

"Well I really couldn't answer that question, Miss Hollister," said Nurse Branner with dignity. "I've never happened to see any statistics in that line. Is there anything I can do for you? Whom did you want to see?"

"I understood there was a young girl living here," said Marietta haughtily. "I came to see her."

"Yes, Miss Fernley lives here, but she is not at home at present. She does not usually return until a little after five."

"Oh! Every day?"

"Yes, every day."

"Very well. I'll call again."

And so Marietta took herself out of the little red house angrily, as if it was definitely someone's fault that she could not attain her object at once. But she did not dismiss her plans. Instead she began to turn over new ones which should further her investigations.

Why, for instance, shouldn't this dance program that she had proposed, work out for girls like this? If the

girls of her crowd thought they were really doing something to uplift other girls less favored than themselves they might even be moved to give larger sums for the furtherance of the idea. That would be the very thing! Invite a favored few of these working girls to the dances and entertainments, and give them the privilege of seeing how the wealthy and aristocratic girls lived. And they, the promoters, could go on and have their own good time while the guests had the privilege of watching them. Of course there would have to be a few young men of the underprivileged class to provide partners for their guests. It would have to be worked out very carefully, or the outsiders might take advantage and make unpleasantness, but she was satisfied she could work it out. So she went to her committees and told some of the other girls about her idea. But she did not find a very enthusiastic response to her suggestions.

"Oh, forget it, Mari," one girl said. "Haven't we got enough unpleasant things to do in this war-torn world without your dragging in something like that? Who wants to do good to every green awkward girl in the county? When I go to a dance I want to have a good time myself and not have to worry about any forlorn wallflowers who don't know what it's all about anyway."

"And there's another thing, Hollister," sounded another dissenting voice, "they won't come if you do invite them, those freaks who haven't any social life of their own. They don't want to be patronized and told how the other half lives. They think they are as good as anybody, and a little better than some. It wouldn't be a success even if you did try it. I'm against it, Holly! Don't do it!"

But Marietta was of the type that always grew stronger under opposition, therefore she determined to go ahead with her plans.

"It all depends on the approach you make when you invite them," she said contemptuously. "You've got to sell them the idea of coming in the first place. Make them see it will be a privilege to come. I know one girl that I'm certain I can bring, and I'll make her dig up some others."

And so, without having even seen Frannie Fernley, Marietta determined to make her the center around which she would organize the whole scheme.

She spent most of the rest of the day in perfecting her plans. In bullying enough of the girls into contributing money for the initial expenses, getting lists of names of young people who were eligible material on which to begin their uplifting work, in hunting up a suitable hall for their gatherings, and inquiring prices; also interviewing orchestra leaders and getting them down to a price commensurate with the amount pledged. Oh, Marietta was most efficient when it came to carrying out her own way. And all this just to find out and nip in the bud this girl who had dared to be seen with Valiant Willoughby.

And Marietta did not waste any time in interviewing Frannie Fernley. She was on hand at the little brick house quite before five o'clock, sitting in the dim little front room filled with the dusk of the evening, and listening to the high-pitched sweet voice of Bonnie in the kitchen talking with the nurse while they prepared the pleasant evening meal that was sending out such delightful odors: the delicious mingling of molasses and butter and a bit of fat browning over the top of a pan of baked beans; the tang of a fresh raw onion cut across a salad of lettuce, green pepper and tomato, with lemon in the dressing; the rich spicy fragrance of cinnamon on the top of a custard pie just being taken out of the oven.

Marietta sat back in the old comfortable chair, in the gathering dusk of a room lighted only by a single dim lamp, and realized that she was both tired and hungry. Those things they were cooking smelled good and tempted her. She didn't try to identify the different smells, but they certainly seemed like an expensive dinner, here in this little tumble-down brick house. What did it mean? Had the neighbors sent in these things because the mother was sick? But then she remembered that the laboring class always were good eaters, and probably insisted on having plenty.

It was almost dark when Frannie at last came home. Marietta had been watching occasionally out the win-

dow for her arrival, but a great drowsiness had come upon her, for she certainly had worked hard all day. So Frannie glided up to the wooden steps and changed her skate shoes to her house shoes, without being seen or heard. She entered the house by the kitchen door left on the latch for her.

It happened therefore that she had a moment or two to smooth her dark curls, straighten her collar, and wash her hands and face before she entered the front room to speak to the guest, whom Bonnie and Nurse Branner had had no opportunity to describe to her. And the big beautiful car had been parked across the street where Frannie could not see it as she entered from the river side of the house. So without any warning, except Bonnie's soft whisper, "There's a beautiful lady waiting for you," she went in to meet the girl who had prepared to hate and humiliate her as far as she could.

But there was about Frannie a grace and gentleness that gave a natural loveliness to her movements, and she was not self-conscious. She had no reason to dread this caller, perhaps just some kindly neighbor like Lady Winthrop, she thought. So the two girls met in the dim room.

"Oh," said Frannie, "you are sitting almost in the dark. And are you warm enough? That fireplace is always needing another log." She stooped in passing and flung a small stick on the dying coals, and it presently blazed up and flung lights and shadows through the room, and over the faces of the two girls. "You are Miss Hollister, they said. I'm sorry, that doesn't tell me anything because I am almost a stranger here."

Marietta stared at the girl she had come to patronize, and then answered coldly:

"Yes, my name is Marietta Hollister, and I understood you were a stranger. That's partly why I came. You see we are getting up a scheme to socialize this side of the river, and give the people living over there a chance to see some of the amenities of life, and to learn how to behave when they go out among really educated, cultured people. An opportunity, you know, to mingle

with young men and women of your own class and have a place where you can have really good times."

Frannie cast a puzzled glance at the imperious young beauty with the glow of the firelight on her long golden bob. Was all this meant for kindness, or did it smack of condescension?

"Why, that's kind of you, I'm sure, to think of other girls and try to help them," she said hesitantly, uncertainly. Was it really kindness, she wondered? "But—I'm afraid I would not be in a position to benefit by anything of a social nature—"

"Oh, well, that's all nonsense of course. Everybody has got to have recreation. I suppose you have a job and you think you can't spare the time, but you owe it to yourself to have some enjoyment out of life. You'll do better work if you relax now and then. You see we're proposing to have a series of dances, and we'll have some suitable young men there who will ask you to dance and will be attentive to you, and in that way you will get acquainted with some really suitable young men. We shall take care to inquire into their characters and shall sponsor no one who is not respectable and steady and dependable. You know, many girls who are employed have no opportunity to meet young men of their own class, in respectable places, and that is one reason why there are so many unhappy marriages. The girls often cannot meet men anywhere except on the street, and they do not have a chance to get to know them. We are trying to provide places for you girls to meet men who would make good husbands by and by."

Frannie suddenly broke down and giggled.

"Excuse me!" she said, suddenly sobering. "I'm afraid I wouldn't be interested. I'm not looking out for someone to marry. I have a job to do and my mother and little sister to care for, and I have no time to waste on such things."

"But that is utterly senseless," said Marietta. "You want to marry and have your own home. Every girl does. Let your family take care of themselves. There is always the Welfare for the family if they need it. And

then you know there are Homes where dependent people can go and be cared for, if they cannot live on what welfare they can get. You have a duty to yourself, and we want to help you with it."

Frannie grew suddenly white and rose to her feet:

"I'm sorry," she said coldly. "You are wasting your time! I wouldn't be interested in anything you have to suggest." And then, with as much dignity as her gentle self could summon, she added: "And now if you will excuse me, I think I will go up to my sick mother. I've been away from her all day. I think that is about all you and I have to say to one another."

"But you don't understand," said Marietta rising to the occasion and putting out a detaining hand. "I have something else to tell you and it's really very important. It's something you ought to know."

Frannie stopped, her head up, her lips and eyes suspicious, and looked her visitor over quietly, with much the same look that she had given to Spike Emberly and Kit Creeber not long ago. The very tilt of her chin showed that she was not in a receiving mood.

For an instant even Marietta was a bit abashed. This wasn't just the way she had planned her approach. Then she flung up her arrogant beautiful head and went on.

"It seems that you——at least I have been told that you have picked up an acquaintance with a young man who is not at all of your class, and that you have been seen skating with him, more than once, holding hands in broad daylight! I felt I ought to warn you that it isn't safe for you to do a thing like that. Not only would you bring disgrace upon yourself, but there would be actual danger. For it happens that the young man you have selected to play up to is quite an important member of our social order, far above you, and his friends and relatives would certainly rally around him, and pay you back for daring to attempt any such bold-faced flirtation with him! It might mean actual bodily harm to you if you keep on having anything to do with him. You probably do not know this, but young men of respectable families do not give *serious* attention to girls from this side of the river, and you might as well

understand at once that such an acquaintance could never come to anything with you. Besides, he is already practically engaged to a girl of his own class, and though he might play around with you a few days it could never bring you anything but heartache! I mean what I am saying, and I'm speaking out of kindness for you, to warn you, for your own good."

Now Frannie had a large sense of humor, and just now it suddenly came to the front in a radiant smile, that was almost a grin.

"Thank you!" she said. "I'm sure you're trying to be kind to me. And now will you go, please? I have other things to do." Frannie reached out and swung the front door wide open, letting in a blast of the icy outside air. And there seemed nothing in the world for Marietta to do but go. Her resourceful mind could not think of another thing to say. And the worst of it all was that she could not make up her mind whether she had reached the real girl in the warning she had just uttered, or whether she was being laughed at.

And then, as she swung across the snowy road, there came a burst of more laughter, gay and sweet, from the little red house behind her. Walking into the dusky night, her cheeks were burning with a new kind of shame. This girl whom she had come to humiliate, had humiliated her. And yet she had not transgressed a single law of courtesy, nor once lost her temper, although she suspected by the look in the girl's gentle eyes that some of the things she had dared to say had cut to the quick.

So this was the girl Val Willoughby had been skating with! She was not going to be an easy one to dislodge. She must think up a better plan to get rid of her.

And tonight she would have the evening with Val, and would see what she could do with *him*.

Chapter 9

WHEN THE NURSE and the little sister who were tiptoeing around the kitchen getting supper ready, heard the front door shut and then a moment later that merry little gurgle of laughter from Frannie, they came cautiously to investigate. Bonnie opened the door a crack and peeped in, and then opened it a little wider, and whispered hilariously, "She's *gone!*" and then the nurse came near and there they stood watching. Frannie was sitting down in the big chair by the door, laughing.

But in a moment Frannie lifted her head, looked at their astonished faces, and laughed again. More quietly now, and softening down to a good-natured giggle.

"What is it, Frannie? What happened?" asked the nurse who wondered if Frannie was so tired that she was near hysterics.

"Oh nothing. Nothing. Only it was so very funny. She came here to invite me to a dance or a series of dances, so that I would meet some respectable young man I could marry and have a happy home," and Frannie went off again into a burst of giggles.

"Was that all?" asked the nurse with a relieved sigh.

"No!" giggled Frannie, "that wasn't all. She wanted to warn me not to take up with strange young men whom I met skating out on the river. She said they would have no serious intentions and I would only get my heart broken, or words to that effect, and maybe even my head too! She said someone had told her that I had been seen skating with one of the young men from the other side of the river, and she felt she ought to warn me that he was somebody important and his friends would never stand for it. But please, Miss Branner, don't tell my mother this! She would want to move away at once. She would be filled with horror that we

had come to a place where people would meddle and gossip like this. She would think I was disgraced. Oh, I thought Bluebell was bad enough with its kindly folk-gossip, but this is a thousand times worse. It's so bad it's really funny."

"Oh, dear me! That girl is certainly a fool!" said the annoyed nurse. "I should have thought she would have known the minute she laid eyes on you that you were not that kind of girl. But I'm glad you're taking it this way."

"Well, why shouldn't I? She seemed to think the main thing that was the matter with me was that I lived on this side of the river. But if that's it I tell you it's *very* funny. I've heard of living on the wrong side of the rail-road track, but this seems to be something a good deal worse."

"Yes. Absurd, isn't it? Well, let's forget her. Come, the supper is all ready, and I've just taken your moth-er's tray up. Let's sit down while the beans are hot."

"Oh, yes!" said Frannie. "And am I hungry! How good they smell. Everything smells wonderful! I noticed it the minute I opened the door."

So they sat down to the simple supper and enjoyed every crumb, and then they sent Bonnie up to talk to the mother while they washed the dishes and got things ready for breakfast.

"But don't tell mother anything about what that girl said, Bonnie dear. We don't want mother to worry."

"Of course not, Frannie. Don't you think I have any sense at all? I'll just tell her it was someone about some 'fense work. It was, you know. I heard her say the dances were for 'fense work, to get money to have 'musements for the soldiers."

"That's the girl," praised the nurse with a smile of commendation, "she's got good sense. She knows what not to tell her little sick mother. Run along, Bonnie, and don't talk any more about it than you can help."

So Bonnie hurried joyfully up to her mother and Frannie and the nurse went swiftly to work. But the nurse could see a little cloud of annoyance on Frannie's sweet face, and knew that in spite of her gay little

laughter she had been troubled by her arrogant visitor.

"Frannie," said the nurse in her most cheery comforting tone, "if I were you I wouldn't waste a minute's thought on anything that cold-hearted selfish girl said. It isn't worth it. Believe me, I know what she is, and I've known her ever since she was a spoiled baby. When she goes around trying to do good, and uplift what she considers inferior people, it's always because she has an axe to grind for herself."

"Yes?" said Frannie with a troubled question in her eyes. "But I don't see what she would expect to get out of it."

"Well, that's the subtlety of her. You never know till afterward, unless you know her pretty well. And knowing her, I can guess what she was at when she came here and tried to warn you against picking up young men on the ice that way. She must have either seen you, or been told of your skating with Val Willoughby. And she would be very jealous of that. She thinks Val Willoughby, and all the rest of the eligible young men of the neighborhood, belong peculiarly to herself."

"Oh!" said Frannie with sudden enlightenment, "that must have been what she meant. She said the young man I had been seen with was practically engaged to another girl who belonged on the other side of the river."

"Yes, I thought it would be something like that. That sounds very Hollisterish. And what did you answer, Frannie?"

"Why, when she got through talking I didn't really answer her at all. I just said I guessed her plans wouldn't interest me, and if she would excuse me I must go up to see my sick mother."

"Good!" said Nurse Branner. "You couldn't have done better. Just keep up that kind of a front and pretty Marietta won't know what to say. She wouldn't be able to understand your not getting angry and answering back."

"Well, she made me get all weak and trembly inside," confessed Frannie, as she gathered up the knives and forks and placed them on the table for breakfast.

"Poor child," said the nurse cheerily. "You certainly

didn't show it when you came out to the kitchen afterwards."

"Well, of course I didn't want Bonnie to see how I felt. She wouldn't be able to keep it from mother, if she found out. She may be very wise, but mother's eyes are very sharp and keen. She would know at once if something worried Bonnie."

"Yes, of course. Well, now my dear, don't you worry one bit about this. It will all pass away and you'll forget it. That girl can't hurt you. You two don't live in the same world. She wouldn't know how to reach you. She couldn't understand you even if she tried. But if she comes again, don't give her any answers back. If she gets disagreeable come and call me. I'll settle her. Just give me the high sign, and I'll come to your rescue. I know all the answers."

"Oh, thank you, Miss Branner. You've made me feel a lot better. I won't worry about her any longer. But I don't think she'll come again. I think she was very mad at me that I didn't let her talk any longer. She probably thinks I'm the rudest girl she ever saw."

"Never mind what she thinks. Just forget it. Now run up and have a little talk with your mother before she goes to sleep. She's been a lot stronger today. Her pulse is definitely losing that thready consistency. I thought you'd be glad to know that."

"Oh, that's grand, Miss Branner. But—do you think it may get worse again?"

"No, not if she is reasonably cared for. She must be kept from worrying."

"Yes, and that's one thing I was afraid of, Miss Branner. If she should hear what that girl said about my skating with a young man she would die of shame, to think I had got to a place where I could be common talk that way. And there really wasn't anything wrong about it at all. He came after me with a message from the doctor and my mother."

"Yes, I know, dear. The doctor told me all about it. And anyway I know Val Willoughby. Nobody would dare say anything against him. It's just as she said, he has friends enough to rally around him. But the whole

thing is that they wouldn't bother you. They would know that anything Val Willoughby did was all right, and that any girl he took up for, even if it was just to skate home from work with her for a while in order to protect her from any unpleasant boors, was to be treated with reverence. Anybody that is a real friend to that young man has to respect what he respects whether they like it or not, or else they will have to settle with Val Willoughby."

So, gradually Frannie's perturbation was quieted, and she was able to forget the unpleasant half hour with her beautiful visitor.

Willoughby had not come home with her that night. He had explained to her in the morning that he would have to leave the plant early in the afternoon and was not sure of returning until late. He had an engagement that evening that was rather upsetting his routine. He had asked her to be very watchful, and go up to another landing before starting to skate home, lest those boys might take advantage of his absence to annoy her again.

So Frannie knew that Willoughby would not be coming that night and was keen enough to realize that this was probably the end of his kindly espionage. Also, probably the end of her seeing him at all.

Which was as it should be, she told herself. He did not belong to her as an intimate friend. He had a different background, belonged to the aristocracy as that yellow haired girl had blandly said. He wasn't her rightful companion. She was a working girl now, and while he was a working man, still it was different with men. They were supposed to work. Even social life recognized that, and she might as well understand and accept it. Of course her own people were cultured and educated, and until her father died she had not had to work. But work was no disgrace, and while she would not for the world assume a social position that those around her would not concede, she had nothing to be ashamed of. Why, even the wealthy girls were running around now trying to find jobs and camouflaging them under the name of "defense." It was just a silly social

notion, and she wasn't going to be bothered about it at all. But of course she mustn't let herself get any foolish ideas about this young man. Probably it was a good thing that that obnoxious girl came to warn her or she might, unaware, have become more interested in him than she realized.

So she resolutely put aside all thoughts of the young man who had for the last two or three days made such a bright thought in the midst of her hard-working hours. She made herself concentrate on getting the house in order. This was Saturday night and she had all day tomorrow to rest up and get herself organized for the life that was beginning before her, and she didn't need any of Marietta's dances either to give it a cheerful slant. She had her little home and her mother and sister, and was glad and thankful for them. Tomorrow, perhaps, she could find a church somewhere near enough for her mother to walk to when she got well. That would be one of the first things her mother would be wanting when she was able to go out again, the right kind of a church.

So Frannie went up and had a cheery little talk with her mother, telling her all the little pleasantnesses she could find in her day of work, describing Mr. Chalmers, and a few of the girls who worked at nearby desks, trying to make her mother see how really pleasant it was, with the frozen river outside making a path straight home when she was done her work. Not an unpleasant moment in the whole tale.

Then they discussed what kind of church they would like to find. Not a large one, the mother hoped, nor a rich one. Only a plain one where the Truth would be taught, and where they would have a good Sunday School for Bonnie. Then Frannie kissed her mother good night and went to wash out some stockings, and get her clothes in good trim for tomorrow and for the week that was to follow. So at last she came to the end of the day where presently she could lie down and go to sleep with a clear conscience, not having taken any time out to hate that interfering girl who had come

around trying to humiliate her. She resolved she would not give a thought to it either while she was on the way to sleep.

It was while she was running the water and working away at her washing, that a low knock came at the back door downstairs. It happened that Nurse Branner had gone down to the kitchen to heat some milk for her patient before she went to sleep.

A little startled, she opened the door and looked out, wondering why anybody would come to the back door at this time of night. But she was not a timid woman so she had no hesitation in opening the door. She was, however, a little astonished as she saw a short heavy set man standing there in front of the door, his hat pulled down over his eyes, and his mouth set in a determined line.

"What do you want?" she asked in a cool voice, setting her broad foot in such a way as to block the entrance of anyone trying to get in.

"Good evening, lady. I was just wondering if you could tell me a few statistics. I been sent here to find out some things. I know it's late, lady, but my work kept me late tonight, and I had so many places to go getting these facts that I got delayed. This is my last stop, so if you don't mind, will you tell me, have your folks bought this house or do you rent it?"

"Rent!" said Nurse Branner crisply, and tried to think what Frannie had told her.

"Oh, you do! Well now, I wonder if you've signed a contract or was it just a verbal transaction?" said the man.

Nurse Branner was clever. She knew it did not do to hesitate.

"A contract, of course," she snapped. "Is that all?"

"Well, no it ain't," said Mike with an apologetic grin. "But if you'll just get me that contract and let me look it over I can get all the rest of the necessary data from it. It will save us both a lot of time."

Nurse Branner was on her guard, besides she had sensed a shadowy form down on the ice in the darkness

of a lot of dead bushes. She was letting no one into that house tonight!

"Sorry," she said. "Contracts are kept in safety deposit boxes in the bank. You will probably have to go to the bank to get that information. Good night!" and she shut the door firmly, turning the key in the lock and then she shot the big iron bolt noisily across into place.

When she turned the kitchen lights out and took a peek through the tiny pantry window she saw two figures, a tall thin one and a short stout one, slipping stealthily away along the shore, and then climbing to a parked car higher up the stream. She began to wonder if after all this river site was so desirable for three lone women.

She went upstairs after a little, settled her patient for the night, and then watched out the window again for a long time, but saw no more stealthy shadows on the ice.

But after she lay down in her bed she couldn't get to sleep for some time, wondering what that man had really wanted. He didn't look exactly like a crook and yet he didn't seem to be the sort of man who would be sent out near midnight Saturday night to get statistics. She must warn Frannie never to let strangers into the house at night. Should she tell her about this strange caller at the back door? Frannie wouldn't have heard him because the water was running in the tub. But maybe she ought to tell her. Or perhaps she had better ask the doctor first, or Val Willoughby if he came over pretty soon. She would have to think about it.

And so the nurse slept, and the two men drove away again.

"I think she was lying," said Granniss.

"No sir, she was talkin' straight," said Mike. "I was there and you wasn't, sir, beggin' yer pardon. I can tell when a dame is talkin' straight."

"She was scared by our coming to the back door."

"No sir, she wasn't fazed in the least. Her voice was that pleasant, and she was one of them dames that don't get scared."

"But people in a house like that wouldn't have sense to demand a contract. Not people that lived in a ratty little old house like that. They probably don't know what a contract is."

"Mebbe they got better sense than the house they live in," said Mike with a touch of his native humor. "They do sometimes. And if you'd been near you'd have seen how quick she answered that 'of course' they had a contract."

"Well, I'd like to know why you didn't ask what bank that safety deposit box is in and what time she'd meet us there, then?"

"Well, because she didn't give me no time. She closed the door that quick, and then shot the bolt. And besides I think that owner will be coming home on Monday and then we won't have to run no more risks of gettin' pinched because we scared a coupla women. We'd cook our goose in earnest if that happened."

"That must not happen!" announced Granniss severely. "If anything like that happened you would find yourself on the spot. Do you understand?"

"Now, Granniss, you promised me that if I tackled this business I wouldn't be in no trouble at all," said Mike in alarm.

"Yes, I told you that, Mike, on condition that you would get this site turned over to me within the week, and the time is up now and you haven't got the initial move started. Another day or two and it will be too late. The conditions I'm counting on for working this deal will be off. Understand?"

"Well, just give me a coupla days more, Granniss, and I'm sure I can pull it off."

"Well, see that you make it snappy then," said the big man as he stopped to let Mike off at his house. "This is the last time I'm warning you. And meantime I'm going to look up a substitute go-between. You see, Mike, this ice is liable to get tacky, or crack or something and we've got to get our materials up here on runners in the night, so nobody will suspect what's coming till it's here, or there'll be a great hue and cry and you'll get the ladies on the other side of the river

all stirred up about commercializing their precious river. We don't want that till we've got so far they can't stop us. Now, Mike, you get hold of that owner and report to me by Monday morning early or else I'm going places without you!"

So Mike and Granniss parted company, and the dwellers in the little brick house slept on unmolested.

Chapter 10

VAL WILLOUGHBY BARELY got back to his aunt's home from the business that had taken him away that afternoon, in time to change for the evening, and snatch a bite of supper from a tray he inveigled the butler into bringing him while he was dressing.

He didn't want to go to this concert. Not that he did not enjoy music, and wouldn't always be glad to hear it whatever he was doing. But he was not especially enamoured of the company in which he was going. He had nothing against Marietta, as a mere concert companion, except that she would talk all the time the music was going on, and not only spoil the delight of the whole program for him, but also bring down frowns and reproof from those people who had the misfortune to be sitting near them. Besides he was morally sure that Marietta had some ulterior motive in thus pursuing him. She was probably plotting in some way to involve him in one of her wild plans under the impression that she was doing a great deal for her country and democracy. He felt that his job this evening was smilingly to refuse her insistence, and pleasantly lead her thoughts to nice safe subjects, giving her the impression that she had had a lovely time. He was wondering as he brushed his hair, meantime humming a strain from the symphony he knew was to be played that evening, whether it would be at all possible really to interest Marietta in the music it-

self. Suppose he set himself to make her see something in the wonderful strains beyond just a big noise that it was smart to seem to enjoy. Why not try it? It certainly would be something worth while if it were possible.

Then out on the road in front of the house he heard a car drive up and an expensive sounding horn summoned him to begin the evening. He quickly swallowed the last drop of his coffee, swung into his overcoat, caught up his top hat, and went down to his task. He had not much idea he would succeed, but he certainly would find out once for all whether there was really anything to Marietta except a big will to have her own way.

And Marietta, down in her luxurious car, watched his room light go out promptly, and rehearsed in her mind the points she meant to cover for Willoughby's instruction during the evening. She had far more confidence of victory in her endeavor than the young man could muster for his own endeavor. He had tried different things on Marietta before, and always failed. But this time he meant to give her a real tryout.

So he climbed into her luxurious car with a fairly cheerful mind.

Then, they had no sooner started on their way than Marietta opened the conversation. Marietta never wasted any time in getting at her latest topic of interest, and she had decided that it would be as well to get the unpleasant part of her evening over first and then she could enjoy the rest. Not that she would own that even her first approach was going to be unpleasant. She had all assurance that she would win, and she perhaps enjoyed the thought of setting Val Willoughby straight. So she began as soon as they were well out on the main road to the city.

"Val, there's something I ought to tell you, and I may as well get it off my conscience first before we get to talking about anything else and I forget it."

"Yes?" said Willoughby, wondering what trick she was going to pull now. Marietta always had plenty of surprises, and he had not been unprepared for some-

thing in an unusual line this evening, but he had hardly expected her to begin quite so soon.

"Yes?" he said casually, looking at her perfect little lips with their unusual set of firmness, or spoiled-childness, which was it? He was not so much concerned about what she was going to say, because he did not intend to do anything she asked, and he had a pleasant "no" with plenty of alibis prepared for every request.

"Well, you see, Val, people have begun to talk about you, and I knew of course you weren't aware of it, and that you ought to be prepared."

Willoughby laughed. Strange that Marietta should be met in all her uplifting tasks by a laugh, but she was so intent she didn't notice.

"Talk about me?" he said with a chuckle. "Heavens! What difference does that make? Though I can't for the life of me imagine what they could find that would be of interest enough to say more than a sentence or two. Don't worry about a little thing like that, Marietta. It won't bother me in the least."

"Oh, but you ought to care, Val," said the pretty lips. "You really ought. It's important. It definitely is! If not for yourself, then for the sake of your friends. It isn't pleasant to have things that are not nice said about someone you've been close to practically all your life."

Willoughby gave her a puzzled look.

"Well, I see you've got something on your mind. Go ahead and tell me and let's get it over. What is it?" he said.

"Yes, I thought so too, Val," said Marietta with satisfaction in her face. "You see, Val, you've been seen skating with a girl from the other side of the river. They are saying that you picked her up, and implying that *she* picked *you* up, and *you let her do it!* And it doesn't do the least bit of good to tell them that you wouldn't do a thing like that. That I've known you all my life and you aren't sordid and horrid like that. They say, 'Oh, my dear, you don't know *men!*'"

"Oh, really, Marietta? And who is this person or

persons doing the talking? Anybody I know?" He said
it in a casual tone as if it were a mere matter of indif-
ference to him.

"Well, I don't think it's quite honorable in me to tell
you who it was, but it was somebody that I knew told
the truth. Somebody who was truly troubled that you
should have done a thing like that, and she told me in
the utmost confidence. She knew I was a friend of
yours and she felt I ought to know. She hoped I would
be able to explain it, perhaps know who it was that
you went skating with and so perhaps there was an
explanation that would leave you without reproach."

"And were you?" asked Willoughby amusedly.

"Well, I told her I thought perhaps it might be one
of your nieces home on a holiday from school, but she
didn't seem to believe that."

"I see," said Willoughby smiling. "Well, that was kind
of you of course. But it isn't important, is it? It can't
do any harm, so perhaps we'd better forget it. It doesn't
seem worth while to bother about it, does it? Certainly
not tonight when we are off on a pleasant evening."

"Valiant Willoughby, how can you be so utterly indifferent to a thing like this? Why, I supposed you would
indignantly deny it, and demand that I help you do
something about it. What do you mean?"

"Why, Marietta, what's the idea? Am I not to go
skating any more, or ever speak to a girl that you and
your friends are not acquainted with? I can't make out
what awful thing I have done."

"But *did* you go skating with that unspeakable girl?"
Marietta's big blue eyes searched his face with horror
in her own.

"With *what* unspeakable girl?" he asked amusedly.
"What is there unspeakable about her? And if she is
unspeakable, why do they speak about it?"

There was a real twinkle in Willoughby's eyes now,
and at one corner of his lips, and Marietta was en-
raged that he should take it so lightly. She felt that he
was making a joke of it.

"Oh, Val, you are impossible! You are perfectly *mad-*

dening! You know why she is unspeakable. You know
she comes from a little ratty house across the river, the
other side of the river, Val, and that's enough to make
her impossible, if there weren't anything else. No girl
from that region would be a fit companion for you,
Valiant Willoughby!"

"Why not?" asked the young man, looking imper-
turbably at the impeccable girl beside him.

"Do you have to ask? Don't you realize that the mention of a girl from that side of the river implies ignorance, coarseness, boldness, irresponsibility, un-
couthness, lack of culture and of course entire lack of
ethics, unwholesomeness, even uncleanness, immoral-
ity—"

"Stop!" said Willoughby. "That will be enough! The
girl I know from the other side of the river is not like
that! She is not any of those things you have mentioned.
And as you have never seen her I don't understand
how you dare insult her by such talk."

"I certainly *have* seen her," said Marietta. "I have
some pity on girls like that, even if you do carelessly
make fools of them. I went to see her this evening, just
before dinner. I wanted to let her know what danger she
was running in picking up young men on the river just
because she was a good skater. I told her that young
men from the other side of the river had no serious
intentions ever toward girls of her class who lived over
there, and that she was likely to have her heart broken,
and lose not only her self-respect but her reputation. I
told her that I was warning her for her own sake, and
that I wanted to help her. I told her that people were
already beginning to talk about her, and that it was a
shame, because if she would behave herself everybody
would be glad to help her to know a few rightminded
young men of her own class, and that would be so
much better for her."

Marietta suddenly finished and Willoughby regarded
her solemnly.

"You say you told her that?" he asked sternly.

"I certainly did," said the girl vivaciously.

He was still a full minute, and then he asked:

"And may I inquire what answer she gave to that?"

"She *laughed!*" said Marietta haughtily. "She was even ruder than I had expected her to be. She *only laughed.* So you can see what she is. She only laughed and went away."

"Yes," said Willoughby thoughtfully after even a longer pause, "I should think she *would* laugh. I think she answered you very wisely. I feel like laughing myself to know what you have done to one of the loveliest girls I have ever known."

"Now Val Willoughby, you don't mean that. You are just saying that because you are angry that I dared to call you down, but I thought you ought to know just what people were saying about you. And now you are acting as if you didn't care at all! I never dreamed that you would react this way. You must have greatly changed since I knew you."

"Just how did you expect me to react, Marietta?"

"Well, I certainly thought you would be ashamed to think you had been caught and recognized. I expected you to be filled with repentance, and give some plausible excuse about her being sick or poor or something and you thought you had to help her out some way, like you used to do with that scrubwoman's child when you were an exasperating kid."

"Oh! I see!" said Willoughby coolly. "But I'm not ashamed, and I'm not repentant, and I do not feel that I have done anything disgraceful. So if people decide that I have, knowing nothing whatever about it except that they saw me skating with somebody they didn't know, I think we can let it go at that and not talk any more about it, can't we?"

"Well, I don't think we can," said Marietta. "I think that respectable people who had supposed you were one of their friends have a right to an explanation of your conduct."

"Why?"

"Because you have gone against all our traditions in having anything to do with a girl on the other side of

the river, exactly as if she were as good as anybody!"

"And yet you, Marietta, not knowing anything of the facts of the case, presumed to go into that girl's home, and according to your own account of the affair, insult her! It seems to me that I have a right to demand an explanation of *your* conduct."

"Oh, indeed! Well, Val Willoughby, I like that! I didn't go there to insult her. I went there to help her. In fact I began by inviting her to a series of dances where I told her she could meet young men of her own class, who would be suitable mates for her. I tried to make her understand that all I was saying was for her own good."

The young man looked at her in growing amazement.

"And she laughed, did she? Well, I'm glad she had the grace to do that after your insults. But now, suppose we forget all this and stop talking about it. We've almost reached the Academy of Music and we certainly won't be in any mood to enjoy the evening if we keep this up."

"But aren't you going to say you are sorry for having gone with that kind of girl? Or at least offer some sort of explanation for your conduct that I can tell people who are inquiring?"

"No," said Willoughby, "I certainly am not. I did nothing out of the way. But even if I had it was none of their business!"

"*Val!* But you can't stop people's mouths by saying it is none of their business."

"Perhaps not, but you don't have to discuss the matter with them, and I do *not* intend to do so, not even through you as a go-between."

"Oh, Val!" exclaimed Marietta in a voice of despair. "How you have changed!"

"Now, look here, Marietta, are we on the way to a symphony concert to enjoy ourselves, or shall we go to a funeral parlor and see if we can find a place to mourn? I really haven't time to waste a whole evening if you are going to carry on like this about something

that you know nothing about, and is none of your affair. Come, Marietta, snap out of it, and let's talk over the music we are going to hear."

"Well, if you'll promise me just one thing," said the girl in a melting tone.

"Not till I know what it is," he said in a matter-of-fact tone.

"Well, it's that you won't ever do this thing again."

"What thing?"

"Why, that you won't ever go skating with that outrageous girl again. That you will not have *anything* more to do with her in *any* way."

"No," said Val Willoughby sharply, "I will *not* promise that! If that is your condition you had better drop me out now. Perhaps you could take the tickets and find some more congenial companion to accompany you. I'm rather fed up with your conversation at present."

But Marietta drove on to the entrance of the Academy of Music, her head high, her mouth wearing the martyr-like downdroop of one who forgives with great effort.

"I'm greatly disappointed in you, Val," she said as the doorman came up to take the car to the parking space, "but I'll forgive you of course. You're one of my oldest and dearest friends. But I'm grieved to death about you," and with great obvious forbearance she took his arm and assumed her haughtiest stride.

Val Willoughby hesitated an instant as she took his arm, and then acceded to her evident wish to go on with their plans for the evening. But he walked silently with stern, set expression, and wished with all his heart that he had never embarked upon this undesirable expedition. However, it was to be got through with somehow, and he felt that before they took their seats it would be best to establish some neutral topic for the duration of their private war, or the concert. So as they stepped into the main hallway and began making their way to the door that led to the aisle where their seats were located, he bent his head and said in a low tone that could not be heard by the gay throngs about them:

"I suggest, Marietta, if we are to go through with this evening as first planned, that we select some neutral topic for what conversation we are likely to have, and confine ourselves to that. And since we are attending a concert of some of the finest program music that is to be heard anywhere, suppose we talk about that. The music, and anything relating to it."

"Oh, if you are going to be disagreeable," said Marietta in her most martyr-like tone, "I suppose we can do that. Though I don't see why you select such a dumb topic. You know I'm not awfully fond of music, and just because I thought it was my duty to try and show you what a great mistake you were making, you get angry and try to punish me by refusing to let me talk about anything I choose; I feel you are most discourteous. I didn't think you were so touchy, Val Willoughby! Didn't you *want* me to tell you the *truth?*"

"Not particularly," answered the young man haughtily, "especially as most of the things you were saying were *not* true."

She flashed an angry look on him immediately.

"I don't care to discuss this matter any further this evening," he went on. "Is that plain?"

"You're just plain *rude!*" said Marietta, tossing her haughty head.

"Sorry," said Willoughby. "I thought you were rather rude yourself. So you see it would be better to take a neutral topic. I've been reading some very interesting items about the symphony we are to hear. Would you care to have me tell them to you? Don't you think that would be better than to spend the whole evening in sulking?"

"Oh, I suppose so!" said Marietta in a furious tone. "But if you want my opinion *I* think *you* are acting like a *spoiled boy!*"

They walked the rest of the way to their very fine seats in utter silence. Willoughby had a grave, almost haughty look on his face, but he was utmost courtesy as he seated Marietta, adjusted her wraps and provided her with a program. But Marietta still had an angry

frown on her face distorting its beauty into anything
but charm.

For the first few seconds after they were seated the
young man applied himself to the study of the program,
and then quite casually began to speak about it.

"Have you read the description of the symphony?" he
asked. "It certainly promises to be quite colorful."

"No, of course not!" snapped Marietta. "I never do.
Why waste time doing that? The music is supposed to
give you the full idea, isn't it? I never could see the sense
of going to work to try to explain what it's supposed to
represent. I think it's all nonsense anyway! As if a sound
could represent people and emotions. You might as well
try to explain a sky or a tree or any part of a landscape
in words. It's there, isn't it? And what more do you
want? Why be sentimental about it? I like practical
things. This trying to mix literature up with art is ridiculous! It's enough to listen to a long program without
having to torture your brains trying to tell what it
means. Of course it doesn't mean anything but what
your imagination makes it mean, and of course every
person has a different idea of it. I think in these times
of war they waste money printing a lot of stuff like
that. It would be far better to save the money and the
paper and put it into war bonds."

"Yes?" said Willoughby with an amused twinkle.
"Well, that's an angle I hadn't thought of, but of course
there might be something in it. Why don't you put that
in writing and send it to the Board of Directors? But—
now that it *is* printed, and put in your hands, don't you
think it is up to you to see that it isn't wasted? What
if you and I put it to a thorough test this evening and see
if there is anything we can get out of it? Just read each
description carefully beforehand and then listen with it
in mind and see whether it makes the music any more
enjoyable. Suppose we try it. Now this first movement.
It starts with a darkening sky, and wind blowing the
grasses and the leaves on the trees, you can hear the
rising wind and then comes the patter of the rain as it
begins to fall—!"

Marietta looked at her escort in astonishment. This was a new phase of Val Willoughby, eloquent and fanciful. Why did he waste himself talking such foolish prattle as this?

"I think that's fantastic!" she said with a sneer. But she listened and watched him while he talked, and finally forgot her annoyance at him in admiration of his handsome face. He certainly was the best looking one of the old crowd of men. How well he would look in a uniform! What a pity he had allowed himself to be tied up to a stupid factory when he might be in some position of high command!

But Willoughby was talking well, and Marietta was fairly intelligent when she allowed herself time off from doing the talking herself. Somehow the story of an oncoming storm began to take form in her mind and when he came to the maiden alone on a desolate road with the rain pelting down, and then the knight on horseback coming to the rescue, she gave over thinking her own angry thoughts and began to take an interest in the tale he was telling. Not that she had as yet any idea of expecting to get the picture again by the sound of music that she was to hear, but at least she was getting the background of the scene, and the hint of a love story, which perhaps alone would have been able to interest her.

Val Willoughby worked hard at the telling because he knew unless he could interest the girl enough to keep her quiet, the whole evening would be an awful bore to him. So now as he talked, and watched a small growing interest in the girl's face, he began to feel that perhaps it would be worth-while after all. If he succeeded in making Marietta take an interest in music, perhaps he might hope that it would keep her tongue still about her own schemes for a little while and let others enjoy the concert. So he put the same zest into this description as he would have put into some experiment in the laboratory, or some delicate execution of government devices to help win the war, and felt really encouraged as he saw her turn toward him and really begin to listen. If he

had known however, that the supreme thought in her mind had been admiration of himself, he would have been disgusted and disappointed.

Yet, back of her observation of the way his hair waved back from his fine forehead, and the curve of his pleasant lips when he smiled, there was forming in her mind that picture of darkening sky, rising wind, lovely girl against an oncoming storm, the sound of horses' feet in the distance. Definitely Marietta would remember that picture when the music began, even against her will. Certainly it would be the first time she had ever formed a mental picture of music she was hearing. And Willoughby was at least comforted by the thought that so far she was listening to him. Perhaps she didn't even realize she was giving him her attention. She seemed to have had her interest caught unawares.

The people had been drifting in rapidly, until now the house was full, and though the young man had lowered his voice little by little until it was scarcely more than a murmur, Marietta had her eyes riveted to the tip of her companion's pencil with which he had idly been sketching on the margin of his program the outline of a mountain, a gnarled tree, and wispy tall grasses with bent heads. Val wasn't an artist. He was merely talking with his pencil for his own help as he went along. But the girl was watching, and making something out of the sketch even though it wasn't very good, as his low voice painted the scene of the music.

And now he was outlining a little bird on wing, flying toward shelter. Then suddenly the audience burst into wild applause. Looking up they discovered that the beloved orchestra conductor had arrived at the front of the stage and was being applauded.

With a deep breath Willoughby straightened up and sat back, feeling as tired as if he had been dragging a heavy burden up a hill. Well, at least he had kept her tongue still for a few minutes, and now, presently, he would have opportunity to discover whether his pupil had taken in aught of what he had been trying to dem-

onstrate. For already the conductor was in his place, and the audience had settled into utmost stillness.

Then came the first soft notes sending forth the shimmer of the summer sky, spreading it out in the semblance of a perfect summer day.

"Listen!" spoke Val softly, but more by the form of his lips, the lifting of his pencil, than by any sound he spoke.

And Marietta was so far under the spell of his pencil that her eyes turned to the platform as if she expected to find that summer day spread out to view.

He watched her. Would the music hold her to the thought, or would she grow restless?

Then all unexpected in the soft summer sky came the distant rumble of thunder menacing, beneath the delicate thread of melody the wind instruments had brought into being, and then again and again, coming nearer each time and more insistently, and Marietta's eyes grew wide with wonder. Nobody had ever made her see anything in music before save a tune that didn't matter to her in the least. But this had caught her. And now Val's pencil touched the sky over the mountains with a smudge of growing darkness, more grass bending low, branches bending, just a line here and there, and that little frightened bird winging its way as the big drops fell, and the storm went on wildly in a tumult of sound.

On to the end of the opening number Marietta's interest held, unaware as she was that she was listening, and when it was over and the delighted applause came she turned to Val:

"I didn't know music could be like that!" she said, half vexed with herself to admit it. "Where does that girl come in?" Val's answer was with the tip of his pencil, for the silence had broken into music again with the theme of the maiden, and softly the pencil kept rhythm, till it seemed the girl was struggling, trying to breast the storm.

It did not require words the rest of the time, nor drawing, only a sort of thought-directing on through

the story, and Marietta sat through the performance like one entranced. Only when the intermission came and everybody was buzzing and talking around them, and some were stepping out into the wide corridors to smoke and meet their friends, was there opportunity to talk, then Val found Marietta was studying her program, reading it all the way through.

By the time she had finished the conductor had returned and the music began again. Marietta listened, aware that here was something worth-while that she had hitherto passed by, annoyed at herself for not having known it before, wondering if all music were like this if only one understood how to listen.

They went quietly out with the throng, meeting now and then some they knew and nodding, but for the most part without speaking to one another. And because he knew she would expect it, he took her to a fashionable place for supper afterward, wishing in his heart this need not be, dreading lest now would be the time when she would start arguing again.

But Marietta sat for the most part silent, absorbed in her own thoughts. At last she roused.

"Well," she said, half crossly, because she always hated to own she had been wrong, "I suppose I'll have to thank you for opening my eyes, or rather my ears, to something great I have been missing. I certainly have enjoyed the evening for its own sake, and I hadn't expected to enjoy it for that reason at all. I think you have a wonderful way of teaching something if you once make up your mind to do it. But watching you all this evening, and seeing how skillful you are with a few crude pencil lines, and how eloquent you are with just the right words to sway my mind to listen, I still feel that I cannot bear it that you should waste your talents amusing yourself with a cheap little ignoramus like the girl you go skating with. I know you made a condition that I say no more on that subject, but the evening is over now, and I can't bear to leave you without your promise to quit her."

Willoughby's lips took on their firm line again, but

he smiled indulgently, and was still for a moment. Then he said quietly:

"I have not changed my determination about that, Marietta, and I do not wish to discuss it further tonight. Sometime perhaps I shall have the pleasure of making you see the loveliness in the character of that girl you despise, just as I have had the pleasure of opening your eyes to the beauties hidden in the music to which you never really listened before. Sometime perhaps I can introduce you to the girl, and make you understand what I mean."

"Never!" said Marietta with the ugly prejudice coming out and sitting plainly on her face. She seemed a different girl from the one who had listened raptly to lovely pastoral strains that evening. "I shall *never* care to meet her as an equal."

"But you know, that is almost what you said about the music when I asked you if you had read the program through. Sometime perhaps you will learn that prejudice often blinds people to some of the rarest things in life. I often wonder if we don't miss out that way in trying to learn about God and things of the other world."

"Oh, for Heaven's sake, Val Willoughby, *stop!* You make me shudder! Don't spoil the whole evening by talk about such gruesome things! I hate solemn stuff like that!"

So they went out to the car and drove home in a strange silence, Val greatly relieved that his evening was over and in a few minutes he might say good night and be free once more to think his own thoughts and go his own way, with no further obligations toward this girl, with whom he had surprisingly been able to spend a pleasant evening listening to thoroughly classical music.

So he rode to her home with her and left her at her door. Said good night gravely, received his thanks, but declined to come in and talk.

"I've given you all the time I can spare tonight," he said pleasantly. "Perhaps some other time we can have a talk about something else we don't agree on, but it

won't be very soon. I've an engagement tomorrow night, and the next night, and I don't know but I may have to go to Washington next week on Government business. Good night." He walked down the pavement to his aunt's home, catching occasional glimpses of the frozen river with the late moon glinting it with silver touches, and wondered if he had utterly wasted this evening.

Chapter 11

SOMETIME DURING THE pale hours when the dawn was beginning to steal into the sky, and rosy lights touched the river of ice, Nurse Branner woke up and decided what to do. There ought to be a telephone in that house, and she decided that she would see that there was one. She would tell Frannie that it was necessary for *her* business that she be within call at any time of the day or night. That she had several "cases" in the future, and one woman in particular had asked her to let her know just where she was, so that she could call her up in a sudden emergency. Frannie might think it queer perhaps, but Frannie didn't know much about nurses' emergencies of course, and she felt she could make her story quite plausible. And it was true that several old patients were in the habit of calling her occasionally, and her own sister always complained when she allowed herself to be more than a day in a house without a telephone.

Besides, Frannie had been saying that she meant to have a telephone, so she would just tell Frannie that she was presenting her with the initial cost, and if she didn't want to retain it when the nurse left, she could always tell them to take it out. So that was settled. She would have it put in the first thing Monday morning.

Next, somebody who could do some responsible investigating ought to know about that man who had

come to the back door so late, and the two shadows
that had moved in the dark across the ice. This problem
would not be quite so easily handled as the other. Besides, this was going to be Sunday morning pretty soon,
and Sunday was a different day from the rest. People
didn't go around and put in telephones on Sunday
even in emergencies, unless some very great person or-
dered it. And there was no one whom she could call
upon to do any investigating or protecting, who would
actually have the right to do it, but the police, and did
did she have a right to go to the police? This wasn't her
house, and the householders didn't even know she was
worried.

So she lay there and thrashed her brains until she
finally remembered the big burly policeman whose baby
she had nursed a couple of years ago, and who had
told her that if there was ever anything he could do for
her please to let him know. She would go to officer
Rowley and tell him all about it. She would go that
very morning. Frannie would be at home, at least unless she wanted to go to church around eleven. Yes she
would tell him all about it. She knew she could trust
him to see if any special vigilance was needed.

So after she had taken the breakfast tray up to her
patient she came down and said to Frannie:

"My dear, I wonder if you and Bonnie could take
turns sitting with your mother for about an hour or an
hour-and-a-half this morning? I want to run over to a
friend's house for a few minutes on an errand. I won't
be long. No, sit still and eat your breakfast. I'll get my
hat and coat. I drank some coffee and had some toast
before you came down, to save time. Now, will you
mind, dear?"

"Mind?" said Frannie. "Of course not. We'll have a
lovely time talking to mother, and take beautiful care
of her. You stay just as long as you want to. We'll be
all right. I didn't mean to go to church this morning
anyway. I thought I would stay and talk with mother.
She wants to ask me a lot of things about the place I
work. But don't you worry, I won't tell her anything to
trouble her. I realize she needs real rest for a while.

And by that time she will be used to seeing me come home safely every day."

So Nurse Branner hurried away. She had carefully planned her campaign for the shortest possible time, so she did not waste a minute. Bonnie, watching out the window, saw her turn to cross the bridge and sighed. She wished the nurse had asked if she might go with her. But Frannie heard the sigh and came with a smile.

"What's the matter, dearie?"

"I was thinking how quick Nurse Branner walks," said the little girl wistfully. "She went right across that big bridge up there. I'd like to go across that bridge."

"Well, you shall, little dear," said Frannie. "I'll take you for a walk myself across that bridge. Perhaps this afternoon, if the nurse gets back."

"Oh, Frannie! And can we walk over to my pretty lady's big white house? I want you to see how pretty it is."

"Why, perhaps so, if it isn't too far."

"Oh, but it isn't too far, Frannie. I runned it across the river when mother was sick."

"Yes, I know. But we'll walk around by the bridge if we go today. Now come on upstairs and let us make the bed and then we'll go in and talk to mother a little while and see how she feels."

So they hurried through the brief housework, Bonnie bustling about with a dustcloth and making a great show of being very busy. Then they had a nice talk with the mother, who seemed brighter, and quite cheerful that morning, glad of the sunshine that came in her window.

Meanwhile Nurse Branner took a taxi to the home of her policeman friend, and as she rode along the sunlit street she was praying in her heart that he might be at home, or at least somewhere that she could reach him.

It was a neat little gray house to which she finally drew up, not more than a mile and a quarter from the bridge, and she could see the round bright face of the little girl who was the baby she had nursed a little while ago, looking out the window, pink cheeks aglow with health, red curls atoss.

She kept the taxi waiting while she went in to see if the man she sought was there.

"Oh, Nurse Branner!" cried Mrs. Rowley in great delight, as she opened the door and welcomed her. "I've been hoping sometime you would come, and now you are here! And see, baby, *see,* this is the nice nurse that saved your life!" Mrs. Rowley seized the baby at the window and brought her forward for the nurse to look at.

"Isn't she wonderful, Nurse Branner? Jim he can't be thankful enough to you. He's always saying he wished he could do something for you, who did so much for us. Sit down, won't you, and let us look at you. It's good to see you again. We love you so much."

"Well, that's very nice, Mrs. Rowley. I'm glad to be here. And I've come to ask your husband's advice about something. Is he here, or could I find him at his station?"

The woman gave a quick glance at the clock.

"Oh, he'll be here in just ten minutes, unless something hinders him. He always comes about this time for his Sunday morning breakfast. He likes fish balls for Sunday, and he wants them piping hot, so he tells me about what time to expect him, and he'll be that glad to find you here. Excuse me just a minute, I think I smell the fish balls burning. I'll just turn down the blaze a bit."

When Mrs. Rowley came back from her neat little kitchen Nurse Branner had the baby in her arms, and was talking to her, and the baby was looking up at her charmed.

"Oh, but she's remembering you!" exclaimed the mother. "She's that bright, Nurse Branner, you'd be surprised. But I'm sure she remembers you. Look at her cuddle down contented, smiling."

And then in the midst of it all in walked the big policeman, with his breezy welcome, and hearty voice:

"Well, bless my soul, if there isn't our Angel-nurse Branner! Isn't this something to honor the day? Did I ever dream to have the blessing of your presence in our humble home again?"

After Nurse Branner had laughingly received his voluble praise, and the usual words of greeting had been exchanged, Miss Branner turned to him seriously.

"You remember I promised two years ago, James Rowley, that if ever I was in need of help I would come to you? Well, I've come. Maybe it isn't help I need, maybe it's only advice, but I thought you would be the one to come to and find out. You see I'm staying with a little family, a mother and two daughters, one a young woman the other a mere child of five. They've just moved into the old Garner house, the red brick, you know, that's been vacant so long. They don't know anybody around, and haven't even got a telephone in yet, though I mean to see to that tomorrow. The daughter works down the river at a defense plant and is away all day. The mother was there alone with the five year old girl, and fell in a faint while she was clearing off the breakfast table. The little girl, all alone and very much frightened, ran across the river on the ice and called for help at Mrs. Winthrop's, who telephoned for Dr. Ransom. He sent his office boy for me. That's how I came to be there. Mrs. Winthrop called in Valiant Willoughby and sent him home with the child, and later sent him down to tell the older daughter. That's the story, and there's nothing the matter with that part, for I happened to be just off a case, and am glad to help these people. They are dear people, and really need me for the present anyway. But last night something happened that worried me. In fact after I had thought about it a little it sort of linked itself up with something that had happened the first night I was there, and I thought I ought to tell somebody about it. I didn't want to tell the family, for they have just about as much to worry about as they can weather. I thought of the doctor, and of Mrs. Winthrop, but I sort of knew the doctor would merely laugh at me and tell me it was nothing and perhaps I ought to take a rest pretty soon. And I didn't like to worry Mrs. Winthrop. So I suddenly remembered you, and I knew you would be the one to come to. I knew if there was anything to it you would investigate it for me, or sort of protect the house for awhile or

something. And if there wasn't anything to it I knew I could believe you. So, that's why I've come. But, there, your wife is calling you to your breakfast, and I want you to have those fish cakes while they're hot the way you like them. Go sit down and eat and I can tell you afterwards."

The big policeman grinned.

"Yes, I like 'em hot, but I like my stories hot too. Sit right down and have a cup of coffee with me, and go on telling. I might get called off, you know, and I wouldn't want to go without knowing what's on your mind."

So Nurse Branner sat down at the table and told the story of the man who had knocked at the back door a little before midnight.

Officer Rowley filled his mouth with one of his wife's delicious fish balls, and while he was chewing he watched the nurse's face as she told her story, his canny eyes twinkling now and again knowingly.

"You say he was short and thick set—stoutish?" he asked keenly as he laid down his fork and picked up his coffee cup to take a deep swig of the hot liquid.

Nurse Branner nodded.

"Have anybody with him?"

"Well, I wasn't sure. He went down the steps to the river and walked out on the ice and I thought I saw a shadow steal out from the bushes and join him. I guess it was a man. Taller than the first one. In fact it wasn't the first time I had seen a couple of men, a tall one and a short one, go by on the ice and look at our house. I didn't think anything of it that first night I was there. And then I happened to look out another night and saw those two going by again—in fact they were going *down* the river that time, and on the other side, so that I didn't realize it was the same two, until I saw them turn and veer over to our side of the river, and then I watched them go by. They were looking up at the house, even stopping an instant to point to the corner of the house. Then I saw they were the same two men. And so last night when that man knocked I realized that I had seen him before, at least I'd seen

his funny chunky outline. But it didn't mean a thing to me even then until I got to thinking it over in the night. And then I saw that while I might be just fancying all this, there *might really* be something to it somehow, and somebody who would know how to handle it ought to hear about it. So, Mr. Rowley, what do you think? Of course it's none of my business at all. I'm just the nurse. But I simply couldn't tell those poor children nor their sick mother about it, nor even warn them not to open the door to a knock in the middle of the night if they should happen to be alone. So I've come to somebody I thought would understand and advise me right. What do you think?"

"I think you did just right, Nurse Branner. And I'll be glad to take over in your place and search this thing down to rock bottom. I'll let you know if I find there's anything to it. But to tell you the truth, your description of the man that knocked at your back door sort of tallies with a man we've been looking for off and on for several weeks back. Where did you say they parked their car?" and the burly officer took out a pencil and notebook and put down some incomprehensible marks.

"Now," he said, looking up with his pencil poised, "what time did you say he knocked at the back door? And approximately what time of night was it on the other two occasions you were sure you saw the two men?"

It did not take long to tell all she knew, and then the officer went on with his breakfast and smiled at the nurse.

"Don't you worry another little bit about this," he said. "I'll be glad to look after it. And in doing so I may uncover something valuable we have been trying to work out for some time. Just keep your attention out the window now and then and let me know any developments. You know there are a lot of Fifth Columnists going around these days. I don't say this is one, but don't let any strange men into your house, and tell your people not to. And if you happen to see me around anywhere don't worry. Though I shall probably not come myself. We'll kind of lay low on uniformed

men to give these men a chance to show their hands. But don't worry, above all things. You folks will be thoroughly protected as long as there is the slightest doubt or danger."

Nurse Branner went out at last with a parting kiss for the baby, and a shower of blessings on her for the visit. She took her taxi quickly over to the place where she had roomed and got a small overnight bag filled with fresh garments. So she hurried back to the bridge, from which she placidly walked down to the little brick house, the light of the pleasant day shining in her face. She had done the best she could with the matter of the midnight visitor and now she meant to send Frannie out for a walk or some kind of a restful interval. If it only were not such a lonely neighborhood just now with all those vacant new houses, some of them not yet finished, she would insist that Frannie go to church. But perhaps it was just as well for her not to go far yet until she had established contact with a church, and could get acquainted with a few young people who might furnish an escort. But certainly not until Officer Rowley had finished his investigation, and reported, she did not want to be the one to urge Frannie to go out alone in an unknown district. Of course it wouldn't be right to count on seeing any more of young Willoughby. He had an important job, everybody understood, and then too he must have his own intimate crowd who would be expecting him. He was a popular young man, and it was wonderful that he had given a strange little girl as much time as he had given Frannie, even sparing time to help put up curtains. People naturally went with their own class, the ones they had been brought up with, and that was right. Only it went sorely against the grain for Nurse Branner to think of Valiant Willoughby as being paired off with Marietta Hollister. She never had liked that girl and felt pretty sure she never would.

If she could have known that Val had spent Saturday evening with Marietta at a concert she certainly would have been disappointed in him. For she wouldn't have known that the young man in question was thinking of

his efforts of the night before with distaste, and wondering what would have been Frannie's reaction to the same lesson in orchestral music he had given, if he had tried it out on her instead of Marietta. Perhaps sometime he would. That was something interesting to look forward to. Provided always that the war had not swept over the land to such an extent that nobody had any time for symphony concerts.

Meantime, why couldn't he take Frannie to church somewhere? He had an idea she was a church girl, and would enjoy going, perhaps to some great rally with a fine speaker. There were often such meetings in the city. He went in search of the Saturday paper and turning to the religious page discovered a number of announcements that sounded interesting. Sometime that afternoon or early evening he would go over and ask after her mother and find out if she had any plans for the evening. Or, if the nurse was going out, perhaps he could sit there awhile and talk, just in a friendly way. Since Marietta's account of her call he wanted to look at Frannie with that in mind. Perhaps she would say something about her caller. He could almost visualize the twinkle in her brown eyes when she laughed at Marietta. He had a passing wish that he might have been present and heard the interview.

Then Val Willoughby chided himself. Was he idealizing that little Fernley girl because he had felt sorry for her, and because she seemed sweet and appealing? He mustn't be that kind of a fool. And of course there was something in what Marietta had said, much as he hated to acknowledge it. One shouldn't go too far out of one's own environment to form intimacies.

Yet Frannie had seemed so well brought up, so altogether refined. He remembered there had been the few pieces of fine old furniture, and some really good pictures, the daintiness of the white curtains, the thin old china on the table. No, surely, those Fernley's had not common tastes. And Frannie conversed well. She used well chosen words naturally, without awkward sentences. Surely Marietta had been utterly wrong. He felt in his heart that Frannie was worth cultivating as a

friend. In fact he felt strangely determined to do it, and let the town gossips say what they would.

So Val did some serious reading that he had been saving for an hour of leisure, hung around until the usual five o'clock tea time that his aunt always made much of on Sunday afternoon, and then strolled out, up the hill to the bridge, and over the bridge to the little brick house with its cheerful friendly light shining down on the icy way.

As he walked he looked down the river, especially as he crossed the bridge, and thought of the lovely things that Lady Winthrop had said about it. Her "street of the city" she had called it. Her fancied way to the Heavenly City. With the silver moonbeams now upon its gleaming breast he could understand her similes. What a lovely lady she was, and how sweetly she was growing old. Taking her hardships and loneliness as if they had been blessings, giving her sons to the war, and taking what pleasure she could from the pictures the river formed for her. Thinking of her Heavenly Home as if she were looking forward to it with pleasure. He wondered if he would feel that way about the end of his life when he got there? That of course was a right way to feel. To meet it joyously, as an end in itself, and not a cessation of all that had been good.

He must not forget that Monday evening gathering she had told him about. He would go at least once and see what it was like. Perhaps knowing a great deal about the Bible and understanding what it meant had been what had kept Lady Winthrop's soul so sweet and young, so full of faith, and ready to look forward through growing old to the time when age should drop away, and life should become new and young and eternal.

So he pondered, as he walked across the river to see the little girl who lived on the wrong side of the bridge, and never knew that Marietta had seen him go by from her window, and attired herself hopefully, for his possible return.

Chapter 12

FRANNIE WAS HELPING the nurse to put away the
supper dishes when Willoughby arrived, and the two
were a bit startled to hear the knock at the door. The
nurse thought at once of the man who had knocked
last night and gave a quick glance in Frannie's direction. Perhaps she ought to have told the girl about it
after all, but the policeman had seemed to think it
wasn't necessary just yet.

"I'll go," said the nurse wiping her hands quickly on
the roller towel and hurrying toward the front door.
If it was that man again she would get rid of him in
short order, and try to do it in a low tone so Frannie
wouldn't have to know about it.

But Frannie was all too willing to let her answer the
knock, for she was thinking of that obnoxious girl, and
wondering if she had come again. If she had she did
not want to see her, and she knew Nurse Branner would
see that she did not have to.

But it was Val's voice she heard instead of Marietta's
and her heart gave a happy little skip. That was pleasant. Nice of him to come over to see how her mother
was, that was what she heard him say as he stepped inside the living room. And Frannie hurried to dry her
hands and go in.

Valiant's smile was warm and hearty, like a very old
friend's, and Frannie felt happy to think he was not going to try to be a stranger as she had feared. He had
come back of his own accord, not just to be polite, but
to be friendly, also. That was what his smile said. He
might be an intimate of that hateful patronizing girl.
He might even be the one she said was practically engaged to her, or some of her kind, but he wasn't going
to look down on other people because of that, and he

wasn't minding that she was living on the wrong bank of the river either.

So she came in without self-consciousness, just a bit of heightened color perhaps, and a shine in her eyes that had not been there before he came. He put out his hand and grasped hers wholeheartedly, making her feel that he was her real friend in spite of that other girl.

He was looking down at her as he stood, her hand still in his, and thinking how pretty she looked, with her hair in little rings of curls around her face, and no make-up at all, her pansy-blue eyes raised to his. Yes, she was lovely. He hadn't noticed it especially before. She had been almost too pale that first time he saw her, when she was so frightened about her mother. But she was beautiful, with those long dark lashes curling back from her wide sweet eyes. He had never been one to stare at a girl, or to analyze her features and think about beauty. He had often acknowledged that Marietta was beautiful, but it hadn't meant a thing to him because he didn't admire her character, and if a girl's heart wasn't lovely what did it matter how her outward features were formed? To be truly beautiful there must be no flaws of soul. The face must match the heart and that, it suddenly struck him, was the case with this girl. This face was no camouflage, it was a true delineation of the life within.

So he stood and smiled down into her sweet eyes, and spoke in an intimate tone:

"I just came over to find out how your mother is tonight, and then I thought if she was able to spare you for a little while, perhaps you would like to go somewhere to church with me."

Frannie's cheeks grew bright and her eyes lighted up.

"Oh, that would be lovely," she said breathlessly, "but I don't know but Miss Branner would like to go out somewhere. I was just going to ask her."

"No indeed," said Nurse Branner decidedly. "I went out this morning, you know, and really I'm a bit tired from it. I thought I'd read a little while to your mother, and when she gets to sleep, I have something I want to

read myself. Go ahead, Frannie. I'd love to have you. Perhaps you can find a church you will enjoy."

And so with lovely happiness in her eyes Frannie hurried upstairs to get ready.

She seemed very sweet as she came downstairs in her slim green coat and her little green turban, her soft brown curls framing her face.

"I hope it's not a very grand church you're taking me to," she said shyly. "I haven't any fine clothes."

"Haven't you?" smiled Val. "They look plenty fine enough to me. But then I'm not much of a judge of clothes. I'm sure they look as if they suited you, and that's altogether satisfactory, so don't let's worry. Have you any choice of churches?"

"Oh no," said the girl. "I don't know the churches around here. I had it in mind to hunt up a pleasant place that would be near enough for my mother to walk to, but that would probably take time, and I'd rather go with you to whatever church you choose."

"Well, I haven't been living around here much until the last three or four weeks, and I haven't settled down yet. I've been going with my aunt to her church the last two weeks since I've been here because it pleased her to have me, but frankly I wasn't very well satisfied. The minister didn't seem to me to believe all he was saying, and I thought I'd like to go where there was a real message. There's one man down in the city who has the reputation of speaking pretty directly from the shoulder, and just now he is talking about what this war means and all the things that are happening in the world today, in relation to the message of God in the Bible. I thought I'd like to hear what he has to say. How about you? Would you enjoy that?"

"Oh yes," said Frannie earnestly. "I've wondered so much how the war can possibly fit in with God's loving the world and wanting to save them."

"All right then, we'll go and see if we get any light on the subject. And about that church for your mother, I'll be inquiring around to find out possibilities. Then, maybe next Sunday we can shop around a little and find a church nearby where your mother and Bonnie

can walk. But tonight we'll go to the Fourth-Avenue Church and see what we can hear. Would you rather walk or ride? My aunt is not going to use her car to-night and she said I might take it. Pretty soon I shall have to have one of my own, but just now I like my skates as well as any form of locomotion. Although it wouldn't be just the thing to skate to church. I suppose the ice will decide to leave us some day and then we'll have to find some other method anyway. But tonight there is no reason why we can't ride if you'd like."

"Oh, I think I'd rather walk if you don't mind. Is it far?"

"No. Not over a mile or a mile and a quarter."

"Well, then let's walk. I haven't been anywhere around here and I think we'd get better acquainted with it walking, don't you?"

"Perhaps," said Val smiling. "I never thought of it that way. But it is a lovely night and I shall enjoy walking down some of the pretty streets that are on the way to church and showing them to you. Then if you are tired we can take a taxi home."

"Oh, I shall not be tired," said Frannie with a little ripple of a laugh. "I don't get tired walking, and you know I have to sit almost all the days at the office. But you—you have to be on the go a great deal. Would you rather ride? Because I could enjoy that a lot too. I haven't had many opportunities to ride of late."

"No, I'd love to walk. I have always enjoyed it. Come, let's go. It is still light enough to see, and we'll go right by Lady Winthrop's home. You've seen it from the river, but I want you to see it from the street. It really is a lovely old mansion, with many delightful facings."

So they went out together, and Nurse Branner smiled and was glad at the way one day had worked out.

So that was how it came about that Marietta saw Val Willoughby and her hated little rival walking by her house together.

Marietta had not turned on the light. She was moon-ing by the window, thinking to open the door for him herself when he came back and stopped to call.

At first she could not believe it was the same girl, the girl from the wrong side of the river. The cut of her green coat was smart, and the little turban was jaunty and becoming. Of course it was beginning to be dusk and the sidewalk was some distance from the house, but Marietta's eyes were sharp, her intuitions were keen, and she knew who it was. She watched for a moment with growing fury in her heart. Had Val Willoughby done this just to tantalize her? Wouldn't he be sure she would see them? He was just trying to annoy her. To show her that he would defy her wish. Her blue eyes snapped like blue flames. She would have to do something extra specially annoying to him to pay him for this.

Perhaps he was even contemplating bringing her in to call. That would be unspeakable! That girl! If he dared she certainly would have things to say to the contemptible creature that would humiliate her forever.

But no, perhaps the best way would be to be out. To seem not to have been at home at all to see him pass. She would go at once, and run no risks of having such a dreadful thing happen. So she rushed up to her room to prepare for an evening with some friends, and watched her opportunity to escape across the lawn to get her car when there was no sign of them on the street.

But meanwhile all unaware of the tumult they were exciting in Marietta's angry breast, the two were walking briskly down Hilltop Road, and taking in all the beautiful homes along the way.

As they passed the Haversett home and Val told her it was where his aunt lived, Frannie gave a little gasp as she eyed the great stone mansion with its massive bay windows and stone arches, and evidences of wealth on every side.

"Oh!" she said softly. "To think that you live there in that lovely home, and yet you are taking time to be kind and go to church with me! *Me,* a little nobody, with shabby clothes, who lives on the wrong side of the river."

He gave her a quick look, and then he laughed.

"You sound like Marietta Hollister," he said and laughed again.

She gave him a quick look in turn now.

"You know her then?"

"Oh yes, of course, I know her. I've known her since she was a spoiled baby younger than your Bonnie. She never had half the sense Bonnie has now. But don't let anything she says or thinks worry you. I understand she's been to call on you."

Frannie lifted wondering eyes.

"How did you know?"

"Why, she told me herself, and my anger rose momently as she enlarged upon her visit. But I beg of you not to worry about it. She isn't worth it. She has money and an expensive education, but she has no soul; she's like a lovely showy flower without perfume. She is essentially selfish, and sometimes cruel in the extreme, if it suits her purposes. I don't like to talk about my acquaintances this way, especially to one who is a comparative stranger to them, but I feel that it is right that you should understand the situation. I hope you won't think me unkind in my summary of her character. You see she is so very beautiful on the outside that it is hard to realize she can be actually cruel. There! Now, have I said enough and can we put the subject aside and forget it?"

He looked down at her earnestly, and drew her arm within his own to emphasize his confidential attitude.

Frannie was looking down, her brow troubled, thoughtful.

"Why, yes, I guess so," she said slowly. "It wasn't exactly pleasant to bear, that call, and I practically knew it didn't matter, because I never would be likely to have my lot cast within even a near approach of hers, but of course I didn't enjoy thinking that a lot of tongues had been caused to wag about you as well as myself, just because you had been kind enough to bring a message to me about my sick mother, and then later to help me out in a free-for-all fight with those two fresh fellows. But I guess if we're not seen skating together any more

the talk will soon die out. You see that girl and I really do live in different worlds, typified to her mind by which side of the river we live on, and we're not likely to cross each other's paths often, so I guess there isn't much damage done."

"Damage? Well, no, I should say not! But if you think I'm going to let that little gossiping baby-doll cheat me out of a new friend I hope I've found in you, you're sadly mistaken. Even if I didn't like you for yourself, and have pleasure in skating with you, which I very much do, I wouldn't let Marietta Hollister beat me out of doing what I want to do. So if you please, keep right on skating down to your work whenever you want to, and if you don't mind I shall join you when I can. I told that snooping little gossip as much myself. So you see you've got to help me keep my word. I told her you were a good friend of mine. And now can't we get to work and find some mutual friends, so we can prove that we didn't 'pick each other up' on the ice, as they are pleased to say we did?"

Frannie laughed.

"Why yes," she said gaily, "I guess we can. Did you have a friend named Ford Harrison when you were in college?"

Willoughby looked at her in surprise.

"Why yes, I did," he said. "How did you know?"

"Well, you see his sister Allison was my roommate in college. I've been trying ever since I heard your name to remember where I had heard it before, and at last it came to me that Allie used to speak of one by that name as her brother's best friend."

"Great!" said Willoughby. "That would surprise Marietta. She didn't know you had been to college."

Frannie grinned.

"She would think a girl who lived on the wrong side of the river couldn't possibly have gone to college," she said amusedly, looking up at him with a comical twinkle.

"No, please, I never said I agreed with that nonsense about the other side of the river. That's a lot of hooey the smart set got up. I never felt that way."

"No, I knew you wouldn't," said Frannie. "I knew you were bigger than that."

"But seriously, Frannie, tell me about your college life. I want to understand why I didn't hear more about you, because I was quite intimate in the Harrison home during my college days."

"Well, you see, that fall I roomed with Allison was the end of my college life. Father got sick, and we had to go west, and I never went back to college. There wasn't money enough after father's health and business both failed, and somehow those were pretty hard days. I had no time for just pleasant correspondence. It's been a pretty busy world for me ever since."

"I see," said Willoughby. "I do remember something about Allison Harrison losing her roommate that she liked so much. But I'm glad to know about it now. We are not just strangers to one another. We have a background of mutual friends through several years. We can start with that, and the next time we have a chance to talk about it very likely we'll find a few others, just for anyone who accuses us of picking one another up on the ice. But—this is the church, and the organ is playing. I guess we are just about on time. Shall we go in?"

Chapter 13

IT WAS A very solemn sermon to which the two listened, after the beautiful singing which preceded it was over. It took up the Bible outline of the national frontiers at the time of the end of the present age, as they are referred to in the seventh of Daniel and elsewhere. It showed how the nations would realign themselves so that two opposing groups would be separated by the line of the Rhine and the Danube, the boundary of the ancient Roman Empire. The speaker quoted famous war commentators' speculations which showed that it would

be possible for the realignment to take place quickly, even within only a few weeks' time."

"Why, I never knew that the Bible told things like this," said Frannie. "Did you? I didn't know that it definitely told what was going to happen on the earth in these days that are so long after the Bible was written. I knew of course that there were prophecies of general things, but I never knew it went into detail. I never even tried to read any of the prophecies. I thought people weren't meant to understand them. Did you know all this?"

"Well, I knew in a general way that there were prophecies that had to do with the latter days of this age. I knew there were prophecies of wars, and one battle in particular, the last one, called Armageddon. Everybody was wondering in the last world war whether Armageddon was soon due. But I gather that not many of the church people have paid much attention to such things, only accepting them as a vague description of matters that would occur in the far distant future, like the Day of Judgment. People who had any Christian background at all have sort of taken these things for granted. It is only within recent years that any large number of Christians have seriously set themselves to study and discover what it is all about. I've been hearing a couple of young Christian students talk, and they mentioned a few of the things we heard tonight. That prophecy about the Prince of Rosh—it interested me a lot, so I thought I would like to hear some more. That's why I suggested coming here tonight. It's rather startling, isn't it? Did you enjoy the talk?"

"I thought it was wonderful," said Frannie. "I'd like to hear more. I suppose there are books or papers perhaps that would tell more about those things."

"I think there are," said Willoughby. "I know those fellows used to have a lot of books and magazines around their rooms, and now and then I would pick up one and read a bit. I'll find out their names and try to get hold of some of them. By the way, Lady Winthrop asked me to come to her house tomorrow night

to a class they have, studying the Bible. Would you like to go? I'll ask her if I may bring you."

"Oh, I'd love it, but I wouldn't like you to ask her about me. You know I'm the girl from the wrong side of the river."

"Now look here! That's not fair. Lady Winthrop isn't like that at all! She seemed anxious to get all the people she could, and she wouldn't even know that your side of the river is not the aristocratic side. She's the most democratic Christian lady I've ever seen. If you'd like to go I'll see that she asks you. I know it will be all right, and I'll be calling for you a little before eight o'clock. I think from what she said that they are studying something along these lines of prophecy."

"Well, I certainly would enjoy hearing more about what we listened to tonight," said Frannie with a sigh. "I wish mother was where she could hear that man sometimes. I don't think mother has ever heard anything like that. Do you suppose that was all true, or is some of it just fanciful, just some imagination added to a few vague facts?"

"No, definitely not," said Willoughby. "This man we heard tonight ranks as one of the foremost Christian scholars in the city, and indeed I understand, in the country. He sifts his facts before he presents them to the world, and he is not only a scholar, but very spiritual, they say. Shall we go and hear him again sometime?"

"I would love to," said Frannie wistfully. "It is all so new to me. It makes the Bible seem real, and brings the prophecies right down to where we live, not as if they were away off and rather uncertain."

"Yes, it does," said Willoughby. "That's what struck me when I talked with those friends of mine. I thought at first they were just fanatical on that subject, but they certainly managed to make me wonder if there was something in it. And then I began to think what if it were true that Christ may appear any day. If it is it makes living in these days seem almost grand. Did you think of that when he was talking tonight about the silver trumpet sounding, and all those signs which pre-

cede the return of Christ to the earth later? Those were very interesting. I always supposed those signs in the sun and moon and so on meant the end of the world and the Judgment Day."

"So did I," admitted Frannie, "and I believe most people do who have read the Bible as carelessly as I have."

"Well, I guess that is true, but it's thrilling to realize that the times of those things may be almost upon us. And of course there were ancient prophecies fulfilled when Christ came to earth the first time. I remember studying that around Christmas time when I was a little kid in Sunday School. But nobody talked to me then about any coming *back* again. I always thought things were just going on and on this way till sometime there would come a day of judgment and then there would be Heaven."

"Yes, I guess I thought so too," said Frannie. "Of course they didn't study about anything like that in college, not even in the Bible course. It was mostly like a history course with some poetry mixed in."

"Yes, that's about the size of it. But I didn't take Bible in my course. In our university it was known as one of those easy make-shifts taken to escape really hard work. Of course engineering was my major, and I just took what went with it. But I see my mistake now. Of course if the Bible really is the Word of God, as my mother taught me, it should be the most important!"

"Yes," said Frannie, "I suppose it should. I never thought of that. And I have never counted it very important at all, although of course I've believed it."

"Well, you're one ahead of me," said the young man gravely. "I'm not sure I have, not always. Though of late, with this war, I've been thinking I was wrong to let doubts in. Doubts don't help the situation much in times like these. Not for men, anyway."

"No, nor for women either," said Frannie seriously. "It doesn't look very happy ahead in life for anybody, does it? Unless there is something to expect like what we heard tonight."

"That's right," said Willoughby.

They walked on till they came to the bridge, and looking down the crystal way they saw the moon shining, making the path of the river into beaten gold. They stood there for some minutes quietly looking.

"It is a glorious sight, isn't it?" said the young man. "I keep thinking what Lady Winthrop said about it. She had some Bible verses about the street of the city being pure gold, as it were transparent glass. I can see what she meant now, can't you? Look down toward the city and see those tall buildings. It isn't hard to imagine the unearthly beauty of a Heavenly City in this light, with the soft mist of the evening about it. That Lady Winthrop is a remarkable woman, and it doesn't seem as if she was old in the least. She has the naive childlikeness of a very young person, or she never would have thought of such similes, even with that Bible verse to start on."

"Yes, she seemed so to me," said Frannie, "though of course I saw her only a few minutes. But I do want to know her better. I thought she was lovely, and I know mother would love her. I hope we can be friends."

"I'm sure you will be," said Willoughby with conviction.

Then suddenly Frannie swung around and looked upstream.

"Look!" she said. "It's wonderful up this way too. Those are 'the eternal hills.' And see that tower of stone among the evergreens, and the river just below like a sheet of silver. It might be a part of the Heavenly City."

"Yes, it's wonderful!" said Willoughby. And then he turned and looked down at her with a great gentleness in his face.

"You're a bit of a poet yourself, aren't you?" he said with a tender smile in his eyes for the sweet girl.

After a minute or two longer he drew her hand within his arm, and they started on again.

"I'd like to linger here till the moon sets," he said half wistfully, "but you and I are both working people. We have to get to work early in the morning. I

mustn't keep you up too late. Of course it isn't to be compared with the hour you would go home from one of Marietta's dances that she tried to tempt you with, but we aren't in her class, so we won't worry about that. Besides, I suppose you have to think about not worrying your sick mother by staying too late."

"Yes," said Frannie. "You're very thoughtful, and most kind. My mother will appreciate it I know. As I do also. But it has been very lovely tonight, and I've learned a lot. I shall never forget that sermon. It made me feel that the Bible is as real today as when it was written, and that it is for me as much as ever it was for the people in the New Testament days."

For answer Val Willoughby laid his hand over Frannie's with a quick warm pressure.

"I'm glad!" he said, and then added: "I'm glad we went. I think that sermon made me see a lot of things also that I've been missing for a long time. Somehow I think that you have helped, too. There's something in having a friend along who understands."

"Oh, thank you!" said Frannie. "Yes, I think I do understand. Because it's something I've never had myself, and always felt uneasy about it. Only I couldn't bring it out in the open, because I had to be strong for my mother's sake."

They were still for a long time as they walked slowly down the paved way from the bridge, and the bright silver street stretched away to where the softly-lit towers and turrets of Lady Winthrop's imaginary city stood shadowy against a star-pricked dome of blue.

As they turned to go up to the little old white picket gate of the brick house, Willoughby said in a tone that was almost like a sacrament:

"I'm glad I have found you. It is good to have you for a friend. In the uncertain days that are ahead of us both perhaps we can study this thing out together."

"Oh!" said Frannie softly, and her voice was so soft it was scarcely audible.

And while all this was going on two men had been waiting silently, back in the shadow of great alder

bushes, up several paces from the inland side of the
house, one a tall man, and the other burly, with a
shovel held in his hard hand, the spoon part of the
implement stuck sharply in the ground where the
outer frozen crust had been removed for a foot or so.
The man was leaning back against the stout handle
of the shovel in an interval of his cautious labor. At his
feet, well concealed by a pile of snow, lay a worn old
tool box with a sturdy pickax beside it, both its pointed
ends caked with frozen mud and ice.

"We oughtn't to have come so early," said the big
man. "You don't have very good sense in your calcu-
lations, Mike. I didn't want any of the family around
while we do this."

"Well, they didn't any of them go out *last* Sunday.
They went to bed early. Every light out at eight-
thirty. I figured they'd do the same this week. But anyhow, don't you worry. The young dame will be all
absorbed in her boy-friend. She won't notice anything
out of the way, and anyway nobody can see us from
the house."

"Okay," said the other. "But it seems to me you've
bungled this all the way through. What exactly did
that agent say about the owner? Tell me again. Tell
me every word."

"Well, he said he hadn't heard from him yet. He
said the old chap was sick and had gone to a sanitarium, and he couldn't get in touch with him."

"But what did he say about a contract?"

"Said there wasn't any. Said they just rented the
house and paid one month's rent down. Their month is
up the seventh. He said if we paid a lump sum down
we could take over, and he'd send a notice to the folks
that the place was sold."

"The seventh! But that's too late! We've got to bring
our stuff here now and get going. I've got big obligations."

"Yep. I tol' him that, and he said there wasn't no
reason in the world if we wanted to, that we couldn't
bring lumber here and park it on the back of the lot.

The tenants never asked how large the lot was. They just wanted the house anyhow. So I told Nick to bring on yer lumber tonight. That okay with you?"

"What? Do you mean he's bringing it here, tonight, *now,* in a few minutes? Why, the folks will hear. You can't get away with that."

"Oh *sure* we can. Not just in a few minutes I don't mean, for I figured it would take us a couple of hours to get these yere wires uncovered and pulled out the way you want. So I told him to begin to load up around ten and come in by the back road. You couldn't get a sledge down the river without making a whole lotta noise, and being an unusual sound it might be noticed, wake somebody up, you know. But coming in by the back road, if we have them boards *carried* in, one at a time, and lay 'em down careful-like there won't be a sound to give us away. And by morning they'll only be a pile of old boards. You know all of 'em are weathered stuff. And if they see 'em they'll just think they never noticed 'em before."

"Well, maybe so," said the big man uncomfortably. "But this ain't the way I intended to work it. I figured on playing safe every step of the way, and we *would,* too, if you had carried out *your* part of the bargain. If anything goes wrong on this deal I'll just lay it to your fault and pay you accordingly, understand that?"

"Say, look here now, you signed a paper saying how much you were willing to give."

"Sure I did, but there were things you were to do, and you haven't done one of 'em on time yet."

"Well, I couldn't help it, could I, if the old guy got sick and went to some sanitarium? I done my best to make things come out anyway though, and I think you'll find everything okay. The only thing I can't figure out is how you're going to get that there mike outta that there cellar. Why, they might discover it was there most any day now, especially when they go to clean the cellar. You know dames like that are apt to be pretty frisky about getting spic and span by spring."

"It's not the mike I'm worrying about," said Gran-

niss. "We could easy get another, but there are incriminating papers, maps, floor plans of defense plants, and other stuff there that we've *got to have!* An' we've got to have 'em before the seventh!"

"I see. But how are you gonta get 'em out without wakin' up the folks?" asked Mike perplexedly.

"You just leave that to me," said the older man. "I'm figuring to wait till some dark night when there's a lotta wind, mebbe even rain, and do a swift job of digging when we start, just tunnel under to that little closet in the cellar and tap the wall. Take out the stuff and the microphone and the recording machine and all and install it in the new shed we're putting up back here. Doing that we can go on using the same transmitter that we had before, and nobody the wiser. An' if the folks in the house discover us working, well, they're just women, and there are ways of handling them. I don't intend to stop at anything."

"You don't say!" said Mike, looking speculatively across the starlight to the other man, secretly planning to leave any "rough stuff" to his partner in crime. "But how come they didn't discover your arrangements when these folks took over the house?"

"Oh, we had that all camouflaged inside. Even if the cops had come into the cellar they couldn't have found it. It was an extra bricked-in addition we built off the far end of the cellar behind the furnace, and it was so finished you couldn't have found the opening unless you knew how. One loose brick that looked solid as Gibraltar, and came out, and then behind a panel there was the key hole. But even that you wouldn't have recognized. It was just a sort of slit, and the key was thin as a knife blade. Oh, we had it all fixed up. It was great. And of course when nobody lived in this house we could come here any time and use it nearly all night without any danger of discovery."

"So! That was the way it was!" said Mike thoughtfully to himself, laying up this knowledge for a time when it would be more lucrative to remember certain things than it now was to keep silence about them.

"Now, Mike, stop right about there where you are

and reach down with your fingers. See if you can strike any wires with your hand yet. I think you ought to have almost got it uncovered."

Mike got down on his knees and worked away beside his prone shovel, running his hand down farther and farther, bringing up handfuls of ashes and small stones.

"Yep," he said, puffing softly with his exertions, "I think I got her. Two wires, ain't there? *Say?* Am I liable to get a shock doin' this?"

"No, no shock, not to amount to anything. Got the two wires you say? Okay. Then we're safe. Now while we wait for the lumber suppose you do a little quiet digging. Go slow, not too continuous you know, else it might attract some dame's attention. Get as far as you can while we wait and have some bushes and weeds ready to put it all under cover in case somebody should come by. Hark! What's that sound? That isn't a cop's car, is it? Over there in the next street?"

"Naw, that there's the ten o'clock bus. She stops at that corner for three minutes and then goes on. I got this neighborhood pretty well memorized. You know I don't go into nothing like this without making sure I won't get caught. But what I don't understand is what you said the first day. You spoke about a powder plant, and I can't just figure how these two things work together."

"Oh, don't you? Well, you're not so foresighted as I thought you were. Don't you see the easiest way would have been to put up a rough building, call it a powder plant, make a small output of the stuff, enough to throw anyone off the track, and have only workmen who are wise to keep their mouths shut. Then we can use our radio all we please without exciting suspicion. That's why I wanted to buy the place. That would have been the easiest way, besides giving us the look of being deep in defense work. And that's what we will eventually do as soon as we can get entire possession. But in the meantime this lumber can be brought in very slowly, a little at a time, until we have enough here to begin to build. Then we can bring our own men here,

put up a rough shell in a hurry, and not attract attention. You see it's wisest to keep attention away from here as much as possible. After we get the shell of a building up we can build a sound proof compartment out of sight. Of course if we could buy the house and put the people out of it at once, offer them a bonus or something, we could use the old arrangement, but if we can't get them out right away, we'll have to fix up something to do till we get possession. But there are always ways to get people out if you offer money enough. I figure this ain't any exception. Hey! What's that? Steps."

"That's the young guy bringin' his gal home. Just lie low. He don't stay long after he comes. He works early somewheres. Guess I'll sort of let up till he leaves."

The big man settled down on the tool chest behind the group of bushes, and the two remained motionless for several minutes, while they watched the lights in the little brick house. Someone came into the kitchen and got a pitcher of water and a tray. They could hear the tinkle of glasses and the clink of pieces of ice. Then the kitchen light went out and there was another interval. But they did not have to wait long until they heard the front door open; voices, footsteps, and then they could hear the young man going down the walk.

"Okay!" said Mike at last in a cautious voice. "The young guy has gone. Now we can work again. It won't be many minutes before all the lights go out, and the house will be asleep."

"Well, don't take any chances!" warned the big man. "What time did you say that lumber would arrive?"

"He didn't say what time exactly. He said he'd be along plenty late so we didn't needta worry. What's that?"

Footsteps! Footsteps! Quiet, steady, measured. A low word now and then stopping a moment, then passing slowly by.

"Sounds like cops!" murmured Mike.

"No brass buttons!" murmured Granniss.

The footsteps passed on, and the sound died away indefinably.

After a little Mike peered into the darkness after them.

"Where do you 'spose them two went? There ain't none of them new houses occupied yet, is there?"

"How should I know? That's your job. That's what I hired you for."

"Well, I guess I'm just getting jittery. I didn't like the way they stopped walking, but there ain't any place down that way where they could rightly go."

He got up and straightened his stiff back, took a step or two out toward the street.

"Hi! there, come on back and get to work," growled Granniss. "They went off toward the bridge. I'm most sure I heard them cross the bridge. Don't be a fool. You'll have that lumber on top of your work before you know it, and we don't want to stay here all night, you know."

"Keep your shirt on, man! You don't have to do a thing but sit still and see your orders carried out. And mind this, fella, I'm just as anxious to earn my money as you are to pay it, so pipe down and keep calm. And—*there,* I hear those footsteps going on now. They were most likely stoppin' to talk a little before separatin'. One has gone on across the bridge, and the other has likely taken the dirt road where his footsteps wouldn't sound. Now, let's get back on the job. You want I should foller them wires now, back to the leanto on the kitchen? Is that right?"

"Yes. Make it as deep as you can and then cover it over somehow. Little sticks across near together, covered with branches. Snow flung across it. Nobody walks across this place anyway. We've checked up on that in the past when we used the empty house."

"Okay!"

Later there were steps in the distance, but the two men were intent on the trench they were constructing, and paid little heed.

The night grew deeper, and the darkness more intense, with only the far dim stars above in the blackness of midnight blue.

And then at last came noiseless wheels and a muffled

engine, rolling down the incline of the back street almost imperceptibly, and Mike striding silently across the ruts of the field to stand in the road and wave and point out the stopping place.

Two dark figures slipped from the driver's seat and approached the load, rubber shod, lifting a single board and following Mike into the field behind the brick house. Mike went like a cat across to the place he had just cleared and indicated just where this first board should be placed. It was all done without talk, the directions given by motions, the men all acting as if they had been trained in a school of silence. Just once a board slipped and went down with a thud, and the crew looked fearfully about and crouched near the ground out of sight. Then after an interval the work went swiftly on till all the boards were neatly piled, low lying, and a few branches scattered over with some snow atop. It was a well camouflaged pile of lumber, and to all casual appearances had been there perhaps all winter. Only one very familiar with the scene would have noticed that the landscape was at all changed. Then the truck that brought them went away like a shadow into the darkness, and after a few minutes the two men slipped as silently away, Mike carrying the old tool chest on his brawny shoulder.

A few minutes later a canny little upstart of a moon peered brightly out from behind a cloud and went on with its journey across the sky, flinging down a flash of silver to the ice-locked river to sail like a bright twin up its length to the west and disappear with it behind the mountains.

And then two silent figures detached themselves from two of the little new empty houses up across the street, and went silently over to the late scene of activities behind the brick house, and carefully examined every inch of the way, bringing small pencils of light to bear in a flash or two upon the broken snow and branches covering the excavation, and the pile of lumber. They nodded at one another, and then together stole away.

And in the little brick house the family slept secure, and the moon rose higher, and smiled down on that

street of the city that two young people had been talking about that evening as they looked down the silver way, till in her dreams Frannie almost thought she saw the tower and pinnacles of the Holy City, and she smiled in her sleep. Rest and peace and comfort and unawareness of the danger and the sinister plans that were working all about her, danger for the whole beautiful world of peace into which Frannie had been born.

Chapter 14

FRANNIE'S PIANO ARRIVED by way of the Bluebell Neighborly Truck Express, about the middle of the morning on Monday, and under Nurse Branner's direction was duly installed in the living room, giving the place a cosy air of homelikeness. With it had come two fine old oil paintings of a quaint grandmother with a white organdy cap and kerchief, and a grim grandfather in old time attire.

"I reckon she wants them pictures hung on the wall, don't she? I brung the hooks they was hung on, and I told her I'd hang 'em for her," said the old man who had brought them.

So the nurse went up to Mrs. Fernley for instructions, and when Frannie came home that afternoon there was her beloved piano in the place that had been left vacant for it, and there hung the old pictures in the same relation to the piano that they had occupied in Bluebell.

"Oh, this is nice, isn't it?" she said with a happy smile as she looked around the room. "It begins to look like home now. When do you think mother will be able to come downstairs, Miss Branner?"

"Well, she's going to sit up awhile today, and if her pulse says so, perhaps the doctor will let her come down tomorrow. He's coming again in the morning, and

I'll ask him. So perhaps we'll have another surprise for you tomorrow night when you come home. But don't get your hopes up too high. He may think she ought to stay upstairs another day or two before she attempts to come down."

Frannie ran up the stairs lightheartedly to see her mother, and her feet seemed to have the old spring, her voice the old ring as she entered her mother's room.

"My dear!" greeted her mother. "You sound more like your old self than you have since we came here. What has happened?"

"Oh, mother, I'm so glad to have my dear piano back again, and it looks good to see the pictures on the wall. Now it seems as if the family had the right setting."

Her mother smiled.

"Poor silly child!" she said smilingly. "I'm afraid you've got a bit of the old family aristocracy in you yet in spite of adversity. Don't encourage it. It always brings discontent."

Frannie laughed gaily.

"Don't worry, mother dear, I could live just as happily without the old family portraits and even the piano, though I *am* glad to have it, and it does make it seem more like home here."

"Yes, I know, dear. I was only teasing you. But now, sit down and tell me about your day, and about last night. I did so want to hear about the church, only the nurse was quite tyrannical. She insisted that I go to sleep before you came back. And most of all I want to know about that young man. Frannie, you've got to be awfully careful. Are you quite sure he's all right?"

Frannie laughed gaily.

"Well, you can feel quite comfortable about him, mother. I am sure you would like him. He seems to have been brought up with very much the same ideals you have tried to inculcate in me, and he's interested in real things. Books and music, and even the Bible. He's interested in knowing what Bible students think of this war in relation to the prophecies. That ought to take with you, mother. I'm sure he would please you."

"Well, yes, he is certainly good-looking, and pleasing in his manners. I saw that in just the few minutes when he carried me up to my bed the day I was taken sick. But—" Mrs. Fernley still looked worried.

"Oh, yes, I knew you'd say 'but' again, mother. But I'm sure you would like the way he talks about churches, and the way he looks at life. He seems what you call 'real.' And he was so interested in the sermon last night. We talked about it all the way home."

"Oh yes, how was that sermon? Is the man a good preacher?"

"Indeed he is, mother. He's your kind. He was most interesting. He knows the Bible so well, and he talks about it so clearly that he makes it most fascinating. Mother, he thinks that the return of Christ to the earth may not be far away! And if that's true, then what they call 'the Rapture' is even nearer. That's the time when He comes to the air to take up out of the earth the people who really believe in Him."

"My dear! That is very interesting. It makes everything seem so very near—as if we were going on a journey in just a few days and might begin to pack and get ready to leave. Of course we don't have to pack for that, for somehow God is going to make us ready, but it makes it seem so very much more real. And of course, it may not be as near as we hope, then again it may."

"But, mother! I didn't know you believed that Christ was coming back again."

"Yes, I have believed it a long time, but in a very vague way. I've read some books about it, in the days when I had time to read. I even joined a Bible class once where they were studying something about that. But then when your father died I felt so down-hearted and there was so much to do, and so much to be planned for, and it seemed so impossible to take hold of life again and go on without your father, that I didn't think much more about it. It almost faded from my mind, and began to seem like a dream, just a mirage. Your father was interested in it too, and after he was gone I couldn't bear to keep on thinking about what he

had talked of so much. It seemed that a door was shut into what had been a bright vision."

"Oh, mother, I wish you had told me this before. I didn't think you knew about this hope that those people tonight seemed to have so clearly."

"Darling! I'm sorry I have been so remiss. Well, we'll have to get hold of things together now. But Frannie, this young man who took you to church tonight, was he really interested in all this, or was it just an excuse to have a good time with a pleasant sweet little girl?"

"No, mother, you mustn't think that about him. He isn't a bit flirtatious. He was really interested. He said he had heard about this preacher and his sermons on prophecy and he wanted to listen to him and see if he could get any light on the subject. I think he is really interested. We talked about it all the way home."

"Well, dear, that sounds pleasant and good. I am glad, of course, for you to have a friend who is interested in religious things. But there is one phase of it that I was thinking about all the evening as I lay here and thought about you. He may be very attractive, and have a wonderful Christian character, and yet he may not be especially interested in you. You'll have to remember that constantly. I hate to spoil your pleasure in the evening right at the start, but I'm sure you ought to be warned. It isn't just like going with the boys at home whom you have known all your life, all your growing-up days. You're a stranger here. You're lonely. And under those circumstances a bit of kindness, an invitation to go to church, means a lot more to you than it would if the boys you have known for years had asked you. What I am afraid of is that you will let your heart get set on this young man, when he really is only being kind and pleasant."

"Oh, no, mother!" said Frannie quickly, her cheeks flushing uneasily. "You mustn't think that. I know he is only being kind. Surely it's all right to talk about hereafter and that sort of thing with someone who believes as I do."

"Of course, dear. And I know I can count on my

girl to set a guard on her thoughts. Remember, you don't know anything of his circumstances. He may be engaged to someone else who is not here just now. Or at least interested in someone else. Miss Branner tells me this young man—Willoughby, isn't that his name?—she tells me he belongs to a wealthy family. She didn't know whether he was wealthy in his own right or not, but his aunt is very wealthy, a woman of society. And he is living with her at present."

"Yes, I know," said Frannie lifting thoughtful eyes to her mother, "we passed his aunt's house this evening. It is very beautiful, and costly looking. But he doesn't act as if he felt that he was rich. However, mother, it wouldn't make any difference. I'm not going to be silly and get a broken heart. I've thought all those things out, and I decided God sent him to help me over these new hard days when I was put in a strange new place, so I could be pleasant and cheerful all the time. But I'll keep sensible. One doesn't have to fall in love, mother, with every attractive man who is kind for a few days. But, listen! He wants me to go with him over to Lady Winthrop's house tomorrow night to a Bible class along these same lines. He says she wants to get new members for her class, and he had promised to go once anyway. He didn't know whether he could spare the time to go again or not, but he said he knew she would like me to come, and if it was all right with me he would call for me tomorrow night. He said she told him it would probably be over before ten o'clock. Do you think I shouldn't have agreed to go?"

"Oh, I don't see any harm in that, dear. He is just helping you to get adjusted to your new life. Going to a Bible study class doesn't mean anything significant. Yes, go, and get better acquainted with that dear lady who did so much for me when I was taken sick. Now don't worry. I just wanted you to be warned, and then I can trust you to be my wise true girl, and walk your sweet natural way, the way you always did at home."

"Thank you, mother dear. I'll remember what you say. And anyway I'm not out looking for somebody to

fall in love with. I have a job, and whatever else comes my way I'll enjoy while I can, but I won't lose my head over it. Good night, mother dear!"

And Frannie kissed her mother and slipped away to her own room, thinking pleasantly of the nice time she was to have the next evening. And resolutely whenever the memory of a friendly smile or a pleasant look came to her mind she put away the thought of it, with a mere recognition that he had been very kind. And then she would go off in memory to the things they had talked over together.

So it was with a very happy heart that she hurried home that afternoon. Val Willoughby was not with her. He had told her in the morning that he had some extra work that would keep him late at the plant so she did not look for him as she sailed out into the crisp air. She had a recurrence of thanksgiving that the weather was still clear and fine and the skating still perfect.

On her way she got to thinking of the two fellows who had so annoyed her before, and wondered why she had not seen anything more of them. Could it be that they were really disabled? Or were they afraid to come back lest the knowledge of what they had done had crept back to the heads of their departments? Well, she was not missing them anyway, and was relieved that they no longer crossed her path. Still, she would be sorry if she had seriously hurt either of them. Of course skates were rather dangerous weapons. But they were all she had, and she felt sure that if she hadn't had them and if Val Willoughby hadn't come along just in time she would have had a serious time.

She ran gaily up the steps from the ice, swinging her skate shoes by their straps, and into the house.

"Ummmmm-m! How good that dinner smells!" she said. "How am I ever going to get along without you when you go to your next case?"

The nurse grinned. She was pressing something soft and blue, and as Frannie closed the door behind her she put down her iron, slipped the garment off the ironing board and handed it over.

"There!" she said triumphantly. "I guess that's all right for you to wear tonight. Your mother said this was what you would be likely to choose."

"Oh, but this isn't a party!" said Frannie with wide pleased eyes. "It's only a Bible class. I don't suppose they'll take off their coats and hats."

"Oh, yes, they will," said the nurse decidedly. "I went to one of those classes myself once, and some people just ran in wearing their bright dinner dresses, coats just thrown around them. A few came from a distance and wore coats and hats, but most of them were quite dressed up. You want a pretty dress on, especially since you are going with a young man. You don't want him to be ashamed of you, you know."

"Oh!" said Frannie with a bit of newly acquired dignity. "This isn't a social engagement, you know. Mr. Willoughby merely thought I would enjoy the study because of something in the sermon we heard last night. I don't think he would need to worry about how I was dressed. He is merely escorting me over there. Nobody will know, probably, that I came with him."

The nurse gave the girl a quick look with a queer little pucker to her lips.

"Oh! You don't say so!" said Nurse Branner. "Well, even so, you might as well look your best. I think Lady Winthrop would like that. Besides, she took the trouble to send word this morning and make sure you were coming with Valiant Willoughby. She said she was counting on your presence."

"Oh, how lovely!" said Frannie. "And you are sure that blue won't be too dressy for just a Bible class?"

"Yes, I'm sure. And what's more your mother was sure too. She told me where to find it in the big chest of drawers."

"Oh, all right. If mother thinks it is the right thing then I'll wear it, but I wouldn't like to feel over-dressed."

"You won't!" said the nurse contentedly. "Take it from me. I've lived in this town long enough to know the customs."

So Frannie took the blue dress, thanked Nurse Bran-

ner with a warm hug and kiss and ran upstairs to kiss
her mother.

"Mother dear, I feel very selfish going out two
nights in succession," she said after the usual greetings
had been exchanged. "Wouldn't you rather I would just
explain when Mr. Willoughby comes that I feel tired
and think I had better stay home tonight."

"No!" said Mrs. Fernley. "No! Not on any account.
I certainly am glad to have you attend a Bible class,
and especially when it is at that dear woman's house.
And don't be a fool, Frannie! Just take this thing as you
would have taken going to prayer meeting at home, or
going to a church social with your Cousin Harry."

Frannie gave her mother a relieved smile.

"All right, mother. I'll do my best."

"And don't you think another thing about what we
talked of last night. I didn't want to make you self-
conscious. Just take it for granted that this young man
is a friendly neighbor and let it go at that. Don't go to
analyzing your feelings and his. I'm sorry I said a
thing."

"There, mother, you needn't be. I'll do as you say.
But do you really think I should dress up so much?"

"Yes. You can trust that nurse. She knows. Now run
down and get your supper and then come up and get
dressed so I can look you over before you go. Besides,
I'd like to hear you play a minute or two on your piano
if there is time. A touch of the Moonlight Sonata would
give me a melody for the evening."

So Frannie ran down to her supper. They had a gay
happy time laughing and talking, and Bonnie looked at
her sister enviously.

"I wish I could go with you tonight, Frannie," she
said wistfully. "I like meetings. I haven't been to a
church in a long time."

"I know, dear," said the sister. "But you shall pretty
soon. When mother gets well and we can all go together
we will have nice times going to church and Sunday
School every Sunday. And I am sorry to have to leave
you behind so much, little dear, but you see I'm getting
acquainted with places for us to go to. And tonight

Lady Winthrop has invited me to a Bible class at her pretty house where you were, and so I shall see it. You know you wanted me to see it."

"Yes, I wanted you to see it, Frannie dear," sighed the little girl. "Yes, I'm glad to stay with mother and Miss Branner so you can see my nice pretty lady. And sometime we'll go there together, won't we, Frannie? And go across the bridge?"

"Yes, sometime. Perhaps pretty soon. I'm sure there'll be a way."

So the little girl gave her sister a sunny smile.

"You have a nice time, Frannie," she said politely, like an older person.

Then Nurse Branner sent Frannie to get ready for the evening and got the dishes out of the way herself.

"You go on. You can't be sure just what time Mr. Willoughby will come for you, and your mother will want to see if you look all right before you go," she said.

So it was still early when Frannie went into her mother's room to be looked over. Presently the nurse and Bonnie came up to help with the inspection and they all pronounced that she looked all right.

"Just pretty perfect, Frannie," said little Bonnie quaintly.

"And now," said the mother, "I want to hear the old piano. Go down and play the Moonlight Sonata, and the Spinning Song, and then if you have time before you go give me one of the dear old hymns I love. But don't hold up your going if your escort comes before you are done. I'll carry the tune over in my heart till tomorrow night when you can finish for me."

So Frannie, in her pretty blue frock, with her coat on her arm, went downstairs and began to play. Softly, sweetly, and then gradually louder till the whole little house was filled with the glorious sound, and it stole out across the frozen river into the stillness of early moonlight, and filled the air about. Two men who were walking over on the other side of the river bank, reconnoitering, heard it.

"Say, if they'd keep that up we could get a lot of

work done tonight without any chance of being caught," said the big man.

"No chance this early," said the other shaking his head. "They're going out somewheres or else there's company coming. We better make it late tonight. They'll be good and tired and sleep sound."

"I guess you're right," said the other, and strode along silently, half annoyed by the tenderness of the lovely music that stole across to them.

But the Moonlight Sonata was only about two-thirds finished when there came a peremptory knock on the door that startled the nurse who had been waiting at the top of the stairs to go down and open the door when the young man should come. Somehow the knock didn't sound quite like his quiet summons the other times he had called.

But Frannie had not heard the knock, so sure she was that her escort would not come yet, and so intent she was upon the music. She knew her mother's critical ear would detect any lapses in her memorizing. So she played on and did not notice the nurse as she slipped down the stairs and went quietly to the door, did not realize that someone was coming in, as she swept on through several difficult passages to the end. And then suddenly it came upon her that there were others in the room.

With a bewildered look in her eyes she whirled about on the piano stool and looked at her guests, expecting to see Val Willoughby. But it was not Val Willoughby. Instead there were three people standing astonished just inside the room, as the nurse, also astonished, closed the door behind them to keep out the cold and looked from one to the other of the three young people who stood there staring at Frannie. It did not take her long to realize that one was Marietta Hollister. The two young men who accompanied her she could not figure out. She seemed never to have seen them before.

But Frannie knew. Suddenly and appallingly it was brought to her startled consciousness that these were three enemies standing before her, and she was so taken

aback that for an instant she could not believe her senses. Then suddenly she lifted her delicate patrician chin and surveyed them, one at a time, coolly, haughtily, with a look that put them in the class of intruders.

She came at once to her feet.

"Yes?" she said in a clear cold voice. "Did you want something?" She addressed her question to Marietta who stood in the forefront, with the two abashed young hoodlums in her wake.

"Why yes," drawled Marietta in her most dominating tone. "I came to find you. I brought a couple of young friends to introduce to you. You remember I promised I would. And we thought we would take you over to our opening night and let you see what we are doing. I'm sure you will want to join us when you see what a gorgeous time we are going to show you to-night."

Frannie swept the faces of the two young men with a freezing glance. She had instantly recognized her two assailants, Kit Creeber and Spike Emberly.

"Thank you," she said turning back to Marietta, "it will not be necessary for you to introduce your friends to me. I have already met them under most unpleasant circumstances, and I do not care to have any further acquaintance with them."

"Oh, now that is rather rude of you, isn't it? They have come to do you a favor. They have come to ask the pleasure of being your escorts to the dance I told you about. If you have had some quarrel in the past just forget it and come along with us. We'll show you a perfectly good time, and you will forget your differences. Come on. Is this your coat? Mr. Emberly, put it on her and show her what a good sort you are."

"No!" said Frannie sharply. "I do not wish his assistance, and I do not wish to go out with any of you. Besides I am going out myself, and I shall have to ask you to excuse me for I must get ready at once." Frannie turned and would have hurried up the stairs, but Marietta angrily placed herself in the way of the stairs.

"Oh!" she said disagreeably. "Do you play in some night club? I wasn't aware you played. We might be

able to offer you a small salary for playing for our dancing if you are interested. You really play rather well."

The very drawl of her voice was an insult, and suddenly Frannie felt tears and laughter coming upon her. But she must not go into hysterics before these, her enemies, sent to try her spirit perhaps. She was enabled to turn an amused smile upon her strange guests.

"I'm not interested," she said, "and I do not play in a night club." Frannie's voice was very quiet and courteous, as if the questions she had been asked had been perfectly genuine.

But suddenly there came another voice, clear, assured, dominating. Val Willoughby, standing in the kitchen doorway:

"Are you ready, Fran? I think it is time we were starting." Then his eyes swept the room, bringing his keen glance to bear straight into the eyes of the two frightened, furtive young men who tried to shuffle unobtrusively toward the door behind them.

"I guess we better be going then," murmured Kit Creeber nervously, edging nearer to the door.

"Yes, I guess you had," said Willoughby fervently, and stepping quickly forward swung the front door wide to let them pass. Then he turned, as they slunk by him, and looked at the startled Marietta who was too astonished even to be angry yet.

"So!" he said scornfully. "Is this the kind of company you keep, Marietta? Is it possible you know what kind of rascals those two fellows are? Or did I arrive just in time to give you protection?"

"Protection!" sneered Marietta furiously, suddenly aroused to the situation. "Just who do you think you are anyway? You're no one to preach? What kind of company do *you* keep? Are you doing slum work too?" Then she turned with head held high and angry eyes flashing and sailed out after her two commandeered escorts, slamming the door of the house behind her and stamping down the walk on her high expensive heels.

Chapter 15

WHEN MARIETTA REACHED her car which had been parked across the street from the brick house, there was no sign of her two escorts.

In vain she looked into the back seat, and turned on her lights to search for her erstwhile attendants, but they were nowhere to be seen. In quite a dignified lofty tone she called their names: "Mr. Emberly! Mr. Creeber! Where are you?" But repeated calls, varying from annoyance to actual anger, and then even fury, brought no response.

Once she thought she heard a cracking sound from over behind the kitchen of the cottage, and a floundering stir in the darkness, but when she took her flashlight from the pocket of her car and started over that way to investigate, she found nothing but a mass of disordered stones and bricks powdered with dirty snow, with sticks and branches in confusion. No sign of the two young men in their shiny dinner coats and rather shabby overcoats anywhere. And finally in disdain she picked her way over the roughness back toward her car. Stepping uncertainly, suddenly she felt one foot go down through the mass of branches into a deep place, so that she fell full length. She was about to cry out for help, till suddenly she remembered the merry eyes of that other girl. She couldn't stand Frannie's scorn. This seemed to be some kind of trough. What could it mean? In the back yard right behind the house! Why did anybody have a right to have a place like that in their back yard?

She called out again, guardedly. If those two horrid boys had any sense of honor they would come back and help her out. But of course what could one expect

from boys who lived on the wrong side of the river and worked down the river at a factory!

Then she heard the front door open, voices, that ripple of a laugh, the memory of which had become so hateful to her! Mercy! She must get out of here. If she called out now Val would come and help her up, but he would read her a lecture, and the memory of his sneer about her erstwhile companions restrained her. Not for worlds would she let him know that her two knights had deserted her.

So she lay still with her hands plunged into the cold dirty snow that Mike had cast over the hole he had dug the night before.

She heard Val and Frannie come out the door and go down the street. She could hear the gay sound of their subdued voices as they walked toward the bridge. And when she heard them turn onto the bridge she tried again to struggle up, but only succeeded in plunging one foot down deeper and entangling it in some wires. Strange! Wires buried in a back yard. What did that mean?

She gave a quick violent jerk to her foot, and succeeded in losing her slipper down in that queer dark hole! What was she going to do now? Oh, she ought to have called Val Willoughby. He was always a gentleman. He would have helped her out, of course, and she would be on her way now. Even if he had tried to read her a lecture she could have given back as good as she got. He, lecturing her, when he was openly attending a girl like that who lived in a little insignificant house and worked down the river! He to presume to lecture her! Perhaps she had better go to Auntie Haversett and tell her what Val was doing, and get this ridiculous business stopped before it got too bad. She probably should have done that in the first place. Well, she'd got to get out of this hole, whatever she did!

So she wallowed about some more, and at last got a firm hold of the edge of this peculiar ditch into which she had fallen, and with edging and struggling was finally free. Out on firm ground again, she shivered; one

stockinged foot was clinging to the brink. How was
she going to get that slipper? Could she possibly hop
over the rough ground to her car without it? No, that
was out of the question. She had to find it. Then she
remembered her flashlight and got it out of her pocket,
turning it downward into the hole. Yes, there was the
toe of her slipper, pointing upward, almost beyond
reach. If she got down on the ground again, flat, she
might reach it. How horrid, with an evening dress on.
She wouldn't be fit to go to the dance afterward. It was
all the fault of—well who was it the fault of? That girl,
of course. If it hadn't been for that girl she would never
have taken up this idea of helping downtrodden human-
ity to rise by means of dances. And she would never
have asked the son of their gardener to bring those
two fellows to help her in her scheme of providing
escorts for the poor girls whom she was to help into a
refined kind of social life in their own social class. But
they were such good-looking fellows, really handsome
in a way, quite challenging. How could she know they
would turn out to be deserters? Cowards! Evidently Val
and that girl had scared them stiff. Well, she had to get
that slipper.

So down she got, carefully, and reaching as far as
she could, just barely escaped touching the tip of the
slipper's toe with the tip of her fingers. Well, she would
evidently have to bend down a little farther!

Over she bent, stretched her arm to its fullest extent
and found that the slipper had somehow entrenched itself in that mess of wire she had got into herself. So she
struggled some more and finally lost her balance, and
fell with her face in the frozen earth, cutting a gash in
her chin on a sharp stone. For an instant she lay there
struggling with angry tears that came unbidden to her
eyes. She, Marietta Hollister, to be left deserted, lying in
a ditch in an alien back yard on the wrong side of the
river! And even the slum boys she had coaxed to come
with her on this expedition had deserted her. What
could possibly have made them do that? Young toughs
they were. Why should they be afraid of Val Willoughby?

But at last Marietta by aid of her flashlight, and a strenuous effort, brought up her slipper triumphantly, and slid her foot into it, and then essayed to hobble over to her car, only to discover that the slipper was minus a heel!

Now what was she going to do? They were new slippers, too, and had cost plenty. Of course that didn't matter much, only to add to the annoyance. But she couldn't go to that dance without a heel on her slipper. She would have to go home, unless she could recover the heel. Even then, how would she make it stay on?

She turned back to the dark hole, and aimed her light down to its depths, but she could not find that imp of a heel. It was gone, away down to the bottom of Mike's excavations. And some day would he, or some other disloyal American, find that heel and wonder, and be afraid?

But Marietta had no idea of that now. She had to get to that dance, for nobody else could run things without her. And now that she had failed to bring the two young men she had promised, she would certainly have to hunt up two more somewhere.

At last she hobbled back to her car and got started on her way, growing momently more and more angry at Val Willoughby. For after all if he hadn't made a fool of himself with that strange working girl from the other side of the river she would never have got into all this.

So Marietta, blaming others for her own misdeeds, gradually in this way soothed her troubled spirits.

Frannie and Val went on their quiet way across the bridge, and when they had put sufficient distance between the brick house and themselves so that they were sure they could not be overheard by any recent enemies, Val said in a low confidential tone:

"Were you having a pretty tough time again, Frannie? I came in while you were talking. The nurse heard me outside and opened the door a crack, motioning me inside, so I got a fair idea of what was going on, but I didn't hear everything. Did I butt in too soon?"

"Oh no," said Frannie with a quick little breath of

a sigh. "I was so glad to see you, and to hear you. Your voice sounded like a refreshing shower on a thirsty day. It was grand of you! But—I hated for you to have to call down—your friend."

"My *friend!* Where did you get that?"

"Oh, isn't she? She implied the first time she came over here that you were something very special in the way of a friend."

"I know," said the young man, "she's been trying to imply that for a good many years, but it happens to be all on her side, not mine, thank you! But don't you worry about her. She's just a very determined girl who is trying to make everything go her way, and to run everything and everybody else. You see I've known her since we were youngsters and she was just that way when she was three. I was rather proud of your quiet voice and your smile in the face of her actual insults."

"Oh, well," laughed Frannie, "it was just funny. But how do you suppose a girl like that, a wealthy cultured girl, came to know those two unspeakable fellows that tried to get fresh with me?"

"Well, I think Marietta has taken up this war work the way she always does everything else, with a great deal of energy and no common sense. I used sometimes to wonder if she *hadn't* any sense. I guess she has, but she doesn't use it. I don't know where she ever picked up those two kids. She probably saw them somewhere and thought they were good-looking, or else some fool told her about them, and she thought they were plenty good enough for the kind of girls she was planning to help into what she calls 'social life.' However it was, they were good and scared when they saw me come in. Did you notice? I never in my life saw anything slink away as fast as those two did. I fancy they were afraid we would complain to the authorities. Have they been seen at your plant since your encounter with them?"

"No, I haven't seen them anywhere. I was almost afraid I might have hurt one of them with that skate. That really wasn't a very pleasant weapon to use on a face."

"Well you used it most effectively. I think I noted a scar on the chin of that one they call Spike. I trust it taught him a good lesson."

"Oh, but I didn't mean to do anything like that!"

"No, of course not, but remember how much worse they might have done for you if I hadn't come along and taken a hand. Well, let's forget them."

"Yes, let's. But why do you suppose that girl wanted to come here again? I'm afraid I was pretty rude to her the first time."

"Don't worry about that," said Val. "I'm quite sure she gave you plenty of reason to be."

"But I don't want to hate her," said Frannie with a troubled voice.

Val smiled down upon her in the moonlight.

"My mother used to tell me that I couldn't always like the things that people did, but I could love them because God did, or something like that. Did you ever hear that?"

"Yes, my mother taught me that, too. She said that we were to love everybody that Christ loved, but we didn't have to love what they did, and that made it possible for us to love them even when they were doing some very unpleasant things to us."

"Well, it's not always easy to get that point of view, is it? But it seems to me you have come mighty near to it. And now let's forget her too, and get ready to enjoy what's before us."

They turned in at the big white gateway and walked slowly toward the house, and then they saw more people coming from every direction.

"Why, they are turning in here," said Frannie. "There must be a lot of them."

"Yes, there are about fifty or sixty in the class, Lady Winthrop said," said Val.

"So many? Isn't that wonderful? I'm so glad you invited me!"

"Even though you had to miss the dance?"

They arrived at the door in a burst of giggles, which perhaps more than anything that had so far happened to them, made them feel better acquainted. And then

they entered the wide beautiful hall and were welcomed by the sweet old lady in a soft gray gown with her pretty white hair in lovely waves to frame her face, and a look of joy in her eyes. And right away she introduced them to this one and that one:

"These are two dear young friends of mine. I want you to know them. I hope they are going to enjoy our study so much that they will want to be with us every week." Frannie's heart gave a pleasant little thrill of pleasure. It was so nice to be taken into the inner circle as it were by this sweet old lady.

"Our Bibles! We didn't bring our Bibles!" whispered Frannie as she looked around at the rustling leaves of the many Bibles.

But almost instantly the need was supplied, for Lady Winthrop touched Val's arm and motioned toward a pile of Bibles on a table by the door, and he quickly brought some, for them and for a few others who had come Bibleless. And then the meeting started with a song—somebody at the piano, Frannie couldn't see who—and everybody taking part. It seemed somehow different from ordinary singing. It was so heart-felt. She stole a shy look at her escort and noted his fine clear voice. His singing bore other voices along.

And then a young man to whom they had been introduced, and who was sitting near the piano arose and began to pray, exactly as if he were seeking personal help for each one for the evening's study.

And so the lesson began.

Frannie found she knew her way about her Bible pretty well, although she was greatly amazed at the startling truths that developed through this well-versed teacher. It had never occurred to her before that the Bible was so linked up together, every word definitely proved by some other word elsewhere spoken.

And as they went on through the lesson Frannie grew more and more absorbed in the thought of how the Bible itself claimed to be the Word of God, not in just a casual way, but in a clear indisputable way, upholding its claims with unanswerable truths that she

had never thought of before. As an undercurrent she sensed its demand to be accepted and put to the test.

It had never occurred to Frannie before, nor perhaps to Val either, that the Holy Spirit was a real Teacher, who was ready to make clear the meaning of the Bible to any soul willing to accept and believe it even before it was proved. But now they were amazed to find that all these people looked on the Holy Spirit as a definite Person. They heard that the moment a soul accepts Christ as his Saviour then the Holy Spirit comes into that soul to abide, never to leave it. That was all new to them. The Holy Spirit had been a part of their traditional belief, inherited from their families, but there had been no knowledge that He was a real Person. If they had heard the words before they had not taken them in. And now suddenly it was as if the Holy Spirit had come into the room, and been introduced to them personally, so that hereafter there could be no Christian life or even thought, without this consciousness of another Person within them who had power and rights and likes and dislikes.

Lady Winthrop sat across from these two new disciples, and watched their speaking faces, saw how new and wonderful it seemed to them, this teaching that was practical. She began praying in her heart for them. For she suddenly knew she loved these two whom she had watched going down her "street of the city" on their flashing skates, and whom she had been praying for. She had so wanted them to come to this class, yet she had been afraid they wouldn't. They were so young and bright and gay looking, and they were of the age when young people want the pleasures of this world rather than study about another world that can only be seen by faith. Yet here were these two poring over the pages, and finding the references as eagerly as the regular members of the class, their faces bright with interest, their eyes shining with each new nugget of truth they took in. And Lady Winthrop's prayers took on the semblance of thanksgiving.

They lingered a little while in the neighborhood of

the teacher. Asking an intelligent question of him now and then, as did others, and when the gathering finally broke up they went thoughtfully away.

"I begin to see," said Willoughby as they turned onto the bridge, "that there are questions ahead of me that I've got to face and settle before I'll be fit to go on. It seems to me that they must even take precedence of my war work or I won't be fit to do it rightly."

Frannie looked up thoughtfully.

"Questions?" she said half wonderingly. "What questions?"

"Whether I'm saved or not," said the young man. "I never considered that at all. I thought I was living a pretty decent sort of life and that would be all that was expected of me. But I see now that I must know whether I've really accepted what Christ has done for me, whether I have my papers all made out, my 'application' as it were. It's just like getting in the army, or enlisting in defense work, only vastly more important of course, and strangely I never gave it a thought before. I thought that people who kept talking about being saved were cranks who wasted a lot of time and didn't amount to a row of pins. But now I see it's the basic principle upon which this whole thing rests. Christ made it so important that He was willing to die to accomplish it and I have just passed it by and tried to get into the procession without filling out my papers. Any day now my work might get more strenuous, even more dangerous, and I don't feel that I want to go on with it any farther until I have this matter settled beyond a doubt, so that whatever comes I've a rock foundation under my feet and some One to trust in. How about you, Frannie? Have you settled this question?"

"I think I did when I was a little girl, just before I united with the church, but I haven't been doing much about it since except going to church regularly when I could. Doing a little church work now and then, like playing for prayer meeting, or waiting on table at a church supper, or even teaching a class in the primary room. But I know those things don't amount to anything. I see now that what God wants is for us to let

His Spirit have His way in our hearts, and it's up to Him then to direct us to do 'church work' or 'home work', the way they said tonight. I never really let Him do anything in my life. I think I'll have a talk with God tonight, and tell Him I want things to be different after this."

Willoughby's hand slid around Frannie's little gloved hand that rested on his arm.

"We'll do it together tonight," he said quietly. "It seems wonderful that we can really talk such things over with the great God, doesn't it?"

"Yes," said Frannie softly. And then just before they left the bridge she pointed down the river to where the lights of the city twinkled and brightened the sky and shone golden in the river.

"Look! Look! See, there's the Heavenly City shining out that way again. It almost seems as if it really were a picture of the City we are to see some day."

"Yes," said the young man gravely. " 'And the street of the city was pure gold.' I looked that verse up today. Lady Winthrop told me where to find it. It struck me as something to look forward to."

Chapter 16

AN HOUR AFTER the little family in the brick house were asleep with every window dark, there came two stealthy figures stealing over the fields and approaching the back of the cottage where the covered trench was located. They halted, and looked about.

"It was right here I fell. Turn on your flash, Spike, and give us a glimpse around. It ought to be easy to find. It was a white card, and there were some other papers with it. Give us a flash. What's the matter? Can't you find it?"

"No, Kit, I don't seem to have it. Guess I must have

forgot to take it out of the pocket of my overcoat when I changed to this sweater. Here's some matches. They'll do."

"Well, go easy! A match scratching might wake anybody, and I don't want to run any risks, not with guys like those two. I don't want us to get pinched. Not at this stage of the game."

A crisp sound and then a flickering light, quavering over the pile of dirty snow and earth, and dying out with a fizzle.

"Heck! Don't you know how to keep a match going? Give it to me!"

Another light struggled out from the damp matches, floated mistily over the heap of rubble, disclosing little, and died away again.

Match after match illuminated the ground for a brief space and faded away, until they were all gone, but not a card was disclosed.

"Well, I guess it ain't here!" said Kit in a discouraged whisper. "But I know this is where I fell, right over that big lump of snow. I cut a big slit in the knee of my pants. What's that you're picking up? Is that a card?"

"Naw, it's only a rag. It's a fancy nose rag. Some dame dropped it here. Got perfume on it. Smell that!" and Spike held out a delicate bit of finery.

Kit sniffed, and then reached for the handkerchief and smelled again.

"Say!" he exclaimed. "That's the same perfume our dame wore when she brought us to this house this evening. It's hers!"

"You poor fool you, how would it get here? Look how far this is from the gate where we came in. And there's no wind."

They stared at each other in the dim night. Then Kit looked around him, turned his head toward the house, and then toward the gate where they had entered earlier in the evening.

"That dame must have chased after us, and likely fell down the way I did!"

"I told you we oughtta have gone across the road and stayed behind that car till she come out and then

told her we found we'd forgot an engagement ur something."

"Not on yer life, I wouldn't have risked meetin' that guy again. Ef he'd slung you across the ice on the river the way he did me you wouldn't either. But say, we've gotta hunt up that dame and get my pass. I'll lose my job ef I don't have it. What did she say her name was?"

"She's that old Hollister guy's kid. They live acrost the river in that house with all them towers and pinnacles."

"They do? Well, we gotta go over there and ask for her."

"Not me!" said Spike. "It ain't my pass that's lost. Go yerself ef yer fool enough to try it, but you'll go by yerself. I don't crash into no swell's house like that!"

"Okay! I'll go by myself then. I ain't gonta lose my pass and lose my job. You know I'll lose my job if I can't find my pass in the morning. Mebbe if I'd go over to that dance we was planning she'd be there yet."

"That won't do any good," said Spike. "Don't you remember she said these dances she wanted us for were over by midnight because all the girls were working girls, and couldn't keep their jobs ef they stayed out too late? So that's out. It's way past midnight now."

"Then I'm in real trouble. That dame won't be up early enough in the morning for me to get my pass."

"What makes you think she's got it?"

"Oh, she likely picked it up ef she fell down. See all these footprints. She fell all righty, and I sure am in real trouble now."

And then a heavy hand fell on his shoulder.

"Yes, you sure are in real trouble, unless you can explain pretty good and quick what you're doing at this time of night, lighting matches around the back of this house."

Spike made a quick movement to leave, but the other shadow that had come quietly up with the first man, put out a strong hand and grasped Spike with a firm hold, and though he struggled his best he was unable to get away.

"I ain't in this," gasped Spike in a scared voice. "I just came along with him because he asked me."

"I wasn't doin' nothin'," growled Kit shakily. "I was just tryin' ta find my pass I thought I might a dropped here awhile ago when I went across lots in a hurry. I gotta have that pass ur I lose my job."

"Yes? Well, you better look out you don't lose something else on the way. What were you doing with matches here? Trying to make a fire this time of night?"

"No sir: I wasn't tryin' to make no fire here. I was just tryin' to find my pass card. It oughtta be around here somewhere."

One of the two men swept his flashlight around the place, but no card showed up.

"You see," he said scathingly. "You just come along with me to the station house and we'll see if we can't get to the bottom of this business."

"No, sir, I can't go to the station house. I haven't done nothin'. I've gotta go see that girl and see if she picked it up and was goin' ta return it ta me."

"What girl?" said the officer sharply.

"Why, she's some rich girl that was takin' us to a social club she started. And she brought us here to get another girl from this house."

The officers exchanged a quick look.

"Did she go? The girl from this house?"

"No, sir. She said she had another engagement, so we beat it. We figured we'd had enough."

"I see. So you came across the back of the lot. But what became of the girl who brought you?"

"We don't know," said Spike gruffly. "We didn't wait ta see."

"Then why did you think she might have your pass?"

"Well, we didn't hear her car right away so we figured she mighta chased around tryin' ta find us, and mebbe picked it up," said Kit eagerly, persuasively. "I've just gotta go ta her house an' see if she's got it. I need it in the morning."

"Who is this girl who brought you. What is her name?"

"Marietta Hollister. She lives across there on the ridge in that big house with a cupola on the top. Her father's some big guy."

"And you expect me to believe a story like that? That a daughter of Foster Hollister was taking a couple of young hoodlums like you to a dance? You must think I'm crazy. Come along with me. We'll see about this."

"Why, you see, it was a dance for young workin' girls an' she hired us to go along and be pardners fer the workin' girls, see? She was payin' us five bucks apiece fer goin' an' havin' a swell time besides, good eats and some fun."

"Oh, she was paying you for going, was she? And yet you two ran away without your pay! Another likely story."

Then suddenly an interruption occurred. A window at the back of the house was cautiously raised, and a moment later a clear voice said:

"Who is out there? What are you doing there?"

The officer who was holding Kit looked up calmly.

"It's all right, Miss Branner. This is Officer Rowley. Nothing the matter. Just a couple of kids hunting something they thought they lost here when they went through the lot awhile back. Don't worry."

"Oh! All right! Thank you!" and the window went softly down with none of the rest of the sleeping household the wiser.

So Spike and Kit went off in the custody of Officer Rowley and the little brick house beside the frozen river slept on quietly.

About two hours later two more stealthy figures arrived among the bushes, and took up a stand alertly.

"Well, I guess we've got the coast clear tonight," said Granniss. "I began to think we'd got every light against us, last night. But it's much better to come at this hour. Practically nobody would be around now. Better go down and look at our digging and see if it's been tampered with at all, hadn't you? Make sure before the lumber truck arrives, and then what nobody

doesn't see won't do any harm. Go easy on that flash though. You know even a sound sleeper is waked up by a light moving around the wall."

"I ain't puttin' any light on anybody's wall," growled Mike. "Whaddaya think I am?"

"Well, now don't get touchy, Mike. This is no time to develop a temper, just when things are going our way."

"Okay!" said Mike glumly, and strode out to the trench he had dug the night before. He stood for a moment turning his light this way and that, studying the ground carefully. Once or twice he stooped and put out a hand, feeling of the roughness of the earth, brought his flash to bear on something on the ground, and finally picked it up, a button that Spike had burst off when he struggled to get away from the second officer as they made their way to the hidden car by which the two officers traveled. Then Mike went back to the covert where Granniss was watching him.

"Well, how did you find it?" questioned Granniss sharply.

"There's been somebody there," said Mike. "In fact several."

"What do you mean?" asked Granniss, anxiety in his tone at once. "How could you tell?"

"I mean there's been some people there," said Mike calmly. After all it wasn't his funeral, he told himself. "I know by the footprints. There's been quite several. And the ground has been considerable tore up."

"What kind of footprints? Men? Or boys."

"Men," said Mike. "It looked like at least three, mebbe four. And there was one girl with spike heels."

"A girl!" said Granniss. "Do you suppose it's the girl that's living here in this house?"

"I couldn't say," said Mike dryly.

"What would a girl want with coming out there?"

"Mebbe heard us the other night. Mebbe got scared, and came to see what was going on."

"Mebbe hired by the government to spy on us," said Granniss bitterly. "Might be, you know."

"Aw, yer dreamin'!" said Mike disdainfully.

"Well, did you make any attempt to find out if our wires had been tampered with? Do you think they could have dug beyond where we went?"

"Could be," said Mike speculatively. "Do you want I should tear it all up and find out?"

"Well, I don't know as we'd have time before those lumbermen get here. Perhaps we better wait till they've gone."

"Not me!" said Mike decidedly. "I gotta get some sleep. I got a job to carry on tamorrow."

"You got a job to carry on tonight, man, have you forgotten? If you do it right it's worth a heap more than any job you have tomorrow. Remember that!"

"Okay!" said Mike getting up with a sigh from the place he had flung himself down. He yawned. "If this has gotta be found out tonight here goes. I ain't waiting on no lumber. I'll have plenty branches to fling in if we hear 'em comin'."

So Mike went to work, carefully laying aside the stones and dirt and branches, where they could be put back in a trice, and now and then bringing a powerful flashlight to bear on the hole. He was working fast. He didn't care to have to do this over again after the men left.

And across the street on the side porch of one of the little new unfinished houses the two officers who had returned from the police station parked themselves comfortably and invisibly where they could easily keep tab on what went on. Somehow they knew that this job about the old brick house was not half finished yet.

But Mike was working away for dear life. He had sighted strange turmoil in the dirt he had thrown in around the wires, and something dark and foreign was tangled firmly, as if a hidden foot were sticking up. Had somebody dug this whole trench up since last night? There was one place where it seemed the fingers of a small hand had been drawn along, burrowing in. Breathlessly he worked and at last was able to dislodge Marietta's slipper heel from the wires where it was as

firmly caught as if the fastening had been intentional. He brought it up and stood bent over, the flashlight turned full on it, and studied it.

"Great jumping goslings!" he ejaculated. "Now how could that get into my nice clean ditch?"

Granniss came near.

"What is it, Mike, have you found something? Have they disturbed our wires?"

"Wal, I ain't just sure yet," said Mike loftily. "It's something mighty queer. It's the heel of some dame's shoe. Down in by them wires, all tangled up in 'em, as if somebody had stepped into 'em, or else was trying to pull 'em out. Some swell dame too, 'cause they don't make heels like that on cheap shoes."

"Where is it? Let me see it," said Granniss in alarm.

He took the absurd high heel and held it in his hand, sensing the soft leather with which it was covered, the art of its lines. Then he held it under his coat and turned his flashlight on it, studying every part of it carefully.

"It's been wrenched off," he announced in a guarded whisper. "Somebody tried to step over there and the ground gave way. She went in unintentionally. Nothing to fear from her, I guess."

"I think you're wrong," said Mike abruptly. "There's marks of hands down there. The whole place has been mauled over, mebbe by more than one pair of hands. I tell you I seen it, I know the signs."

"Well, if that's so there's nothing for it but to get at the wires and see if they've been tampered with. Get a hustle on and be quick about it before the truck gets here."

"But what's so important about them wires? We could replace 'em, couldn't we, ef they've disturbed 'em?"

"Oh, it's not the wires. They are only the beginning of the aerial that goes up a tree. It's what they lead to. Man, there's papers in with that transmitter in there that would put us all where we don't want to be, and no mistake about it. Besides if they've tampered with those wires we've got to destroy all evidence and then beat it

with no time to lose. What I want you to do is find out if
those wires are still uncut between this ditch and the wall
of that kitchen. Find out if anybody has traced 'em to
their source this evening. And do it mighty quick, too."

"Okay," said Mike in no hearty voice. "But I ain't
partial to workin' in double quick time. Not after I've
worked all day in the plant."

The whispering ceased. Mike climbed down in the
hole again and went to work, wishing he'd never taken
over this job, no matter how big the pay promised. But
at last he reached the place where he had ended his
digging the night before and found the wires still un-
disturbed as they came out of the solid ground about a
foot from the brick wall of the kitchen. So he laboriously climbed out and went back to the big man who was
seated on the tool chest.

"Well, they're all okay. Just look as if they'd been
pulled a bit, kind of taut, that's all. I guess they didn't
think it was worth while going no further. Ur mebbe
they got tired and decided to come back another night."

"Well, that looks bad," said Granniss. "I guess we
better arrange somehow to make a grab right away and
get out of this for good. If those wires are still there as
you say then that's a perfect guide to the place where
we expect to break through the bricks, and since someone has tried to get down there tonight they must have
discovered the wires. Lost a heel doing it. That would
be enough to make a thoughtful person suspicious. Say,
Mike, you don't think you could go on and break
through tonight? It can't be much farther, and in case
we can locate the loose brick we might be able to do
the whole job tonight and get away. I don't like this out-
look. It means somebody is suspicious, and once get
somebody suspicious, it's first come first win. Mike, we
gotta get that stuff tonight!"

Mike dropped down on the hard ground wearily and
shook his head.

"Nothin' doin'," he said shakily. "Whaddaya think I
am? A machine? You'd better get some other man if
you want the world moved in a night."

"What's the matter with you, Mike? Getting cold feet

with the goal just in sight? I didn't think you'd play out right at the end and lose all that dough."

"Lose it?" said Mike excitedly, raising his voice above the stipulated whisper. "Who said I'd lose it? If that's the kind of a guy you are, I can quit right now, and make more money snitchin' on you than I can diggin' solid ice caves an' breakin' into honest people's houses while they're sleepin'!"

"Look here, Mike! If you're a stinking yellow sucker like that I could put you in the jug in no time for digging this trench into honest people's houses, and taking part in an act of treason to your country, and how much of a chance do you suppose you would stand, your word against mine? I'm a respectable business man, well dressed and educated, and you're a poor laboring man. So get down off that high horse and get to work. See what you can accomplish before those lumber fellows get here. Remember, you don't know what evidence I could bring against you when I get my hands on those papers."

"You wouldn't dare!" muttered Mike in a low undertone, but he went slowly back to the trench and lowered himself out of the other man's sight. He was getting angry clear through, and thinking out a plot whereby he could get Granniss into real trouble with the government.

Then suddenly they heard the lumber truck coming, and Granniss arose in a panic and began to kick branches and stones into the trench.

"We better take a couple of those shortest boards," he said, "and lower them into the hole, and then cover them up. We can't have our men falling in there, and getting tangled up in this jam. Get outta there, Mike, and help me move a couple of boards, quick, and shovel some of that snow back over them."

Mike was glad enough to get out of the hole. He had reached the place where nothing short of a good strong blow or two with the pickax would get to the brick wall, and he was scared to try it on a calm clear night like this. He had in mind the voice of the quiet elderly woman who had opened the door and looked him down the night he first came here. He had a feeling that

she was capable of doing almost anything, certainly calling for the police. He was sure there wasn't any telephone in here yet, but there was no telling how soon one would be put in with a woman like that nurse on the job.

Halfheartedly he helped lift two boards and sprinkle some rubble over them, piled a couple of branches and some snow atop, and went out to the road to meet the truck.

The truck men knew their job. They carried their lumber swiftly and silently and put it in place, received their pay and went their way, as the moon slipped over the rim of the horizon and left the world in darkness.

The two men stood for a moment discouraged, looking at one another, and then by common consent stepped over to the trench.

"You made a pretty good job of camouflage if you did do it in a hurry. Suppose you just fling a few more shovels full of stuff across the top, and we'll let her go for tonight. I guess we'll be safe. One more night ought to get us through the wall. If the weather would only favor us. A good warm rain, or even a melting snow would melt that ice, and cause it to crack, and then if a wind would come up we'd have plenty of noise to hide our movements. There! Put some of that snow on the top. Now come on, let's go! Tomorrow night we'll break through that wall and get our stuff, and then we can take our time getting the rough building put up. I been figuring it out while I sat here, and it's going to seem just like another operation of the same carpenters that built those houses over there. I think we'll get by. You're a good fellow all right, Mike, and here's an extra ten bucks for a little velvet for you, so be here on time tomorrow night."

They went away toward the parked car which had been left in a new place that night. And as soon as the sound of the car's going died away two figures separated themselves from their hiding place and slowly made their way over to the scene of the night's action.

Their rubber shod feet made no stir of sound in the silence of the place. They picked their way over to the

trench, and with their flashlights bored into the carelessly placed covering to the enlarged trench. Quietly
with heavily gloved hands they removed enough of it to
discover the boards. These they studied for some minutes, conversed with sketchy gestures, now and then
a whisper, finally removed more rubble until they could
move the end of one board enough to get a narrow view
of the concealed wires sticking out of the brick wall.
After carefully examining the layout, which included
reaching in and tapping the wall gently, the two men
softly returned the rubble into place, and stepped over
to the newly arrived lumber, which they looked
over carefully. Then they retired to a distance and
turned their glances up to the tree tops.

"Say, Tom, if that's a radio there's an aerial around
here somewhere. Which tree do you think had it?"

Tom looked up speculatively at the tree tops, and
finally pointed to the tallest one.

"I think that there one, Rowley."

"Yes, I shouldn't wonder. Think you could climb that
tree and find out? We gotta get this thing all figured out
before we clamp down on them. We gotta know just
what to expect."

"Sure thing!" said Tom. "Yep, I'll take a try at her,
but it ain't necessary to go all the way up ta find out.
Them wires will be going up the tree trunks somewheres around here, ef it is an aerial."

"Okay! Look around and cipher it out. I'm figuring
they'll have to show their hands pretty soon. Maybe
tomorrow night, maybe the next. We better have a posse
ready when the time comes. You can't tell just what
those babies have got up their sleeves, or what they're
figuring to do. We've gotta be ready. You know it
might just be they're planning to put dynamite under
that brick wall."

"What fur would they do that?"

"Well, fer some reason they wantta get possession of
that house. Look's like they've had an illegitimate radio
hid there somewhere, and mebbe some incriminating
stuff. You know there's been a lotta messages leakin'

through to the enemy. There's bound to be several places where they send off messages."

"Okay, Boss," said Tom, and was off.

It was sometime before he returned.

"I found the aerial all right," he said. "Far side of that tallest tree, behind them evergreens."

"I thought so," said Rowley. "They must have a radio transmitter hidden away. They may have had it going there for some time. It's good and lonely here. Nobody would suspect. You had to look hard to find that aerial. Nobody would notice it, going by, and nobody even went by here for several years."

"But if it's a mike, they could easy get another."

"Yep. It's something more than just a mike. Something incriminating or I miss my guess."

"Watcha goin' ta do about it, Rowley?"

"Ain't sure yet. Gotta think it over. Come on, let's go!" and the two men slowly faded out of the picture.

But up in the third little bedroom where Nurse Branner had been sleeping since Mrs. Fernley was better, she was lying awake listening. She hadn't heard anything definite, but she was almost sure someone had been whispering. Yet when she slid over to the window she couldn't see anyone, for it was very dark. The little moon was tired of its walking across the sky and had dropped down behind the hills to rest until another night. Yet Nurse Branner was much comforted by the thought of Officer Rowley, and his reassuring voice, and also by the promise that the telephone would be installed tomorrow morning. At last she too dropped off to sleep again.

About that time Marietta Hollister, driving home from an evening of revelry, passed just across the river from the little brick house, and cast a baleful glance in that direction. To think that Val Willoughby had dared to come into that house while she was there and openly taken that girl out somewhere! Where had they been going? And why had he mentioned Lady Winthrop? She had scarcely had time to consider that point since it happened, so excited she had been about falling into

that hole at the back of the house, and about the two missing escorts. Besides, one of them had called up that morning to know if she had found a pass into the shipyard where he worked. And then he asked her when they were going to get their "dough." Imagine it—when they had simply checked out and left her alone!

Chapter 17

WILLOUGHBY HAD TOLD Frannie on the way home from the Bible class that he was probably going to be called to Washington for a conference, and it might be several days before his return. He had arranged for someone to look after his job while he was gone, but he was worried about her.

"If I were you I wouldn't go down on skates for a couple of days. The weather reports say there is going to be milder weather and a likelihood of the ice melting. Also storms in the offing. It won't be too safe on skates. Ice is treacherous, you know, when it begins to melt. I wish you would promise me to stay off the ice for a few days."

"But surely I could tell if the ice wasn't safe," said Frannie. "I've been used to skating since I was a very little girl."

"Well, it isn't always easy to predict what weather will do to a frozen river. Besides, there are undercurrents to be reckoned with. And besides number two there are those two fellows. If Marietta has them under her wings there is no telling what the three of them might not plan. Just go quietly downtown on the bus that passes the next street over behind your house. It goes down and crosses the river at the lower bridge, and comes around by your office. You will get there a little ahead of your opening time. Will you do that? If you don't I shall be uneasy all the time I am gone, and re-

member I haven't settled my score entirely with those
two hoodlums, and if they find out I'm gone they may
take advantage of you. They are cowards, I know, but
I think they are fairly scared of me, and would delight
to get the better of you in my absence. Besides Marietta
hasn't helped matters for us any by what she did tonight. So, stay off the ice while I'm gone, will you?"

"Why, yes, I can if that will help you any, but really
I don't see why you should worry about me. I'm not
in the least afraid."

"Then all the more I'm worried. You see I feel as if
you had in a way been put in my hands to look out for
until you get thoroughly acquainted with the place. And
anyhow I want you to, please."

So Frannie smiled and promised, and told her tumul-
tuous young heart not to make anything out of that. He
was just courteous, and felt that a gentleman ought to
protect a lady. Any lady. He wasn't singling her out because he had any particular interest in her. And then
their talk drifted back to the subject of the Bible class,
and how pleasant it was to have opportunity to get this
study.

"It's going to be a great privilege to go to that class,"
she said. "And when mother gets well she'll want to
go. Bonnie can go too. She always behaves beautifully
in church."

"That's a fine idea, only won't she get pretty sleepy?"

"No, she's been used to going to church evenings all
last summer, and she can sleep it out the next morning
if she will."

So Frannie did not expect to meet Willoughby the
next morning, and got up a little earlier to be ready
for the bus. She cast a wistful eye toward the ice, as
she started out to the bus corner, but after all it was
milder, and there were gray clouds with a sullen look
off toward the east. As she got out of the bus she felt a
drop of rain. Rain? So soon? Perhaps the weather man
had been right about it, as the young man had suggested. Probably he usually was. Frannie never read the
weather man. She usually took weather as it came with
a smile, whether dark or bright. Well, she was glad

that she had come by bus. It certainly would not be good to have to skate home in a torrential rain, but as for safety, she smiled. Surely a little rain couldn't break up that thick ice that she had traveled so happily on for so many days. But it made her feel sad to see the rain come pelting down now. She hurried into the office and as she hung her hat and coat away she looked out the back window and saw the rain come down in a regular torrent, as if it had come to stay. It made her sad to see it pelting down so hard that it fairly leaped up again, it had such a determined destructive look, and she almost felt a pity for the clear ice that had carried her so safely. Would it come again that winter? Would there yet be cold fierce enough to make a solid street of it again? Probably not until another year. As she went to her desk there was a heavy sadness upon her. This threat to the ice meant more than just losing the skating. It probably meant an end to her acquaintance with the young man whose friendship had made such a bright spot in her drab life. Probably that was a good thing, for it could not naturally go on to a lifelong friendship. That Marietta had made quite plain, even if she herself had not had sense enough to know that he belonged among a different class of people. Even if he was sensible and democratic and all that, he had a family, hadn't he? An aunt at least, who lived in that beautiful house, and companied with people on the other side of the river where she, Frannie, did not belong. Yes, it was probably a good thing that this storm and separation had come before it was too late for her to realize that she was getting far too much interested in this young man who had been so very kind.

So Frannie went hard to work, and accomplished a great deal on that long gloomy day, and did not allow herself a moment to turn aside to think. She must be true to the right and the life that God had marked out for her. And she tried to think, every breathing space that came, how grand it was going to be to have mother come downstairs again.

The rain continued according to schedule, all that day, growing harder and harder, steadily through the

night. The two figures that crept through the darkness at the back of the old brick house on the wrong side of the river, came in an old car of ancient make, and parked it this time up the back street, hidden behind bushes. Also they wore rubber coats and rubber hats, and they waited until the nightly load of lumber was landed safely before they began operations. But when the lumber truck was gone they went at it in earnest.

"You get that trench cleared right up close to the brick wall, Mike," directed Granniss, who was togged out in old clothes and looked like a laborer himself. "Get a pile of stuff each side of the trench and then we'll lay those two boards across to cover us while we work. Maybe a couple more. We gotta work fast, and this is just the kind of a night we wanted. Listen at that ice cracking. Sounds like a gun. A little pounding won't be heard. This is great. The river'll be breaking up pretty soon. Come, let's get to work. I'll get the car ready to receive the stuff when we get it out. I brought some boxes along so we won't get the papers wet. Got some important maps and plans in there."

So Mike went down on his rubber shod knees with pick and shovel, and soon had the upper end of the trench cleared, placing the rubble in a pile either side, and laying the boards across.

The wind arose and howled about the place, and shook the bare branches of the trees until now and again one fell with a crash, but there were so many crashes that it would not be noticed. And in a short time the bare brick wall lay close ahead, with the wires sticking out. Mike found himself quite excited to think he was at last so near to the goal, and actually working now out of sight under cover, where he could guardedly use his flashlight.

Of course Mike could not know that there watched two across the street, who were well aware of strange activities going on, and that the guarded little flashlight whose sharp brightness danced and gleamed through the rain like diamonds, was entirely within their sight. Mike did not know that when he had accomplished the feat of chiseling a brick or two loose, so

that he could put his hand inside and feel around
for things he had been told to locate, one of the two
across the street in hiding, had quietly slipped from
his covert to his secreted bicycle, and noiselessly
pedaled away to a telephone station not too far off,
where he had arranged to call the Police Station and
give instructions. Then he went back to Rowley who
was carefully watching developments, listening to every
movement.

And about that time Frannie, who had not been
able to get to sleep with her usual promptness, thought
she heard a sound like a blow on the back wall of the
house. She listened for a moment to see if it could be a
tree fallen with the wind which rose now and then
with sudden vigor, and then died down again. There!
There was that sound of a blow again, as of a sledge
hammer, on the back wall, down low, as if it were
striking the foundation. The wall seemed to tremble.
Could that be a slight earthquake? Did earthquakes
ever come to that part of the country? Or was this
purely imagination?

Then suddenly she remembered the new telephone
which had been put in that morning. It was located
down in the living room so that it should not annoy
the sick mother, and it seemed a long way downstairs
in the middle of the night. But again she heard that
dull thud that seemed to shake the little house. Strange
Nurse Branner hadn't heard it, but she was sleeping in
mother's room tonight because she was afraid the wind
and noise outside would make the invalid restless.
Frannie's room was partly over the back of the house,
and that was where the sound seemed to come from.
There it was again! She must do something about it.
What was a telephone for if not to use in emergency?

But she mustn't let the nurse get awake, for that
would likely waken mother, and she mustn't turn on a
light for if there was really somebody outside trying to
get in they might have a gun and see her through the
window and shoot her. Oh, but this was fantastic. It
probably was nothing at all but the wind rattling some-

thing, a loose shingle perhaps. But even if it wasn't any safer to go down in the dark than the light, she felt much more comfortable going in the dark. So softly she stole up, careful not to waken Bonnie, threw her bathrobe about her, stepped into her soft slippers, and stole slowly, cautiously to the head of the stairs. Maybe she was a fool! Maybe she ought to go back and try to go to sleep again, but at least she could go downstairs and see if the same sound was clearer down there. Perhaps she could find out what it was, and calm her mind and then she could go back upstairs and go to sleep like a sensible girl. She needed her sleep if she were going to be alert and worth her wages tomorrow. She was a working girl. She had no right to stay awake humoring herself with fancies and fears. She was brave!

So she went on step by step, avoiding carefully the stair that squeaked. She had had plenty of practice at that while her mother was so very sick at first.

And in due time she arrived at the foot of the stairs, went across to the little alcove between the bottom step and the coat closet where the telephone had so newly come to reside, and then tried to think what to do next.

Of course. She must call the police. But she didn't know their number, and she mustn't make a light to look it up. But surely the operator would know! So with shaking hand she took down the receiver, half hesitated, and then in a trembling voice spoke, very softly:

"Will you please give me the local police, quick!"

"What is your number, please?"

Her heart was beating so wildly now she could scarcely answer, and then almost at once she heard a man's voice, cool, deep, dependable, like one who was used to constant emergencies, and it gave her reassurance.

"Is this the police station?"

"Yes, what's wrong?"

"Oh, I don't quite know, but it sounds as if somebody was trying to break into the back of our house. It's number ten, Rosemary Lane, the little old brick house that has been vacant so long, they tell me. Would

you please tell some officer who is near here to go behind our house and look? It sounds as if somebody was pounding on the bricks and it sometimes shakes the whole house. There it is again. Oh please, quick, could you send someone?"

"Number ten, Rosemary Lane. Why sure, we'll take care of it, sister. Don't you worry. Is the house lit up?"

"No, I was afraid to turn on the light."

"Well, that's right. Keep it dark till we get there. Then if everything is all right we'll knock on the door and tell you."

"Thank you. But please don't knock loud. My mother is sick and I don't want to frighten her."

"Okay, lady. Just keep the house dark till we come. We'll take care of you."

So Frannie dropped down in the big chair by the front window and tried to stop trembling. Somehow calling the police had made her more sure than ever that there was something dreadful the matter, as if she had created the interloper herself out of her imagination.

It seemed to be very still here in the dark living room, and then she began to think it had all been a mistake. There wasn't anybody pounding on the back wall. There wasn't a sound anywhere except the snapping of great branches, their thud as they fell to the ground. And how like a fool she was going to feel when the police came, and found nothing was the matter. Her face grew red in the darkness at the thought. Everybody would hear of it. Maybe it would get in the papers, and people would laugh. Only there was nobody around here to laugh whom she would care about, except Valiant Willoughby, and he was away. Maybe he would never hear of it. But if he did he would think she was a little blunderer and a 'fraid cat, always getting into trouble and needing to be taken care of, and she simply couldn't have him feel that he had to go around feeling sorry for her, and taking care of her all the time. And then have that girl, that horrid girl, maybe come and laugh at her in her own house and

tell her that was what it meant to live on the wrong side of the river, with no servants around to guard the place.

Then suddenly into the deep quiet there came an extraordinary blow, as if given by a heavy sledge hammer, pounding over heavy folds of canvas or some heavy cloth, and the whole kitchen floor shook, so that the dishpan which Bonnie had left in the sink rattled.

Frannie jumped and caught her breath. "Oh!" she said, and put her hand over her heart. She struggled to her feet and stood staring around her, wondering what to do next, and yet mindful of the officer's warning that she was not to turn on the light.

The rain was still pelting down and rattling on the improvised roof over the trench where the two men worked. And now the big man was by the side of the stout man, sliding into the trench beside him as the rattle of bricks in a shower could be heard mingling with the rending sound of breaking ice. Then all was suddenly still. Frannie, creeping trembling to the kitchen window to look out, saw two dark figures step across the street swiftly and come up close to the house, and two more follow behind, and then two more. Had the police come so soon? It didn't seem possible since she called. She knew the station house was at some distance from their home. But now she could hear voices.

One voice, Miss Branner, who had been wakened by the last rumble of the wall, recognized as belonging to Officer Rowley. He was speaking with clear authority, that could be heard in the little house even above the roar of the storm.

"That will be about all," he said, putting a mighty grip on the flabby shoulder of the big man. "Just what do you men think you are doing breaking into another man's house at night while the people sleep?"

"Oh," said the big man clearing his throat importantly. "This isn't another man's house. I've just bought it, didn't you know that? And I'm going to make some changes in the place. I wanted to see the architect tomorrow and have the plan drawn up so I thought I better come over and do some measuring up tonight."

"Yes?" said Rowley. "Well you can just walk out of here and down to the police station with me and do your measuring up there. I fancy somebody else will need to measure you before you go any farther. Come on, step out of there. Brewer, snap those bracelets on him and look out for him."

"Now, man, who are you?"

"Oh, I don't know anything about this business," said Mike airily. "I'm just a laborer he hired to do some digging for him. Getting extra wages because of the storm, you know. Comes in handy when you have a big family, see?"

"Yes," said Rowley, "I see. Well, come on over to the police station and see if you can make them see. Come on. Hustle out of here. We haven't any more time to waste."

And then into the noise and storm of the night came the clear siren of the police car in front of the house, and Frannie stole to the front door and opened it, to find two policemen standing there, and a red car with bright lights standing at the gate.

"Well, ma'am," said one of the policemen, "I guess it's all over. They've just arrested your two men, and I think there's men here enough to take care of the house tonight."

"Oh, thank you," said Frannie, with a sound of tears in her voice. "I was afraid you were going to scold me for being scared at nothing. I've been hearing sounds several times, other nights, but I thought I was silly."

"No, ma'am, you weren't silly. You did the right thing callin' us. But you see our men were onto the fellows. They'd been watchin' several nights, only they wanted them to give themselves away completely before they pinched 'em."

"Oh!" said Frannie. "But what would they want to get into our house for? We're not rich people. We haven't anything much to steal. The few solid silver things we had mother put in the bank for safe-keeping. She was sort of afraid to live in such a secluded place so near to a big city, and yet not in it."

"Well, that's what the men wanted. The seclusion.

They're what is called Fifth Columnists, I guess. Anyhow they've been operating a broadcastin' station illegally, givin' away our American secrets to the enemy, and this was a nice quiet place where they could send messages. At least that's what we figured was the matter. I haven't been in charge of this case, but there's others like it nowadays, and I guess they musta had some of their stuff hid in the cellar. You folks come unexpected and moved right in and they had to get it out before it was discovered. But you don't need to worry any more. Our men will take charge of the premises, and nobody can't bother you any more. Them fellers are gone to the police station, and there they'll stay tonight, and there ain't any chance of anybody else gettin' into your house. There's too many police around."

"Oh, thank you," said Frannie, relieved.

"You're welcome, miss. Call us any time you need us!"

And then Nurse Branner stepped up.

"Officer, is Mr. Rowley anywhere about here tonight?" Her voice was crisp and self-possessed, and Frannie looked up penitently.

"Oh, did I wake you up?" she asked. "I'm so sorry. I tried to be quiet."

"No, you didn't wake me up," said the nurse, smiling. "It was the pounding on the wall woke me. Did you say Mr. Rowley is around here, officer?"

"I think he is," said the policeman politely. "Would you like to see him?"

"Yes, I would very much," said the nurse. And in a moment more Officer Rowley appeared dressed in a rubber uniform, dripping from every point and fold of his coat and boots.

"What was the matter, Mr. Rowley? Did you find anything down there?"

The big policeman grinned.

"We sure did, Miss Branner. Just a little matter of a radio transmitter used for spy purposes. You see they've been using this as a hideout till you folks moved in, and they had to vamoose in too much of a hurry.

So they just sealed everything up, and planned to come back and get it later. I haven't looked everything over, but I guess there's some pretty important papers for the government to see. Anyhow we're taking possession of them and will keep them safe till the government expert gets here. Sorry we couldn't have pulled this off sooner and saved you any further worry, but we had to keep them under espionage till we could find out just what they were at, so we could catch them red-handed. But we watched them carefully, and you weren't in any danger, we made sure of that. So now you can get your family back to sleep and you won't be bothered any more tonight. I'm leaving a force here to guard the house, and I'm having the break sealed up. If you'd just let us go down cellar a minute or two, then we'll be in a position to take care of everything."

Quietly the men went down the narrow cellar stairs, investigated everything including the movable brick and the slit of a keyhole, and then as quietly returned and went out into the rain, bidding Frannie and the nurse get a good rest. And so as the stormy morning grew toward dawn, sleep gradually came to the excited little household in the brick house.

While down the beaten silver way the rain continued to fall, unlocking the icy fetters, and making it into a river again.

Chapter 18

THEY WENT TO sleep after a little, just as the dawn was creeping into the sky, but they did not sleep long. Their nerves were too tense, excitement stirred in their blood, and they were up early, tiptoeing around, careful not to waken the mother who mercifully had slept through the night. Lulled by the storm which she believed to be harmless, she had not heard the excitement.

They slipped out into the bright morning that had come to succeed the rain and wind, and went cautiously around to the back of the house where a couple of grim policemen still patrolled the yard. They looked curiously at the trench, now lying exposed, cluttered with bricks and mortar and other debris. They stood back and looked into the gaping hole, now large enough for a man to enter, but they saw only a large caselike frame against the side of the wall and an old wooden chair. Everything else had been taken out by the officers. They did not know yet what significance there had been to this night raid. They wondered about the men who had been found battering into the wall, trying to obtain entrance. They looked and went away in awe.

"Well, I'm glad your mother isn't able to walk around yet," said the nurse. "She would have had to know all about this thing, and I'm afraid she never would have felt comfortable in her home again. She would want to move right away."

"Yes, I'm glad she can't know about it yet," said Frannie, "but my mother is very sensible. She would not be frightened if she had to know. She might take some extra precautions against any further possibilities, but she would never run away from here. And after all, Miss Branner, those men, even if they were still at large, wouldn't be likely to do the same thing in the same place again, now that they have been found out."

"Well, perhaps not," said the nurse. "Still I think the memory of what happened in the night might be hard to forget."

"I don't feel that way," said Frannie thoughtfully. "I think there is great comfort in the knowledge that the police could get here so quickly in any time of need. And then——Miss Branner, don't you think God may have had something to do with taking care of us?"

"I surely do," said the nurse in a fervent tone. "And I guess He always takes care of His own that way, whether there are any police around or not. Only sometimes. He does use the police."

"Of course," said Frannie.

Then they suddenly looked at the clock and found they had to hurry to get Frannie off on time.

So, with two policemen wandering about the back yard, and a big hole in their back cellar wall, Frannie had to get on the bus at the corner above the house and go quietly to her work in the city. As she settled herself in the bus she cast an anxious glance back, and a quick trustful prayer upward for a guard over her dear ones. Another hard day to go through and she needed keeping power herself that she might be calm, and keep her mind on her work.

Two or three times she wondered what Willoughby would think if he knew what had been going on, but she quickly chided herself for that thought. With his innate courtesy, of course, he would have wanted to do something about it right away for her reassurance and her comfort. But she mustn't let that longing for his presence well up in her heart. It was a good thing he was not at home, and could not possibly find out about last night, for it would just have been another excuse for his protection, and she knew very well she had no right to expect protection from him, nor to think of him as in any way her property. She was a working girl and as such was beginning to experience some of the annoyances and anxieties that other working girls in the days of war probably had to experience. She must just take things day by day as they came, and try to remember some of the wonderful things that had been said in that Bible class Monday night.

"Nothing can possibly come to one who is God's own child, that God does not permit. And even though it may be hard to bear, and seem to be a calamity, whatever it is it will work out for good and to the purpose of God. For that purpose is to make His redeemed ones into the image of His Son Jesus Christ."

So when there was a moment of time she cheered her heart with these thoughts.

Willoughby hadn't told her just how long he was to be gone. Perhaps he didn't know himself. There were a great many secrets and mysteries in these days about the movements of any man connected with war work.

He would come back when he came, and maybe—her heart shrank from the thought—maybe he would not come back at all. It was perfectly thinkable that he might be transferred to another place or country hastily, with no time even to come back and say farewell to anyone, even his closest friends. Well, here was something that was possible and she must be quite prepared for it. Why should it matter to her? He was only a casual acquaintance who had been kind to her.

For three days this went on, and then the fourth night when she got home, there was her mother sitting up in the big chair in the living room!

"Mother *dear!*" she exclaimed, rushing swiftly over to the chair to kiss her. "Oh, this is good, *so good!*" and there were actually tears of joy on her face.

A little later there was a knock at the door and there stood the young man from the agency where they had rented the brick house. Frannie opened the door and let him in, glad that her mother was back in a sheltered corner behind the piano, and wouldn't feel the draft from the door.

"I just stopped by," said the young man, "to tell you the deal's all off for the sale of the house. The fella that wanted it has gone to jail for a good long term, enemy alien, and the deal's off. You can go on staying here as long as you want. The owner telegraphed this morning he didn't wantta sell, anyway. So you don't need to worry."

Frannie gave the young man a bewildered look.

"But of course we understood the house was not to be sold," she said with dignity.

"Yes, but I stopped by last week and told the lady somebody was buying the house, and you'd havta get out. But now that's all off. You can stay!"

Then Nurse Branner stepped forward.

"Yes. I am the lady you saw when you called last week. I understand. And now, did you bring that contract? I don't think we'd care to stay here any longer without it. Not after the way you've acted. Did you bring the contract?"

Frannie turned a frightened look at the nurse, and Mrs. Fernley arose from her chair and stood watching the young man alertly.

"Why, no, ma'am. I didn't bring any contract, but the owner said you could stay."

"Very well, then you can bring a contract. Make it out for a year. Don't you think so, Frannie?"

"Why, of course," said Frannie, catching the idea quickly. "We certainly wouldn't want to have any uncertainty about it. There are other houses we can get. I saw one today."

"Why, yes, ma'am. You can have a contract. I'll bring it around tomorrow night. I'll have it all fixed up for you to sign."

"All right," said the nurse firmly, "you may bring it, and in the meantime we'll talk it over and decide whether we want the house for another year. You know there are a lot of things about it that need fixing, repairs on the roof and so on. We'll talk it over. You bring the contract and we'll see. The quicker the better."

"Why, I could go back to the office tonight and get a contract," suggested the alarmed clerk. He knew he had overstepped himself in trying to break the lease with these people in the first place, and didn't want them to move away and leave him to bear the blame.

After the young man had gone, the Fernleys turned in bewilderment to Miss Branner.

"What is it all about, nurse?" asked Mrs. Fernley.

"Well, Mrs. Fernley, you just sit down in your comfortable chair and I'll tell you all about it. That's it. Now pull that afghan over your knees again and don't look so frightened. Nothing has really happened, and nothing is going to. I may have overstepped my rights perhaps in talking up to that washed-out youth, but when he came here last week and tried to tell me that you had to move by the seventh I felt it was up to me to keep you from finding out anything about it until I had a chance to inquire into things and find out what your rights were. I meant to tell you last night about it, Frannie, but I forgot entirely with all the things we were

doing. I did try to call up a lawyer I know to ask him, but he was out, down in Washington on business, and I thought it wouldn't matter if we waited a few days till you were able to think about things, Mrs. Fernley. But now it seems to have settled itself, and of course in case you want to stay here I suppose you can almost make your own terms. Demand a few repairs, you know, or something like that. If you ask me I think that youth is plenty scared at what he did, telling you to move when he had no orders from the owner, and I guess he'll be as reasonable as you want him to be."

"Why, that's all right, of course, nurse. You always know the right thing to do I'm sure, and we're very much obliged to you for taking the initiative in our interest, aren't we, Frannie?"

"Yes, indeed, mother. Miss Branner has been simply wonderful. I don't know what we would have done without her."

So the matter was smoothed over, and they talked a little of the different houses that were to be had, deciding from what they knew of rents that the brick house was really the only one they could afford. And then suddenly in the midst of their talk the young agent arrived back breathless with a crisp new contract. After reading it carefully over they finally signed it, and Frannie drew a breath of relief as he rode away on his bicycle.

"Well, the house, such as it is, is ours for a year," she said as she locked the door.

"Yes, and that clause that allows you to sublet in case you find something more suited to your purpose will help too," said the nurse.

"Yes, I'm glad you suggested that, Miss Branner," said Mrs. Fernley. "I've thought of that possibility several times."

And so quite contented they all went to bed and to sleep.

The weather was mild for several days, and the thick ice broke up, and floated away down the river to the sea. The beauty of the great silver street was gone, the

skating was gone. Would it come again before another
year, Frannie wondered, as she rode daily to her work,
and sighed a little? She loved to skate.

Lady Winthrop took advantage of the mild weather
to drive over and call on the Fernleys, and it happened
that Mrs. Fernley was downstairs, doing a little mend-
ing, carefully watched over by the nurse who wouldn't
let her work long at a time.

Bonnie, always wanting to do whatever her mother
or sister were doing, sat near on a little stool painstak-
ingly sewing two patches together which she asserted
were for a quilt for her doll.

Lady Winthrop had brought a roasting chicken all
stuffed and ready for cooking, a basket of apples from
her farm, some sweet potatoes and two jars of fruit
for the invalid. She settled down like an old friend and
talked. The two ladies had a delightful hour together,
and told each other bits of their life history, until when
the car came back for Lady Winthrop they felt very
well acquainted, and Frannie's mother had promised to
bring Bonnie and come over with Frannie to the next
Bible class, if she was allowed to go out so soon.

"I'll send the car over for you," called back the dear
Lady Winthrop happily, as if she were talking to an old
friend.

"Oh, but I shall soon be able to walk," said the
other woman, with a pleasant ring to her voice and a
light in her eyes. "That isn't far."

So when Frannie came home that night there was
good cheer in the brick house, the smell of roasting
chicken, and a dish of big red apples on the table in the
living room. It seemed almost cheerful as she entered,
and she was able to put aside her sad thoughts about
how lonely she was every day with no young people
around with whom she felt like being friendly. Well,
perhaps she would find some congenial companions at
the plant pretty soon, that is, when things at home were
going well, and mother was up and around all the time
to make home a place where she could bring some
girls now and then. That would be nice.

So she entered into the gala spirit, enjoying the

chicken and sweet potatoes and fruit with the rest. It was almost as pleasant as it had been when they first arrived in the house and felt that they were anchored for a while and were going to be happy, as happy as they could be without the husband and father who had been so much to them all.

Frannie was congratulating herself that she had scarcely thought all day of the young Mr. Willoughby who had been such a delightful companion before he went away. He hadn't said he was not returning, just said he didn't know how long he had to stay. So perhaps he knew there was a possibility that he would not be sent back. Perhaps Washington had some bigger, more important job for him, and she was glad if that were so, for his sake, but she sighed a little that perhaps she would never see him again. And to cover up that sigh she smiled.

"It's so good to have you down at the table again, mother dear!" she said happily.

And the mother smiled.

"Yes, it's nice to be down," said the mother.

"Are you warm enough?" asked the nurse. "Wouldn't you like Bonnie to run up and get your little shoulder shawl?"

"Well, perhaps I would feel more comfortable with it," said the invalid. "Isn't it getting colder again?"

"Why yes," said Frannie, looking up from her unconscious absorption. "I noticed it on the way home. I had to turn up the collar of my coat. My, wouldn't it be nice if it would get cold again and the river would freeze over? I promised Bonnie I'd try to find my old skates and teach her to skate."

"Oh, well, it will be time enough for that next year," said the mother. "I don't believe it will freeze solidly again, after melting off entirely this way. That wouldn't be likely to happen."

"It might," said the nurse. "It does sometimes. I can remember one winter in my girlhood when it did that three times before spring, but of course that was unusual. Still it isn't late in the winter yet, and I read somewhere that this was going to be an unusually cold

winter. That would be nice for you, Frannie. You really
need the exercise you get skating back and forth to
work. And, of course, you can't walk all that way."

Frannie looked up, smiled, and was about to burst
into eagerness, but then she suddenly remembered. She
had promised Val Willoughby she would not skate down
to her work while he was gone. Surely that promise
would not be binding indefinitely. He had spoken as if
he were returning soon when he bade her good-by, but
suppose he never came back? Surely she would not
have to refrain from skating the rest of her days. How
silly! If he never came back he would have nothing
more to do with her, and of course she had a right to do
as she pleased.

But from that moment the hope that the ice might return lost its thrill. Certainly she didn't want to go skating
without him so soon after her promise, even if he did
not come back this winter.

So she plunged into the ceremony of dishwashing
with a vim, making a game out of it with Bonnie for
helper, and tried to forget the ice and all the nice evenings and mornings she had spent on it, for somehow
they seemed to be running away from her with a sort
of a hopelessness that she could not conquer.

Later that evening there came a timid knock at the
door. When Frannie opened it thinking it was the little
girl who sold magazines she found Kit Creeber standing there with averted face.

"Oh," she said as he stepped inside the room. "It's
you again. What is it now, another dance?" and she
smiled at him amusedly.

He twirled his cap embarrassedly, and grew red in
the face.

"Aw naw! Say, we didn't get that dance stuff up. It
was that fool girl with the yellow hair. She offered us
five bucks apiece to take some girls to a dance, and of
course we were out for the dough. But we didn't mean
any harm. We meant to carry it through, honest we
did, till we saw who you were, and then we beat it.
And say, I wantta apologize for the way I treated you
that first day at the plant. We didn't mean anything

but just kidding. But when you took it that way Spike got mad. But afterwards we saw you were a real lady, and I'm sorry. I hope you'll forget it."

Frannie looked at the embarrassed boy in astonishment.

"Why, of course," she said coldly. "I guess I didn't quite understand. But you didn't need to come and apologize."

"Well, you see I lost something that time I came here for the dance, and I thought I'd come and ask you, did you find it? It means a lot to me. It's a pass I had, and I'm expected to show it at the gate where I work. I can't find it anywhere. The gate man is getting awful hot about it, and I thought I'd take a chance asking you if you found it. It was in an envelope in my coat pocket, and when I got home it wasn't there."

"I'm sorry," said Frannie, "we didn't find anything. I'd be glad to give it back to you if I had. But if you go to Mr. Chalmers the head of the second floor department and explain it to him, he'll maybe fix it up for you. He's very kind and fair."

"Well, but I don't work there any longer. I'm over at the powder plant."

"Oh, I see," said Frannie. "Well, I'm sorry, I don't know what to suggest then. But usually if you are frank about a thing and tell the truth they will meet you half way."

"Thanks awfully," said Kit, and took himself away with haste.

Frannie sat down weakly in her chair and stared at the wall.

"Well, did I ever!" she exclaimed softly to herself. To think that boy would come and apologize! What did he do it for? Was he afraid that somehow he would get connected with the men who were running that queer radio? Or did he maybe have something to do with it? Well, probably not, but at least she needn't be afraid of him any more. It was good that he no longer worked in the same plant with herself. He might try to get fresh with her again sometime if he was still there. She was glad the nurse and Bonnie were still upstairs

and wouldn't ask questions about him. She didn't want
to tell about that trouble with those two boys. Her
mother must never hear of it.

She didn't think long about it because she found
that such thoughts inevitably brought Val Willoughby
into her mind, and that was what she was strenuously
trying to avoid.

When she went to bed that night and looked out
of her window there she saw the river spread wide and
dark, with a sheen of silver beginning to gather from
the rising moon which was growing nightly larger. It
gave her a twinge of sadness. Why did the moon have
such power to take one back over past days, or nights,
and spread sorrow over one's heart? But there! She
must hurry and get her garments ready for the mor-
row, and then get to bed. She had no time to sentimen-
talize. It would be hard enough to get up early in the
morning without that! Then when she opened her window the fresh breeze swept stingingly in. Yes, the
air was decidedly colder. It wouldn't take long at a
temperature like this to freeze that river again. But
what good would that do her when she had promised
not to skate while Willoughby was away?

Chapter 19

THE COLD CAME steadily down that night, freezing everything it touched. It laid an icy clutch on the river
and began slowly turning it to glass. The moon lingering late showed a solid stillness where there had been a
dark limpid heave and quiver at sunset hour. The river
had definitely succumbed to the cold again, and if there
were any little fishes in it anywhere they must have hurried shivering to their homes to put on their seal overcoats. And sharply and smoothly down the glassy surface shone the pale silver of moonlight.

Frannie looked out before she crept into her warm bed, and said sadly: "The skating will be coming back soon," and sighed as she laid her dark head down on her pillow. Sighed and shivered, and fell asleep from sheer weariness of trying not to think.

"No, I will not be silly," she said over and over to herself. "I shall never give in to disappointment nor have a broken heart. Everything works together for good to those that love the Lord. It will all work out right. I must just trust and wait till He helps me to see how right it is, and then I shall be glad and not feel badly any more."

Lady Winthrop looked out of her window in the early morning and saw the ruby light of the first flash of sunrise stealing in a wide crimson sweep over her river, like a flaming carpet. She could see it from her bed, as she lay softly there in the great old-fashioned four-poster, with its fine linen draperies. It was a sight she loved to waken early just to see.

"The street of my city has come back!" she said softly to herself. "It has come back to stay awhile longer. And I shall again see those dear young people go down to the city on their flashing skates. They will go down together this time and I shall watch them, many times perhaps before the springtime comes and takes away my street of silver."

She lay looking at it for sometime, as the sun rose higher and flashed over tall buildings and towers and pinnacles, studying out her vision of the fair city that hovered in her imagination. And then she went on softly to herself again:

"And some day, some great day, *I* shall walk down that street that is 'made of gold, as it were transparent glass,' and I shall step up the crystal way to the bank of the city. I shall go on into the city and see the face of my King, my Saviour, my Lord Jesus who died for me. I shall look on Him, and be like Him, incredibly like Him. With all my mistakes and sins; it is so wonderful that He can make me like Himself some day. And I shall not be afraid nor ashamed."

Silence again as the sun climbed higher, and the way

where the darkness of the river had been grew broad and rosy.

Then the soft voice went on:

"And I shall live there among those Heavenly mansions, far more spacious and beautiful than my dear earthly house, and I shall walk those golden streets. I shall stand on the crystal banks and see the fire mingled with glass that will sometimes come in that great street of the city, my city, my Heavenly Home. Please God, make me ready for it when the time comes, dressed in the white linen garment of Thine own righteousness, because try as I could all my life I can get no righteousness of my own. And I shall dwell by my street of the city, all the days, that shall never end! And my dear ones whom I have lost awhile on the journey here will be there! My City! My street of the city. Oh, I'm glad it has come back again for awhile!"

Three days later when the supper dishes were done and the Fernleys were just settling down to a few minutes' pleasant talk before the mother was remanded to her room, Frannie stepped to the window and looked out. The great hole in the back of the house had been thoroughly bricked up and cemented and reinforced, so that they felt secure from unexpected intrusion, and there was a cosy cheer over the whole place. They all felt it. And yet there was a sadness in Frannie's heart. She couldn't but think of the days, though they had been very few of course, when she and Willoughby had had pleasant companionship. Was it possible that even those few days had spoiled her sweet content, her joy in life? Well, that was silly, and she had told her mother that she didn't intend to be silly, she *would* not. So she put on a cheerful tone.

"Oh, mother, you should come to the window and look out! It is such a lovely sight. The ice is like a piece of glass, and the moon is almost full. It is worth while living here just for this sight even if for no other reason. Come, mother, come and look. You can see Lady Winthrop's 'street of the city' as she calls it."

For Frannie had long ago told her mother all the

lovely tales of the sweet old lady that Willoughby had told to her.

So Mrs. Fernley went over to the window and stood with her arm around her daughter looking out on the winter beauty.

"Yes, it is indeed a lovely sight," she said, "and a lovely idea. I am looking forward to the time when I can go over to that Bible class and get to know that sweet woman better."

But Frannie said nothing about skating to her work yet, and her mother, knowing little of how long it took to make ice safe for going, was glad. Somehow it always seemed a big risk for her little girl to go sailing off alone down a river of glass.

"And now," said Nurse Branner, "it's time you and Bonnie went to bed."

It was just then that there came a low tap at the front door, and then the knob turned and in walked Valiant Willoughby!

Frannie turned and looked at him, her eyes wide with a great joy, her face blooming out in smiles.

"Oh, you *did* come back!" she said, almost as a little girl would have said it.

And Val had eyes for no one else, his rare smile filling the room with good cheer.

"Why *sure!*" he said. "Didn't you know I was coming back? That's what I've been intending to do all along." He went and stood by Frannie and took both her hands in his, looking down at her as if she were the sweetest thing on earth.

And then, with her hands still in his he turned to the others. "Hello, Bonnie, and Nurse Branner. I'm glad to see you all looking so well. And now, Frannie, aren't you going to introduce me to your mother? You know I've never rightly met her, just picking her up off the floor and putting her to bed. That isn't an introduction."

And so he led her over to her mother, who had gone a few steps toward the stairs as he came in.

Frannie laughed.

"Mother, this is Mr. Willoughby. I know you'll want

to thank him now you've got well for all he did for you when you were taken sick."

"Oh, yes," said Mrs. Fernley, giving him a smile that made him think of her daughter, it was so sunny and kindly.

Val reached for one of her hands and folded it with Frannie's within his own clasp, a kind of symbol of the united friendship they all felt. "You know," he said gently, "I *like* mothers. My own is gone Home, and so I almost envy everyone who still has one left here on earth. I am very glad to know you."

Mrs. Fernley gave his hand a warm pressure and smiled again, trying to thank him for all his kindness to herself and her daughter, but he waved her thanks away.

"It was nothing," he said. "But I mustn't keep you standing. You are still an invalid, aren't you? May I help you upstairs? Is that where you were going? And may I ask a favor of you? Do you mind if Frannie and I put on our skates and go out on that ice for a few minutes, just to celebrate my getting back? They tell me the ice is solid as the Rock of Gibraltar, and I'm aching to try it. Do you mind?"

"Oh, is it safe? Why of course, go for a little while. Frannie has done nothing but work since you went away. She needs a bit of exercise."

"Well, that's all I've done too, so I think we can both enjoy it. The ice is perfect. You look out your window and you'll see us skimming along."

"I will," smiled the mother. "Go, Frannie dear, and have a good time."

"Oh, mother, and can *I* go sometime too?" pleaded Bonnie.

"Why, of course, you can, Bonnie," said Willoughby, "I'll come over sometime before it is bedtime and Frannie and I will take you out, one in each of your hands, holding you up, till you learn for yourself. I think I can find a pair of skates at my aunt's that will about fit you. My little cousins used to skate and I'm sure I've seen some small skates over there. Will that please you?"

"Oh, muvver! *Can* I?" asked Bonnie entranced.

"Why yes, dear, that will be wonderful!"

So Willoughby gathered up the little mother and carried her easily up the stairs, and they said good night. And then Frannie got her skates and they went out together into the clear cold night.

He helped her down the steps to the ice, and knelt before her to help her on with her skates. Then he looked up to her face and caught the starry look in her eyes.

"Oh, Frannie, Frannie *dear!*" he said suddenly, taking both her hands in his, "it is so good to get back to you! It seemed forever before I could get away and come back. Did you miss me at all, Frannie? Or is it too soon to expect that from you?"

Frannie lifted shy eyes.

"Yes, I missed you—very much," she confessed. "I thought I ought not to, but I did."

"You darling!" said the young man, stooping suddenly and laying his lips on hers. "Frannie, I love you! Oh, my *dear!*" Then he lifted her up, and put both arms about her, drawing her close in his arms, laying his firm cold cheek against her glowing one, his lips on hers again. Frannie thrilled to his kisses, her heart full of wonder and joy. He loved her! Think of that! And she had been trying to forget him, because she thought he didn't belong to her world, because she thought he did not care for her, was even perhaps engaged to some other girl. But he wasn't. He loved her! The thoughts tumbled themselves over and over in her brain until she was just in a tumult of joy.

Then suddenly Val remembered.

"Can they look out the upstairs window and see us?" he asked with a comical grin. "We might be a couple of gold-fish in a glass bowl for all we remember the world now. I don't care if you don't, of course, but we don't want the whole world in on our sweetest privacy, even on a moonlight night. Wait till I get my skates on and we'll go away by ourselves for a little."

He made her sit down on the step while he adjusted his own skates, and then together they glided away from the shore and out into the middle of the

stream, remembering to turn and wave to the three shadowy figures in the upper window who stood watching them, and waving back, especially the smallest one most vigorously.

On down into the silver pathway they flew, joyful in the touch of shoulders, the clasp of hands, the look in their eyes as their glances met.

"Oh, I *love* you, little girl," said Val. "Do you think you can love me enough to want to marry me, so that we can be together always?"

Such sweet converse they had that they scarcely saw the gold in the silver way before them, as they glided on and on, almost down to where the river joined the sea.

And when they turned and came back they went more slowly and touched in their talk on the sweetness of loving one another. Val began to tell her how she looked to him when he first saw her, and how different she seemed from the silly girls he had always been so bored with. And little by little she told him how desolate her young heart had been after he went away.

"But it was only a few days," he said. "I told you I would be back. I did not know before I went that they would keep me so long, but sometimes it seemed to me it would never end. I did not realize I would feel that way for just a few days, when I left. But when I got away where I could not see you any more I began to realize what you were. I met a couple of girls I used to go around with when I was in college but they only made me long for you."

Frannie's hand lay warm in his as he told her this, and she nestled closer as they glided on.

"What were you doing down there anyway?" she asked suddenly.

"Oh, just the kind of work I was doing here. You see, I was taking the place of another man who was very sick and couldn't keep on. It was work that one had to have special training for, the kind of training I have had. That's all I can tell you now, because on account of the war these things have to be kept secret. So it was important there should be someone there who understood. The man I was substituting for is

rather high in his profession, and he turned out to be sicker than they thought at first, but at last he got better and then they let me off. I got back early this morning, but I went straight to the plant. I haven't been home yet. I wanted to see you so much. But there was a lot to be done at the plant. I couldn't get away any sooner. You see the men I left in charge here were rather green at the job, and I found a lot of mistakes to be rectified. But oh, I'm glad to be back, and glad, *glad* to have you again."

He suddenly flung his arm about her and drew her closer, and so they glided on in the silver night, so close they were like one body, so much a part of one another that they seemed a single figure.

And in the dim distance the mountains girded round about the river, the towers and turrets of earth's mansions took on their unearthly semblance, and seemed like outlying parts of Heaven to which they were traveling.

And then they looked up at the beauty of it all.

"Look, look!" said Frannie. "How beautiful. Doesn't it seem like a picture of what Heaven might be?"

"Yes," said Val reverently, "our Heavenly Home. And to think that we can be *sure* that we are both going there. All our lives we can go on looking ahead to going there, to being with the Lord, *our* Lord, forever. Oh, I am so glad we are both saved. There doesn't have to be an uncertainty about it ever, because we accepted His word, and He has promised. I've been thinking a lot about these things while I was away. In fact that was one of the main reasons why I was so sure I loved you, because you were interested in these vital things. Because we thought alike. I can't imagine a happy married life without that. People have to think alike to enjoy life together, I guess."

"I guess you're right," said Frannie softly. "I couldn't feel the same toward one who didn't understand my deepest thoughts and feelings."

"Dear!" said Val pressing her little mittened fingers tenderly. "Of course. And now, Frannie, I think I ought to take you back. Mother will be watching for us

to come even if she has retired, and besides we both have to be up early in the morning, remember. But tomorrow night I'm coming over early and have a little talk with your mother about all this, and *we'll* talk it out together, you and I. Make our plans, you know. I don't want to be away from you any longer than I can help."

"Oh!" said Frannie with sudden dismay in her voice. "Plans. Yes, of course. But listen. You know I have responsibilities. I couldn't leave my family high and dry—"

"Of course not!" said the young man heartily. "But your responsibilities will become my responsibilities now, you know. There'll be two of us now to take care of your mother and sister. And remember I haven't any mother or sister of my own, so I'm going to enjoy yours a lot, and shall delight to make life happy for them both. Shall we do it together, dearest?"

Frannie looked up at the eager face above hers and a great joy flashed into her eyes.

"Oh, you are wonderful!" she said in exultation. "I didn't know there were men like you. And to think the *only one* should be mine! I can't see why God could be so good to me!"

"And just for that we're going to stop till I kiss you again," said he, whirling her over to a wooded place in the bank, and holding her close in his arms to lay his face against hers for a moment. "You darling!"

Slowly at last they glided on back to the little brick house, and took off their skates.

"I heard at the plant today that you folks had had a little excitement up this way a couple of days ago. Is that true? I meant to ask when I first arrived, but I was so taken up looking at you that I forgot it. What happened? Or didn't you know about it?"

"Know about it?" said Frannie. "I should say I did! For a few minutes I thought I was the only one who knew about it. I heard a noise and slipped to the window. It was during that worst storm. The wind was shrieking, it was raining fiercely, and we heard a great pounding on the back cellar wall. At least I did, and

the nurse came too, pretty soon. But I had slipped down to the telephone and called up the police and asked them to see if someone was trying to break in."

"Brave girl! I wish I could have been here to help! But what was it? Was someone trying to get in?"

"Yes, it seems they had a radio transmitter walled up in our cellar. They had been using it to send messages, intelligence about war plants and such like to the enemy, and when we suddenly moved in that spoiled their plans. So they wanted to get their paraphernalia out, and they didn't dare come and tell us about it. It seems they had some incriminating papers there, hidden behind the furnace in a walled-up place they had built while the house was vacant several years. They couldn't come and open the place from inside lest they would be arrested, so they chose a stormy night and tried to work in from outside. They dug a trench, and when they got close in they began with pickax and sledge hammers, and it was pretty awful for a few minutes in the middle of the night. But just think, mother didn't hear it, at least if she did she thought it was just branches breaking off the trees in the storm, and she slept all through it. Wasn't that great?"

"Pretty great I should say. Oh, I'm sorry you folks had to go through all that without me here to help. I shall have to begin right away to take care of you all very hard to make up for it. And by the way, you won't need to work any more, you know. I mean you shall have a beautiful and comfortable life from now on."

"Oh, but I'm doing defense work now, you know, and all the women of the land are asked to do that, so I guess I should keep right on at my job for a while, as long as I'm needed. I guess our work at the plant is pretty important, and it isn't good for them to have to change helpers when they have someone taught."

"That's true, I know, and of course if you put it on that score I'll have to withdraw my objections. We've all got to help win this war. But as much as I can I mean to take care of you and make life easy. Of course I'm talking rather 'biggity' for a man who hasn't

even asked permission of your mother to court her daughter. Do you think she will offer serious objections?"

"Oh no," giggled Frannie, "only she will tell you, I am afraid, that you are thinking of marrying a girl from the wrong side of the river, and that isn't being done, you know."

Valiant threw his head back and laughed loud and long, and the echo of that laughter, mingled with a ripple from Frannie, reached up through an open window in the Hollister mansion and caused a beautiful young lady to turn uneasily and sigh in her sleep.

Then Frannie spoke more soberly.

"Mother admires you very much. I'll tell you later all the nice things she said about you, and she was glad that you are a Christian. The only thing she is afraid of is that you may not care for me and will break my heart, and she warned me not to let my heart get entangled. She has heard that you belong to a wealthy family and live in a fine house, and she has no aspirations toward wealth. She doesn't trust it, perhaps. She had some wealthy relatives herself."

"Well, if that is all the objection she will offer I can easily quiet her mind. You can tell your dear mother that I am anything but rich. I have a few thousand invested that was left over after my father's estate was settled, and beyond that I have only my salary for the work I am doing. I have an aunt who is fairly well off, but that has nothing to do with me. She has children of her own who will inherit her money, so you see I'm not a poor little rich boy, and your dear mother needn't worry on that account. You can tell her too, if you like, that I have a fairly promising education which will probably make it possible, if all goes well, for me to support you in a modest way, so she needn't think I am a lazy-good-for-nothing, either. Just a plain young man with health and a job, who loves you more than anything in life. Now, do you think I will pass?"

"I'm sure you will," whispered Frannie with her face against his, her lips close to his ear.

"And oh, here's another thing," said Val, suddenly

holding her back and looking into her face. "How do I rate with Bonnie? Is she going to be terribly upset to have a big brother?"

"Oh, no," said Frannie, her face wreathed in smiles. "She simply adores you. She will be delighted. But truly, you know, none of my family have been presuming enough even to dream that you would ever want to marry me, a plain working girl from the wrong side of the river." And then her eyes twinkled merrily and her laugh rang out again with his hearty one.

"Well," said Val, recovering from his mirth, "hadn't we better call it a day and quit? I don't know how I'm going to tear myself away, but I guess it's got to be done if we want to keep our jobs till the end of the war."

As they reached the door and turned to go in, Val pointed to the river, bright in its silver sheen.

"Look," he said, "our river! *'The street of the city'* where we met. By which we may travel to the end and find the City Eternal waiting to welcome us some day."

"Yes," said Frannie softly. "I found a verse this morning in my Bible. It sort of fits now. 'Here we have no continuing city, but we seek one to come, a house not made with hands, eternal in the Heavens!'"

And so they said a tender good night, and Valiant Willoughby went on his way. And the next day was a new day!

Novels of Enduring Romance and Inspiration by

GRACE LIVINGSTON HILL

BRING ROMANCE INTO YOUR LIFE

With these bestsellers from your favorite Bantam authors.

Barbara Cartland

- [ ] 23499   LIGHTS, LAUGHTER AND A LADY #177 $2.50
- [ ] 23445   TEMPTED TO LOVE #176 $2.50
- [ ] 23561   A DUKE IN DANGER #175 $2.50
- [ ] 23297   HELP FROM THE HEART #174 $2.25

Grace Livingston Hill

- [ ] 20911   MISS LAVINIA'S CALL #64 $2.50
- [ ] 23467   MAN OF THE DESERT #63 $2.50
- [ ] 23558   CHRISTMAS BRIDE #62 $2.50
- [ ] 22903   MYSTERY FLOWERS #61 $2.50

Emilie Loring

- [ ] 22860   MY DEAREST LOVE #4 $2.50
- [ ] 22763   WITH THIS RING #8 $2.50
- [ ] 22671   UNCHARTERED SEAS #31 $2.50

Eugenia Price

- [ ] 22583   MARGARET'S STORY $3.50
- [ ] 22798   BELOVED INVADER $2.95
- [ ] 23158   LIGHTHOUSE $3.50

Georgette Heyer

- [ ] 22596   REGENCY BUCK $2.75
- [ ] 22762   THE CONVENIENT MARRIAGE $2.50
- [ ] 22508   LADY OF QUALITY $2.50
- [ ] 22934   BEAUVALLET $2.50

Prices and availability subject to change without notice.

Buy them at your local bookstore or use this handy coupon for ordering:

Bantam Books, Inc., Dept. RO, 414 East Golf Road, Des Plaines, Ill. 60016

Please send me the books I have checked above. I am enclosing $_____
(please add $1.25 to cover postage and handling). Send check or money order
—no cash or C.O.D.'s please.

Mr/Mrs/Miss _____

Address_____

City_____ State/Zip_____

RO—9/83

Please allow four to six weeks for delivery. This offer expires 3/84.

INTIMATE MOMENTS™

is proud to present

Romancing the Crown

*With the help of their powerful allies,
the royal family of Montebello is determined
to find their missing heir. But the search for the
beloved prince is not without danger—or passion!*

**This exciting twelve-book series begins in January and
continues throughout the year with these fabulous titles:**

January	(IM #1124)	THE MAN WHO WOULD BE KING by Linda Turner
February	(IM #1130)	THE PRINCESS AND THE MERCENARY by Marilyn Pappano
March	(IM #1136)	THE DISENCHANTED DUKE by Marie Ferrarella
April	(IM #1142)	SECRET-AGENT SHEIK by Linda Winstead Jones
May	(IM #1148)	VIRGIN SEDUCTION by Kathleen Creighton
June	(IM #1154)	ROYAL SPY by Valerie Parv
July	(IM #1160)	HER LORD PROTECTOR by Eileen Wilks
August	(IM #1166)	SECRETS OF A PREGNANT PRINCESS by Carla Cassidy
September	(IM #1172)	A ROYAL MURDER by Lyn Stone
October	(IM #1178)	SARAH'S KNIGHT by Mary McBride
November	(IM #1184)	UNDER THE KING'S COMMAND by Ingrid Weaver
December	(IM #1190)	THE PRINCE'S WEDDING by Justine Davis

Available at your favorite retail outlet.

Silhouette®

Where love comes alive™

Visit Silhouette at www.eHarlequin.com

SIMRC

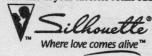

Welcome to

Silhouette
DREAMSCAPES...

a world where passion and danger mingle together...and the temptation of dark, sensual romance awaits.

In December 2001, look for these four alluring romances:

FROM A DISTANCE
by Emilie Richards

THE PERFECT KISS
by Amanda Stevens

SEA GATE
by Maura Seger

SOMETHING BEAUTIFUL
by Marilyn Tracy

Available at your favorite retail outlet.

Silhouette®
Where love comes alive™

If you enjoyed what you just read,
then we've got an offer you can't resist!

Take 2 bestselling love stories FREE!

Plus get a FREE surprise gift!

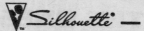

CALL THE ONES YOU LOVE OVER THE HOLIDAYS!

Save $25 off future book purchases when you buy any four Harlequin® or Silhouette® books in October, November and December 2001,

PLUS

receive a phone card good for 15 minutes of long-distance calls to anyone you want in North America!

WHAT AN INCREDIBLE DEAL!

Just fill out this form and attach 4 proofs of purchase (cash register receipts) from October, November and December 2001 books, and Harlequin Books will send you a coupon booklet worth a total savings of $25 off future purchases of Harlequin® and Silhouette® books, AND a 15-minute phone card to call the ones you love, anywhere in North America.

Please send this form, along with your cash register receipts
as proofs of purchase, to:
In the USA: Harlequin Books, P.O. Box 9057, Buffalo, NY 14269-9057
In Canada: Harlequin Books, P.O. Box 622, Fort Erie, Ontario L2A 5X3
Cash register receipts must be dated no later than December 31, 2001.
Limit of 1 coupon booklet and phone card per household.
Please allow 4-6 weeks for delivery.

**I accept your offer! Enclosed are 4 proofs of purchase.
Please send me my coupon booklet
and a 15-minute phone card:**

Name: _____

Address: _____ City: _____

State/Prov.: _____ Zip/Postal Code: _____

Account Number (if available): _____

---

097 KJB DAGL
PHQ4013